By Ramsey Campbell
from Tom Doherty Associates

PACT

of the

FATHERS

PACT
of the
FATHERS

Ramsey Campbell

A TOM DOHERTY ASSOCIATES BOOK
NEW YORK

PACT OF THE FATHERS

Copyright © 2001 by Ramsey Campbell

This book is printed on acid-free paper.

Design by Heidi Eriksen

A Forge Book
Published by Tom Doherty Associates, LLC
175 Fifth Avenue
New York, NY 10010

www.tor.com

Forge® is a registered trademark of Tom Doherty Associates, LLC.

Library of Congress Cataloging-in-Publication Data

Campbell, Ramsey.
    Pact of the fathers / Ramsey Campbell.—1st ed.
      p. cm.
    "A Tom Doherty Associates book."
    ISBN 0-312-87869-9 (acid-free paper)
    1. Human sacrifice—Fiction.   2. Father and child—Fiction.
3. First-born children—Fiction.   I. Title.

PR6053.A4855 P33 2001
823'.914—dc21

                                                              2001040478

First Edition: December 2001

Printed in the United States of America

0 9 8 7 6 5 4 3 2 1

For Chris and Geoff
—something else from an old wreck

Acknowledgments

I owe the underlying notion of this story to Patrick Tierney's *The Highest Altar*, and in particular to his conversations on the subject with the Hebrew scholar Hyam Maccoby, which led me to Maccoby's own remarkable book. However, the greatest strengths of *Pact of the Fathers* are the work of my editor, Melissa Ann Singer, who sent me the most detailed and perceptive editorial letter I've had in the nearly forty years since August Derleth showed me how to write. Is my daughter Tammy in here? Her time in York is, though I may have taken liberties with the university syllabus.

PACT
of the
FATHERS

By the time the island bobbed up on the horizon under the blazing blue sky Daniella had lost count of how often she'd stopped herself wishing she were somewhere else. Before she was even out of sight of Athens the sea had begun to throw itself and the small smelly motorboat about, and that was more than an hour ago. Fixing her gaze on the horizon convinced her that some part of the world was staying as still as she hoped her airline lunch would. She clung to the drenched prow with both hands and told herself all this had to come to an end—the heavy stench of petrol mixed with the fumes of the boatman's cigar, her unprotected eyes flinching from the glare the sea threw up, the salty gusts that lashed her bare arms, already tender with sunlight that was a hot mask clamped to her face. Now a line of boats much like hers swayed into view ahead, and an object as white as the edge of the waves rose beyond the boats. "Nektarikos," the boatman said.

She assumed he would be pointing at the island. It was the first word he'd addressed to her since she had stepped on board. The white object raised itself above patches of green, and she realised it was a villa on top of the island. She tried to hang onto its steadiness while the island took shape, reaching out a claw of rock to shape the bay. As the boat passed to the left of the line of tossing vessels and the

fishermen exchanged Greek shouts with her ferryman, she
saw buildings at the foot of the bleached island. Long slow
waves drew the boat towards little more than a sketch of a
harbour as her stomach and the inside of her skull risked
recalling how it felt to be settled. When the boat sidled
against a landing-stage short of several planks, she had to
swallow only once.

A road as white as the pebbles of the beach led past a
handful of tavernas, outside one of which a fat man naked
to the waist and basted with sweat was scraping a barbecue
grill, and vanished uphill between squat unadorned white
houses to reappear below an olive grove. The boatman
stepped deftly onto the landing-stage and twirled the thick
rope around a splintered post before extending one large
hairy hand to Daniella. She'd hardly grabbed her jacket and
her underweight suitcase when she was swung onto the
shaky planks so fast it took her brain a moment to catch
up. He let go and strode towards the tavernas, and she
stumbled after him as fast as her renewed dizziness per-
mitted. "Nana Babouris?" she pleaded.

Whatever he answered was accompanied by a swing of
his left hand to indicate the villa. "You mean," Daniella
protested, "I'm going to have to walk?"

He scratched his curly greying beard and shrugged. She
appeared to be faced with tramping uphill at least a mile,
a prospect that filled her mouth with dryness. She needed
water, and was trudging after him in the hope that English
money would buy her a bottle when she heard a screech of
brakes and saw dust rise among the highest trees. "Babouris," the boatman assured her with a smile that exposed
all the gaps between his teeth.

Around a dozen rubbery screeches preceded the arrival

of a sports car that would have been silver but for dust. The driver's eyes were hidden by wrap-around sunglasses. She hurried after the boatman over the unsteady pebbles as he seized her case and marched to the car, and had to support herself on the passenger door while he threw the case into the boot. "Do you mind," she asked the driver, "if I just get a drink for the road?"

He raised his bristling reddish eyebrows that the road had turned pale and offered her the emptiness between his considerable hands, and she would have mimed her need if the boatman hadn't opened the door for her as she let go. "Babouris," he repeated helpfully.

"Babouris," the driver confirmed.

Nana would have all the water Daniella could drink, and suddenly the girl yearned to be with someone to whom she could talk. She sat in the car, only to jerk forward with a gasp at the heat of the white leather. Despite his knife-edged trousers and crisp shirt the driver smelled so intensely of sweat it brought back all her fear. There was nothing to be afraid of now, she told herself as he jerked up a V of his fingers and jabbed them so close to her eyes she could see every whorl of the fingertips. When he indicated his own face with his other hand she said "I didn't bring any glasses."

She had to point at her eyes and flap her hands on either side of them before he seemed to understand. She'd barely tugged the seatbelt across herself when the car swerved with a clamour of pebbles and raced uphill. Three scrawny kittens survived scurrying across the road and chased through a hillside garden into a less than vertical cottage in front of which sat an old woman, her brown face wrinkled small, and then the tiny village fell behind. The

road veered between the trees, which were keeping their
shade to themselves, though not the shrill insect rasping
they passed back and forth as if Daniella's approach was
being announced all the way up the island. The car didn't
slow for even the sharpest bend, and neither digging her
nails into the seat nor squeezing her lips together did
her any good. Blurting "Can you slow down?" brought her
nothing but the taste of dust. She shut her eyes in case not
watching the road slew about might stabilise the contents
of her skull, but she was ready to get out and walk—
preparing to haul on the handbrake if a request failed to
halt the car—when she felt it swing around a wider curve
before it stopped with a squeal that stank of rubber. As she
willed it to have come to rest she heard a clatter of sandals
and a cry of greeting. "Daniella."

She opened her eyes to see Nana hurrying along a path
composed of the same white marble as the villa. Her sun-
bleached blonde hair spilled out of a jewelled silver comb
and down her back, over a long silk dress yellow as the
centres of the sunflowers standing guard in a small labyrinth of paths through sprawls of blue and purple blossom,
between pine trees and glossy shrubs. "Didn't you enjoy
your ride? Stavros," Nana said, and more of a reproach in
Greek. "Sometimes I think he wants to drive like they did
in that chase in my first film."

She'd been in her twenties then, two decades before
Daniella was even born. Forty years seemed hardly to have
aged Nana, no doubt partly thanks to the cosmetics her
firm manufactured. Daniella opened the hot door and
leaned on it, then on Nana's arm. "Have you luggage? Let
him bring it," Nana said, placing a cool hand over Dan-

iella's grasp. "Tell me what you'd like now. Anything I can give."

"I'd . . ." She almost gasped that she would die for a drink, but the thought made her mouth even drier. "I'd love some water," she said, and bore down on Nana's arm.

Nana's sea-blue eyes and long classical face turned to her. "Is something else wrong?"

"The boat trip wasn't too much fun."

"It wasn't my choice of a welcome, I promise you. My boat is away for repair. When it's brought back I'll show you round my ocean."

She prolonged an apologetic smile as she led her guest up three broad shallow steps into the wide single-storey building. The vestibule was more than twice the size of Daniella's room in her house in York, and furnished with a pair of low couches and several vases spilling vines. Daniella tried not to shiver at the sudden coolness, but she did. "You poor girl, what now?" her hostess said.

"I wonder if I could lie down for a little while. Maybe stuff is catching up with me."

"I won't ask what kind unless you want to say."

"I'd rather not start just now."

"Then you shan't. Come with me to your room."

Daniella's hand was pressed to Nana's arm as she was escorted along a marble corridor, past a closed door opposite a bedroom with white walls stained blue by sunlight through drawn curtains, and into a similar room. "Make yourself comfortable or tell me if you can't," Nana said and swept out, closing the door.

Daniella stripped to her panties, slinging clothes onto a tall straight-backed pine chair, and fumbled her wristwatch onto the stubby-legged table level with the mattress, then inched beneath the single purple sheet. It felt cool as an autumn breeze. She slid down and laid her cheek against the pillow. The contents of her skull had almost ceased rotating when Nana's footsteps crossed the vestibule and grew more compact in the corridor. She was only starting to sit up as Nana filled a glass from the jug of iced water she set on the table before supporting Daniella's head and holding the crystal glass to her lips. Daniella sipped the glass half empty and swallowed a last mouthful on her way back to the pillow. Her hostess stood the glass beside the jug and leaned down to plant a dry kiss on Daniella's forehead. Daniella's eyes had closed by the time Nana spoke from the doorway. "Rest as long as you like. Nobody knows you're here but us."

EARLIER THAT YEAR

ONE

The smile the young receptionist behind the steel-grey horseshoe of a desk offered Daniella was by no means purely professional. "Can I help?" he said.

"I want to go up and surprise my dad."

"I'd like that if I were him, but you'll need to tell me who he is."

"Teddy Logan."

"Mr Logan." The receptionist lowered his head an inch to regard her under his brows, incidentally presenting her with a better view of the wet black turf of his scalp. A drop of gel glistened on the right shoulder of his collarless jacket, which was only slightly greyer than the desk. "You're his daughter," he said.

"Right so far."

"Are you planning an acting career?"

"I've done a bit. Does it show?"

"It mightn't to most people. Nice try, but you missed one detail."

"Tell me."

"Mr Logan's American, and you'd know if you heard him talk."

"You're new, aren't you?"

"Not so new I don't know how to do my job."

"He isn't going to like you doing it this hard. Why

don't you call upstairs and tell him I'm here."

"Someone's pitching him an idea for a film."

"Call his secretary, then."

"You're saying you didn't know she's gone for lunch."

"Right, I didn't. Listen, you've been good, but—"

He crooked a finger until she leaned close enough for the scent of gel to oil her nostrils. "What would it be worth for me to say you took me in?"

"Not much. I'm a student."

"I don't look as if I need your money, do I? Just company for dinner."

"I've already got a boyfriend."

"Must be pretty insecure if you can't accept an invitation for a night out on the town."

She was wondering resentfully if the accusation was aimed at her when the glass doors admitted a burst of the rumble of traffic on Piccadilly before sweeping it out again. "Any messages, Peter?" the newcomer said.

"Nothing for you or Mr Logan, Miss Kerr." To Daniella he murmured "That's his secretary."

"I know. Hi, Janis."

"Hi, Daniella."

The receptionist struggled to maintain a smile as his words began to flee him. "Excuse me, Miss Kerr, this young lady isn't, that's to say, is she . . ."

"She's the great man's best production."

"I'm sure. Will you take Miss Logan up to him, Miss Kerr?"

"Happy to," said Janis, but stayed Daniella with a negligently half-open hand until the receptionist looked up from the clipboard he'd abruptly found interesting. "Even though she's who she is you'll need to give her a visitor's pass."

"Absolutely. I was just—" Just relieved, Daniella thought, that Janis headed for the lift without waiting for his stumble at an explanation. He shoved the visitors' book across the desk for Daniella to sign and crouched off his seat to hand her a plastic badge. "Sorry," he pleaded in a whisper.

"I believe you," Daniella said as Janis restrained the lift on her behalf. The box of mirrors full of images of Janis— tall, elegant, sallow, ebony-haired as a film in glossy mono-chrome—and of herself—slim enough, face too round to be really interesting, small nose that annoyed her by ap-pearing to want to look cute, blonde hair in which last month's rust was lingering—had barely closed its doors when Janis said "Any problems with our new boy?"

Daniella remembered how she'd had to search for a summer job—how hard it was for so many people to find work. "No," she said.

Janis snapped open her suede handbag to touch up her black lipstick. "So what brings you to town?"

"I was supposed to have lunch with my mother, only one of the companies she looks after, their computers crashed this morning. I was on my way out when she called, so I thought I'd use my ticket anyway."

"I know Mr Logan will be glad you did. Stop him brooding over whatever's on his mind," Janis said as the doors revealed the London offices of Oxford Films.

A carpet greener than grass after rain led along the wide blue corridor. Framed posters from the fifties showed suited people accompanied by slogans that grew less discreet

as the decade progressed, until by its end they were prom-
ising horrors in bright red before discovering sex for the
sixties and seventies. Nana Babouris's face appeared on
some of them, and occupied more space as the posters abandoned sex to become steadily braver and weepier. Two posters for *Help Her to Live*—Nana beaming as she lost a
wheelchair race to her adopted daughter for the British
market, Nana lifting her high above the child's chair for
America—guarded Janis's door, and Daniella recalled using
up a boxful of tissues when, at ten years old, she'd watched
the film. She grinned wryly and dabbed at her eyes as she
followed Janis into the office.

Janis sat behind her wide thin pine desk and tugged
her charcoal skirt over her darkly nyloned knees as she
thumbed the intercom. "Mr Logan? I thought you'd want
to know your daughter's here."

His response was audible through both the speaker and
the connecting door. "I'm on my way," he shouted and
flung the door open to stride out, his white shirt bulging
with his stomach but not quite straining at its buttons, his
arms and his bright blue eyes wide, his bushy eyebrows
crowding creases up his high forehead all the way to the
temples that used to boast more of his grey hair. He hugged
Daniella and rubbed her spine until he yanked her T-shirt
out of her jeans, and she did her best to match his fierceness,
however overstated she'd begun to find it recently. "Good
to see you too," she gasped.

"That isn't the half of it. You're a picture." With some
reluctance, as if he hadn't finished assuring himself she was
there, he left off hugging her and led her by the hand into
his office. "Say, you can be the audience," he said.

Beyond the window flanked by posters a bus without a roof passed soundlessly, its sightseers turning their backs on the Logans with a movement so unified it might have been choreographed to gaze across Green Park towards Buckingham Palace. Fat bags of soft black leather sprawled on the tubular frames of chairs in front of and behind her father's massive antique desk. A man with a briefcase gripped between his gleaming coaly brogues sat perched on the edge of the chair facing the desk as though he was afraid to relax. "Isaac Faber. He wants to make movies," her father said. "Isaac, meet my only child."

The man sprang up to shake her hand, nearly tripping over the briefcase, and sat again at once. His scalp was only slightly hairier than his unshaven chin. His pudgy youthful face was doing its best to be ready for whatever came next, and she felt sorry for him. Her father sat on a couch and patted the portly cushion beside him, and said as she joined him "Try and sell my daughter. She's your target audience."

"It's," Isaac Faber told her, "well, as I was saying, it's about searching for a myth."

"Who's doing that?"

"That's right. I mean, it's interesting you ask. I was thinking while you fetched your daughter, Mr Logan, it could be a knight, Arthurian, he could be. Brought to life by magic or he's been in like suspended animation till people need him again."

"That part sounds better," Daniella's father said.

"He sets out to look for others like him," Daniella was eagerly informed, "but he can't find any, so he goes searching for what people believe in like they used to believe in the Holy Grail. And he finds the world's more savage than it was the last time he was alive. The only myths left are success and wealth and power, and people will do anything to get them."

"Sounds pretty true."

"But would you pay to watch it?" her father said.

"I don't know," she had to admit.

"Sounds like no to me. There's your answer, Mr Faber, from a young lady who goes to the movies every week. People need myths to live by. That's why *The Flood* broke records. My daughter and her friend Chrysteen saw it twice."

He was directing a thumbs-up at the posters for the film, the ark balanced on a dripping mountain-top beneath a rainbow, the column of Oscars—best cinematography, best effects, best original song (*The Engine Of My Heart*: "No oars, no sails, just the engine of my heart...") all dwarfed by the image in the clouds of Shem (Daniel Ray) embracing Sarah (Nancy Hilton). "We fancy Daniel Ray," Daniella said.

"That's what movies are about, Isaac, giving people what they want, not what you think they ought to. Lots of animals and fart jokes for the kids, and romance for the ladies, and action for us men, and spectacle for the family, and wonder on top of it all to send everyone out feeling they've been somewhere they want to go back."

"I thought you might want to consider investing some of your profits in a movie that could earn you a different kind of award."

Daniella's father grew monolithically still, as he did on learning she'd behaved in some way he thought wrong. Whatever she might have dreaded he would say to Isaac Faber, it wasn't "Want to teach me about investments too?"

"Only—"

"Some of the television companies have public money to risk is what I hear. Try them. Now if you'll excuse us, it's been too long since what's left of my family had a talk."

Isaac Faber grabbed his briefcase and stared at it until he was out of the chair. "Thanks for your time," he said, his attention shuttling between his listeners, "and your advice." He closed the door with a painful gentleness before making a rapid escape. "What a monster," Daniella's father said.

"I didn't think he was that bad."

"Not him. Me."

"You were only doing your job. You're still my usual dad." Nevertheless he'd given her the chance to ask "What's the matter?"

"What should be?"

"I'd say you had something on your mind."

"Plenty of room for it." When the quip didn't turn her gaze aside he said "I guess, I guess I just don't understand how anyone could think I'd care to put my name anywhere near the kind of message that guy wanted to send. Maybe you can tell me what I must be doing wrong."

"Nothing I know about."

He reached out to her with the hand that used to sport his wedding ring, but refrained from touching her. "I wish you'd told me you were coming."

"Don't worry, dad, I wasn't trying to catch you out."

"At what? How do you mean?"

"At nothing. That's my point."

"I meant Mr Faber could have waited and we'd have had lunch," he said, tramping to his chair behind the desk. "So how's your work shaping up?"

"I like having to act and not just being a waitress."

"Your university work, Daniella."

"Good."

He rubbed his forehead, but the creases stayed as deep. "You didn't need to get yourself a summer job. You could have come home to me and had more time to study."

"I don't need more time, honestly, and I want to earn a bit. You always said how hard you had to work to get a break." She could have added that she valued her independence, but she knew that wouldn't please him. "I thought you'd be happy I got a start in life."

She didn't expect to see his eyes grow moist and turn upwards as his hands closed into fists on either side of his gold pen standing tall in its golden holder. She could only assume he was growing nostalgic. "Anyway," she said, "don't you want me to use my student house when you bought it for me?"

"Make the most of it, yes. I know you're doing that, even if you could ask your tenants for more rent. I know they're your friends, but that's all the more reason to do business properly with them." He drew a breath that reddened his face and blurted "Listen, Daniella—"

He could hardly have been inviting her to hear the footsteps that became audible just as the door was edged open. "Teddy, we need to talk," the newcomer declared. "Oh, hello, Daniella."

He was her father's partner Alan Stanley, and she didn't believe he hadn't known she was there. He stalked past, lanky and stooped and round-shouldered, bestowing scents of soap and after-shave and deodorant on her, and leaned down to grip the edge of her father's desk. "It's been long enough," he said.

Her father lifted his hands as though to seize his partner by the lapels and pull him conspiratorially close. Instead
he muttered "I'll be with you in a minute."

"Don't let anything prevent you." Stanley laid his gaze
on Daniella as he retreated to the door. "Please," he said.

Her father seemed anxious, but not to stand up. "Will
you wait till I'm through?" he said to her, barely a query.
"Then I'll drive you back and we can talk. No, you'll be
bored waiting." He turned to the safe and typed the combination fast as a stenographer. "You go shopping and be
back in let's say two hours."

"Thanks, dad, but..." As he lifted out a wad of
twenty-pound notes she saw a slim white wooden box at
the rear of the safe. "What's that?" she said.

"My wad for emergencies."

"Not the money. The box."

"Nothing." His face appeared uncertain whether to
grow pale or red as he shut the metal door. "How much
shall I give you?" he said, hurrying around the desk.

"As much as you want, only dad, I'm not going to be
able to stick around that long. I have to get back to meet
someone this evening."

"Someone."

"Right, someone I know."

"With a name."

"Blake."

"Which end of the someone is that?"

"His front. His first name."

"You don't know the rest of him?"

"Of course I do. Blake Wainwright."

"Have I heard of him?"

"I've only known him a few weeks. He's okay."

"You think you can know a person in that short a time? I guess it depends how you mean knowing."

"Not the way the Bible does."

"Don't, either, if you care whether I sleep nights. You won't thank me for saying this again, but it isn't like it used to be when I was your age and you could go to a clinic if you had to. These days sleeping round can kill you, and let me tell you your mom and I never did. Never slept with anyone till we were married."

His concern for her had grown even more stifling since her mother had divorced him. She saw him waving notes at her like a fee for keeping herself pure, which seemed almost as demeaning as the reverse. "Maybe I won't either," she said with some resentment.

"I pray it's more than maybe. Keep faith with me over that at least. You're enough of your own person to have that respect for yourself. This Blake of yours, you can't know if he's been with anyone else, can you? Even if he says he hasn't."

"Believe it or not, I haven't asked." She saw her father preparing to worry the subject further, but she'd had a good deal more than enough. "I thought you had to talk to Mr Stanley," she said.

"I have to talk with you." For a moment he looked paralysed by the conflict, only the skin around his eyes moving, and then he snatched a sheaf of notes off the wad. "Take this anyway," he said, planting the money in her hand. "It'll help you keep me in mind. Spend it however you like."

It must have been at least two hundred pounds. He threw the rest of the wad in the safe, which he shut again so fast she scarcely glimpsed the white box. "You don't have to give me this," she said. "It wasn't why I came."

"I want to. Won't you let me?"

The present was a gesture, she understood then—a means of pretending to himself that he was taking care of her in whatever way he secretly wished he could. "Thanks, dad," she said. "Really, thanks a pile. I'd stay if you didn't have your meeting."

"Can't you call your friend and put him off?"

"He'll be in a lecture." Before she could grow vexed at the threat of further interference she stuffed the notes into her purse and embraced her father. His hug was fiercer than before, so that when eventually it relented she had to search for breath to say "We'll get together again soon."

"Very soon," he said, so tonelessly that all the way to her train to York she wondered what he had in mind.

TWO

It wasn't supposed to be dark by the time she reached York, but the sky had other ideas. When her little nippy cute snub-nosed bright blue Ford emerged from the car park, the clouds were pretending it was dusk above the high steep roofs of narrow winding Micklegate and challenging the streetlamps to catch up. She drove across a river bridge and past Clifford's Tower, where families of mediaeval Jews had failed to hide from being massacred. A second bridge carried her across a different river to follow the curve of the Roman city wall before swinging away to the suburbs. Ten minutes' worth of long streets packed with small quiet houses, in front of which the occasional mower prowled the enclosure of a garden, brought her to the campus.

She parked outside the Drama Barn, watched by three student Cossacks who were celebrating an interval with heartfelt cigarettes, and headed for the lake. She'd arranged to meet Blake at the far end of the footbridge, but only trees and huddled shrubs were waiting there, and so she leaned on the handrail and gazed across the water.

Boxy concrete buildings pressed low by the slaty sky lent a shifting whitish glimmer to the lake. Someone's birthday was being sung and drunk to in the Godric Bar. Footsteps rattled on the bridge, and its reflection seemed to quiver with them, but none of them was Blake's—all of them were bound for the birthday. He was a minute late, then five, then a darker ten. It took her half an hour to admit to herself he wasn't going to appear.

She might have given him up sooner if she hadn't felt watched. Shrubs scraped their leaves together whenever a breeze attempted to shift the July mugginess, and kept suggesting how much their foliage could hide. The chorus in the bar only emphasised her isolation. Her lips rehearsed a shout and let it fly. "Blake, is that you arising about?"

Shrubs creaked and shook their dim leaves in a wind that was breathing down her neck. She shoved herself away from the handrail and strode furiously to prove that nobody was hiding. A gathering of shrubs around a tree, and darkness behind them—another clump of bushes, and nobody behind them either, nor any room. A curve of the lake brought her to a huddle of shrubs through which she could see the end of the bridge where she'd waited. Close to their roots, two footprints glistened in the soil.

They were so deep that whoever they belonged to must have stood there as long as Daniella had been on the bridge, perhaps longer. Moisture was sinking into them as if they had only just been vacated. At once she remembered how much money she was carrying. She thrust a hand into her bag to grasp her attack alarm as she retreated to the bridge.

Blades clashed in the Drama Barn, and she heard a rush of footsteps over wood. As she groped for her keys, a face and then another sprang up in the car next to hers. A couple had been busy with each other on the back seat, and she managed a grin and a disinterested wave before shutting herself in her car. She had to keep braking to restrain her speed once she was on the road. She drove across both rivers, through crowds of tourists and natives the lights of the streets had attracted, and under the arch at Micklegate. Two minutes later she was turning along Scarcroft Road towards her house.

It was in the middle of a row of tall houses facing a park. Four boys who had stripped to the waist to wad themselves goalposts were playing football on the grass combed by shadows of the railings. She found a parking space as close to home as she was able, four houses distant, and verified twice that the car was locked before hurrying to her exhausted iron gate and lifting it so that it wouldn't scrape yet more of an arc on the cracked hump of the path. She sidled past the weeds she and the others kept agreeing needed more than stern words and unlocked the blue, though black from the orange streetlight, front door.

Duncan's bicycle was leaning against several of the silver tulips of the wallpaper. Beside it the phone stood mute on the small unfolded table beneath the lamp wearing the party hat Chrysteen had draped over the shade the day the two of them had moved into the house. As Daniella set foot on the lowest stair Chrysteen shouted from the bathroom "Did someone come in? Danny won't be back yet, will she?"

"Afraid I am."

"Come and see what Maeve's done to my film," Duncan called from the front room.

Daniella adopted a careless expression as she went to find them. He and Maeve were sprawled on the couch in front of the television, her long fishnetted legs outstretched from her wide short skirt across his lap, while the rest of the fat floppy suite was occupied by her computer magazines and a list of websites she'd printed out for Chysteen

to consult for her psychology essay. Chinese takeaway car-
tons and a lingering aroma had taken up temporary resi-
dence too. "On your own?" Duncan asked Daniella, poking
his large face forward until his mousy hair trailed over his
ears to frame his dimpled chin. "No man?"

"None of those."

"Shit." When Maeve frowned he enquired "Aren't I
being couth enough again?"

"I'd say you found the right word for Blake," Daniella
said.

Maeve shook back her glossy auburn hair from her pale
oval face peppered with freckles. "First tiff?"

"More than that or less. He didn't turn up."

"Must be a," Duncan said, and suppressed an epithet.
"A steaming stool."

"Who is?" Chrysteen asked from the stairs, her small
pert green-eyed face flushed beneath the turban of a towel
even pinker than her bathrobe.

"Daniella's date let her down," said Maeve. "Sorry,
Daniella."

"Danny." Chrysteen joined her in the doorway and
stroked her arm. "We're never lucky with our men, are
we?"

Daniella thought it was more that their fathers had lost
them all their boyfriends by making them aware they
weren't good enough. "Do you want to leave my movie till
another time?" Duncan suggested.

Daniella transferred the printouts to the sideboard nobody ever remembered to dust, much like the rest of the
house. She tucked her legs beneath her on the vacated chair
and clasped her knees. "Show me."

For some seconds after Duncan set the videotape rolling

she thought she was still watching a blank screen, and then she noticed characters forming. Very gradually the words grew clear, one behind the other. PHOTOGRAPHED. EDITED. DIRECTED. Just as she wondered if Maeve had to finish working on the credits, tiny letters swarmed from within the larger to spell BY DUNCAN MCDONALD. Behind all this activity the title of the documentary had been taking shape. UNNOTICED, it announced while the rest of the words faded, then followed them into blackness to make way for the opening scene, the first of several prolonged observations of people living on the streets of York and ignored by practically every passer-by. It occurred to Daniella as Duncan switched off the television and rewound the tape that the title could describe both the subject and the camera. "See, now it looks like a real film," he said.

"Don't be so Glaswegian," Maeve rebuked him. "It always did."

"Now it looks like more of one," Daniella said.

"I want to make an online broadcast, but I don't know what of yet. She won't let me put the camera in her room."

"You keep me to yourself," Maeve said, rewarding him with not enough of a slap to pinken his cheek, as Chrysteen proclaimed coffee in the kitchen.

He set about washing up at least a day's accumulation of everyone's plates while Daniella sipped coffee from her old Care For Children mug with its chipped slogan A CHILD FOR LIFE. Maeve watched her across the round table through the intertwining fumes of both their mugs before murmuring "I didn't finish saying I was sorry."

"For what, Maeve?"

"Someone phoned for Blake while you were out. Sounded like a girl."

"And you told them . . ."

"Where he lives and where you were meeting him. I
didn't think it could be anything suspicious when they'd
rung here."

"Don't let it bother you any more, then."

"It does, specially when you let me and Duncan pay
such a piddling rent and then I go and do that to you."

"You wouldn't be paying any at all if my dad didn't
keep insisting. You know you two were the ones Chrys and
I liked best that wanted to share our house. Anyway, if you
hadn't you mightn't have met."

"There's that," Maeve admitted, perching on Duncan's
knee as he sat down.

"And as for Blake, it was better known than not,
agreed? Now I've definitely had enough of him."

Nevertheless Maeve turned on Duncan. "What are you
squirming about now for?"

"Just finding something to take her mind off," he said
in his best injured voice.

"Get on, then," Maeve said as magnanimously as she
ever treated him, and stooped forward while he produced
from his shirt pocket the thinnest of hand-rolled cigarettes.
"Have a blast on England's finest," he said to Daniella.

"I won't, thanks, not while I'm a bit on edge with
things. Maybe I'll have a beer. But you go ahead."

Chrysteen leaned into the refrigerator for a bottle of
Dutch lager and flipped off the top for her as Duncan lit
the joint and clanked his Zippo shut before inhaling with
a hiss between his teeth. Maeve indulged in a token puff
and passed the joint to Chrysteen. By the time the remaining half returned to Duncan, he was grinning with aston-

ishment and delight—was still grinning when the doorbell rang.

He turned most of a cough into a giggle, having exhaled with a gasp. "It's the police."

"Don't be doing that." Maeve dealt his shin a vigorous slap that helped send her to the window. She opened a finger and thumb between two slats of the blind, then pressed her cheek against it, scraping plastic on the glass. After a pause that everyone but Daniella greeted openmouthed she said "It's the police."

There was silence while the others decided who would lead the hilarity. It was Chrysteen who cried "It's the police" as if repeating the punch line of a choice joke.

"No," Maeve said, not loud but so clearly it cut through the laughter. "I mean it. It's the police."

"You're f—" At a warning look from Maeve, Duncan kept the rest of the word to himself. "You're not. You aren't joking. Help," he muttered, sticking out his tongue to extinguish the joint with a hiss and dropping the bent bedraggled stub in his pocket before devoting himself to waving off the spicy smoke.

"Everyone stay in here," Daniella said. "I'll see what they want."

It was her house, after all, though she had time to reflect as she ventured along the hall that ownership made her more responsible in the eyes of the law. Her fingers needed some persuading to turn the latch. The door gave a nervous sound on her behalf as she pulled it open, spilling the light of the party hat over the solitary officer on the path.

He lifted his peaked helmet to display more of his worn

middle-aged face, the nose so broad it might have been flattened to conform with the rest of the features, whose plainness was only underlined by a thin rigid black moustache. If he'd allowed himself any expression while he was waiting, he had dispensed with it now. "Is Miss Logan here?" he said.

"Daniella Logan, right, that's me. What—"

It wasn't just the unmistakable herbal smell straying through some chink in the kitchen window-frame that caused her to falter; it was that, having raised his head to acknowledge the smell, the policeman ignored it, so that she understood how much graver the reason for his visit had to be. A surge of guilt made her blurt into the silence that had spread from the deserted park to the house "Is it Blake?"

A frown too faint to trap a shadow vanished as she glimpsed it. "Can you say that for me again, Miss Logan?"

"Blake Wainwright. He's a student. Has something happened to him?"

"We haven't heard so." The policeman held his hands by his sides and levelled his unexpectedly deep brown eyes at her. "Not to him," he said.

THREE

The motorway from London fell miles short of York. Daniella had never driven to it nearly as fast as she was being driven now. Even when the road ceased to be a dual carriageway the policeman didn't slow down. Cars flinched to the side of the road, away from the pulsing lights and the siren, and a van that was venturing out of the car park of a pub retreated like a snail into a shell. Once she saw a translucent decoration twirling in the headlamp beams, a moth; once she glimpsed a fountain that was a man urinating brightly into a ditch. Once she sucked in her breath as a rabbit froze in the road, its black eyes huge and gleaming, but when she felt a soft thud beneath one wheel and then another she made no further sound. She knew there was worse ahead.

She didn't speak until the car raced past the junction for the motorway. "We should have turned there," she protested.

The policeman moved his grip higher on the wheel. "I'm afraid not," he said.

The road twisted back and forth as though desperate to avoid the probing of the headlamps, and then it described a long curve, the outer edge of which broadened into a layby shaded by trees. The single permanently parked vehicle was a double-decker bus that had been converted into a roadside café where truck drivers drank murky tea from mugs. Just now there were no trucks, only three police cars whose warning beacons jerked the underside of the foliage alight, leaves glaring red or blue like cheap illuminations. Daniella's driver sped to the far end of the lay-by before swinging across the road into the entrance, and she saw the Mercedes pointing in the wrong direction and resting against trees beyond a police vehicle in front of the bus. Though the Mercedes didn't look as damaged as she'd feared, her innards stiffened. It was her father's car.

The policeman hadn't braked when she unclipped her safety belt. He began to speak as she fumbled the door open and dashed across the rutted earth to the Mercedes. Its silver body was being turned into a throbbing bruise by the roof lights of the police cars. There wasn't a scratch on the passenger side, and she dared to hope until she realised what else she was seeing. Half the car was gone.

For a moment her mind let her imagine it was a fake, a prop of which only as much as an audience needed to see had been built. The trees had smashed in or sheared away most of the driver's side of the car. The wreckage of the driver's seat sprawled almost horizontal in the back, and was sprinkled with glass that glittered dark red, perhaps not just with the flashing of the police lights. She bowed towards her three palpitating shadows on the hood and planted a hand on the unyielding metal, which was so cold it added to her shock. "Where's my dad?" she said.

She had no sense of how loud she'd spoken until a chubby big-boned policeman abandoned his interrogation of a young man in motorcycle leather and made his weighty way to her. "Daniella Logan?"

"Where's my dad?"

"They've taken him."

Her voice was seeking refuge in her throat, and when she forced it free it came out sharp. "Who has? Where?"

"The medics. To the hospital."

"Which?"

"The nearest is Leeds. He'll take you," the policeman said, turning a slow thumb towards her recent driver.

"What happened?"

"That's what I'm now in the process of ascertaining."

He rounded with deliberate if unnecessary gracefulness on the motorcyclist, who stepped forward. "Are you Daniella?" he said.

His thin angular face was white as paper. A vein at his temple throbbed with light or anxiety or both. She didn't know what she might be inviting by saying "Yes?"

"He talked about you. He said your name."

Her eyes blurred, and she supported herself on the remains of the hood while she blinked her vision clear. "Who are you?"

"I called the police and the ambulance and stayed with him till they came," he said, patting the mobile phone on his belt. "I didn't make him crash, I wasn't even close. I was nearly on the road when I saw him coming and I stopped." His accent was retreating northward as he spoke. "I think he saw my light and thought this was part of the road. That's how fast he drove onto it, and then he tried to stop when he must have seen the bus. He skidded round, and—well."

Though he restrained himself from indicating the wreck, his glancing away from it while he avoided talking about it was as bad. She stood back from it and wobbled only a little on her rickety legs as she saw her driver trudging over, having spoken to his radio. "Can we go to the hospital?" she said almost before her voice gave way.

"I was coming for you."

He stayed close to her as she returned to his car, but she managed not to need to grab his arm. Once she'd donned her safety belt he eased the car into the road. He built up speed gradually, by no means as much of it as before, and left the warning lights and siren off. She tried to speak more than once on the way to saying "Can't we go faster?"

"I'm sorry," he said and breathed hard through his nose, either expressing some emotion or delaying his next words. She saw the oncoming road grow artificial and irrelevant as a video game when he said "I'm afraid there's no longer the need."

FOUR

E xperts on the cinema have described Theodore Daniel
Logan as the last of the old-fashioned producers and the
first of the new. He started his career as a production assistant in Hollywood. By the mid-1950s he had risen to
become an assistant producer at Worldwide American Pictures, in which capacity he visited this country to oversee a
series of co-productions with our own Oxford Films. He
enjoyed his stay so much and was so impressed with our
native talents that he chose to make his home here and
build Oxford Films into a vibrant force in the international
market. From creating the world-famous Ripper Jack series
he moved on to invent the even more successful concept of
Uplift Cinema, a term that can be found in the latest dic-
tionaries. He himself was wont to say he could never have
affected the hearts and souls of the world without his star
Nana Babouris, who I see is here today, having travelled
from Greece to pay her respects to the memory of the man
who discovered her. I think her presence and that of so
many other famous names shows how Theodore—Teddy—
Logan was loved even more than his films, both by his
family and everyone whose lives he touched . . ."

Daniella felt the priest was packaging her father in a
way that blurred his awkward aspects, sealing him up even
more hermetically than the coffin that hid the body only

her mother had seen at the hospital. She stood in the front
pew of the plain white church, her mother on her right
and Chrysteen on her left, and couldn't help thinking that
they were competing at how blackly they were dressed. As
her gaze lingered on the gilded handles of the coffin she
told herself he would have appreciated the luxury, and tried
to believe he might be looking down on it or in some other
way aware of it. Her attempts saw her through the eulogy,
at the end of which speakers above the abstract triangles of
stained glass on either side of the unadorned altar struck
up a hushed melody not unlike an accompaniment to va-
cating a cinema. The similarity made her dab hard at her
eyes as she followed her mother out of the church.

The rituals were far from over. Every mourner needed
to be shaken by the hand, every one of the procession of
utterances had to be greeted with not too much of either a
smile or a tear, and then there was the coffin to be watched
as it descended into the earth, and a handful of soil that
gritted under Daniella's fingernails to be cast with a soft
rattle on the lid. As she joined her mother in the elongated
black car that had led the stately parade she remembered
the first time her father had given her a ride in a limousine,
following so digressive a homeward route from the studios
that it included all the places whose names on signposts had
amused her: Ot Moor, Brill, Worminghall, Ickford, Shab-
bington, Fingest (which she'd thought must be like a finger,
only more so), Berrick Salome, Toot Baldon . . . Now the
vehicle scarcely had time to gain speed along a sinuous lane
green with shade before it and its dozens of followers arrived at the Logan house.

It stood at the edge of Oxford, facing fields and surrounded by a garden crowded with several varieties of rho-

dodendron. Sunlight scoured the tall bay windows set in
sandstone on either side of the massive oak front door, windows that displayed the absence of Daniella's father in every
room. As she unlocked the door she remembered how he'd
sprinted down the wide oak staircase to hug her breathless
the last time she'd come home. Now the rooms seemed
unnaturally clean from the attentions of the housekeeper,
and the buffet with which the caterers hired by Alan Stanley had loaded every available surface in the panelled
dining-room only made it feel less lived in than a
restaurant. But the guests trooped in and set about the food
and wine, and as the conversations grew louder Chrysteen
brought her a lager to go with her plateful of snacks. She'd
seen that Daniella needed a drink, since all the guests appeared to be determined to top the observations they had
made to her outside the church.

"He thought the world of you," said Reginald Gray in
the tone he reserved on his television show for welcoming
inexperienced guests. "He made you the best life he could."

"He gave you everything you wanted, didn't he?" said
Loony Larry Larabee, not attempting to live up to his epithet on this occasion.

"Don't take this the wrong way," Anthony St George
said, "but you can't know how important you were to him."

He was the surgeon who'd had himself flown to the
hospital, though not quite in time to save her father, and
so she told herself he still meant to be kind. Meanwhile
Norman Wells was informing her mother "You and Teddy
created the most precious thing anyone can, Isobel."

He would say that, Daniella thought, since he ran the
Care For Children charity. The approach of Simon Hastings, Chrysteen's father, saved her from blushing too much.

"Rest assured I'm keeping both eyes on the investigation," the chief constable said.

"Thank you," Daniella's mother murmured.

Daniella considered leaving it at that but couldn't. "Why my dad was drunk, you mean. So drunk he didn't even know which way he was going."

A hint of a quizzical expression he might have directed at someone half her age appeared on his jowly pinkish face. "What do you think that could tell us?"

"I don't know, but he never drank and drove."

"Till then, you mean. Up to then, agreed, he was an example to us all."

"If there were more men like he was," said Bill Trask, owner of the *Beacon* newspaper, "the world would be a steadier place."

Daniella saw Nana Babouris frown at his back, and felt encouraged to retort "Just men?"

"I didn't mean to denigrate your mother," he said, lifting his fat piebald face to sight down his luxuriant purplish nose at Daniella, "but you'll remember we're here for your father."

"I'm not likely to forget it, am I?"

Perhaps she'd spoken too loud or too sharply, because he was raising the pair of pressed-together fingers next to the one that was swollen around a wedding ring, either to wag them at her or to bless her, when Eamonn Reith put a gentle arm around her shoulders. "Is it all proving a bit much, young lady?"

"I think she's behaved like a credit to the family," her mother said.

"I've been observing that," the psychoanalyst said, giving Daniella a squeeze that felt close to proprietary. "I just wanted to say, Daniella, if you find you'd like counselling, my services are free to Teddy Logan's daughter."

"You're kind."

She was doing her best to appreciate his concern, even though it made her feel as if some delayed reaction to her father's death was lying in wait for her. As Reith moved away, Nana Babouris beckoned her over to whisper "If you need somewhere to help you recover I'm not too far away. You'll find me in your father's book. Easier still," she said, and palmed it, "here's my card."

There had been times when Daniella might have gone abroad if the prospect hadn't made her father so openly anxious. "I'll remember," she said.

Chrysteen and her parents were the last to leave. As the Hastings family drove away, Daniella's mother expelled a breath that trembled her wide pink lips and drained her pale blue eyes and flawless oval face of nearly all the animation she'd maintained throughout the wake. "Well, now I can be myself."

"You didn't need to pretend you weren't," Daniella said. "Everyone knows you and dad split up."

"You wouldn't have wanted me seeming less of a wife than the rest of them."

"I couldn't stand it if you were like Mrs Trask."

"The *Beacon*'s perfect woman, you mean. Little and demure."

"Some of the others weren't much better, were they?"

"Maybe it was the occasion. No wonder Ms Babouris looked out of place even if she was toning herself down."

Daniella might have mentioned Nana's invitation, but there was a question she wanted to ask. "Mum?"

"I fancy a coffee to liven me up. Are you feeling a bit

sludgy in the head as well after all the effort you've been making?"

"Let's have one and talk."

Her mother seemed uncertain as a house guest in her old kitchen heavy with mahogany units, and Daniella took that as another cue for her to wonder "Why did you leave dad?"

"I didn't until I thought you could look after yourself." The dripping of the percolator appeared to demand most of her attention as she added "You were at university and I felt it was time to make a move too. Shouldn't I have?"

"It was a shock, that's all."

"You mean I should have let you know my plans, but then he would have known too."

"He wouldn't have been able to do much to stop you, would he?"

Daniella's mother took an inadvertent step towards her as the percolator hissed. "He seemed happy enough with me not around, so you're right, I should have had more thought for you."

"You always had lots." As she stroked her mother's back she felt bound to add "Both of you did."

"The truth is I only really decided I was going once you did."

"Why, didn't you like being alone with him?"

"Once you'd gone there didn't seem to be much left between us," Daniella's mother said, and gazed hard at her. "Was anything wrong when you were with him?"

"I just felt whenever it was time to leave I hadn't given him enough."

"He made you feel that way, do you mean?"

"He tried not to."

Her mother lifted two earthenware mugs down from the hooks beside the stack of ovens. "I hope you'll keep on using my spare room whenever you need it. Don't feel compelled, but don't you dare feel anything but wanted."

This was far less oppressive than her father's insistence on her coming home as often as she could. "I never have," she said.

Her mother passed her a fuming mug and cupped her hands around her own. "So what do you think you may do with it all?"

"All what?"

"This house, for instance. I can't imagine he will have left it to me."

"You can have it if you want."

"That's lovely of you, but I should wait and see what else comes to you."

"Do you think I might be a partner in the studio?"

"I won't be surprised if you find you have some interest in it."

"I'll be a movie magnate. Maybe I'll have my name on films." The blaze of amazement faded before it could illuminate prospects more precise. "I'd rather still have dad," she said.

"I hope I'm some consolation."

"You know you're a lot more than that." Nevertheless Daniella didn't want to feel she was the subject of some kind of emotional auction, especially when one of the competitors could no longer bid for himself. As twilight set about subduing the colours of the long garden and intensified the silence of the house she said "I don't suppose you'd like to go and visit dad before it's dark."

"It's a little soon for me. Would you?"

"I wouldn't mind now everybody's gone. I'll be back in York tomorrow, and I don't know when I'm coming home again."

"I'll tag along if you'd like me to."

"It's all right, mummy, you stay and rest," Daniella said, having glimpsed her mother's need for it. "By myself I'll have more chance to think."

"How are you going?"

"I've been drinking. I'll walk."

"Best be off then, while there's some light on the road."

Daniella hurried upstairs to change. On the horizon beyond her window framed by green curtains printed with vines, the Chiltern hills were turning blue with an oncoming chill. Nearly all her clothes from the fitted wardrobe and the drawers had accompanied her to York, but she felt as though her father's absence had emptied her bedroom. She took off her black dress and pulled on the jeans and thin sweater she'd travelled in, and trotted quickly past the echoes of her footsteps in her parents', her father's, nobody's room.

Her mother was taking up less than a third of the massive burgundy leather settee in the front room. A gin and tonic and the control of the giant widescreen television, which had opened its oaken doors, were doing their best to keep her company. "I shouldn't be long," Daniella said.

"You be all the time you have to be."

Daniella picked up speed once she left the squeaky gravel drive for the secluded grass-verged road, on both sides of which poplars fingered the dimming sky as if to determine how solid the dark blue glassy surface was. Infrequent breezes startled creaks out of the dense hedges. She walked on the right to face the traffic, but there was

none to face. Twice as she rounded a bend some small crea-
ture darted across the road, and once a lithe black glossy
shape vanished with a plop into the ditch alongside the
roots of the hedge. Otherwise, for most of the half an hour
it took her to come in sight of the churchyard, she was
alone with shadows stretching to combine with the dusk.

When it occurred to her that her father wouldn't have
liked her walking by herself out here so late, she had to
halt and dab at her eyes. She felt as if she was rebelling
against his protectiveness at last, but she would rather not
have had this chance. She would almost have preferred to
be back at the convent school to feel constantly watched by
the stern pale faces pinched by wimples in case she might
even think of transgressing any of the rules, far more than
made sense. She and Chrysteen had hardly ever broken one
for fear of letting down their parents—mostly their fathers,
who'd insisted on sending them to the high school that
would keep them safest, though the families were at best
token churchgoers. At first university seemed almost too
unconstrained for her to brave without Chrysteen—sometimes it still did.

How much was her mother to blame? Just now Daniella blamed her more for leaving her husband for so little
apparent reason—if she hadn't he might still be alive. He
must have been feeling lonely to have welcomed Daniella
on the day of his death so forcefully it had seemed close to
violence. She found herself remembering her last day at
school, her ascending the steps to the stage to receive a
distinguished old girl's handshake and an award for excel-
lence in English, her parents' proud faces a few rows of
folding chairs away, her father raising a triumphant fist
before he opened it and brought it to his face as though to

gaze at it, instead fingering the edge of his right eye: had he been reflecting that one day he must lose her? But it was she who'd lost him, and now they could be no closer than the churchyard.

The church looked less than ever like one. Only the irregular arrangements of stained glass in the assortment of angular windows relieved its resemblance to a stone vessel half buried in the earth, its low concrete roof straining up to a spire like a primitive prow, and the light was gone from the windows. Three crows sailed up from the tallest of the fir trees beyond the church as she closed the hushed side gate in the high stone wall. The birds flapped to add themselves to the blackness on the horizon while she left the path for the grass and picked her way between the graves, which were youngest behind the church. She rounded a corner that boxed in the altar, and saw how her father's grave lay in the shadow of the building. For a moment, as her brain refused to accept what was there, she thought only the shadow was preventing her from seeing the headstone and the mound. But they were hidden by at least a dozen figures dressed in black.

Each of them held a flame above its head. The flames were steady in the abruptly breathless air, but so dim she had to convince herself she was seeing them. She stepped forward a pace she was barely conscious of taking, and another. Her foot caught a fragment of gravel that had strayed off a grave. The pebble struck the church with a click like the snap of a camera.

Only the closest of the figures turned. Daniella had frozen, but when she saw that each of them was hiding its face with its hand she retreated a step. She heard a murmur—a very few words. At once there were no flames, and the gathering vanished around the church with hardly a whisper of footfalls on the grass. She barely had time to distinguish by their clothes that they were all men. One stooped to the grave, then he too dodged around the church.

She faltered and then dashed after them, almost tripping on the unkempt fringe of a grave, supporting herself on the slimy pelt of an old moss-topped memorial. She hadn't sighted the intruders when she stumbled to a halt. The turf the diggers had laid that afternoon had been disturbed. One of the green squares meant to cover up her father's plot was askew.

As she bent to it she heard car door after door slam beyond the main gates. She sprinted past the church and along the slithery gravel drive, and panted to the gates in time to see the last vehicle swing around a bend in the direction of the motorway. The car slewed across the road, its brake lights flaring. She was able to read most of the registration number before it was snatched away. She bolted after it, but when she reached the bend the cars were only a low blurred sound that merged with the oncoming dark.

She stood in the middle of the road, digging her knuckles into her hips, and then she walked back through the gates to adjust the grassy cover of her father's resting-place. She couldn't say goodbye now—there was too much of a clamour in her head. She hurried through the gates and made for home. As she marched fast into the darkness, clenching her fists whenever anything unseen stirred in or beyond the hedges, she whispered over and over the letters and digits she'd glimpsed reddened by the brake lights.

FIVE

When Daniella closed the front door and crossed the hall, her mouth widening with the urgency of her news, she found her mother asleep in front of a screen as blank as fog. A half-full glass of gin and tonic stood between her suede-slippered feet like a tribute. She looked unexpectedly old and vulnerable, exhausted by playing the widow. Rather than waken her, Daniella picked up the glass and drank—mostly melted ice cubes, but at least they moistened her mouth. She eased the door shut and tiptoed fast along the hall into her father's study.

When she was little, and recently too, she'd enjoyed sitting in his capacious office chair that spun and reclined and sank and rose behind the desk, but now she felt as if she was trying to take a place that could never be taken—his. She switched on the overhead light and the long rectangular desk-lamp on its segmented snaky neck. As she hesitated over which number to call, the spines of books in the glass-fronted case snagged her mind with titles: *When Men Were Men, The Secrets of Finance, The Bible Decoded*, in which a place was marked with a Midas Books compliments slip. Victor Shakespeare of Midas Books was abroad but had sent a lavish telegram for Alan Stanley to read aloud at the funeral. She had to clear her mind of Alan Stanley's voice as she resisted dialling 999, instead sprawling the directory open on the ornamental green blotter.

"Oxfordshire Police."

"Can I report—"

"Will you speak up, please? I can't hear you."

Daniella didn't want her mother waking until the call was finished. Not much more loudly she said "I want to report some people messing with someone's grave."

"Is the incident taking place now?"

"Not right now. Just now. Well, maybe half an hour, a bit more than half an hour ago. They've gone."

"Who has?"

"Whoever they were. I saw them and I got their number."

"Can I take your name?"

"I'll tell you, but let me give—"

"I'll need your name first."

"Daniella Logan. It was my dad's grave. He was buried today."

She wasn't expecting that to affect the briskly efficient voice, but there was a pause before the woman said "Would that be Teddy, I ought to say Theodore Logan? The gentleman from Oxford Films?"

"He was my dad."

"You say someone was interfering with his grave?"

"Right, and I got nearly all a registration number. I don't know what year, but the rest is nine four nine cue you something."

"Can you say what kind of car?"

"Black. Some sort of hatchback, and it was heading for the motorway."

"You're at Mr Logan's house, are you? Someone will be with you very shortly, Miss Logan."

"It's on Chiltern Road," Daniella just had time to add, and was holding the vacated receiver when her mother wandered into the room, blinking and rubbing her eyes. "I hope that's a boyfriend," she said.

"It's nobody now."

"It was one though, was it?"

"No boyfriend. I'm doing without those."

"Tell me it's a temporary arrangement."

"Maybe. I've plenty of friends."

"I'm glad, but all the same..." Daniella's mother waved the fingertips of one hand at her mouth as if to dissuade it from further interference. "Who was it, then? I'm no great fan of secrets."

"I only didn't want you to be shocked when you've just woken up. It was the police. I called them."

Her mother seemed to rouse her brain with a single hard blink, and Daniella was about to explain when she was silenced by a crunch of gravel outside the house. Her mother hurried into the front room. "Why," she said, "it's Simon Hastings."

Daniella ran to open the front door as Chrysteen's father reached it. "Is Chrys all right?" she pleaded.

"I certainly hope so. She was when I saw her onto the train." He rubbed his crew-cut scalp and gave his head a quick shake, quivering the jowls that spoiled the squareness of his face. "Has she been in touch?" he was already saying.

"No, I wondered if she's why you're here."

"I'm here because of your call," he said, and closed the door behind him. "I was looking in at the station to see an old friend and I heard your father's name come up."

"You were quick," Daniella's mother said, padding into the hall.

"I moved as soon as I heard. Where shall we, ah . . ."

"Teddy wouldn't rate me as a hostess if he could see me, would he? Forgive me, I've been snoozing." She strode into the front room and sat stiffly upright on the edge of the sofa, where she reached down for her glass and focused her dismay on it, perhaps wondering if she had forgotten finishing her gin. "Should I be offering you a drink, Simon?"

"Not when I'll be at the wheel soon, thanks." He leaned against the piebald marble mantelpiece as Daniella sat deep in an armchair. "You say someone was interfering with the grave, Daniella?"

"About twelve men. They'd tried to dig it up."

"You saw someone digging?"

"No, I must have got there after they had. Only when they all ran off the grass on top of it was crooked. I didn't see them doing much, just—"

"You're sure you saw them," her mother said, meaning well on the way to the opposite. "I know you're more upset than you've been letting people see, and it must have been dark, mustn't it?"

"She's a perceptive young lady, all the same. What do you think you saw, Daniella?"

"I don't just think. They were all holding lights up. Lights or wands."

"Were they using them for any purpose you could see?"

"No, but I didn't watch long. They saw me and ran off."

"Could you identify them?"

"They didn't let me see their faces, but I got most of a registration number."

He nodded with apparent satisfaction as her mother

said with the start of a laugh that would be either fond or nervous "So what do you make of all that, Simon? Have you ever heard anything like it?"

"I rather think I may have. I suggest we scoot along for a look."

"All of us?"

"That way there can't be any argument over what's to be seen."

Even if that was aimed at her mother, Daniella couldn't help feeling reproved too. She locked the house and sat in the back of the Triumph. The house swung away, blackening, as poplars trooped out of the dark beyond cut-out silhouettes of her mother and Chrysteen's father. The curves of the hedges sloughed off the headlamp beams, the black carapace of the road slithered beneath the light, and in less than five minutes the churchyard wall produced the gleam of the gates. "If you'll let me in, Daniella," Chrysteen's father said, "I'll drive up."

She pulled the bolts out of the concrete and pushed the gates back, caging a stone cherub and an angel with the shadows of the bars. As she walked ahead of the car up the drive, black rectangles widened behind headstones, crosses printed their negative images on the grass. Her father's stone blazed white, displaying just his name and years. The headlamp beams rested on it as the passenger door echoed the driver's—her shadow was pinned to the stone until she moved aside. "It doesn't look disturbed," Chrysteen's father said. "Can you show me where?"

"I fixed the bit they'd messed with. I don't suppose I should have."

"I'm sure you were acting out of respect. What did you touch?"

As she leaned down to point at the square of grass a blacker version of her fingers swelled out of the mound, and a man's appeared to clutch them as he stooped to peel back the turf. He peered for some moments at the earth he'd revealed before murmuring "Is this how it was when you covered it up?"

"It looks the same."

"Then put your mind at rest. You too, Isobel. Daniella must have interrupted anything they meant to do. This hasn't been dug since the funeral."

"They might come back," Daniella said as a breeze like a breath of the stones parted the hair at the nape of her neck.

"I think they'd be afraid you saw more than you said, but I'll look into having the place patrolled just in case they return."

"Who?" her mother protested. "You're talking as though you know who they are."

Having adjusted the square of turf he'd replaced, he straightened up. "I believe it's possible to make a fair guess on the basis of what Daniella says she saw."

"Satanists, you mean?" her mother said with a fierce glare at the surrounding darkness.

"There's quite a lot of that style of behaviour all over the country just now. Not necessarily Satanists. People who want to throw away the Bible and everything it ever stood for. More to be pitied than scared of, mind you, but they can't be ignored if they start troubling the law-abiding public, especially friends of mine."

He opened two passenger doors and held Daniella's mother's for her. "Shall I take you somewhere happier?"

"Please." Her voice sounded weighed down by other

thoughts, even when she added "Thank you."

Once Daniella was seated he climbed in and saw her staring at the headstone, which looked increasingly unreal in the midst of so much darkness. "They must have wanted a new grave for whatever they get up to," he assured her as the car crept backwards with a gravelly whisper. "It could have been anyone's. What you saw had nothing to do with Teddy or his life or yours."

"Thank God for that at least," her mother said, and the stone was extinguished like a thought Daniella had failed to grasp.

SIX

Daniella emerged from her philosophy tutorial full of ideas about the origins of belief, most of them from disagreeing with her tutor. She was absolutely unconvinced that the need to believe was just another evolutionary mechanism— for one thing, it didn't help the human race survive. More people had died for beliefs or from them than even nature had succeeded in killing off, and she couldn't see that had much to do with the survival of the fittest or of the sanest either, but her instincts told her the compulsion to create a belief or to find one that seemed to make sense of your life was more than simply a means to provoke conflicts that kept the human numbers down. Wasn't the yearning for belief the most human of qualities, perhaps the sole uniquely human one? She found herself imagining the birth of the first beliefs, infant humanity striving to shape its raw experience of a world where everything might have appeared to conceal a supernatural force, even a god. However naïve these perceptions were, mightn't they have been purer than hers or anyone's now, closer to some source of belief? She was hurrying down the path to the car park, eager to be at the computer in her room, when her walk grew less sure of itself. A vehicle was nosing out past hers, and it looked increasingly familiar.

It was black. It was a black hatchback. Its registration

number crept into view around the left side of her car: D, 9, 4, 9 . . . She was peering fiercely at the driver's face in the shadow of the sunshield of the windscreen when the remaining letters produced themselves. They were JRC, and she sent an apologetic smile to the bespectacled grey-maned professor of popular fiction who blinked at her before he drove off. She had to stop feeling followed and watched.

She would have preferred not to notice on her way home quite so many registration numbers that contained a Q like a question she had to answer. None of the vehicles was both black and a hatchback, but she had begun to wonder if the one she'd glimpsed outside the churchyard might have been robbed of colour by the dark. Once she'd avoided the crowds by using Skeldergate Bridge she was followed along Nunnery Lane by an ominously dark red hatchback. Not until it carried on as she swung into Blossom Street was she sure that its plate didn't contain a single character she was on the lookout for.

Chrysteen's amber Accord and Maeve's mauve Mini had left her a space in front of the house. The edge of a wind as large as the park flapped the party hat on the lampshade in the hall, a fluttering that spread to the notebooks in the wire basket of Duncan's bicycle. The cover of the topmost book drew a chime from the bicycle's bell, and either Maeve or Chrysteen whispered in the kitchen "She's back."

Daniella's voice came out sharper than she intended. "What's wrong now?"

Maeve and then Chrysteen appeared in the kitchen doorway, and Duncan poked his large face out of the dining-room as though he was being led by the dimple in his chin. Both girls were wearing dresses, not a common sight in the house. "We thought we'd celebrate our anniversary," Chrysteen said.

"Which one?" Daniella had to ask.

"Ten months and three days," said Duncan, "of all being in the house."

It was clear to Daniella that they meant to take her mind off her troubles and that only her paranoia hadn't let her understand this sooner. As she gathered everyone together for a hug she smelled Maeve's Thai vegetable casserole simmering in the kitchen. "Have I time to do a bit of work first?" she eventually said.

"Half an hour if you're feeling inspired," Maeve said.

Daniella hurried upstairs to her room and tidied the bed by tugging the black and white quilt up to the solitary pillow. She sat at her desk and switched on the computer, too late. In the park a small spotted monochrome dog was helping footballers make a noise, but they weren't the problem. She typed the ideas she'd had during the tutorial and saved them, then she changed into the short black dress she was glad to realise had never had a chance to impress Blake, and took the question downstairs that had interfered with her thoughts. "Did anyone phone while I was out?"

"We'd have told you if they had," Maeve said with a frown that drew her freckles together.

"Do you think I ought to call them? It's been a week."

"You could." Having read Daniella's face, Chrysteen added "You should."

Another trip upstairs fetched Daniella's address book. She dialled the number she had only pencilled, and played with Duncan's bicycle bell in time with the ringing in Oxford until a woman announced "Oxfordshire Police."

"Hi, it's Daniella Logan. Someone tried to dig up my dad's grave last week."

This sounded even more inappropriately offhand once it was finished, but no comment was audible in the response. "And you were calling because . . ."

"To see if you'd found out anything."

"I think we may have. Can you hold?" It was barely a question: at once the line was not much more than dead. At the end of a generous interval the woman said "I'm afraid the officer you need to speak to isn't on duty."

"When will he be?"

"Tomorrow afternoon, so if you'd like to try then—"

"Can't someone else help?"

"There's nobody else available at present."

"You said he'd got something. What did you hear it was?"

"I'm sorry, I'm not authorised to discuss cases."

"You mean you won't," Daniella said with a resentment that made her feel childish, and hung up. "Let's eat," she called.

The popping of a cork appeared to speed Maeve out of the dining-room. "Anything?" she hoped aloud.

"There's nobody I can talk to. I'm not going to care," Daniella said, and helped her carry avocados stuffed with prawns to the dining-table, on which someone had lit slim candles. The flames, dim in the early evening glow, roused a memory she quelled as she sat on the fourth high-backed fat-bottomed chair. Duncan poured her a glass of wine that, while it wasn't champagne, produced streams of bubbles just as endless, and raised his. "To Daniella's house," he said.

"Daniella's house."

"Our house," Daniella said, and dug a spoon into her half of a thick-skinned pear. "Thanks, everyone. This is just what I needed."

Chrysteen watched her finish scooping out the pear before she said "What didn't we do that you're thinking about?"

"I'm only wishing I didn't have to wait till tomorrow to know what the police have found out."

"Do you want to phone my dad?"

"Not if I'm spoiling our evening."

"We'll enjoy it twice as much," Duncan said, "when we're sure you are."

"I'll turn the pot down," said Maeve, already pushing back her chair.

Chrysteen followed her out of the room. Daniella heard the whir of the telephone dial, and Chrysteen's fingers drumming on the plastic, and then "Dad? It's only me ... Nothing. I'm fine ... Trundling along like always ... Just a psychology essay ... We're having dinner ... Just the four of us ... You know you'd know if I had someone ... Anyway, I wasn't really calling for me. Can Danny have a word?"

A trace of Chrysteen's warmth lingered in the earpiece as it said "Daniella. What use would you like me to be?"

"I was wondering if you knew anything about that car I saw."

"Indeed we do. Has nobody been in touch?"

"I rang them but they weren't there."

"Then let me tell you we've tracked down all the possibles, not just the couple of vehicles that fit your description but all those that tally with the number you gave us. Nearly all the vehicles can be accounted for that night. The rogue is a dark blue hatchback owned by a couple in Banbury, not too far from Oxford."

"That sounds like it. It would have looked black. Who—"

"Unfortunately that's the question we can't answer."

She felt as though he had been lifting weights from her brain only to drop them back in place. "Why can't you?"

"Because the car was stolen from the owners that night. Next day it was found abandoned in Aylesbury."

"Why didn't someone tell me then?"

"I should say because they couldn't be sure it was the one until they'd checked the rest. Presumably the driver realised you might have taken his number and that's why he abandoned the vehicle."

"Did you get his prints?"

"The car was burnt out, sadly. Even our expert couldn't lift a print from the remains. Try not to trouble yourself any more, will you do that for me as a friend? It must have been distressing for you, but you'll agree these people didn't do any real harm."

"Maybe they didn't have time. I keep feeling I'm being followed."

"Have you seen anyone?"

The answer was no, but it didn't take away the nervousness his question aggravated. "I don't think so," she said.

"I'm sure you won't. Can you think of any reason why any of your mysterious gathering should want to bother you? Don't you think they'd make sure you never had an opportunity to identify them?"

"I expect so. I just—"

A doorbell rang beyond him, playing a phrase from the

part of the *William Tell* overture everyone knew. "Could you answer that, dear?" he called, and brought his voice back close to Daniella. "Time to play host to some important people, but whenever you need a father's advice you know where to find me. Never be afraid to get in touch."

"Thanks. I won't be," Daniella said, feeling no clearer than her words, and wandered down the hall to tell her friends what he'd told her. "Good riddance to whoever they were," Duncan declared, and she agreed as everyone else did—but she was agreeing only aloud. While she wasn't yet sure why it was so important, she'd realised she had to know.

SEVEN

The Bible had been written to justify beliefs that already existed and to answer awkward questions in a way designed to stifle further argument. So women were appendages of men and admonished to behave as if they were, presumably because in those days men couldn't cope with independent women any more than too many couldn't now. Too much knowledge or inquisitiveness was bound to lead to evil. The memory or legend of some kind of great flood had been turned into a warning that if humanity acted against Biblical law the world as they knew it would be brought to an end. Even the diversity of language was the fault of human ambition. Daniella would have thought languages were something to celebrate rather than to find a culprit for, but perhaps the writers of the Bible, not to mention whoever had originally told the stories written there, had felt closer to the chaos that had preceded themselves— felt compelled to invent beliefs that would consign chaos to the past. She thought her ideas were enough for at least a page of her essay, but she had only just switched on the computer and scrolled to the end of her work when she realised someone was watching her from the park.

He was behind a bush beyond the railings almost opposite her window. Only his head and his white-robed shoulders were visible. His brownish hair was cut too high, a tuft of parched grass sprouting from a whitish block. His small mouth was rounded in an ambiguous grimace, his dark eyes resembled holes in stone. Daniella met him with a glare that stung her eyes, and was about to leap to her feet and crane out of the window, past caring what she might shout, when he lurched sideways, tugged by a Yorkshire terrier. As an additional explanation of his presence he dug a plastic bag out of his pocket and struggled to duck behind the bush to collect an item he bore away to the nearest concrete bin.

"Crap," Daniella muttered. That was why the dog had been there and hence the man, but it would also do as a description of her paranoia. She'd had enough of feeling at the mercy of her ignorance. At least she wasn't under pressure from the university; her philosophy course gave her three weekday afternoons off, and the tutor had granted her until the beginning of the autumn term to finish her essay, out of sympathy over her father. Only noting down her thoughts for the essay and switching off the computer kept her from striding downstairs at once.

She locked the house and jogged to the box on the main road to phone Directory Enquiries free rather than pay to call from the house. A trace of someone's aftershave crept into her nostrils as she scribbled on the back of her hand the number she obtained. As she emerged into the heavy July sunlight a man wheeling a toddler too small for her push-chair glanced at Daniella's hand as though to read a secret sign. She let herself into the house and left the door open to admit more sunlight while she dialled and then fingered the faint graze Duncan's bicycle handle had imprinted on the wallpaper. She had traced the mark three times when a woman's bright voice said *"Beacon."*

"Can I speak to Mr Trask?"

"May I take a name?"

"Daniella Logan. He knew my dad, Teddy Logan. Well, he knows me."

"I'll see if he's available," the receptionist said and turned into a march by Elgar. Before the tune had time to advance far the receptionist interrupted it. "Putting you through now."

"Daniella," Bill Trask said at once. "Are you in town? Come over. Come up."

"I'm in York."

"Usefully employed, I hope."

"I'm writing an essay and I've got a job as a waitress."

"Sounds a steady enough life to me. Stability, that's the state to aim for. I know you appreciate how hard your father worked for it," the newspaper proprietor said, and she heard him breathe hard through his nose swollen with all the reds and purples of the wine that, if his performance at her father's wake was representative, he devoted a good deal of his time to drinking. "He was never one for staying in the background if he didn't have to, any more than I am. You'll always find me here keeping an eye on my staff. I like to see them on their toes."

"That's why I rang, because I thought you'd be there."

"Something not right in the paper? If we've been in-accurate, just you tell me where."

"I was wondering if you ran a story about my dad."

"You'd know if you read my paper, wouldn't you?" This appeared to be meant lightly, since his tone didn't change as he said "Rest assured we did. 'British Film Paragon Dies,' that was our headline. Two full pages on Teddy's career and not too much about the circumstances that took him from us, just that he was in a crash."

"Thanks. Only I meant did you have anything about the stuff after the funeral."

"What might that be?"

"Didn't Mr Hastings tell you? I thought he would have when it was my dad and you both knew him. Someone tried to dig him up after we'd all gone."

"God help us, there are some devilish people about these days. It goes hand in hand with the collapse of the family, the kind of behaviour we're seeing." He sounded ready to paraphrase more of a *Beacon* editorial, but said less fiercely "We'll have to take it Simon didn't think it was for the paper."

"You ought to put something in, shouldn't you, if it makes you as angry as that?"

"It was the night of the funeral, did I understand you to say?"

"That was when."

"It's old news then, regrettably. Even though it concerns old Teddy I couldn't justify having it written up so late."

"They've only just found the car one of the people used that night."

"Let me have a word with the police and then I may be back in touch."

Daniella hung up and sat on the doorstep, tugging out of the flower-bed those weeds that were within reach. In the park unseen birds emitted single notes bright as fragments of the sun. She had just decided to return to her essay when the phone rang. She dropped a handful of dead stalks and shook earth off her hands onto the path and grabbed the receiver. "Hi? It's me."

"Chrysteen?" She hoped his impatience was directed at

himself as he said "You're not my daughter."

"She isn't here, Mr Hastings. It's Daniella."

"You're why I'm calling. I've just been speaking to Bill Trask."

"I have too."

"Precisely."

Since he seemed prepared to let that stand as a reproof she blurted "What did you say to him?"

"We agreed it wouldn't have been advisable for the paper to report any of that business."

"Why not?"

"His position is that it's too long after the event. The fact that a car has been tracked down isn't newsworthy enough in itself. My objection—do give this some thought for Teddy's sake—is that all the story would be likely to achieve is attracting the wrong people to his grave, sensation-seekers or worse. How would you feel if that happened?"

"I wouldn't like it, but ..."

"Don't feel guilty. We know you meant well. May I suggest as a friend you should take a little time to sort out your feelings about Teddy's death? Didn't Eamonn Reith offer to counsel you? You might want to consider him."

"Thanks," Daniella said, and a few more things she felt were expected of her before dropping the receiver on its hook. She gazed through the doorway at the park in its cage, which helped remind her the world as she knew it was real. She felt as if nobody except her cared what had happened at the graveyard. She might have thought she was expected to believe that nothing significant had.

NEKTARIKOS

Daniella was in the desert. She had been walking for so long it seemed the world had turned to sand. It was impossible to see where the sky, which was the colour of brass and so parched it had shrivelled the sun, met the horizon. She felt as if she was trapped under a bowl by a watcher. When she looked back she saw sand trickling into her footsteps to erase them, though there wasn't a hint of a wind. When she faced ahead again she saw a figure almost shapeless with the squirming of the air. She couldn't tell if it was approaching or receding or simply waiting for her to have to go to it, but as she began to run towards it the sand that had hindered her by sinking underfoot grew solid, rendering her tread so fleet she might have been racing across the wasteland to her fate. In an instant the figure was vaster than a man would appear to even the smallest child—than anything alive had a right to be. She was still unable to distinguish its shape with so much turmoil in the air, especially before its face. She would have cried out, but her tongue was thick with sand, her throat felt stuffed with it. At her back she heard drumming, and sensed someone close behind her. Before she could turn she glimpsed a flash of metal, and she grew dry as sand from head to foot while the desert was stained red all around her. Perhaps the moment only resembled eternity as she jerked awake.

Her mouth was dry, at least partly with fear, and her neck ached as though her skull had been clamped to force her to watch the dream. The drumming hadn't ceased. The rapid clattering, a babel of rhythms that seemed unlikely ever to settle their conflict, was outside her window. She kicked off the single twisted sheet and drained the glass of water on the table level with her head, then refilled the glass from the jug she was surprised to find not just topped up but musical with ice. The drumming persisted beyond the blue curtains in the white wall, making her feel she had yet to waken properly. She stumbled to the curtains and slid them as wide as her arms would reach.

There was the sea, so calm it toned down the racket in her head. Only a path of ripples flawed the immense blue jewel. The ripples trailed behind a power cruiser loaded with people in swimwear, whom it was ferrying away from a cove at the far side of the island from the harbour. Close to the villa, beyond a pale blue swimming-pool, half a dozen women were hitting trees with sticks, dislodging olives that circular nets had been placed to catch. Nana was sitting at an elegant slim-legged table on a marble terrace in the shadow of the villa, sipping from a tall fluted glass before typing rapidly but daintily on the keypad of a mobile phone. "Have Berthold call me urgently," she said and gave her guest all her attention. "Daniella. Feeling better? I hope my islanders didn't disturb your sleep."

"Don't worry, I needed to wake."

"Would you care for anything before dinner?"

"Dinner?"

"You've slept a night and most of a day."

That made Daniella feel even less awake. "I think I'd like a shower," she said.

"You'll have seen there's one directly off your room, will you? If you find anything lacking, don't hesitate to let me know."

A broad marble shelf next to the curtainless shower beside the toilet in the pale capacious room contained soaps and shower gels and shampoos and conditioners, every one of them a Nana's Glamour product, and a sponge bigger than her head. She showered and shampooed until the onslaught of water and her fingernails on her scalp chased some of the dullness out of her brain, after which she dried herself on an extravagantly plump towel. She put on underwear and a short thin dress, then hung the clothes that needed hanging in the walk-in wardrobe and stored the rest in a floor-level drawer while the clattering of sticks on trees lessened and ceased. Though the air was still laden with the rasping of cicadas further down the island, she heard Nana's ominously quiet voice. "Let me speak to him."

Daniella took her time about emerging from the villa. First she wandered down the corridor to the vestibule, beyond which were servants' rooms and a kitchen where half the surfaces were marble and a casserole tended by a woman in black was simmering on a spotless hob. When the woman only smiled at her, Daniella ventured onto the terrace. Nana gestured her to sit and touched the twin of her own glass with a fingertip, then poured wine into it from a red clay jug and tilted her head against the phone. "I've listened to you, Berthold, now you hear me. My business can't afford your mistakes, so you pick up that cheque and close the door behind you, and when you've done that you could offer up some thanks that I'm treating you no worse. And don't think of suing because you'll lose, and I'll get your handshake back from you as well."

Her sea-blue gaze had stayed on Daniella throughout
the monologue. She killed the phone and laid one soft cool
hand on Daniella's wrist. "I can't be softer than the men,"
she said. "Didn't that sound like your hostess?"

"Not to me."

"Maybe an actress never stops being one."

"I used to think that's what I'd like to be."

"Try not to feel the way I think you're feeling. Sometimes when I was your age I thought my life was coming
to an end."

Daniella took a gulp of wine, dry though it was. "It
was just getting started, wasn't it?"

"Thanks to your father. Thanks to him needing a new
face to say a few lines before I was stabbed in the back in
his Greek spy film."

"You must have said them well."

"I'd vowed someone would notice me while I had my
chance. You have to know it when it comes. They said I
stole the scene, even the star did. That's why Teddy trusted
me to play the nursemaid in his next film."

Each time her father was mentioned Daniella felt as
though a knife was twisting in her guts. She took another
mouthful of murky amber wine and swallowed, and had
to pinch her lips together with her teeth. "Not your taste?"
Nana said.

"It's okay. It's fine."

"Friends make it on the mainland. I have it brought
over whenever I run low."

"Were there people here before?" Daniella pointed
across the stridulating trees to the jagged cove, from which
the path of ripples had long since vanished. "I thought
maybe they came for a swim," she said.

"There's a trip twice a week in the holiday season. A friend of mine runs them. Nobody comes to my island unless I invite them."

That reminded Daniella of too much all at once. Sensing her mood, Nana touched her wrist again. "Just remember you're here to recover, and you don't need to tell me anything until you have."

Just the same, Daniella felt the need to change the subject. "Do you think you'll do any more acting?"

"I'm in the other kind of glamour business now. I retired while I still had my looks, before I had to change my image." She gave her guest a smile that revealed a single wrinkle in each cheek and said "Theo will be serving dinner shortly. Is there anything you want to do first?"

"Could I call home?"

"Of course you may," Nana said, handing her the chunky mobile phone. "Shall I leave you?"

"If you wouldn't mind, Nana. It might be a bit..."

"No need to explain. Let me know when you've finished," Nana said, and took her glass into the villa.

Daniella waited until the clapping of sandals on marble had reached the kitchen before she typed Chrysteen's Oxford number. The phone beyond the sea hadn't started to ring when she walked past the pool and stepped down among the netted trees. The nearest beetles fell silent, and Chrysteen's mother said "Adele Hastings. Hello?"

The beetles renewed their chorus, and Daniella was afraid they would give away where she was. She was trying to open her mouth to ask at least one swift question when she heard Chrysteen call "Is it for me?"

That had to be enough for now. Hearing Chrysteen's mother had made Daniella feel guilty for not calling her own. She broke the connection and keyed her mother's number. The bell had barely repeated itself when her mother said "Hello?"

She sounded desperately anxious and so close Daniella yearned to be able to hold her. "Mummy, it's me."

"Daniella." The word was both a heartfelt accusation and something like a prayer. "Where are you?"

"I'm safe."

"Where?"

"With someone who's looking after me. Don't worry, mummy, I'm absolutely safe."

"So you keep saying. Why won't you tell me where?"

"I'd rather not at the moment, all right? Just in case someone I don't want knowing asked you and you felt you had to say."

"Such as who?"

"Lots of people," Daniella said, and it wasn't stepping into the shadow of an olive tree that caused her to shiver.

"Suppose they have your best interests in mind?"

"They haven't. I know."

"Oh, Daniella, listen to yourself. Try and hear how you're sounding."

"I know how."

"Then can't you see you need help? Nobody wants to hurt you. There are people who care about you almost as much as I do, and I just want you back the way you were before you got yourself so upset and confused over your father. That's all it must have been, and I'm not the only one who says so."

Daniella was on the edge of revealing far too much for her mother to believe or cope with, but then her mother said "What kind of a place are you in? It sounds awful. What's all that noise?"

"Just insects, mummy. They're harmless."

"It doesn't sound at all harmless to me where you are. When am I going to see you? When are you coming back?"

"I don't know yet. I have to do some stuff first."

"What? Can't you tell me that at least?"

"I promise you'll know soon. I'd better go now. I don't want to run up the bill. I'll try and call you again, but remember I'm with someone I trust."

"How far away are you? Have you gone out of the country?"

"Maybe," Daniella said, and wished she hadn't admitted even so little. "I've got to go. Love you," she said and switched the phone off.

She was dismayed to have to think her mother would be unable to trace her; the exchange couldn't identify a number calling from abroad. Or might her mother's phone be monitored, perhaps without her knowledge? Daniella had to believe not—she mustn't let herself be panicked when she had nowhere to flee. The insect chorus grew louder at her back as she returned to the villa.

Nana was in the kitchen, watching the old woman stir the casserole and conversing with her in rapid Greek. "Daniella, Theo," she said. "Theo, Daniella."

Daniella took the leathery brown hand that went with the wizened angular face beneath the tight grey bun. "Hérete," Theo said.

"Theo says hello."

"I wish I could speak a bit of your language."

"I'll see if I can find you a phrasebook. I've none here,"

Nana said, clipping the phone to her belt. "Thanks."

"Can I pay for the call?"

"Most emphatically not, my dear. You keep your money to yourself."

"I brought some, but I haven't any Greek."

"You won't need any while you're my guest."

"You're kind," Daniella said, and felt awkward for asking "Do you need me for anything?"

Nana spoke to Theo, who sipped delicately at the ladle before passing it to Nana to taste. "Why, for dinner," Nana said. "Come to the sunset."

On the terrace she poured glasses of wine from the replenished jug while the old woman ladled the casserole onto two plates. "Stifado," Theo said.

Even though Daniella hadn't eaten for more than a day it came as a surprise to find she was ravenous. When Theo left her and Nana alone she thought she would be expected to make conversation, but her hostess seemed to understand she would rather be quiet in the hope of feeling peaceful. The sun shrank and grew redder, and a scarlet comet's tail spread across a sea as still as the cloudless sky. As the sun sent up a crimson glow from behind the horizon Daniella poured herself another glass and refilled Nana's. "Thanks, really, thanks so much for letting me come," she said. "You saved me. I'll always remember."

"No need to think of remembering now." Nana gazed through her reddened wine towards the world elsewhere. "You must stay as long as it takes. You're more welcome than you know," she said, and placed a hand over Daniella's. "I feel as if I've been given the daughter I never had."

NINE

"Shouldn't you be talking old-fashioned when you're dressed like that?"

He had a mop of bleached blond curls and the face of an overgrown schoolboy: not the class bully, perhaps, but one of his gang—the member who echoed the leader or made cracks similar to his. Daniella was tired, her ears were ringing with the uproar trapped by the exposed rafters, her eyes had begun to ache with the dim flickering light of the artificial flames of torches shackled to the bare brick walls of The Trencher, her throat was dry with smoke from the dining area that adjoined the bar, but she had to take him as a challenge. Producing her pad from the bodice of her serving-wench's outfit, she said "Marry, sir, of what viands wilt thou partake?"

He sat back hard enough to scrape his end of the bench over an unpolished floorboard and let fly a chortle that was meant to sound surprised. "What which?"

"What meats wilt thou choose? Hast perused the list of provender?"

"She means the menu, Desmond," one of his trio of chubby male friends translated.

"I know that," Desmond said, taking care to be heard to chortle while he did. "What do you recommend, love?"

"Wilt have a mediaeval patty that with fried slivers of potato doth arrive, and also salad?"

He peered at the Gothic script on the unwieldy oversized menu and stubbed out his cigarette before saying "You mean the Trencher Burger?"

"The same, forsooth, and no other."

"Sounds my kind of meat. I'll have it. Medium," he added in a tone intended to demonstrate he was in control.

"I'll have that too," said his companion on the bench, and their friends concurred, perhaps to avoid an exchange with Daniella. She wrote down their order and enquired "To imbibe?"

"Beer all round," Desmond said.

"A flagon of ale," Daniella corrected, gently enough. She handed in the order and bore the ale to the table, where Desmond's boisterousness dwindled at her approach, shrinking further once she'd rendered the party even more schoolboyish by the plastic bibs she'd tied on them. She cleared several tables in the rapidly emptying restaurant, and talked to Lucy and Maud about nothing very much until it was time to pretend that carrying the trayful of dinner didn't require all her concentration and strength.

Drinking had restored Desmond's self-assurance. "We'll have another of these," he said, hoisting the empty flagon, "and we were just saying you were pretty good. We like girls who can take it."

"Why, sirrah, I relish a bout of words as well as any man."

"No need to keep it up," he said somewhat plaintively, but when she brought the refilled flagon he'd prepared his next sally. "What time do you finish?"

"This style of speech fits me so well I may choose never to doff it."

"No, come on. When do you get off work?"

"Alack, a poor menial's work never ends."

"Look, I'm asking if you'd like to join us for a drink."

"Pray do not take me for an innocent. My father warned me where such dalliances lead."

"Nothing wrong with a bit of fun."

"Valiant of you to admit you've no more than a shrimp in your codpiece," Daniella said, to such mirth from his friends that he stuffed his reddened face with burger. She stayed well clear of the party until it was time to present the bill, and wasn't surprised that when all the money had been fumbled onto the table it included hardly any tip. She displayed its meagreness to her colleagues on her way to change back into a student before emerging into the late afternoon.

The stout door gave onto three plump steps that led up to the flagstones alongside the river. To her right a bridge reached down to embrace a drowned sun with its inverted arch. A narrow cobbled alley took her to the street that paralleled the river and thence to the hot close crowds on Micklegate. Beyond the arch in the city wall she left the crowds behind. She'd turned the corner of her road when she missed a step on the uneven pavement cracked by parking. An unfamiliar car—a green Mazda—was almost nuzzling the rear of her Ford outside the house.

She strode up her almost equally green path and dug her key into the lock. As she slammed the door with the sole of her foot, Maeve and Duncan and a smell of coffee emerged from the kitchen. Maeve looked secretly pleased,

Duncan the reverse of both. "Someone's here to see you,"
Maeve said.

"First you've heard of it, I'm betting."

"Then you'd clean up," Daniella told Duncan.

"Hope it was all right to let him in."

"We can't just shut doors in people's faces," Maeve protested under her breath.

"So long as you're around if I need you," Daniella said,
consigning her bag of clothes to a kitchen chair, and made
for the front room.

The man seated on the couch and leafing through a
glossy magazine stood up at once. He was a head taller
than Daniella and, she thought, a few years older. He had
deep earnest brown eyes, a broad nose, fleshy lips whose
sensuality was contradicted by severely combed black hair.
He wore pale blue trousers sharply pressed, a dark blue
shirt and darker tie. "Daniella Logan?" he said, and stuck
out a hand. "Mark Alexander."

His hand was soft but firm. He could have been a sales-
man, given his briefcase on the couch. "Should I know
you?" she said.

"Not unless you read this," he said, proffering the magazine.

Since it was called *Filmfile* she'd assumed it to be Duncan's. The cover fell open at the contents page, displaying
her visitor's name and his passport-sized photograph, the
youngest face in a totem pole of contributors. He'd written
an article—*Missing Giles Spence*—about lost British films
and, she found on flicking through the magazine, had con-
tributed several reviews. "Duncan might like this," she said.

"It's for you to keep, and these."

From the briefcase he produced three more issues of

Filmfile, including that month's. He had an article in each one: *Michael Powell's Palette, How British Movies Lost the Space Race*, and in the most recent, *Selznick and Logan: The Producer as Auteur.* "What have you been writing about my dad?" she asked as she turned to the piece.

"That he was even more successful than Selznick at imposing his view of the world on the films he produced."

"I'll look at it later," she promised, having read the words he'd just spoken, and laid the magazines on the sideboard, raising a sparkle of sunlit dust. "You didn't come just to bring me these."

"I wondered if it'd be on to ask you about your father."

"Couldn't you have phoned?"

"Sorry if I should have, only I like to see people's faces when I'm talking to them and have them see mine."

She preferred that herself. "Have you driven far?"

"London."

"Then you'd better sit down for a while."

He waited until she swung her legs over the arm of a chair before resuming his place on the couch, at which point Maeve looked in. "Is anyone having coffee?"

"I'd love one," Mark said, "but no sugar."

Daniella watched Maeve suppress a comment about a sufficiency of sweetness and was even more irritated to have thought of it too. Once Maeve took her knowing smile away Daniella said "So what were you planning to ask me?"

"I should ask first if anyone's working on a book about your father."

"Not that they've told me. Unless they went to his partner," she said with more resentment than she managed to conceal, "and he hasn't bothered saying."

"You'd rather they came straight to you, I can tell. So here I am."

"You want to do a book about him."

"If I get enough material. Certainly a major article to start with that looks at the man as well as his productions. You know some people think they're camp these days, what with Nana Babouris being a gay icon, but I think there's more to them. If I wanted to sift through his papers, would you be willing?"

"I don't see why not."

"I should clear it with you rather than his partner, or is your mother the best avenue?"

"She left dad last year."

"That's so, of course."

He seemed to have confused himself, and glanced away from her as Duncan tramped into the room to thrust a mug at him while Maeve handed Daniella hers. "Are you going to be paying her for her dad's secrets?" Duncan said.

"I don't need that, Duncan." When he stayed in front of her visitor, Daniella said "Do you know the magazine Mark writes for?"

Duncan dropped a scowl on the glossy heap. "I've seen it around."

"Thanks for the service."

"Our pleasure," said Maeve, gripping his elbow with her nails to steer him out of the room.

Daniella chased away the silence with the first question she could think of. "Do you write about anything except films?"

"Only people connected with them. That's what I've made a bit of a name for."

"I expect you deserve it." She had simply been reflecting

that if he were more of a journalist she could have told him about the men at the grave. "I hope you don't think I was putting it down," she said.

"Not if you weren't." He set his mug on the carpet and reached for a notebook, but left his hand in his pocket as he said "Will it be too soon for me to interview you about your father?"

"I don't see why."

"Even about"—he withdrew his hand, still empty— "the accident?"

"What about it?"

"Well, the drinking."

"How do you know about that? None of the news said."

"They told me at Oxford Films when they gave me your number. I did ask them a few questions."

"You must be good at your job." She saw him wonder if that was less than a compliment as she said "He'd never driven drunk before. He told me once he hadn't and I shouldn't. Maybe he should have got used to it and then he mightn't have crashed."

"Why that night, do you have any idea?"

"He was coming to see me," she said, not as an answer. "I don't suppose I'll ever know why."

Mark sat forward, barely parting his lips. His sympathy revived the sight of her father's car beneath trees throbbing red, of the vehicle that had tricked her by proving to be less than half of itself. "I'm sorry," she mumbled, knuckling her eyes. "I'm seeing the car."

"I'm the one who should be." Mark rose from the couch as though his outstretched hands were hauling him towards her, then held up his palms. "I didn't mean to trespass."

"It isn't your fault. I have to remember."

"Will you be all right?"

Once she'd taken a breath that tasted of tears and made her head swim she felt able to say "Am."

"I only really wanted just to sound you out about whether I could interview you soon."

"I don't mind seeing you again."

"That's perfect, then."

As Duncan's mutter and Maeve's low rebuke drifted out of the kitchen she said "Maybe here isn't."

"I'll give you my number." He picked up the briefcase and slipped a card out of a pocket in the lid. MARK ALEXANDER, MOVIE JOURNALIST, it said in lightly embossed red type on white cardboard, with a Whitechapel address and phone number. "Do you want to make a date now?" he suggested.

"Let me have a couple of days while I try and finish some of my coursework. But call if you find out anything about my dad I mightn't know."

"We'll talk soon. I'll leave you alone, then, or I should say with your friends."

Daniella imagined Maeve's fierce grimace exhorting the silence she heard in the kitchen while Mark let himself out of the gate and raised one cupped palm. She collected his half-full mug and took it with hers to the sink. Maeve met her with an expectant look, Duncan kept his face expressionless. "I must say he seemed quite a charmer," Maeve said.

"He only wants to interview me, you know."

"Then I'd say someone would be missing their chance. What are you muttering about, Duncan?"

"I said let's hope that's all he wants."

Daniella didn't know which of her friends she was agreeing with as she said "Why, don't you like him?"

"Bit old for you, isn't he? Old enough to know better."

"He won't find any better than our Daniella, and it's about time she met someone worth meeting."

"Don't argue over me, you two. I've told you, all he's after is an interview."

She was about to lose patience with their imperfectly concealed skepticism, not to mention with feeling less than honest with herself, when Duncan said "Sounded more like he was upsetting you to me."

"He wasn't, Duncan. I just did some of that to myself."

"What was he saying about a car, then?"

Maeve dealt his ankle a padded kick with a trainer. "You shouldn't have been listening."

"Don't worry, Maeve. Mark didn't really bring the car up, I did. I was remembering what happened to dad." She felt a little too cared for, the way her father had so often made her feel. "I'll let you know if I need protecting," she said with a wry smile at them both.

She was carrying the issues of *Filmfile* to the couch when she heard one of her friends set about clattering mugs in the sink to cover up a further burst of muted disagreement. If that was how Maeve and Duncan got on together, perhaps it wasn't up to her to object, not least because she hadn't the experience. She sat down and opened the topmost magazine, only to lose her grip on the glossy pile, which slid off her lap and splayed across the couch. Duncan's last question to her had belatedly focused her thoughts as if a murmur in her brain had suddenly grown audible. At last she'd realised what she should have asked about a car.

TEN

The receptionist at Wendell, Wendell and Rumer had a perfectly smooth face that looked as though some of the rust from her tiny tight curls had spread to the centres of her cheeks. She kept issuing bulletins about the imminence of her employer. "Mr Wendell senior just has to finish this call," she said now.

"Thank you," Daniella's mother said, and turned back to Daniella, lowering her voice. "Don't feel I'm blaming you for being like your father. He would never let go of things either. But sometimes you have to let go, don't you, Mr Stanley?"

Alan Stanley leaned across the low table scattered with financial magazines towards the Logans as though to present Daniella with an invisible bouquet of his various scents. "Sometimes," he admitted. "You have to know when to."

She didn't see why he had to be there. She felt he would be intruding on the reading of the will: his mottled overfed roundish face would, his unnecessarily long eyelashes that seemed designed to add appeal to eyes so pallid they were as bad as colourless, his habit of keeping his lips straight while he decided what expression was expected of them. "When I know I'll do it," she told her mother.

"Oh, Daniella. What more do you want?"

"Maybe time to think."

"What are you saying needs any of that?" This was no question, as became apparent once she said "Will you say if this makes sense to you, Alan?"

"It'll be a privilege to help."

"I don't know if Daniella's told you what she thinks she saw while she was saying goodbye to her father."

"Simon Hastings did mention it."

Daniella felt altogether too discussed. "Why did he have to do that?"

"Alan was your father's partner, you know," her mother said, and told him "The upshot being that she got the number of one of the cars, but the police have found out it was stolen."

He cocked his head at Daniella and produced a rueful grin on her behalf. "Dead end, then."

"You'd think so, but this young lady won't leave it alone."

"Should I ask why?"

"Unless you know," Daniella blurted. "Unless Chrys's father thought he had to tell you that as well." The sight of Alan Stanley and her mother competing to appear patient angered her so much that it cost her an effort only to murmur "Why was just that car stolen? Wouldn't they all have to be if these men wanted to make sure nobody could trace them?"

"You might want to think so," Alan Stanley said.

"That doesn't make sense."

"I'm glad you see that," her mother said. "So can we—"

"I mean it doesn't make sense that they'd have stolen all those cars. They never would have when they didn't know I'd see them, so why just one?"

"What's your alternative?" Alan Stanley said.

"Maybe the one that was stolen wasn't the one I saw. It could just have had nearly the same number."

"Excuse me," the receptionist called, apparently louder than she already had. "Mr Wendell senior is free now."

Nothing much else happened for so long Daniella had started to wonder if the receptionist had intervened simply to end the argument when the nearest door in the corridor beyond the white pine crescent of the receptionist's desk sprang open and a small man darted out, thrusting a gold ballpoint into the breast pocket of his elegant grey suit. His quick eyes were a startling blue. He was bald and beginning to wrinkle, with blue veins tracing a route from the ends of his silver eyebrows to his temples. "Mrs Logan, do accept my apologies for the delay," he said in a light high voice. "Miss Logan too, of course, not to mention Mr Stanley. Will you come this way? Have you not been offered a drink?"

"We were fine," Alan Stanley took it on himself to answer.

Notwithstanding the sunlight that shone from the white façades on the opposite side of the Strand, the office seemed dark with oak panelling and brass plaques and stiff leather furniture. The elder Mr Wendell took a creaky seat behind an oaken desk that would have dwarfed even the average man, and picked up a manila folder only to put it down again so as to rub his loud dry hands together. "May I commence?"

Daniella's mother glanced at Alan Stanley, but Daniella wasn't having him speak for her. "May as well," she said.

"I never refuse a lady." The solicitor produced a pair of gold-framed spectacles from the pocket of his waistcoat and placed them on his nose so as to inch them downwards and peer over them. "We'll retain the formalities, shall we?

I think they indicate the dignity of the proceedings," he said, and lowered his voice at least half an octave as he began to read the contents of the folder aloud. "I, Theodore Daniel Logan, being of sound mind..."

Daniella had only ever heard such a reading in old films, and she had to tell herself that nobody in the room was acting a scene. Perhaps she simply felt ashamed of her eagerness to learn how rich she was destined to be— ashamed of holding her breath in her suddenly tight throat when she heard her name.

"...to my daughter Daniella, all my investments and the income and interest therefrom, my shares in the production company known as Oxford Films, the property at 11 Chiltern Road in Oxford and all furnishings and move-ables therein, and all other moneys and possessions that shall be deemed to form part of my estate."

The solicitor raised his spectacles with a fingertip to frame a blink at her. "Is that everything?" she heard herself manage to pronounce.

"I should say so," Alan Stanley said with some reproach.

"I mean it's everything. It's too much. You ought to have some of it, mummy. You ought to have half."

The solicitor cleared his throat. "If I may continue..."

"Sorry," Daniella said, abashed for having interrupted the formalities he valued.

"...these bequests to be held in trust for her until she attains the age of twenty-one. Should this not come to pass, my shares shall be transferred to my partner Alan Henry Stanley, and the rest of my estate shall be bequeathed to my ex-wife Isobel Harriet Logan, formerly Thorne."

This was even more like a film, and Daniella had to laugh, though neither the sound nor her words emerged quite as she intended. "But that's, it's silly. I mean, I don't care, I can wait, but you're supposed to be an adult when you're eighteen."

"That is the law," the solicitor admitted.

"It must have been Teddy being old-fashioned," Alan Stanley told Daniella's mother.

"I really don't care," Daniella insisted, as much to herself as to anyone. "I've still got two years at university. I can be thinking what I'll do when dad's stuff comes to me."

The solicitor coughed so discreetly the side of his fist almost silenced it. "Mr Stanley, will you . . ."

Daniella suppressed most of her instinctive anger. "Will he what?"

"Isobel. Daniella." Alan Stanley sat forward and up-turned a hand on each of his thighs and made his mouth hint at drooping. "I thought it best to leave this until now. I hope you'll understand."

This was said largely to Daniella's mother, who responded with not much less impatience than her daughter was experiencing. "What, Alan?"

"I'm afraid Teddy turns out to have made some rash financial decisions."

"How rash?"

"Let's just say his investments and accounts are having to be investigated."

"You are? You're looking into them?"

"Sadly, no. The tax people. They're going back into all his dealings for the last six years, and Daniella, I'm afraid that means they're freezing the estate."

She'd lost nothing that she had, she told herself; it was having Alan Stanley bring the news that was close to intolerable. "How long?" she had to ask.

"I wish I could say. Let's hope everything comes to you by the time it's needed."

"Please add my hope to that," the solicitor said.

"Never mind, you've still got your house in York," her mother said. "They'll let her keep that, won't they, Mr Wendell?"

"Is it in Miss Logan's name?"

"Her father gave it to her for going to university. He didn't want her having more on her mind than she had to when she was studying. You hear of students killing themselves with worry, even killing themselves because of it."

"Do try and put your mind at rest," the solicitor said, perhaps to both the Logans. "It should be possible to defer the duty on the gift until the issues concerning the estate are settled. Feel free to contact me if there's any query in the meantime."

"Thanks," Daniella said, and stood up, wanting to be out of the confusion of sunlight and gloom to discover how she felt. "I need to get back to my essay. I can catch the next train if I hurry," she told her mother during a hug and kiss that she tried not to make too perfunctory. She had reached the corridor when a voice snagged the tangle of her thoughts. "Daniella?"

She carried on several paces before feeling seized by her own politeness. "What is it, Mr Stanley?"

"Alan, please." He sidled alongside her and raised the corners of his mouth to say "Are you all right for cash?"

"I've got a job."

"I gather so, but didn't Teddy slip you a few notes whenever you came to see us?"

"He liked to."

"That cash wasn't accounted for. He kept it for emergencies, which meant you. I thought it might be prudent to transfer it from his safe to mine once I saw how things were developing. I left everything else where it was, of course."

It wasn't the money that made her say "I could use some if you've got it at the office."

"I should have brought it. Thoughtless."

"It's okay. I'll go over with you."

As the stately lift lowered itself a floor her mother said "At least now we know what your father was keeping from me." Perhaps Daniella's unsureness about that was visible— was why her mother gave her a smile contradicted by a frown as the doors shut her and the lobby out. Twice as much of a descent produced the basement car park, where pillars as broad as a large man supported a concrete roof studded with blocks of harsh light. As Daniella followed Alan Stanley she heard a stealthy creaking behind a pillar, and faltered before she saw it came from a Jaguar that was cooling down. Alan Stanley's car was a white Volvo hatchback with leather seats plump enough to furnish a room. "Big car," she said, to say something.

He reached across her from the driver's seat and tugged her seatbelt until the tag snapped into place. "Room for all the family."

"I didn't know you had one."

"I couldn't live without them."

The car swung up the ramp onto the Strand. Sunlight added a smell of hot new leather to his scents as the Volvo avoided the pigeon-ridden cliché of Trafalgar Square and edged into Pall Mall. It was turning along St James's Street into Piccadilly, moving slower in a tarry stream of taxis than she could have walked, when he said "You realise your mother was right."

"When was she?"

"You understand now why your father was troubled. Why he'd been drinking the last time he was going to see you."

"He still shouldn't have."

"I agree with you, but I very much doubt you appreciate what he was going through."

The car put on a spurt into Piccadilly, then had to wait fuming until the last of an implacable procession of buses gave it leave to swing across into Half Moon Street. It sped down the ramp into the garage under the Oxford Films building, and so fast into the space with Alan Stanley's name on it that she pressed her spine against the leather as the sidelights swelled on the concrete wall. "I expect I didn't frighten you," he said, springing her seatbelt out of its lock.

"I expect you didn't mean to," she retorted, and was at the lift and thumbing the button before he was out of the car. "Do I need to get a badge from reception?"

"Not when you're with me if I say you don't."

In the corridor that used to lead to her father and his urgent warm embrace the monochrome posters looked drained of colour and the coloured ones too garish. She didn't want to linger when the place felt emptied of all it had meant to her, but she halted outside her father's office. "Where's Janis?"

"I had to let her go. I already had an assistant," he said, leading the way past the person referred to, a thin pale girl in a skimpy black dress and with several colours of spiky hair, into his office.

It struck Daniella as doing its best to equal her father's: a view of Green Park and of the tops of buses, their strips of windows stopping and starting in both directions as if a film editor was trying to locate a frame; a desk the delivery men must have cursed over carting upstairs, that was guarded by hulking cabinets and overlooked by posters; metal-framed leather bags to sit on. "Can I call for anything before we deal with business?" Alan Stanley said.

"Thanks, but I really need to get home. To York, I mean. To work."

"Then let me give you everything Teddy would have," he said, and went quickly to the safe behind the desk. He was halfway through confiding the combination to it when he paused. "Will you want both your houses, do you think? Are you likely to keep both?"

"Why?"

"I'm sure you'll agree that the place in Oxford is too much for one person, and it would make sense financially to put it on the market before anyone else can do so for less of a sum."

"Like who?"

"Whoever may gain control of his estate. If you speak to Mr Wendell I'm sure he could arrange for the house to be put up for sale, even if the money realised will have to be held as part of the estate until the situation is resolved."

She didn't want to be distracted by all this. "I'll think about it."

"I should," he said, and opened the safe. His shoulders stooped further before he turned to her, elbowing the metal door shut, a wad of notes in his fist. "This is all there was of what Teddy used to call his petty cash, though we knew he meant it for you. Eight hundred pounds. You may as well take it all."

"Thanks. Really, thanks."

He must have glimpsed her preoccupation as she stowed the notes in her purse. "Is there some other way I can help?" he said.

It was the reason she was there. "You can open my dad's safe, you said."

"There's no longer a reason, but yes."

"There was something else in there last time he didn't let me see. Some kind of box."

"A box." Alan Stanley hesitated, then the corners of his mouth rose. "I have it," he said.

"Can I go and look?"

"It's here. I transferred it." He reopened the metal door and reached in to drum his fingers on a lid. "Here's your box."

She ventured close enough to be assailed by his scents and by a tang of sweat they failed to conceal. He was resting his fingers on a carton less than a foot square. "That isn't it," she said.

"I think it is, you know. It's where Teddy kept your cash. That would have been what he didn't want you to see."

"Why wouldn't he have?"

"Perhaps so you didn't feel too secure. No, that wouldn't . . . I don't know. I can't speak for him."

"This isn't what I saw. Let's look in his safe and I'll show you."

"I do assure—" Replacing the lid, he returned the carton to the safe and shut the door. "As you prefer," he said.

The swiftness with which he headed for her father's

office must be intended to convey dissatisfaction, but it
didn't give her time to care. Her father's leather furniture
looked slumped, brought low by the spectacle of his bare
desk, and she thought she smelled dust in the air. The view
of buses and the park would have resembled a back-
projection if she had let her senses slip that far. She watched
Alan Stanley type the combination and haul the safe open.
"See for yourself," he said.

The safe was empty apart from a sparse heap of papers.
"It isn't there," said Daniella.

"As I told you. I put it in my safe in case anybody tried
to take it from you. Will you trust me in future?" he said,
and met her eyes.

For several moments she was unable to look away or
to move. When she spoke her lips felt thick and not much
less stiff than stone. "Why shouldn't I," she said, hoping it
didn't sound too like a question. "Thanks for my dad's
money. I've got to run for my train."

She'd given him an excuse to drive her when she
wanted to put distance between them. She did indeed run
to the lift, where mirrors displayed her bewilderment
whichever way she turned. The doors were still parting
when she dashed across the lobby, past the receptionist who
had taken her for an actress when she'd asked to see her
father. She heard him start to tell her to return a badge she
hadn't got, and then she was beyond the glass doors and
struggling through the crowd enclosed by the merciless sunlight, the uproar of traffic. She was seeing Alan Stanley's
eyes and the look in them. She'd seen that look in those
eyes before. She'd glimpsed it the night he had recognised
her at the graveyard.

ELEVEN

Forget I called," Daniella told the receiver, which was buzzing as though she'd caught a wasp in it to chase the unhelpful female voice, and was gripping it fiercely out of frustration when the creak of plastic was bitten off by the shrilling of the doorbell. She dropped the receiver on its plinth and opened the front door an inch, then pulled it and her foot back. "Mark," she cried, and brought her voice down. "I wasn't expecting you yet."

"I was on my way north when you called. I have to write about the Museum of Film in Bradford."

He looked earnest as ever, if more casually dressed in jeans and a short-sleeved blue shirt with a pen and notebook peeking from the breast pocket. "So long as you'll be able to cover that as well," Daniella said.

"Shall I come in?"

"Or we could go out," she said, less than ready to be alone in the house with him. "For a drink or just a walk."

"If it's a drink it's on me."

"I'm not exactly a penniless student, you know."

"It'll be my pleasure all the same."

So presumably the condition of her father's estate wasn't yet news. She shut the door and followed Mark down the path, feeling unexpectedly ashamed of the weeds he had to sidestep or trample. Several assorted terriers raced to snarl and yap at him through the railings of the park as he fell into step beside her. When the canine chorus gave way to the stuttering of traffic on the main road, he said "You had something to tell me about your father."

"I will," Daniella said, but had to raise her voice. "Let's find somewhere quieter first, shall we?"

Increasingly crowded Micklegate led them beneath the stout arch to the bridge, on either side of which sunlight kept up a soundless chatter on the corrugated silver river. Beyond the bridge the twisting road extended narrow streets that led to alleys crammed with shops. At the far end of an alley that smelled of fresh cakes Daniella saw a portly corner pub, its black timbers bulging with white-washed walls and small fat one-eyed panes. "Is that your sort of place?" Mark said.

"Let's find out."

The interior was as dark as the low thick beams—so dark that the drinkers in the corners were distinguishable from the old theatrical posters adorning the walls only by an ability to talk. A dumpy door led to a plump-flagged courtyard where three tree-stumps were surrounded by lesser versions of themselves with token backs to show these were seats. The inn proved sufficiently touched by the times to sell Budweiser. Mark brought out two and watched Daniella take a mouthful from her bottle, and another. "Quiet enough?" he said.

It occurred to her that she'd walked most of a mile without experiencing any awkwardness in his hushed company, but she was feeling uncertain now. "More than," she said, and told herself to stop holding back. "Mark, do you write any of the stuff at the front of your magazine?"

"*It's Only the Movies, Ingrid?* Any of us can if we've got

a story that's peculiar enough. I wrote the piece this month about the porn stars who made the crew and the director strip off too."

"I won't ask how you knew about it."

"I heard a rumour and followed it up. There's nothing about films that doesn't interest me."

That sounded like the cue she needed, but instead she found herself saying "Were you actually there?"

"For a day's shoot."

"Did you have to be naked as well?"

"They let me off, but they did say they could have offered me a part."

"You mean you could have offered them one," Daniella said, straightening the grin that had taken her off guard. "Would you write something if it was just about a film person but not films?"

"If it's true and strange enough it could go in."

"It's both of those." She took a sip of Budweiser before setting down the bottle with a gentleness that let her feel in control. "After my dad's funeral," she said, "hours after, when it was dark, there were about twelve men at his grave."

"Doing what?"

"Some kind of ritual. Holding things up, but I'm not sure what. Maybe wands."

"You saw this."

"I just wanted to be alone there for a while. I still haven't been," she said with sudden bitterness.

"Did they see you?"

"One did." She couldn't name him, not without evidence. "I got most of the number of his car," she said.

"I expect you gave it to the police."

"Yes, and they said it was stolen when I saw it, but I don't think it was the same car."

"That's some coincidence."

"I don't care. It can still be true."

"Hey, I'm on your side."

"Good. I think the man who owns the real one will have got rid of it, either that or just hidden it if he has another car."

"How would you find out?"

"I was trying before you came today, but the police won't tell me who owns cars with numbers like the one I saw, and the car licensing people won't either."

"I should have asked if you saw the man's face."

"He had his hand over it," Daniella restrained herself to saying. "I need to find out what they wanted. If the public gets to hear about them, maybe I will."

"Which is why you called me."

"You're the best journalist I know."

"Out of how many?"

"I'm sure it would have to be a lot before you weren't the best."

"Even better than Bill Trask?"

"Especially than him and any of his crowd."

He smiled—whether at the flattery or her raw resourcefulness she couldn't tell—then regained his earnest look. "Suppose what you saw was made public," he said. "Aren't you afraid these people might try and shut you up?"

"If all your readers knew about them I should think they'd be scared to try."

He gazed at her until she expected him to say something less mundane than "I'll see if I can talk it up with my editor. I may want to come back to you in case you remember anything more."

She saw Alan Stanley watching her over his mask of a hand. "When might you be able to get it published?" she said.

"Not in our next issue, so not for six weeks at least." More of her disappointment must have been apparent than she considered worthy of her years, because Mark said "If she doesn't want it for that page there's always my feature on your father."

"Will that be six weeks too?"

"Longer, I should think." He exhibited a grimace not unlike the one she was keeping to herself, and pointed to the bottle as she drained it instead. "Another?"

"I've had enough, thanks."

"I'd buy you lunch but I really need a few hours in Bradford."

"Never mind, I'm working on an essay."

"I hope I haven't distracted you from it too much."

"You've only been a help, Mark."

He seemed uncertain whether to agree. He pushed back his seat, which rumbled drunkenly over the flagstones, and preceded her through the mumbling dimness of the pub. As they emerged into the street she murmured "Thanks for not saying I must have imagined it all."

He blinked at her or at the sunlight. "Why would I want to do that?"

"Some people seem to think I did."

"You'd wonder why."

She found herself wishing they were somewhere quiet again in case they discovered they had more to say to each other, but he was already heading for the main road. They were still inside the city wall when he turned towards the car park by the Trencher. "I saw last time you have to be a resident to park in your street," he said.

"Next time I'll give you a notice to say you've come to see me."

"I'll look forward to it."

"Me too," Daniella said, leaving him with a smile and just as swift a wave.

She was hardly aware of the crowds or the heat as she made for home. She was content to stroll while her mind felt as if it had floated free of thoughts. As she passed beneath the arch at Micklegate Bar her footsteps grew close and flat, as did those behind her. She was telling herself not to feel pursued when a voice she knew overtook her. "That was him then, was it?"

"Hello, Blake." She wished she wasn't compelled to ask "Who?"

Her ex-boyfriend's wry mouth grew more crooked. "The feller you were going out with."

"Talk sense. When?"

"The night we were supposed to meet by the lake."

"The night you let me down, you mean. I don't know why I should tell you, but I hadn't met him then, so don't try using him as an excuse."

Blake raised his left eyebrow and the skin beneath the eye and jerked up that corner of his mouth. "So who was I warned off about?"

"I don't remember ever warning you about anything," Daniella said, no less loudly when a tourist couple hurried their children past her, "except about not handling me in public like I was your property."

"I said I was sorry about that, twice."

"After you did it twice, and anyway what do you mean, warned off?"

"Someone rang me that afternoon and said you already had someone at home and I'd better stay away from you unless I wanted, what did they say, my career to come to a sudden end."

The odour of baking from the shop behind her swelled up, suddenly too sweet and thick, in Daniella's throat. "Who said?"

"He didn't say. He was whispering."

"Why didn't you—why didn't you call me at least?"

"I tried a couple of times, but I never got through."

"You should have tried harder," Daniella said, not sure how unreasonable she was being—as unreasonable and confused as the world was growing, perhaps. "Well, I don't know anything about it. There was nobody, but we've finished anyway, and I hear you've got someone else since."

"Do you mind?"

"Not at all. I'm glad for you. Now, sorry, I've got to work," she said, and hurried through the sunlight that was one reason her throat was dry so soon after her drink. She didn't want to ponder Blake's story yet—she was too conscious of the question Mark had posed. She felt as though he'd made her aware of having tried not to admit it to herself.

TWELVE

B eliefs are necessary to the survival of the human race," Daniella read, "but maybe they are also necessary to the survival of the fittest." The sentence impressed her no more when read aloud than it did by lying on the page—not as a final line, at any rate, even if it was worth keeping. "Beliefs," she said, "can't live with them, can't live without them," and found her fingers reaching for the keys until she clicked the mouse to save the file instead. She was due at The Trencher soon, but first there were calls she wanted to make.

The sun was sinking beyond the park, drawing brightness out of the grass and leaving trails of weak shadow on the pavement in front of the railings, as she closed the computer down. She was alone in the house. Chrysteen was on a birthday pub-crawl for one of the other psychology students, and Duncan had taken Maeve for their first anniversary dinner. An unnecessary echo of her footsteps followed Daniella into the hall, where the paper hat on the lampshade struck her for the first time as childish, left over from a time before she'd learned how much there was to life. She dialled the number that had a rectangular box all to itself in the phone book.

After three rings a female voice so bright she took it at first to be live spoke to her. "This is the Care For Children switchboard. If you have abuse or any danger to a child to report, press 1 now. If you are a child in need of our care, press 2. If you wish to make a donation, press 3. If you wish to speak to an operator, press 4 . . ."

Daniella did and was rewarded by several bars of a computerised version of *The Teddy Bears' Picnic*. She'd begun to sing along with it as an alternative to growing tense when a voice not unlike that of the taped message said "Stacy speaking. How may I help?"

"Can I speak to Norman Wells?"

"I should think he's probably gone for the day. May I ask who's calling?"

"Daniella Logan. Can you give me a number where he'll be?"

"I'm not authorised to pass out that information, I'm sorry. Would you like a word with his—"

"I need to speak to him personally. He was a friend of my dad's. Teddy Logan, if you've heard of him."

"Most people have, I'm sure," the operator said and adopted a tone she might have turned on a child who had called for help. "Our sympathies to you in your loss. Will you hold while I see if I can locate Mr Wells?"

The bears reappeared, dancing on the computer keyboard. Daniella heard two choruses of them before the operator told her "Putting you through now."

Daniella heard more of the bears and couldn't help joining in: ". . . sure of a big surprise . . ." "You sound pleased with life," Norman Wells said.

"Some of it."

"A good deal, I hope. That's how it should be at your age."

"Why?"

"That's the least you deserve, to be content with your life. I know Teddy—" He didn't quite suppress a noise that might have been rebuking his own tactlessness. "Anyway, what's the occasion? I presume it's not an official call."

"Well," she began, and had scarcely paused when he said "It's not, is it?"

She wondered if the prospect always made him so anxious. "Not at my age," she told him.

"My point entirely, absolutely, that's to say. Our concern here is children, which you aren't any more, are you?"

"I don't know what my dad would have said to that."

"You're at university. You ought to be your own person by now," Norman Wells declared with a fierceness she wasn't prepared for. "However, I'm sure you didn't ring up for a lecture, so I wonder what you expect of us oldsters. You've plenty of friends there, I trust."

"I've a few in my house."

"The closer the better. Now, was there something urgent? Don't think me unwelcoming, but I'm just in the midst of organising a tour of events."

"We needn't talk now. I wanted to find out when I can come and see you."

"That would be a pleasure, for me at any rate. Why would you like to?"

"I'm helping someone who's writing about my dad."

"I'm sure it must be time for a study of his films. Is that the sort of thing?"

"And about his life."

"You couldn't leave that out, of course. Please let me wish you success with it, but I don't think there would be any point in your coming all the way down to Sussex, not when you must have so much else to do."

"I quite like driving places. It makes me feel like you said I should be."

"Surely not if you'd be wasting your time. I wouldn't be able to tell you anything about him everyone else doesn't know."

"I thought you were friends."

"Many of us were."

"Close, though."

"He made some extremely generous donations to the charity, even more than most of our mutual friends, and I'm sure he was aware how his generosity was appreciated, but I wouldn't say I was any closer to him than, than various people you'll have thought of."

"I'd still like to meet for a chat. There might be things I'd find important that you wouldn't, maybe things you've forgotten I might help you to remember."

"Let me see if anything occurs to me in say the next few weeks and if it does I'll be in touch."

"Will you be there if I think of something to ask you?"

"I won't. As I said, we're about to start a tour and we're having some last-minute problems."

"What kind?"

"People who sold themselves as reliable turning out not to be."

"If I can fill in for anyone, since I've done a bit of acting, and you're coming up this way—"

"That's most thoughtful of you, Daniella, but they're one-man shows, and the performers I've booked aren't the trouble. Besides, we won't be heading your way, we'll be nowhere near you. I do thank you, but I'll ask you to excuse me now so I can get back to making sure of the arrangements."

"Go ahead," Daniella told him, only just before she was cut off. She jabbed the receiver rest to quell the sharp metallic command for her to replace the handset and dialled the number she'd inked on her wrist. Once she'd explained that she wanted to thank the motorcyclist who had stayed with her dying father, an Oxfordshire policeman was happy to give her a name and a Darlington number.

A woman answered with a briskness that sounded designed to leave any trace of an accent behind. "Who's this?"

"Can I speak to Nigel Burgess?"

"Are you one of these girls from his night class? He's at his studies if you are or if you aren't either. He doesn't want to be a despatch rider for the rest of his life."

"It's about Teddy Logan. I'm—"

"You're not his counsellor."

"I'm not," Daniella said, and refrained from adding that she'd never had recourse to one. "I'm Teddy Logan's daughter."

"Oh, I see." There were few condolences in that, and less in "And?"

"Nothing bad, I promise. I was grateful to him for waiting with my dad. I've just got a question."

"What would that be?"

"I'd like to ask him."

"You would." The woman paused before relenting or resigning herself enough to say "It's for you, son. Don't let her keep you."

Some time, much of it occupied by a shifting of hands near the mouthpiece, passed before he said "Who's this?"

Unlike his mother, he sounded as if he wanted to know. "It's Daniella Logan," she said. "We met the night my father died."

"I remember. How are you now?"

"I've survived."

"I'm sorry."

"No, I mean it. I hear you're being counselled."

"I was told I had to be," Nigel Burgess said apologet-ically, and she wondered if the instruction had come from his employer or his mother. "It was that or drink too much, no good with my job. It preys on your mind, being re-sponsible for someone's death."

"Well, it shouldn't. I was going to thank you for look-ing after him."

"If I hadn't been there in the first place there might have been no need."

"If it wasn't you it would have been a different accident with all he'd had to drink."

"Thanks for saying that. Thanks for calling."

"Hold on. Can I ask you something?"

"I'm still here."

"You said my dad talked about me. Do you remember what he said?"

"Your name. That's how I knew what to call you when we, you know, met."

"That's all. Just my name."

"No, he said something about—I'll be finished shortly, mother. It's helping to talk. Sorry about that," he said to Daniella, and no more while she swallowed dryly. "He said something about a day."

"A day for what?"

"Your day. He said your day. Let me think exactly, he said your name and then he said 'her day.' Was he coming to see you on your birthday?"

"That isn't for months."

PACT of the FATHERS

"Were you graduating? Up for some kind of prize?"

"Not that I know of. I mean, no. Are you sure that's what he meant? Could he have started to say he'd heard something?"

"I don't think so. He sounded as if he was finished."

In at least one sense, Daniella reflected bleakly, he had been. "So was that all he said?"

"It was. He said it like he was talking in his sleep. I'm not even sure if he knew I was there. I'm certain he didn't suffer."

"Thanks," she had to say to that. Indeed, she thanked him again before ringing off, although talking to him had only further confused her. She had time for one more call, and she meant to see that it resolved something. When the Care For Children switchboard began to utter its message she pressed 4 at once and was answered by an operator named Susan. "How may I help?"

"I was wondering where your tour will be going."

"It starts in London, then we're in Cambridge, Birmingham, Sheffield, Bradford..."

"What day is that?"

"Bradford? Thursday. Would you like the details?"

"I'd love them," Daniella said and, having pulled a ballpoint from the pocket of her shorts, not only uncapped it one-handed but fitted the cap to its rear end with a deftness that made her feel in control at last. She wrote the address and time of the Bradford event on her wrist and dropped the receiver on its hook, and hurried upstairs to transfer the details to the notepad beside her computer before she washed and changed for work. She was going to find out why Norman Wells was anxious to avoid her. Despite what he'd told her, next Thursday would bring him within an hour's drive.

THIRTEEN

A coach full of chattering pensioners in summer dresses was being unloaded for a matinee at the Alhambra, and she thought she'd reached Bradford in plenty of time. Above the theatre clusters of shops curved up a hill beyond which another was ribbed with narrow red-brick terraces, their highest chimneys bristling against the horizon of the Yorkshire moors. She hurried down an underpass to a paved flat hollow where the sounds of a guillotine—a rapid sliding followed by a clump—proved to have been made by a lone skateboarder. As she emerged beneath three lanes for the moment bare of traffic, the steep red roof of the town hall loosed a clatter of pigeons like slates of the wrong colour. The hotel facing the town hall displayed a glassed-in poster for the Charming Child Contest hosted by Loony Larry Larabee for the Care For Children Fund. Anybody passing would have noticed that, Daniella reflected as the automatic doors deferred to her with hardly a whisper.

A red carpet the width of the extensive lobby met her feet. Several businessmen were sitting forward in a circle of wing chairs taller than themselves and holding a discussion no less hushed than whatever music was suspended in the air. A receptionist whose hair and makeup were on their way to growing as autumnal as her uniform awaited Daniella well before she arrived at the counter, beside which a man in a russet outfit was fitting plastic letters to a board. "What can I do for you today?" the receptionist said.

"Is Norman Wells, he runs Care For Children, is he around?"

"I believe he may be with us. Shall I see?" Her fingers scurried over her keyboard, and she barely paused before saying "He's checked in. Would you like me to try his room?"

"You could."

"Who shall I say?"

"I'm just here because I saw the poster."

The receptionist ducked her head towards the receiver she lifted and widened her eyes twice. When none of this brought her a response she said "He's not upstairs. Shall I page him?"

"Or I could see if he's helping set things up."

"He will be, knowing him. I'm sure they won't mind if you go through. They're in the Priestley Suite."

At the end of a short corridor beyond the lifts a pair of doors was wedged open, showing a room by no means full of about twenty large round tables. Waitresses were draping cloths over them and setting each of them with a china figurine of a Victorian child, fresh flowers sprouting from its cranium. On a stage framed by photographs of children's beaming faces six feet high a purple-cheeked man with his arms outside his jacket was informing a microphone that it was being tested, only to have it emit a screech that drew a pained note from the chandeliers. "Leave it, Bill," said a woman who was sorting entry forms on the table nearest the door. "We'll have headaches once the cherubs are assembled as it is."

Daniella cleared her throat, the carpet having muted

her approach. "Excuse me, do you know where I can find Norman Wells?"

"He went up for a shower," the thin-faced woman said, "not ten minutes ago."

"Do you happen to know which room?"

"I might, but who's looking for him?"

"I met him at my dad's funeral."

The woman shrugged her right shoulder, which Daniella took as her reply until she saw it was intended to adjust the Care For Children T-shirt. "Three oh," the woman started, and repeated it before deciding "It's either three or four."

"Three—" Daniella said and fell silent, hearing a voice at her back. "Was that you squealing, Bill? Thought you only did that at weekends with a man behind you."

The comedian strode into the room, thrusting his round big-mouthed face with its comically inadequate nose forward as though it was the beginning or end of a joke. "You haven't wrecked the mike, have you? Don't say I'm going to have to shout when the little sweethearts mightn't like it. We don't want them clinging to their mummies."

"It's still working, Larry," the man on stage said, provoking another electronic whine.

"There's nothing like an expert, Bill, and you're nothing like. I haven't heard anyone squeak so loud since the last time I pinched young Ivy here's bum."

He was gesturing at the woman next to Daniella, whom he appeared not to notice as he bore down on the stage. "Which was it?" Daniella murmured urgently.

"Four," Ivy said in much the same tone.

Daniella was beyond the doors when the microphone boomed in Larabee's voice "Why all the happy chappies and music continued to drum like a woodpecker in the other corridor as a man who sounded close enough to touch her said beyond the door "She's here now. Do you want her?"

She twisted around to retreat and saw a figure lurch at her. It flung up a hand that looked ready to arrest her as she recognised herself in another mirror. She heard the man shout "Sophie" and a woman's answer from the adjoining room. The light beyond its spyhole went out, and Daniella heard the woman's voice enter the man's room. The man wasn't Norman Wells. The woman in the Priestley Suite had meant to direct Daniella to the floor above.

She managed to grin at her approaching self as she hurried down the corridor to a pointer for the stairs. Only the lack of a number betrayed that the door didn't lead to a room. The stairs were grey and bare and sharp-edged, with a chilly metal banister. They seemed determined to make her footsteps ring out harshly under the blocks of icy light set in the rough white pockmarked windowless walls. She was breathing hard with haste by the time she reached the door painted with a red 4 as big as her head.

Another of the mirrors she was beginning to dislike greeted her with her infant-sized self. She thought she heard a vacuum cleaner, and then she realised it was a hair-dryer in a room ahead. The one she wanted surely had to be either 403 or 404. When she brought her face close to the spyhole of the latter she saw only darkness. The hair-dryer was in the adjacent room. She knocked on the door hard enough to bruise her knuckles. "Who is it?" Norman Wells called.

She opened her mouth and then pinched her lips shut with her teeth. She moved aside, out of range of the spy-hole, and knocked again. The dryer wound down into silence, and footsteps padded to the door. It was on the move, releasing a warm wet scent of shower gel, as Norman Wells said "I won't be—"

He saw her, and his ostentatiously patient look collapsed. She had the impression that his jowls instantly gained weight, dragging at his pudgy face, undermining his thick lips and flaring his nostrils and almost closing his eyes. If he weren't so tanned she was sure he would have changed colour. The right side of his scalp was dry, but a trickle of water emerged unchecked from the parting of his grey hair. He grasped the lapels of his white towelling bathrobe as if to haul his back straight, then tugged the belt tighter with both hands. "Daniella," he said in a voice a little too determined to be firm. "As you see, you've surprised me."

"Sorry."

"Good heavens, no need to be sorry. It isn't that serious."

Her awareness of being about to say things that until now she would never have imagined saying tautened her forehead and ached in her skull. "It wouldn't be if you were just surprised."

"Now what can you mean by that, Daniella?"

"I didn't know you'd be upset to see me."

"Good Lord, I don't think so. You're letting your imagination run away with you a bit there. Do I really look upset? Harassed, more like."

"I'm sorry if I'm harassing you, but—"

"I don't mean you. I hope you wouldn't, not the way you were brought up." He gripped the edge of the door as his gaze dodged away from her towards the junction of the corridors. "I'm desperately busy, that's all. I need to be dressed and downstairs or they'll be wanting to know where I am."

She might have believed that was the whole of his reason for panic if the trickle of water hadn't reached his left eyebrow without being dabbed. She saw him take a backward pace she thought he hoped was surreptitious, and moved forward so that he would have to push her out of the way in order to close the door. "Just tell me one thing, then," she said.

"Look, Daniella, this is hardly the appropriate time or place, is it? Just imagine what anyone passing will think, me half dressed and letting a girl your age into my room."

"There isn't anyone," she said, just as a lift bell rang in the transverse corridor. She saw his eyes flinch, and heard herself say "Who don't you want seeing you talking to me?"

"Who indeed. Really, do forgive me, but what a foolish question. I thought you were supposed to be more mature than that. Have you been watching some of those old thrillers Teddy made before he worked out what he could be proud of?"

His fingers on the door shifted, ready to shut her out, but she only moved her feet apart to stand firmer. "I haven't, but it's about my dad all right," she said.

The trickle ran down from his brow to his eye, which blinked twice before he let go of the door in order to dab. "I told you when you phoned—"

"What are you afraid I'll ask?"

"What on earth are you—why in God's name should I—"

"I know it's about him. I already know part of it. I saw something he kept in his safe he didn't want me to see.

Whatever it's about, I can stand it. Tell me. Someone's coming. Tell me, quick. Tell me what he kept in a box in his safe."

Someone was indeed approaching, having been announced by the bell of the lift. As she leaned her head back to glance along the corridor she glimpsed Norman Wells' lips working and his tongue pushing them apart. He muttered a few rapid words, less than a sentence, and she was trying to grasp what he'd told her as she saw Larry Larabee sweep into view. "So it was Teddy's treasure," he said, just loud enough for her and Norman Wells to hear. "I thought that was you downstairs."

The door nudged Daniella's foot, then pretended it hadn't as it winced back. "Is that you, Larry?" Norman Wells said too loudly, and shoved past her into the corridor. "Am I needed?"

"Always. We couldn't do a thing without you. You're the man in charge."

"I'm coming right now."

"I should put your other togs on first, and it wouldn't be a bad idea to do something with your hair. We don't want the mumsies and their troupe wondering which of us is the comedian."

"I meant when I'm ready, of course," Norman Wells said, wiping the breadth of his forehead with the back of one hand. He stumbled backwards into the room, out of Larabee's range of vision, and gave Daniella a look as intense as it was unreadable. "I wish you luck elsewhere," he said, and shut the door.

The way out was past Larabee. The light from the wall-lamps kept lending his eyes a sly gleam as he came for her, thrusting his face forward as though searching for a joke

ahead of him. "There's a sad sight, a young girl chucked
out to fend for herself," he remarked. "Take my arm if you
like and I'll escort you where you're going."

"I'm going home."

"Where all good girls should be."

As she sidled past him he pirouetted with a swiftness
she wouldn't have expected of his bulk and took her elbow
in a soft clammy grasp. "So what do we thank for the
pleasure?" he said.

She felt as if he was trying to drive out of her mind
any sense of what Norman Wells had confided to her.
"How do you mean?"

"What brought you here besides your tootsies?"

"I saw the poster and I thought I'd see if there were
any jobs."

"What use did you think we could make of a young
thing like you?"

"In the show, maybe. I've done a bit of acting."

"I can tell," the comedian said, and gripped her arm
harder as they reached the junction of the corridors.
"Where are we off to now?"

"I'm parked by the station."

"Then I'll show you the short cut." He led her to the
door that gave onto the stairs. The clank of the metal bar
echoed down the stairwell, accentuating the emptiness. "We
don't need the lift, do we?" he said. "Walk where you can
and you'll live longer, that's my motto."

At least she could free herself of his clutch and stay
ahead of him. She advanced so quickly onto the stairs that
she was three treads down when he dragged the door shut
with another harsh clank. "You should have come to me,"
he said.

She grabbed the banister, which felt colder than before, so as to continue walking while she glanced up at him. His first step set his face quivering as though its petulant expression was about to change. "What for?" she said, her voice flattened small by the walls.

"I thought you said you wanted to perform."

"I've got a job right now, but I'm always looking."

"Both eyes on the future, eh? There can't be many would deny you that. You're a student, aren't you, here in Bradford."

She turned the corner of the stairs and met his gaze. "I'm at York."

"Did we have posters up there?"

She thought he might know they hadn't, particularly since his face had grown blank. "I was here to get some tickets for a concert," she said.

"At the Alhambra? I didn't know they catered for your age."

"You'd be surprised."

"Not often."

As she hurried down the next flight she sensed his gaze on her back. It felt as clammy as his grasp had, or perhaps that was just heat clinging between her shoulders. Her heels scraped the edge of a stair as she swung herself around the next bend. The noise grew hollow above and below her—the corridors beyond the barred door she'd just passed might as well have been miles away. "Are we having a race?" Larabee said close behind her. "Only asking. You'll find me up to it if we are."

She stared at him from the bend halfway between two floors, and saw amusement turned inward in his eyes. "I'm just in a hurry," she said. "I thought you would be, to fix things up."

"There's still a chunk of time left."

His murmur didn't sound addressed to her. Of course nobody was behind her except him. She didn't quite run— she kept telling herself there was no need—but she wished he wouldn't follow her so closely that she could sense his clammy heat like a breath engulfing the whole of her back. She was growing dizzy with taking the bends so fast when he said "So would you like me to do what I can?"

"About what?"

"I sometimes have a stooge. I'll add you to my roster of hopefuls, shall I? Then you'll have something else to look forward to. No point in living if you don't have hope."

She no longer knew if he was joking. "Thanks," she nevertheless said.

"That's it, carry on down."

She'd stepped onto the next descending flight when she checked herself. "Those go to the basement," she said.

"Why, so they do. Blame your charm for muddling up my head." He crossed to the fire exit and closed a fist around each of the bars on the double doors. "Well, how's that for a feeble payoff?" he said, having shaken the bars. "They're stuck."

She darted across the concrete and slammed the heels of her hands against the left bar. It gave at once, almost trapping Larabee's fingers. The door swung wide, revealing pedestrians on a pavement. As she joined them in the sunlight and restrained a gasp of relief, Larabee called "Remember you're on my schedule now. Don't be surprised if I'm suddenly after you."

The door clanked shut as she dodged around the side of the hotel. His words and the heat felt as if he was at her back, but she had to clear him out of her head so that she could concentrate on the information she'd received. If Norman Wells had said what she thought she'd heard, surely that made sense of other events too.

NEKTARIKOS

I'm just going to down to the shop."

"I'll call you back in a few minutes," Nana said, and laid the silenced phone on the patio table. "What do you need? Perhaps I have it here."

"I thought I'd see what I might like."

"I'd guess nothing. It's merely a peasant shop, you should realise."

"Sounds like it could be fun."

"Then you must see for yourself. Shall I have Stavros drive you? He's only dealing with my weeds."

"I was going to walk and get a bit of exercise."

"My pool hasn't given you enough, then."

"It's given me plenty," Daniella said, feeling the afternoon sunlight dry the water on her and the bikini Nana had given her. "I'll want to jump in it when I come back."

"Do you have a sense of how long you may be?"

"I should be down to the harbour and back in a couple of hours, shouldn't I?"

"There's nothing I can think of to delay you."

Daniella peered at Nana's sea-blue eyes before deciding that hadn't been a question. She was heading into the villa, leaving a trail of increasingly less wet footprints on the marble, when her hostess said "You won't go dressed like that, will you?"

"You think I'll offend someone."

"Only if you enter the church. No, I thought you might catch too much sun."

"That's one thing I do need to buy, sunglasses."

"Save your money." Nana stood up, dropping the phone into a capacious pocket of her ivory ankle-length dress, and placed her cool hands on Daniella's shoulders to guide her into the building. As Daniella shrugged herself into a beach dress that fell below her knees, Nana brought her a pair of sunglasses much like the visor Stavros had worn in the car. "The latest thing," said Nana. "Try them and you'll never wear any others."

Daniella shortened the adjustable arms and fitted the glasses to her head. "They don't seem to make any difference."

"You won't notice what they're doing," Nana assured her, and passed her a wide-brimmed straw hat. "Is there any other way for me to help?"

"Can you tell me where to go to change my money?"

"Nowhere else but here, except you haven't to buy money from me. I'll make you a present of some."

"You mustn't, Nana. You've already done so much."

"Not yet enough," the actress said, but took the fifty pounds Daniella extracted from her purse. "Are you doing some writing?" Nana wondered. "Noting your impressions down?"

Daniella resisted an urge to thrust her old school exercise book deeper into her handbag. Her neck was throbbing with tension, and she had to lick her lips before she could speak. "Just some old stuff," she succeeded in saying.

"Nostalgia? I understand. We all look back," Nana said on the way to her room, from which she reappeared with a handful of large crisp colourful banknotes. "I think you'll find it hard to spend all that."

"I may try, though."

"You'll find more use for it when I take you for a cruise around the islands. Perhaps tomorrow now I have my boat back. I can watch out for my business just as well from there," she said, indicating with the phone the powerboat alongside the fishermen's vessels it dwarfed. "If you aren't back in your couple of hours, shall I send for you?"

"Send . . ."

"Stavros with the car."

"I'm sure I'll be back by then," Daniella said, not wanting to seem ungrateful but feeling a little trapped. One reason for her walk was to experience some freedom from being thoroughly looked after. "I'll make sure," a promise she wished she didn't have to undertake, and slipped the bottle of water Nana handed her into her bag.

The rasp of cicadas surrounded her as she walked along the marble path, sandals clacking. The insect sound was the ancient voice of the island, she thought; it must be almost as old as the sea and the rocky slopes. A single cloud hovered at the zenith, matching a white sail perched on the horizon, and only the waspish buzz of a moped down by the harbour reminded her the centuries had moved on. She ducked to inhale the scent of a sprawl of purple blossom as she descended three steps to the patch of bare earth above the road.

Cicadas fell silent as she tramped downhill and struck up again once she'd passed. The olive trees on which they were indistinguishable from the bark, except for one beetle she glimpsed inching out of sight around a slim trunk, offered some intermittent shade, though they had been unable to save the grass beneath them from being parched the same pale gold as Nana's hair. At least Nana seemed to have been right about the sunglasses: they prevented the glare of sunlight from reaching Daniella's eyes but left colours undimmed. They were so nearly weightless she might have forgotten she was wearing them, except for a sense of their presence flanking her vision.

By the time she reached the bend at the foot of the first slope of road, the villa had been reduced to a series of white gleams through the tattered canopy of leaves while the empty sky pressed the sea lower. By the second bend the villa had withdrawn out of sight, and the roofs above the harbour were floating on the sea. She could still hear the buzz of the moped, and once a goat fled precipitously upward between the trees with a clatter of rubble that put her in mind of the casting of dice. As she passed the third bend the moped was silenced, having emitted a curl of grey fumes that hung like a signal above the roofs until it was absorbed by the sky. Now the only prospect was the sky itself, resting on the bright sharp edge of the sea. She could have been walking for a quarter of an hour, her sandals gathering dust at every step, when the trees ahead writhed and began to melt as though the relentless sunlight had distorted her glasses, because she had burst into tears.

A lizard greener than the grass had any chance to be skittered away from the large flat rock she found to sit on. She fumbled off the glasses to plant them on the rock before cupping her face in her hands and giving herself up to sobs. She wasn't sure why she was crying: perhaps at being safe, or at knowing she should have done more than she'd felt able to risk, but mostly at the betrayal that made her clutch at her face. She wept until her head was stuffed with the taste of tears, and then she wiped her hands on her dress and found barely enough tissue in her bag to blow her nose. She hadn't finished when the bag fell over, spilling the plastic bottle, which hit the road with a decisive crack.

She rubbed her eyes clear with the backs of her hands just in time to see the last of the water stream downhill. "Bye," she told it with a moderately successful version of a wry laugh at herself, and shoved the empty bottle into her bag so as not to litter Nana's island. There was bound to be water on sale by the harbour. As the glare of sunlight on the road began to throb in her eyes, she warded it off with the sunglasses and sent herself towards the next bend.

She was glad when at last she saw the red tiled skullcap of the church. Her memories—only those and the sunglasses, she had to keep telling herself—had begun to make her feel she was being kept company on the deserted road. When she came abreast of the gravel path to the open door beneath the rough white tubular tower surmounted by the dome, she made for the church.

Beyond the token porch the cramped interior smelled of incense and of the multitude of candles grouped in brass holders close to the walls, from which images of stern-faced haloed saints, their fingers raised to bless their visitors, were flaking. Several dozen folding chairs were stacked against the wall to the left of the entrance. In the middle of the stone-flagged floor a heavy table displayed under glass the icon of a saint, a flat thick brownish shape disconcertingly suggestive of a gilded steak. Beyond the table a priest dressed from tall hat to foot in black was on his knees before the brightest and most elaborately populated of the walls, swinging the crucifix at the end of a rosary in circles as if to drive away demons as he prayed. He half-turned

his massive bearded head to frown at her beneath wiry
black eyebrows—at the way she was dressed, perhaps, or
at whatever sound she had been unable to suppress as the
candle flames reminded her of the mistake she'd made in
the graveyard. "Sorry," she mumbled, but the priest had
already ducked to his beads, and so she tiptoed out of the
church.

A line of squat white houses not much less rough than
rocks straggled down the lumpy road to the harbour. Old
women sat unmoving outside two adjacent houses, their
faces wizened as dried fruit, their eyes black as their head-
scarves and the dresses that hid them from the neck down,
their expressions no more welcoming than the priest's had
been. A moped leaned in a doorway beyond which she
heard the thumps and grunts of a martial arts game a solitary silhouette was playing on a television almost blank
with sunlight. A boy who looked too young to have left
school rode a motor scooter uphill with a boy of about six
standing between him and the steering column. The scooter
slewed around and raced downhill, the passenger clapping
his hands with delight, his and the rider's white shirts fluttering. The frantic movement revived the dizziness she'd
suffered during her first day on the island, and she had to
rest a hand on a low hot crumbling wall. The dizziness left
her mouth even dryer than her expenditure of tears had.
Once she felt steadier she tramped down the road in search
of a drink.

A shop occupied the corner by the harbour. A wire
stand loitered outside, nothing like full of a few yellowed
paperbacks in Greek with their dog-eared pages taped shut.
There wasn't much to read at the villa: some feminist volumes that told her nothing she didn't already know or feel,

a few novels not unlike Nana's films, shelves of books in Greek but no dictionary or phrasebook to help Daniella if she'd wanted to attempt them. The topmost rack of the tottering stand, which looked incapable of swivelling without losing its balance, displayed three postcards of Nektarikos curled by the sun and rendered nearly blank, as if the island was fading into a past before there were photographs. In the open front of the shop some planks had been laid across upturned crates to exhibit an array of dusty vegetables, behind which shelves held cans of food, packets of cereal, a variety of other supermarket items that looked abandoned in the dimness rather than for sale. To the right of the shelves was a glass-fronted cabinet containing not too many bottles, to the left was a counter built of unplaned planks on which a boy perhaps twelve years old was resting his bare feet while he leaned back in a rickety straight chair and listened to a tape through earphones. Daniella went to the cabinet, but it was padlocked shut. "Excuse me," she said.

She had to repeat it before the boy raised his head. His dark eyes looked sleepy with indifference, and the corners of his lips couldn't be bothered to raise themselves. "Could I get some water?" she said.

His fingers were splayed on his smooth bare thighs. His hands rose on the sides of their palms just enough to express either incomprehension or lack of interest. "Water," she said and cupped her hand before tipping it towards her open mouth.

Though the gesture aggravated her thirst, at least it seemed to reach the boy, who pointed in the direction of the cabinet. "Locked," she said, twisting an invisible key in the air.

He jabbed his finger at the cabinet. When she repeated her mime with as much additional vigour, he padded across the boards to beckon her impatiently out of the shop and jerk his thumb at the tavernas he had in fact been indicating. He stumped back to prop his heels on the counter with a thud of great finality. "Thanks," Daniella said, and no quieter "Funny way to run a shop."

She could only assume he resented being left in charge, no doubt by his parents. Nobody was to be seen outside any of the tavernas, nor by the harbour. She couldn't blame anyone for staying out of the heat. She moved under the faded striped awning of the nearest taverna and cleared her dry throat. "Hello?"

The motor scooter sped uphill and abruptly cut out, leaving a smell of diesel fumes and a silence broken only by the whisper of the waves. "Hello?" she called again, loud enough to make herself cough.

Beyond the few cheap tables and flimsy chairs the kitchen had nothing to say. She was still coughing as she hurried next door. When she managed to shout "Hello" before another parched cough overcame her she heard a commotion in the kitchen, and a large thin ragged cat ran out, dragging a half-eaten eyeless fish. She told herself the owners of the two tavernas must be in the next one, but the only response that met her call there and the cough it revived was the dripping of a tap.

However many films she'd seen in which that was supposed to be ominous, the sound of water didn't strike her that way now. The kitchen was little more than a recess open to the hillside, with a barbecue grill taking up much of the room. One of a pair of rusty taps was dripping rapidly into a stone sink. She bruised her fingers in the inter-

stices of the metal cross while twisting it. A violent
knocking in the pipe signalled the imminence of a jet of
water, muddy for some seconds and then clear enough for
her to risk. She cupped it in her hands and ducked her face
to them, tasting earth in the first mouthful. The taste had
faded, and so had her cough, by the time she used both
hands to quell the spurting of the tap.

As she retreated into the sunlight she wondered what
kind of mime she would have to perform by way of explanation, but there was nobody to need one. Beside the nodding boats Nana's vessel stood almost as still as an outpost
of the villa whose whiteness it shared. Daniella could see
no reason to linger by the harbour. Her drink from the tap
wouldn't last her all the way back, but she'd noticed a flask
in the shop. She found the wad of Greek notes as she
stepped into the dimness. The boy had gone, leaving the
tape player mute on the chair.

"Hello?" she called, and was answered by a voice—an
impossibly deep voice that seemed to rise from some un-
derground hollow, and grew even deeper as it chanted an
ancient song. Her mouth had tightened dryly before she
realised that she was hearing the priest. Of course, it was
Sunday, and the villagers must have used the back alleys as
their route to the church.

She left her largest note on the counter. Another day
she would ask for her change—Nana could tell her how.
She weighed the note down with the tape player and
reached for the blue plastic flask at the near end of the
middle shelf. Suppose it was the boy's? It seemed to be
empty, which was going to have to mean it was for sale. A
dozen pebbly paces took her back to the taverna, where she
rinsed out the flask and filled it with clear water. She hung

the flask on its strap around her neck as she emerged onto the deserted track.

The priest was singing from deep within himself. His voice sounded dark as his clothes and his frown, and made a stone bell of the church. Its stern ancient message grew louder and stronger as she trudged uphill, and she felt as though it and the tiny village had cast her out—as though the voice might even be singing about the intruder who sneaked into people's kitchens while they were at worship and who took away merchandise without asking. She'd paid over the odds for it, and she mustn't let herself feel alone and surrounded, not again, not here on the island. Nevertheless she was glad when the voice sank below her as if it had been caught by the trees. By the time the island swallowed its last resonance she was at the third bend.

She found the least patchy shade the bend provided and unscrewed the stopper of the flask. The water was already lukewarm. She swallowed some and choked, and spat out the mouthful, which for a moment darkened the road like an unreadable symbol. The flask must have belonged to someone—a child, she thought, who had used it for a purpose other than drinking while at play on a beach. A sizeable amount of her mouthful had been sand.

She could only assume the inside of the flask had been so caked that rinsing hadn't dislodged the crust. She spilled water into her palm and threw it into her mouth to help her spit out the gritty residue. As she raised and lowered her head, a band of trees about halfway between her and the villa appeared to move. She thought it was an effect of the sunglasses until she removed them. There had to be a concentration of heat-haze on that stretch of road; the trees alongside weren't merely quivering, they were writhing as though close to bursting into flame. She donned the glasses, though they failed to shut out the sight that was making her feel dizzy and vulnerable, and tramped uphill.

She was trudging up the length of road below the one from which the haze had disappeared when the heat found her. Her mouth was instantly dry as sand, her skin seemed to wither on her flesh. Wherever she looked, rock and trees and bleached grass shifted as if the very absence of moisture made them appear to be underwater. She felt close to fainting as she stumbled under the nearest shady tree, where all the heat followed her. She opened the flask so hastily she almost dropped the stopper, and flung her head back to fill her desiccated mouth. Though she took care over tipping the flask she had to shut her lips to fend off the contents, barely in time. There was no longer any water, only sand.

How could even the heat of the island have dried up the water so fast? She might have wept if that wouldn't have wasted any moisture left to her. The stopper on its cord rattled repeatedly against the flask as she sent herself out of the useless shade. She tried climbing the slope below the next stretch of road, but the ground was too steep, and as unstable as the rest of her surroundings looked—as her legs began to feel long before she'd finished staggering up the road.

She couldn't tell when she left the worst of the heat behind. She thought she sensed it following her up the slope. The scent of the trees behind her had been suffocated by a smell of dryness, but glancing back would only aggravate her dizziness; even the thought of the quivering haze did. She imagined she felt it shrink from the marble as she floundered onto the outermost path, beside which Stavros was spraying blossoms with a hosepipe. As the purple flowers sparkled with drops bright as the sun, her mouth produced a trace of saliva in sympathy. She stumbled into the coolness of the villa, and was concentrating on the last few paces to her room when Nana looked out of hers. "Daniella," she began, and then "Whatever's wrong?"

"I got too hot. I think I'm dehydrated," Daniella croaked, and would have hurried onward if she hadn't heard a masculine voice in Nana's room.

Heat lurched at her through the coolness, and she flung out a hand to support herself against the marble wall. Nana's smile at her reaction looked just a little pained. "Let me introduce you," she said, pushing the door wide. "This is my partner Daphne. She's come over from the mainland."

The woman was short and muscular and smelled of Greek cigarettes. Her dark hair was cut severely level alongside her thick lips, which straightened themselves as she presented Daniella with a nod and a strong swift handshake while her large grey eyes held off deciding in her favour. "Good to meet you," Daniella said, and hurried into her room to pour herself a glassful of iced water followed by another before she lay back gingerly on the bed. It didn't matter how much of a shock Daphne had been, so long as she wasn't a man. Seeming to hear a man's voice where she'd expected none had reminded Daniella of everything she'd fled, and she was unable not to think of Norman Wells.

FIFTEEN

Daniella was washing up the contents of the sink, which nobody had touched during the weekend, when Chrysteen came back from the end of the road with a newspaper. They all took it in turns to buy a daily paper, if hardly ever in the order they'd agreed in their first week at the house, even though Daniella had written it on a sheet of paper she'd taped to a kitchen cupboard, where it fluttered as a breeze from the open window met Chrysteen. Maeve favoured the *Guardian* and Duncan the *Times*, while Daniella was a buyer of the *Independent*. Chrysteen tended to buy whichever had gone unbought longest, which would be the *Independent* today, and so Daniella was taken aback to see her with a tabloid—even worse, the *Beacon*. "Was that all they had left?" she said.

"I thought you'd want to see it."

"I hope I've grown up a bit more than that," Daniella said, and then she saw the front-page headline. "That isn't—"

"It is, you know."

CHILD CHARITY MAN HAS KIDDIE PORN

In a dawn raid today on the home of Norman Wells, the man behind Care For Children, police found Internet pornography featuring children as young as six.

Police also raided the headquarters of the charity, which receives millions of pounds a year from donors. They took away computers and disks.

Wells was travelling with this year's Care For Children tour, which invites parents to bring young children to perform for audiences. Police are anxious to interview him. They confirm he has not been seen since last night's Care For Children show in Reading. They ask anyone who knows his whereabouts to contact

"I don't believe it," Daniella said.

"Me too. My dad always says he can tell a paedophile just by looking at them, and then all he needs is to find some evidence to prosecute them, but he gives money to Care For Children and went to some of their shows. He took me once when I was little and let Norman Wells take me to the zoo."

"Which you're saying means . . ."

"My dad must have been wrong for once, mustn't he? Maybe he couldn't tell because Mr Wells was too close."

"When I said I didn't believe it I mean I really don't. It's too—I mean, I just saw him."

"That's why I brought you the paper."

"What I'm getting at, Chrysteen, when I met him I could tell something was wrong."

"And now we know what."

"Not that. I honestly don't think so. He was scared."

"Scared of being found out, you mean. He must have known the police were on to him."

"No, scared that someone would see him talking to me.

He tried to put me off going to talk to him."

"Maybe he was scared he'd give himself away to you. Maybe he thought you were on to him and that's why you wanted to see him."

"Why on earth would he think that, Chrysteen?"

"I don't know, I'm sure."

"Right, because you weren't there. You have to take my word, it was nothing like you're saying."

"You ought to know, only I wonder why you'd want to defend someone like him."

"I'm not. I'm trying to work out all sorts of stuff, and you aren't helping much."

"Well, I'm sorry. I wouldn't have bought the paper if I'd known it would make you like this. I can't help it if it isn't news you wanted."

"Don't sulk," Daniella pleaded, capturing her not especially resistant hand. "I don't want all this crap that's happening to lose me my best friend."

"Then it won't."

"You can understand I'm edgy after, you know, everything."

"I would be."

They had a swift but forgiving hug, and Daniella let the *Beacon* flop on the table. "The thing about Norman Wells," she said, "he knew I wanted to talk to him about dad."

"Maybe that was it."

"Was what, Chrys?"

"Maybe your dad suspected him. Did he ever leave you alone with him?"

"No, but I can't think of a time when he would have. He didn't keep us apart that I know of. Not like Blake. I think it was my dad who rang him to say I already had a boyfriend."

"Why would he have?"

"Maybe because he wanted me to himself that night. He must have been coming to tell me how his money had gone wrong."

"Why didn't he just tell you he wanted to talk to you alone?"

"I don't know, do I? Maybe it was after he got drunk he decided he was coming and being drunk made him call Blake too. I'm not trying to figure that out just now. I'm still wondering about Norman Wells."

"Why, Danny? Why are you concerned about him?"

"Because I don't . . . I'm not sure if . . ." Daniella turned the newspaper towards her and brought her hand away blackened with newsprint from the bland ambiguous photograph of Norman Wells. "It's not as if this says much. They found some porn at his house, but how do they know it was his?"

"Whose else could it be?"

"Wasn't he married?"

"Was, but they split up after their little girl was murdered, and not only murdered either. That was supposed to be why he started Care For Children, to try and save them from anything like that, and then it got into all kinds of caring. Only now I'd wonder who really killed her."

"I thought the guy who did it hung himself in prison."

"Yes, before his case came up."

"They must have had some evidence, though, mustn't they?"

"Just like there has to be some about Norman Wells."

"Why, because it's in the paper? That doesn't follow,

Chrys, especially not when it's the *Beacon*. Half the time they put in stuff because Bill Trask wants it to be true."

"He wouldn't want that to be true about Norman Wells if they're friends, would he?"

"I don't know if they are friends. They needn't be just because they were both at my dad's funeral."

"Well, why don't you call Mr Trask and find out what he knows?"

"I will," Daniella said and flicked through the *Beacon*, filling her nose with the smell of recycled paper, until she found the number. Before she'd finished dialling she wasn't sure why she had begun: in the hope of proving the newspaper wrong about someone she had preferred to Bill Trask, or because she was dismayed not to have seen through Norman Wells? She hadn't decided when a bright brisk receptionist announced "*Beacon*."

"Can I speak to Bill Trask? It's Daniella Logan."

"Who, sorry?"

"Teddy Logan's daughter."

A pause made Daniella wonder if she was about to be asked the question again. "Please hold," the receptionist said, and replaced herself with the same old Elgar march. Several cymbal-clashes later she said "Mr Trask is in a meeting. Can anyone else help?"

"Whoever wrote your story about Norman Wells."

"That would be Eleanor Donnelly." The march returned, tramping unstoppably onward, and Daniella had begun to conclude she had been given all the information she could expect to receive when the receptionist said "Putting you through."

The next sound was a shrill throat-clearing that heralded a woman's sharp voice. "Who is it again, please?"

"Daniella Logan."

"I thought that was who she said." The reporter slowed her voice down and lowered its pitch. "I was so distressed to hear of your sad event. I hope you saw my tribute."

"I don't believe I did."

" 'Shine on, Starmaker,' that was my head."

"I wish he could have seen it."

"Perhaps he can."

The reporter's solace was a little too ready, and Daniella regretted having seemed to invite it. "Anyway," she said, "I was calling about a friend of his."

"I'm sure he must have been a friend to anyone he thought deserved it. I suppose sometimes even his judgment may have been at fault."

"Maybe."

"Since it must have been in the case of the person I gather we both have in mind."

"Norman Wells, you mean."

"I was told he was the story you rang about. Please don't think I intend any criticism of your father. Anyone who's mixed up in the sort of thing Wells is learns to hide what he is from normal people, even his own family."

"What sort of thing is that exactly?"

"I really hope I needn't say. I should think a caring father must have warned you as soon as you were old enough to understand."

"He did," Daniella assured her, remembering how she hadn't quite grasped her father's meaning when she was four. "I thought there might have been stuff you couldn't put in your sort of paper."

"I believe we have a duty to inform our readers of anything they ought to know about."

"But there would have been things you didn't want kids to see."

"We most certainly didn't print the filth Wells kept at his house. No publication that was legal would have, let alone a family paper."

"Did you see it yourself?"

"I'd no wish to do so. I know perfectly well what it must have been. May I ask—"

"When did the police let you know?"

"Know what, Miss Logan?"

"You tell me. Did they say in advance they were going to raid him?"

"I'm sure you must realise I can't give out that information, and I have to say I don't see the point of the question."

Daniella was trying to discover as much as she could in the hope that something would grow clear. "I'm figuring they told you they were going after him."

"I've a story I must write, so unless you've anything for me—"

"Yes, I've got another question. Why did you run the story before he was caught?"

"Because he hadn't been."

"I don't follow."

"Because people needed warning about him, particularly parents who might have trusted him."

"Whose idea was that?"

"I beg your pardon?"

"It had to be Mr Trask's, didn't it?"

"I'm sorry, I'm not—Please wait a moment."

If Norman Wells had been a friend, might the proprietor have published the story as a warning to him to take cover, however untypical of the *Beacon* that would have been? Daniella had realised she could hardly say that to the journalist when the phone spoke. "Daniella? Bill Trask. Why are you pumping my reporter?"

"I wanted to know why you ran the stuff about Norman Wells so soon."

"Why?"

"Yes, why."

"That's what I'm asking you."

"Because, because I saw him just a couple of days ago."

"Thank God you only saw him. Thank God you weren't a younger child."

"I didn't feel I was in any danger. If anybody was—"

"How in heaven's name can you—ah, forgive me. The news won't have broken yet, of course."

"Which news?"

"To deal with your other question first, we published because we were advised to do so."

"By the police."

"Who else?" he said, and even more bleakly "There's nothing more to be discussed about that when it has been overtaken by events."

"Why, what's happened?"

"Our friend who was nothing of the kind to anyone is dead."

"You mean he—"

"The phrase some of us might use is he was executed."

Daniella had thought he was saying Norman Wells had killed himself, but this was worse. "You sound pleased about it."

"I won't pretend I'll be mourning him."

"Don't you think killing him was a bit extreme? We

don't know if he did anything worse than look at pictures."

"Oh, but we do." The newspaper proprietor sighed at the knowledge or at her and said "It's bound to be all over the media in a matter of hours, so you may as well be told. Whoever dealt with him must have come on what he was doing just too late to stop him. Wells had killed Alan Stanley's little son."

SIXTEEN

D ad, how's the salad?" Chrysteen said.

"Even better than your mother makes."

"Can I get you another lager?" said Daniella.

"Not when I'll be driving later," he said with the briefest of frowns. "Coffee would come in handy at some stage. Don't think I'm not glad to have taken up your invitation finally, but you're a good way to come just for lunch."

"Dad, you said I should be where Danny was so we could carry on looking out for each other."

"Did I? Shows how things you say come back to haunt you, but always do what you say you will, otherwise life comes to bits." He seemed to regret lecturing them, and held up a loose fist to consult his watch. "I'll have to be on my way soon. Anything I should do while I'm here?"

Daniella had to hope one drink would keep him talkative. "You could tell us about Norman Wells."

"Why would either of you want to know about him?"

"I saw him just a couple of days before, before all that happened."

"Where was that?"

"I was in Bradford and I saw he was there, so I went in to talk to him. He was my dad's friend. That's why I'm asking you about him."

"I hope I don't seem callous. Ask away, then, and I'll tell you what I can."

"What exactly happened?"

"We heard that. It was on the news."

"It wasn't all, Chrys. How did he get hold of Alan Stanley's little boy? Hadn't he been in the paper by then?"

"Sadly not," Chrysteen's father said. "He stayed overnight with the Stanleys on the basis that it wasn't worth his while driving back to London when he'd be in Wales the next day. Apparently he and the Stanleys had quite a lot to eat and drink. The Stanleys did, at any rate."

"You mean you think he made sure they'd sleep."

"It would seem so. All we can be certain of is that your father's partner got up in the early hours and found both Wells and the elder boy, two years older than the four-year-old, had gone. The boy sometimes walked in his sleep, and his father thought he might have strayed out of the house and Wells had gone after him, so he went to look for them without wakening his wife. He found them."

"What could Mr Wells have been thinking? He must have realised everyone would know it was him."

"We've concluded he knew he was about to be exposed and meant to take the child hostage while he planned his escape, unless the pressure he was under had twisted his mind even further. Did he seem nervous when you met him?"

"Worse than. Did he know who was going to inform on him? Do you?"

"You must know I can't give that sort of information out, even to Teddy's daughter."

"Does it matter?" Chrysteen said.

"I was just wondering how much they told you," Daniella said to the police chief.

"Enough to justify a warrant. As Chrysteen says, all that matters is the information proved reliable. Is there anything else I ought to make clear?"

"What did Alan Stanley find?"

"Danny, do we need to know that?"

"I do. I want to understand."

Chrysteen's father's gaze lingered on her before it turned to Daniella. "There's a children's playground near the Stanleys' house," he said, "and not near much else."

"Yes?"

"That's where the boy was."

Daniella wondered if she was about to sound or indeed be only morbidly curious. "He'd been . . ."

"Knifed to death."

"With what?"

"What do you think with?"

"All right, Chrysteen, it's a reasonable question," her father said, but stared at Daniella before adding "The weapon hasn't yet been found."

"You mean he got rid of it somewhere before . . ."

"No, quite the contrary. It was used to kill him."

If he hadn't hesitated over the last words Daniella might not have said "How?"

"Slowly, I hope," Chrysteen said, and immediately "I don't want to hear."

"I do."

"I rather doubt that, Daniella. Be advised," Chrysteen's father said.

"Truly I do. I'll only imagine things otherwise, and that's worse than knowing."

"I wonder if you'd find that's always true," he said, and expelled a breath that made his nostrils gape. "He was tortured to death."

"In the open? Wouldn't someone have heard him?"

"We assume he was knocked out to begin with, unless he was so frightened he didn't dare to make a noise until he couldn't. Whoever took revenge on him"—Chrysteen's father paused as she pushed back her chair—"stuffed his mouth with sand from a sandpit in the playground."

"I really don't need to hear this," Chrysteen declared. "I'll be in my room when you've finished."

Daniella felt bound to continue, though her friend left her a censorious look. Once Chrysteen was well on her way upstairs, Daniella risked asking "Did they just stab him?"

"No."

The word and its tone conveyed enough that she might almost have made do with it, but he was already saying "They cut his muscles so he couldn't crawl very far, though he tried. They stripped him and took off a lot of his skin as well."

"Oh."

Perhaps she sounded insufficiently distressed, or he was determined that she should hear everything she'd driven Chrysteen away for. "Then other things beside his skin, and then it seems they heated up the knife, presumably with a lighter."

"Okay."

That was meant to silence him, but he appeared to be convinced she was inviting more. "He'd dragged himself into some woods behind the playground by then. He was going away from the road, but he wouldn't have seen, if

you get my drift. As well as the knife someone got more
sand—"

"Don't tell me any more."

"You're sure, now? There's a good deal yet."

"Mustn't he have been dead by then?" Daniella heard
herself pleading.

"Our surgeon thinks not. Wells would have been conscious for the best part of an hour."

She had to swallow before she was able to say "Who
could have done that to him?"

"You might be surprised how many people could."

"You mean they'd say so, but there's someone out there
who did. Doesn't that scare you?"

"I should think it's the likes of Wells who should be
scared."

"Don't you want to catch whoever did all that?"

"We've officers working on the case, I assure you. So
far there are no leads."

It was less than an answer to her question, but perhaps
she didn't want to hear one after all. "You said Mr Wells
was in some woods," she said. "How did Mr Stanley find
him, then?"

"I should have thought you might have guessed that,"
Simon Hastings said, and before she could silence him by
revealing she just had "Wells left quite a trail, I hear."

She squeezed her eyes shut and opened them at once,
having only seen Norman Wells as he'd looked when she'd
last met him, pink from the shower and vulnerable in his
robe. "Anything more you'd like me to tell you?" enquired
Chrysteen's father.

"No thanks," Daniella said, and took a drink of lager
that tasted unpleasantly metallic. "Nothing."

"Then have you anything to tell me?"

She had, but couldn't now. Compared with the tragedy
that had befallen Alan Stanley's family, her having recognised him at her father's grave seemed insignificant. She
could imagine the policeman's distaste if she raised the subject now, but she had another piece of information for him.
"You need to know what Mr Wells said."

"Has it any bearing on how he was found?"

"I shouldn't think—no, it couldn't have."

"Tell me anyway."

"I know my dad was hiding something. I asked Mr
Wells if he knew what, because he was a friend of dad's—"

"So were quite a few of us."

"You were, but I just thought he might say."

"You couldn't know he had secrets of his own. But
you're going to tell me he gave you information about
Teddy."

"He said dad forged something."

"Is that all?"

"It's all he had a chance to say."

"Money, do you mean? Does that strike you as remotely
like your father?"

"Maybe not money. Maybe some kind of a document
to do with it, I thought."

"Connected with his financial troubles, you're implying.
Wouldn't it have surfaced by now?"

"Not if—" As quickly as she saw the answer she suppressed it; she wasn't going to be accused yet again of making assumptions on too little evidence. "Not if he'd
destroyed it," she said.

"I'll pass on the information to the people who are investigating his affairs, all the same. May I suggest we keep

it to ourselves until it's definitely proved? You wouldn't want to undermine your father's reputation without a good reason."

"You know I wouldn't."

"Then we're in agreement," Chrysteen's father said, and went to the doorway. "It's safe for you to come back now," he called, "and I'd appreciate that coffee if it's still on offer."

Chrysteen gave Daniella a searching look that threatened to revive all she'd learned of Norman Wells' fate, except that she was preoccupied with the trip she wouldn't be able to make until tomorrow. She'd assumed her father would have had no opportunity to hide whatever she'd glimpsed in his London office, but he had. He needn't have driven straight to her—he must have detoured via Oxford. He'd kept safes both at the studios and at the house.

SEVENTEEN

At first she wasn't sure if the studio gate-keeper, whose sad-eyed face with its loose bottom lip was rendered comical by its minor nose and major ears, was joking. "Of course you can let me in," she laughed.

"I don't know you, miss."

"How long have you been here?"

He propped his elbows on the windowsill of the hut and clasped a fist in his other wizened hand. "Nearly a year."

"That's why. I haven't been here for almost that. I often used to come and see my dad until I started university."

"So you say, miss."

"I'll more than say, I'll show you," Daniella told him, and offered him her driving licence over the window of the car. "See, I'm who I said."

"All right, miss, I believe you," he said with some reluctance and no enjoyment. "I still don't think I can let you through."

"You need to tell me what the problem is. My dad left me this whole place."

"Not till you're older, Mr Stanley says."

She managed not to snatch the licence as he passed it down. "That's only two years, and it certainly should mean I can come in now."

"Mr Stanley's in charge, and he says nobody gets in without his authority."

"You know he couldn't have been thinking of me. You know he wouldn't mind."

"He might, Miss Logan."

She made her hands unclench on the wheel, relinquishing the temptation to accelerate as a character had in at least one of her father's early films, to smash the barrier that was too flimsy to be more than an indication of how civilised people behaved. "Tell me why."

"Everything needs to be left as it is till the investigators have been, Mr Stanley says. If it looks as if I've let anything be tampered with I'll be out of a job."

"I wouldn't want that. I'm just looking for something I know my dad meant me to have that I think he must have left in his office."

She was trying not to act her lie too much, but found she couldn't blink until the gateman responded. "Does Mr Stanley know?" he said.

"Only me and my dad."

"Mr Stanley would have to decide."

"Fine, so call him."

"I don't like to trouble him just now."

"I wouldn't either after what happened. So let's not bother him. Come with me if you want to see."

"I'm not supposed to leave my cabin. What if the investigators turn up while I'm gone?"

"Okay, fine. I'll call him myself. I'll tell him you wouldn't let me in even though you knew who I am and that's why I'm having to bother him."

The gateman removed his peaked cap, freeing a ragged

halo of grey hair, and used his knuckles to rub his scalp. "Supposing you got in, how long d'you think you'd be?"

"Not long at all. I know where to look."

He tugged the cap down, putting away most of his hair except for a rebel tuft above his right ear, and set the barrier hoisting itself. "I hope you'll remember I've a family to keep," he said, handing her keys from the board.

"I won't spoil anything for them," Daniella said, and drove under the barrier.

The high blank walls closed in, excluding all sense of the Oxfordshire fields and hushing the motorway less than a mile distant. The wide bare concrete road led between sound stages, long windowless brick structures that might conceal a street with no back or a series of rooms missing some walls or a reconstructed landscape from anywhere, or even nowhere, on earth. Her father's office was in the executive building, beyond the costume department and the scriptwriters' block. Last time she'd visited the studios she had passed several Roman legionaries in conversation with a group of Victorian maidservants—she'd felt as if she was an extra in a film about a film—but now the only movement was that of a sparrow bathing in the dust of the road. The bird darted over the perimeter wall as she parked beneath her father's window and left the car, awakening a curt flat echo with a slam. She waved at the gateman along the road as she twisted the key in the lock and pushed open the hot white door.

The building smelled of too much sunlight and too little air. Framed stills, mostly of Nana Babouris, kept her company up the stairs to the left of a short hall. She was halfway up when the stairs emitted a loud creak to complain of their disuse. She thought the carpet underfoot had grown less firm than she remembered as she let herself into the office.

The room seemed too large and empty, uninhabited by the filing cabinets and the empty desk. She went quickly to the safe behind the desk and twirled the tumblers. All the digits of her eighteenth birthday released the door for her to haul open. Beyond it was nothing but a capacious metal hollow. Her father must have cleared out the safe when he knew he was to be investigated, she thought. She was leaning against the door to close it when one of the trio of phones on the desk rang.

She swivelled the tumblers to hide the combination, then she held a fist over the receiver before making an impatient grab. "Hello?" she demanded, and sucked in a dry breath.

"It's the gate, Miss Logan."

For a moment she felt in charge of everything, even her life. "I'm through here," she said.

"That's lucky, because I've just had Mr Stanley on."

"And?"

"He says the investigators are on their way."

"You don't need to worry. I haven't touched anything. I'm coming out now."

"I'll be lifting the barrier."

She surely didn't need to be quite as fast as he seemed to be implying. As she stepped onto the road she remembered the first time she had done so, clinging to her father's hand to be led across the road into a magic land brighter than midsummer, where a glittering path wound between cottages that sparkled like crystals and women shimmered on the arms of knights in silver armour. Her father had been producing a musical of *The Sleeping Beauty*, but she'd felt as if he had opened a door to magic for her—a door to a place (she had thought at the première of the film, where cameras had gone nova at the sight of her being led on her father's arm along the red carpet) in which a girl as old as she was now needed only to lie at peace to be crucial. The vividness of the memory stayed with her as far as the gates.

The gateman was just hoisting the barrier. "Did you find what you wanted?" he said.

"It must be at my dad's house."

"Well." That could have concealed any number of meanings if he hadn't added "Good luck."

"Hope to see you again soon," she said, handing him the keys, and drove off.

The long wall of Oxford Films gave way to trees that patched the narrow winding road with shadow. In a few minutes she was on the motorway, which she left for Chiltern Road at the next exit. Several prolonged black limousines were making their slow way down the central avenue of the churchyard, and she promised herself she would visit her father's grave once she'd retrieved whatever he had left at the house.

She wasn't prepared for how much more deserted a FOR SALE sign made the house appear. The rhododendrons looked dusty, the front rooms too bright—bright as sets onto which nobody was about to step to greet her from a window. Her key to the front door turned less than halfway and balked with a metallic squeak. She was wondering furiously if the investigators could have changed the lock when it gave. Someone, perhaps the estate agent, must have pressed the catch partly down. She had one foot in the hall when the phone rang.

Though her father's study was at the rear of the house, the sound was closer. Who had left the phone away from its base? The slam she gave the door sent her across the hot breathless hall to the front lounge. A twist of the door-knob, which must feel clammy because her hand was, admitted her to the room.

The receiver was perched on the back of the armchair nearest the hall. The plastic was so warm with sunlight that she could have imagined someone had just placed it on the chair. She switched it to receive and held it not quite against her cheek. "Who's there?"

The line immediately went dead. "Go on then, be rude," she told it, and silenced it as she made for the hall.

Apart from the phone, the study appeared not to have been touched. Perhaps the Midas Books compliments slip that served as a bookmark in *The Bible Decoded* had begun to droop. The drawn curtains were keeping sunlight off the books, but the air tasted dry. She fitted the receiver to its base on the desk and hurried to the poster for *David and Goliath* behind the office chair. Her brain started to perform the song that accompanied the final credits—"I'll make a pebble be a stone, I'll turn that stone into a rock, I'll raise that rock to be a tower, To look down on the ones who mock me"—as she swung the glazed poster up on its hinged corner and set about spinning the tumblers on the door she'd revealed.

The key was the date of her twenty-first birthday. When she'd learned the combination it had seemed to promise her a secret in her future. She rounded it off with the year after next and heaved the door open with both hands, and released a sigh that sounded caged by metal. The solitary item in the safe was a passport—her own, which her father had offered to keep for her once he'd persuaded her not to go abroad last summer. She leaned in to convince herself there was nothing else. She was squinting at the unrewarding dimness when she heard a stealthy noise beside her or behind her. The heavy door swung towards her, trapping her neck against the edge of the safe.

More darkness than the safe contained rushed into her skull. A stench of metal filled her nostrils and spread into her gaping mouth. She grabbed the edge of the door and struggled to free herself, her feet shoving at the rug behind the desk only to rob her of balance. The door put on weight, and her right hand lost its grip on the edge. Her fingers skidded across the metal, and her elbow struck an arm—the arm of whoever had closed the safe on her.

She clawed at the fist at the end of the arm. It flinched away, but the door dug harder into the side of her neck. Her head ballooned with darkness, and she felt her limbs slacken as though they were melting. Her breath rasped helplessly at her throat; she couldn't breathe or swallow. One thought had lodged, a jagged ponderous lump, in her brain: what was happening to her was pointless, since there was nothing but her passport in the safe. Her mouth was as incapable of protest as it was of sucking in the stale metallic air. The rug slithered away from beneath her toes, and she slumped forward. She was flailing her arms and kicking just as feebly as she watched the colour of the blood that massed behind her eyes when the weight of the door lessened, by no means enough. Somewhere in the distance, even further away than her body, she thought she heard footsteps. They hesitated before turning into the slam of the study door.

It required all her strength and at least a dozen painful breaths for her to haul the ponderous door away from her neck. Some time later she planted her hands against the bottom of the safe and levered the door wide enough to let her stagger backwards. She clutched at the revolving chair for support as she tottered around to face the room, and heard a key in the front door, then voices in the hall. The chair spun with her, and she sprawled across one corner of the desk, which didn't prevent her from sliding to the floor. The room tumbled away into blackness, though her mind made a lurch to keep hold of it. She wasn't only trying to stay conscious. She was desperate to hold onto the sight she had just seen.

EIGHTEEN

She would be fine, Daniella told herself. She was better than any number of people who needed her hospital bed. Her neck was only bruised, and she had been able to lie on her back without too much discomfort—she had even slept for a total of perhaps almost an hour, despite the heat that had felt like a pile of blankets, and the surgical collar that had added clamminess and awkwardness to the aches in her neck, and the disinfectant smell that had kept growing too reminiscent of the smell of the safe, and the incessant hushed activity that had made her stiff and breathless whenever it had sounded like footsteps creeping near her bed. She'd survived the night, and now it was late morning, and there was no reason for her to be troubled by the busy noises outside the screen she'd been lent while she changed back into her clothes. When she'd finished easing the collar of her T-shirt over the tender skin on both sides of her neck and replaced her fat ruff she tucked the T-shirt into her jeans and wheeled the screen open. At the far end of the ward, beyond the ranks of animated busts propped up by pillows, were Simon Hastings and her mother.

She faltered at the sight of Daniella's neck before giving her a prolonged though cautious hug, at the end of which Daniella said "I thought it'd just be the local police."

"I am the local police," said Chrysteen's father.

"Not someone so high up, I mean."

"Nobody else will do when the child of an old friend gets into bother on my patch."

"Thanks," Daniella couldn't very well not say, and turned to her mother. "You shouldn't have come all that way."

"I wish I'd been here sooner. I was spending the night with someone and I came as soon I picked up the message. I'm glad I'm still in your purse to be contacted."

"I wouldn't have anyone else."

"Are you sure you're fit to leave?"

"The doctor says so. He says they wouldn't have kept me in overnight if I hadn't been falling all over the place."

"He says that, does he? I'd like a word with him."

"He'll have gone home. He's been up two nights. Don't worry, it just hurts to turn my head."

"You're not going to drive back to York in that state."

"It only hurts, it doesn't mean I can't turn it. Can we go to my dad's house now?" Daniella said to Chrysteen's father.

"We should, I think, Isobel. It's the quickest way to clarify the situation."

"Then I'll drive her," Daniella's mother said.

Once she had manoeuvred out of the labyrinth of cars parked even where they weren't supposed to be outside the hospital, she drove at significantly less than the policeman's speed around the edge of Oxford and through the winding lanes to Chiltern Road. Daniella was aware mostly of her neck, a fragile lagged support for the burden of her head, and of the sunlight that swiped her face whenever a tree passed. She tried to relax as the car coasted onto the gravel in front of the house.

She climbed gingerly out of the car and then walked as fast to the front door as she could without jarring her neck. Simon Hastings was on the doorstep, but she made certain she was first into the hall, to prove she wasn't nervous. She marched to the study and threw the door open.

The rug was flat on the floor behind the desk, and the chair stood on the rug. "Who put those back?" she protested.

"The chap who called the ambulance said he did," Simon Hastings told her.

"The estate agent, you mean. What else did he say?"

"That they found you on the floor there, he and a young couple did. They must be planning quite a family if they were looking at this house," he said to Daniella's mother, and to Daniella "The chair had fallen over and the rug was kicked up. They thought you must have lost your balance and hit your head on the desk."

"Then they couldn't have been seeing much."

"I assume it didn't take them long to notice the marks on your neck. Apparently the young woman thought you'd been strangled and was quite upset. I rather fear you've lost that sale."

"I'd been choked, so she was right." When they only gazed at her, Daniella closed and locked the safe so that she could sit in the chair. "I had," she said.

"That's it," her mother said, "you sit down if you're not feeling too well."

"My brain's fine. I remember exactly what happened."

"Tell us by all means," Chrysteen's father said.

"I was looking in the safe and someone shut the door on me."

"Oh, Daniella," her mother cried and shook her head.

"The estate agent did wonder if there'd been a robbery, since there was almost nothing in the safe. What were you expecting to find?"

"What we were talking about when you came to see Chrys."

"I thought you were under the impression it had been destroyed."

"I couldn't know, could I? I had to check."

"Is anybody going to let me into their confidence?" her mother said.

"Daniella had the idea that Teddy might have faked something because of his financial problems."

"Whatever gave you that notion?"

Daniella didn't want to mention Norman Wells when that would involve so much more explanation. "We don't know what he might have done if he was desperate, do we? You said yourself you thought he was hiding something, and you were right."

"So presumably now you're satisfied it was destroyed," Chrysteen's father said. "Nobody would want to steal it, would they?"

"Not even the man who stuck my head in the safe?"

"You're saying someone pushed you into the safe."

"Not pushed me in, no. I was leaning in and he shut it on me. I didn't see him, but I felt him all right, as maybe you've noticed."

"I know you've been through a lot, Daniella." Chrysteen's father cocked his head to turn his concerned gaze a little askance and said "What are you saying someone wanted to do to you?"

"What does it look like?"

"I have to tell you the estate agent and his party didn't see or hear anyone."

"Neither did I till he caught me, but he was already here. He must have run in the front room when he heard my car and taken the phone with him, because that's where it was."

"Why would anyone have done that, Daniella?" her mother not so much asked as pleaded.

"Maybe he was waiting for a call. Someone called and when I answered they rang off. Maybe they were parked up the road and meant to be keeping watch."

"You're saying there was more than one person now."

"I only said maybe. There had to be a car, didn't there, and I didn't see one."

"If you can't see something," her mother said, stretching out her hands as if to demonstrate the emptiness between them, "mightn't that mean it isn't there?"

"Like whoever tried to, to hurt me wasn't there, you mean. Except I felt his hand and he felt me scratch it. So," Daniella told Chrysteen's father, "you just need to find someone with a scratched hand."

She meant that as some kind of a joke, and followed it with a sample of a laugh, but her audience gazed mutely at her. After a pause Chrysteen's father said "Can you say why the rug was disturbed?"

"Because my feet slipped while I was being choked. Go ahead, tell me it sounds like I slipped on the rug and stuck my head in the safe and it was only my weight that was holding it shut."

"Couldn't that have been it," her mother said eagerly, "and you imagined someone was there while you were passing out?"

Daniella's skull had begun to throb worse than her neck. "No," she said.

Her mother's eyes grew close to tearful. "Why not?"

"Because something was stolen. A book."

"Which book?"

"It was there," Daniella said, pointing at the gap she'd glimpsed as she'd fallen away from the safe. "*The Bible Decoded*, it was called."

"What makes you so sure?" Chrysteen's father said. "Do you know the book?"

"No, but I noticed it because it was the only one with a bookmark in."

"Why do you think anyone would want to steal it?"

"Yes, Daniella, why, for heaven's sake?"

"How am I supposed to know? I just know it's gone. Maybe they thought it was special because it was marked. Maybe they thought it was hollow inside like the one in that old film of dad's, *Money Isn't Much*. Maybe it was."

Her mother attempted a smile that didn't quite hold up. "How many maybes is that?"

"Being stolen isn't one of them."

Her mother turned away from her as Chrysteen's father stooped to the bookshelf. He lifted out the books on either side of the gap and peered into the space. "Well now," he said, "here's a book."

The possibility that *The Bible Decoded* might simply have been pushed out of view made Daniella's brow tighten with rage. She watched as Chrysteen's father laid the books on top of the bookcase and reached into the gap, and then she more or less laughed. "Why, it's one of my old school exercise books," she said.

"Daniella Logan, English Language," he read. "It must

have fallen down behind at some point. Would anyone like it?"

"I've got plenty of your schoolwork. You have that if it'll remind you of happier times."

Daniella was painfully aware of the appeal her mother was making. She leafed through several pages of her early teenage writing, which looked as childish as the scrutiny she was continuing to undergo caused her to feel, and then she let the book fall shut and raised her head. "Anything else you need to know?"

"Only that you're all right."

"We'll do whatever's necessary to set your mind at rest," Chrysteen's father said.

Daniella wasn't sure if he was addressing her or her mother. She shoved the book into her handbag and stood up steadily enough. "I'll head back now while there isn't too much traffic."

"Are you really fit to drive?" her mother said as if she didn't dare to seem too concerned, and once Daniella had done her best to reassure her "Will you ring me when you get there? Leave a message if I'm not back."

Daniella promised, and managed not to wince or grimace as she ducked into her car. She rested her head against the seat and drove slowly onto the road, from where she saw her mother and Chrysteen's father starting to talk. She knew they were discussing her. She felt their concern dragging at her, but it couldn't hinder her. Being disbelieved as well as assaulted only aggravated her determination to read the book that had got her attacked.

NINETEEN

I s it a book?"

Though the woman at the enquiry desk might have been years older than Daniella, she sported pigtails and wore a skimpy spotted dress. "That's why I came to a bookshop," Daniella said, mildly enough.

"We don't just sell books. We're selling less and less." Having paused, apparently to give Daniella time to be impressed, the assistant said "It'll be in Religion if it's anywhere."

Daniella went where the assistant's glittery fingernail indicated, past pens and computer games and films on videocassette, quite a few of them produced by her father, and greetings cards. A bookcase at the rear of the shop seemed to be the place, displaying several copies of just the Bible as well as *The Good News Bible*, which she took to be the Bible minus the unpleasant or contradictory bits, and the Bible in Welsh and in Yorkshire dialect. There were also books about it, whose spines she had to tilt her head to read, chafing her neck on her fat collar. Since none of the books was the one she was seeking, she approached a middle-aged man who was rearranging a display of books as fat as the Bible. "Have you got *The Bible Decoded*?"

"Have we—ah, you think there's a book called that."

"There is."

"I've never heard of it."

"Would you have?"

"I've been in books for thirty years. If it's religious I'd know," he said, and rubbed the bald patch at the summit of his greying hair as though to increase his monkishness. "I should try Games and Puzzles."

Despite his mournful tone, that was presumably advice, and so Daniella searched until she found that section. Among the few books for which jigsaws and board games left room were a couple about cryptography, nothing like the title she was after. "It isn't here," she complained to the pink-domed man.

"Then it sounds like fiction to me."

Unsure how to take that, she returned to the enquiry desk. "If you haven't got it, can you order it?"

"Who's it by, do you know?"

"I don't, but it's published by Midas Books."

"Are you certain? It doesn't sound like anything they'd do."

"It's them all right."

"If you say so," the assistant said, and shrugged as well, uncovering one bony freckled shoulder, before typing the title on a computer keyboard. "Bible bible bible," she read aloud, though Daniella heard her babbling. "No, sorry. Not here."

"Here as in your shop?"

"Here as anywhere. Not published, or not in print, anyway."

"That can't be right," Daniella objected, then realised what the compliments slip she'd seen in the stolen copy might have implied. "Hang on. They must be just going to publish it."

"We'll see," the assistant said, and rummaged through a heap of glossy catalogues until she found one for the next six months of Midas Books, its cover embossed with the brand names of half a dozen authors. She barely glanced at the index before saying "Not here either. Like I said, it's not their kind of thing at all. They only publish best-sellers."

"Maybe they've changed the title," Daniella said, sounding desperate even to herself, and leaned over the counter to peer at the index while her neck twinged. The nearest words to Bible were Bad and Bare and Bed and Biggest, and there was no title remotely likely to relate to it. She found the phone number of Midas Books in the catalogue and scribbled it on her wrist with a splintered splinted ball-point from the desk. "I'll call them," she declared.

"Good luck," the assistant said, possibly ironically.

Daniella tramped out of the shop and made for home. She extracted her keys from her bag as she stepped over and around the weeds on the front path. She read the number on her wrist as she closed the door behind her. She was lifting the receiver when she heard footsteps in the kitchen. Anyone who wanted her would have to wait, she vowed, not expecting it to be Mark.

He was trying not to look too earnest, but his deep brown eyes were wide, and the corners of his mouth seemed not to know which way to turn. "Hi," he said.

"Hi."

"Chrys told me what happened when I rang, so I came over to see how you were. I hope you don't mind. She let me in and then she had a lecture."

"I don't mind at all. Just let me phone someone and we'll talk." She lifted the receiver again but couldn't wait to ask "Any luck with putting what I told you in your magazine?"

"It looks as if it'll have to wait for my big piece about your father."

That was frustrating, but he looked so apologetic that she couldn't make her feelings known. "You did your best," she said.

He was lingering in the hall, apparently awaiting some direction from her, when a by no means especially welcoming female voice said "Midas Books."

"Can I speak to Victor Shakespeare?"

"You would be . . ."

"Teddy Logan's daughter."

The voice didn't quite succeed in pretending to be unimpressed. "Please hold."

Mark had been struggling to keep his face blank since her first sentence to the phone. "I know," she said. "What a name for a publisher."

He swung one hand towards the kitchen and turned that way. "Shall I . . ."

"You could make us some coffee or even some tea for a change if you like."

He was in the kitchen before she'd finished speaking, and it was a different, not to say friendlier, female voice in her ear that said "Pardon?"

"Sorry, I was just . . . Is Victor Shakespeare there?"

"He's away from his desk. This is his assistant. Can I help?"

"Can you tell me about a book called *The Bible Decoded*?"

"I'll do my best. What would you like to know?"

"When you're going to publish it."

"I don't believe we are."

Just because the stolen copy had contained a Midas Books compliments slip, Daniella thought in dismay, that needn't mean the slip had come with the book. "Then how can I find out who is?"

"I understand that's going to be nobody."

"That can't be right," Daniella heard herself protesting like a child. "I've seen the book."

"Oh, so have I. We had copies all over the place for a few days. It made no sense from what I heard, but it was here."

"I don't get it."

"You wouldn't want to," Shakespeare's assistant said and, before Daniella could demand an explanation, gave her one. "Victor somehow got it into his head it was something we might want to publish, so he had the States send us all the copies there were to be had. That was when he was thinking of starting a non-fiction imprint."

"But he isn't."

"I wouldn't be surprised if that book was enough to put him off the idea. I've never seen him take against a book so much."

"I'd be interested to read it, then."

"I don't know how you would. It was out of print once we got hold of it, and Victor sent all our copies for recycling."

Except for one, Daniella thought, and said "How would I find the author?"

"I can tell you who he was, still is as far as I know, or do you mean how would you contact him?"

"Both of those."

"You can write care of us. On second thoughts, as long

as you're who you are I don't see why I can't give you his address. Excuse me a moment."

She was gone so much longer that Daniella began to fear she couldn't locate the information. Mark's sounds in the kitchen had ceased. She started, jerking her neck, when Victor Shakespeare's assistant said "Here he is. Timothy Turner. Lives in Venice."

Daniella wasn't too surprised to be given a Californian address, which she wrote on the pad that was keeping company with a stub of pencil on the seat of Duncan's bicycle. She tore off the page and slipped it into her bag as she went to Mark. "Looks like I'm on the way to finding something out at last," she said.

He handed her a mug of milky tea out of which dangled a string and turned to pick up a mug for himself. "What's that?"

"About a book that was stolen from my dad's house. Someone wanted it so much they did this to me."

"Bastards." He was on his way to facing her as he said "What's important about it, do you think?"

"I hope I'm going to know. I told my mum and Chrys' dad I thought it might be hollow, but I didn't really. I couldn't stand arguing with them any more when I don't think they're even sure I was attacked."

"Then they should be. So you haven't any idea what the book's about," Mark said, and the phone rang.

She made a wry face at him before hurrying to lift the receiver. "Hello?"

"Hello, Daniella. Victor Shakespeare. How are you these days?"

"I've been worse."

"I'm glad to hear you're better." He seemed to be trying

to render his flat clipped Northern voice light and high.
"People have been looking after you," he said or asked.

"I've got my friends."

"We all need those if we want to get anywhere in this
life," he said, and emitted an unexpectedly feminine prim
cough. "I was sorry not to be at Teddy's funeral."

"Your message was."

"At least I paid my respects, but he deserved more. I
believe you're still affected by your loss."

"I would be, wouldn't I?"

"We all are. If you're looking for consolation you might
try watching some of his uplift films."

"I don't know if I am looking for that just now."

"I was thinking of the book I hear you rang up about.
Had you got it into your head it might help you cope somehow?"

"You sent my dad a copy," Daniella said for him to
take how he liked.

"Did we? It must have been when he was making *The
Flood*. I couldn't have looked into the book when we sent
him one. It's complete shite from one end to the other, and
we don't do shite at Midas. Written by some Californian
that must have taken too many drugs and thought he could
see things nobody else could see, and found someone as
crazy as him to print it. They'll print anything over there,
but I can promise you it's not the sort of thing Teddy would
like to think you'd turn to because he's gone."

"Why did you have it, then?"

"Even Britain's best-selling publisher can miscalculate
sometimes. Maybe I was forgetting the secret of our success."

"Which is?"

"Books are goods like any other, and if you want to compete in the market you need trademarks. That's what every one of our authors' names is. I bet if I mentioned any of them you'd see in your mind how they're lettered on our covers. Once you've got that recognition into the mind of the public it sticks, and we guarantee they know what they're buying every time."

Daniella remembered the Midas Books catalogue—remembered the look of each author's name on the cover—but wasn't about to admit it. "You didn't think they would with Timothy Turner."

"They'd know they were buying shite."

"I was thinking of writing to him."

"What about? Ask me if you've got a question. I'm here to help."

"I thought he might have a spare copy."

"You don't give up, do you? You're Teddy's girl and no mistake. Fair enough, you win. If you write to him care of us I'll see it gets where it should."

"I will if I need to. Thanks," Daniella said and thumbed the receiver rest to cut him off, only to call Directory Enquiries for Timothy Turner's number. As soon as a recorded voice put the digits together for her she dialled, rousing only a machine that told her, so slowly and sonorously she wondered if the tape was running down, to leave a message. She asked the author to call her urgently about his book and left her number.

Her neck felt constricted, not least with frustration. She pulled off the hospital collar and trudged into the kitchen, trying to massage her shoulders. "Any use?" Mark said.

"I can't reach."

"Want me to?"

"I'll let you."

He stood up so eagerly that a corner of his wallet poked out of a pocket of his thin snug trousers. As she sat on a chair he moved behind her and rested his fingertips on her shoulders. His fingertips found her collarbone and his thumbs set about rubbing her shoulder blades. He was massaging harder than Chrysteen did. Daniella took an open-mouthed breath only to discover she didn't want to protest after all. Warmth was spreading from her shoulders to her neck, towards which his thumbs were working. She held her breath for when they met, and gasped as they did. "Shall I stop?" he murmured in her ear.

"I'll tell you when."

She was feeling no pain, only heat that focused itself in her neck. Heat climbed her spine, carrying her aches with it, and seemed to float them out of her tingling scalp. "How's that so far?" Mark said.

"Too good to stop."

His hands drew apart, massaging, and converged again. One of them kneaded the nape of her neck while the other began to rub her back. Her T-shirt pulled out of her shorts at once. He hesitated just long enough for it to be noticeable, and then he stroked her exposed back, pushing the T-shirt higher. It felt inevitable, the end of a wait she hadn't let herself be aware of. When his hands lingered over discovering how flat her stomach was, she pressed her shoulders against him. When his hands closed gently over her bare breasts under the T-shirt, she shifted until her mouth reached his. It was her tongue that opened the proceedings, and she felt as if she was finally gaining a freedom too much of her life had been designed to deny her. She rose slowly to her feet so as not to dislodge his hands. "Not down here," she freed her mouth to murmur, and was covering his hands with hers so as to lead him to her room when a key was thrust into the front door, which thumped open. "Hello?" Duncan called. "Anyone home?"

Daniella's neck renewed its stiffness. She disengaged herself from Mark and tucked her T-shirt in. "Just us," she responded. "Me and Mark."

"Have you seen Maeve since this morning?"

"I didn't even see her then. Where did you lose her?"

"We were drinking by the river and talking about the future. Maybe I oughtn't to have said I wanted her to be in it. She said I was trying to box her in, and we had a row and she trotted off."

He was staying out of sight, so that she wondered how discreet he imagined he needed to be. "Come here if you want to talk about it," she called, and glanced at Mark. "You're hanging out," she told him.

It was only his wallet that had emerged further, but he started so vigorously that it sprang out of his pocket and sprawled on the floor, loosing several plastic cards. She was stooping to retrieve them when he tried to catch her hand. "Daniella—"

For a second she couldn't see the problem, and then she read the name on his Visa card—all the name. She let the card lie with its cronies and stepped back. "So that's who you are," she said.

"It's not my professional name."

"What a professional. No wonder you hid when I was phoning," she said, and raised her voice. "Aren't you coming, Duncan?"

Mark retrieved the wallet and shoved the cards into it. "Daniella, if you'll give me just a few minutes—"

"I nearly gave you a lot more than that, didn't I? Piss off before I call the police, Mark Alexander Shakespeare."

His face was growing earnest, but she was familiar with that trick. As he failed to move, Duncan tramped into the room. "Hey, she asked you to get going," Duncan said.

"Don't interfere, what's your name, Duncan. Daniella, I was trying—"

"You don't want to fuck with anyone from Glasgow that's had the day I've had, my wee man. Do as she says and make it hasty. It's her house."

"Duncan will see you out," she said, lowering herself onto a chair. "I'd make sure you went except I feel sick."

Mark loitered, apparently unsure what to do with his hands or his face, until Duncan stepped in front of him and brought his head close, at which point Mark retreated as far as the doorway. "I'll be in touch," he said.

"No you won't," Daniella told him, "because if I hear you I'll hang up, and if someone else picks up they won't get me, and if you try to come anywhere near me again I really will call the police."

"Sounds like you aren't welcome," Duncan said, walking at Mark until he had to step back. Daniella heard them tramp to the front door. It opened and stayed like that, and she imagined Duncan playing doorman as he watched Mark retreat. There was a pause that struck her as far too lingering besides entirely pointless before she heard a car door slam and the snarl of the departing vehicle. "Has he gone?" she called.

"Like a rabbit," Duncan assured her.

"That's all I want to know," she said and closed her eyes, trying to relax. Even the massage felt false in retrospect. Mark's father must have sent him with his magazines to find out how much she'd seen at the grave. At least she hadn't told Mark the very little she had learned from Norman Wells, she thought—and then her eyes widened and her head rose, rediscovering aches in her neck. She didn't care about the pain. She'd realised what Norman Wells might have intended her to understand.

TWENTY

B y the time she reached the edge of Oxford it was nearly dark. Two hours out of York the motorway traffic had slowed as though it had joined a funeral near Leicester, only halfway to her destination. When at last she came abreast of the problem she found it was a tangle of three smashed cars, or rather how every passing driver braked for a look. Later there had been several miles of crawling in first gear past Rugby, and again outside Northampton, but the reasons for those delays were nowhere to be seen, just a couple of gratuitous mysteries to add to her life. The accident had put her in mind of her father, and both the possibility of more of them and their absence aggravated the tension in her neck. At least once she left the motorway she was met by fewer glaring headlamps as she followed miles of winding road on which she was unable to catch up with the afterglow on the horizon while twilight seeped out of the fields. She had to join a second motorway for the stretch between two adjacent exits, and the headlamps on it seemed to extinguish the last of the evening. When she drove onto Chiltern Road the trees shut out the lights and the murmur of Oxford, the better to concentrate on gathering the dusk.

The pale prow of the church sailed glimmering out of the dimness beyond the trees. She parked on the yielding verge not quite opposite the main gates and straightened up from the car, massaging her neck. Dimness carpeted the empty road and merged leaves overhead with the blackened sky and appeared to shrivel the bars of the churchyard gate as if they were charring. She fetched her flashlight from the car boot, which she shut as quietly as possible, whether so that the sound wouldn't emphasise the loneliness or for fear it might be heard. There was nobody, she told herself angrily as she stalked to the entrance beside the locked gates.

The gravel of the drive whispered shrilly underfoot, and then a path did. The church loomed beside her, its thin windows glinting like slivers of coal. Headstones, negative images of archways, reared around her where the darkness wasn't crossed out by stones that resembled broad strokes of whitewash. In the trees behind the church bits of the night were audibly restless, and she had to remind herself they were crows. The whitish path fell silent as she stepped onto the turf. She switched on the flashlight and shone it ahead.

She'd known it to be stronger. The beam only hinted at her father's carved name and dates until she ventured forward. Darkness etched the inscription deeper as a crew-cut shadow of grass sprouted at the base of the stone, but she couldn't distinguish individual squares of turf. She lowered herself to her knees beside the shallow mound and trained the beam on it. "Sorry, dad," she murmured. "I won't disturb you, I just have to know." With that she ran her fingertips over the mound until she located the remnant of an edge of turf.

It lifted with a soft tearing sound and a faint patter of earth. A smell of exposed soil turned her mouth dry. She held her breath as she laid the turf aside, its glistening underside upturned, and poked her fingernails into the earth. Of course she should have brought a tool. She couldn't stand the gritting of earth under her nails, and so she used the rim of the flashlight as a scoop. The beam sprawled across the turf and drew into itself and spilled wide again as though it was signalling, and she was still holding her breath when she heard a response—voices whispering in the dark.

She sucked in a breath that tasted of earth. Her head jerked up, and aches met across her throat, so that for a moment she felt that the collar was choking her. Everywhere she looked were figures, all of them as still as the stone she had assumed they were composed of. Then one stirred behind a drunken cross, and another peered around an angel. Three faces sprang alight, and the luminous balloons of their heads came bobbing towards her.

She stopped being scared before they advanced very far. She was only furious that her startled heart was taking so long to slow down. They were girls in their mid-teens. Two of them were almost as thin as their bones, but their friend was large enough to make up for them both. All wore black, and the pictorial T-shirt under the large girl's singlet was her skin. She and one of her companions had cropped hair, hers white, the thin girl's green as moss, while the third girl's scalp was tattered with black tufts. The lowest of several rings in her face glinted from her bottom lip as she announced "She's digging someone up."

The flashlights they had been holding under their chins converged on Daniella. "You can't do that," the large girl told her.

"This is our place," said the girl with green hair.

"It is at night," their pierced friend said.

"There's lots of old sods here like everywhere else," said the green-haired girl, "but these can't tell us what to do."

"Then you won't want to tell me."

"That's different. You're in our place and we make the rules."

"And they say no digging people up."

"I won't be digging anybody up. Maybe you could take your lights out of my face."

"More like we couldn't. We want to see who thought they were all by themself."

The girls were surrounding Daniella with a smell of alcohol. Beyond the beams that poked at her eyes she could see their heavy boots and the word BUTT carved in the stubble on top of the large girl's lowered head. "I'm his daughter," Daniella said, pointing her own light at the headstone.

"Never heard of him," the pierced girl said.

"You don't need to have. He was my dad, that's all that matters."

"We're someone's daughter too."

Perhaps the green-haired girl sounded too close to being proud of it to suit her large friend, who said "Wish we weren't."

"Doesn't mean you can go digging him up."

"I keep telling you I'm not going to. I just need to find something that's here."

"What's it doing there?"

"Dropped in."

"Is it money?" the large girl said, and with more of the first enthusiasm any of the trio had shown "We'll help you look."

"Help me see, then. Put the light here."

The three beams swung to the uncovered patch, where the soil blazed black. Daniella sank to her knees again and gouged at the earth with the rim of the flashlight. The girls leaned so close their beery smell grew constant. The only sounds were the scraping of metal and the spattering of dirt across the turf. An object gleamed in the hollow that was now an inch deep: a black pebble that grew legs and antennae before scuttling away from the light. An inch deeper there was nothing but soil, and then another inch or more. The girls had started to mutter; one beam, losing interest, had begun to play with Daniella's face. As she dug up a lump of earth and hurled it across the turf so hard it shattered against a toecap, she heard another sound—a clink of metal on metal. "What's that?" the large girl demanded.

"She got mud on my boot," the pierced girl complained, stamping on the edge of the grave.

"Not you. What went ding?"

Daniella used the flashlight to sweep soil away from the item she'd unearthed. All the beams were intent on it, revealing glints of metal inches apart. "I'll get it for you," the mossy-haired girl said.

"Don't bother," Daniella told her, and cleared away more soil. Both glints came from a single surface. The girls were reaching out their hands, eager to push hers aside. She slid her fingertips under the metal and winced. An edge had nicked the end of her longest finger; soil added to the sting. Nevertheless her fingers were able to lever up the object hidden in the earth.

The point rose first, and then almost a foot of blade. Despite its length, it wasn't much of a knife. The point looked perilously thin, and the edges weren't quite straight.

The handle, which she thought was oak, had been planed smooth, but the blade was slightly askew in it. The metal shone gold in the flashlight beams as she held the knife while she scooped most of the scattered earth back into place and spread the square of turf over it, patting that down before stumbling to her feet. The girls had been commenting throughout: "That's a knife," and no more usefully "That's so weird" and "That does my head in." Now the large girl stepped forward. "Let's have a look," she said.

Daniella trailed the flash of the blade across the girl's not entirely focused eyes. "There, you've seen it. It's real."

The others blocked Daniella's way as the large girl held out a hand worthy of a boxer. "A proper look."

"I'm keeping hold of it. It belongs to me."

"Who says?" demanded the pierced girl. "You found it in our place."

"And I'm taking it out."

The large girl raised her flashlight like a club. "Who says we'll let you?"

The aches in Daniella's neck seized the back of her head. She'd let someone hurt her with her father's safe, and now she'd had more than enough: she wasn't letting three young girls overpower her while she had a knife in her hand. "This does," she said, and waved it.

The girls laughed, and the largest spat past the grave. "Thinks that makes her big," she said with a renewal of enthusiasm. "Come on then, let's see you—"

"I don't know what it makes me, but I know I'm pissed off. Just let me through."

The girls glanced at one another but didn't move otherwise, and Daniella had had double enough. As she jabbed at the large girl's face with the knife she didn't know if she was more afraid of harming her or that the point would snap off. The girl retreated, nearly tripping over the stone rim of the next grave. "The bitch tried to cut me," she shouted as though she was summoning help.

"I will if anyone gets in my way. Just stay back," Daniella said, slashing at the air as she stalked forward. The green-haired girl dodged out of reach, but her pierced friend seemed unimpressed if not actively interested in how the pain would feel. Daniella was still expecting her to move when a swing of the knife traced a red line across her throat. "Shit," the girl said, not without admiration, and backed off.

Though Daniella's mouth had turned dry, she couldn't show her dismay. She headed for the gates without looking behind her. She heard the girls' voices: "Look, she cut me" and "Shit" and "Shit." Pebbles rattled on a grave, and then handfuls were flung after her. Most of them clattered against the church, but a few stung her shoulders, and one fragment added a bruise to her neck. She marched along the drive, her head pounding with her determination not to run. Before she reached the exit beside the gates the hail of missiles had ceased. As she bent painfully to climb into her car she saw the girls following their flashlight beams past the rear of the church.

She couldn't drive back to York now. She was glad it was the second of her nights off from the restaurant. The journey and her encounter with the girls had both caught up with her, and her skull was a thunderhead of tension above her throbbing neck. She dropped the knife into her bag and twisted the ignition key. She kept having to brake as hedges flared ahead in too much pointless detail on the way to her father's house. She swung the car onto the gravel and trudged to the front door and let herself in.

The emptiness felt like her inability to think. As she switched on the light in the study, having illuminated the hall, she had the impression that some of the night remained stuck to her eyes. Her neck gave a reminiscent twinge at the sight of the locked safe. She grabbed the phone and typed her York number, and was answered faster than anyone could have walked out of the nearest room. "Hello? Hello?"

"Hi, Chrys. It's me."

"Where are you?"

"I'll be at my dad's tonight. It's too late to drive back."

"Why did you go home? Duncan said you didn't say."

"I'd rather show you than tell you. Maybe by then I'll have figured out what it means. Did Maeve come back?"

"They're upstairs making it up to each other. When will you be back?"

"Tomorrow afternoon, I should be. I haven't got a lecture till then."

She had to think what to do with the knife. She might have locked it in the safe, but preferred to keep it nearer, not least because the notion of opening the safe made her palms sweat. She switched off the light in the study, and the light in the hall once she was upstairs, but couldn't bring herself to do without the one on the landing. The desertion of the house made her room with its denuded dressing-table and depleted chest of drawers and wardrobe feel barely hers. At least it had her old bed. Once she'd hurried through getting ready for it she laid the knife under the bedside table and turned off the light and slipped into the dim bed.

At first she couldn't sleep for trying to ignore the collar.

When she'd had enough of turning in search of comfort she pulled the collar off and consigned it to the table. Now there was nothing between her and exhaustion. She slept before she expected to, and awoke to broader daylight than she'd intended to sleep through. She thought that had roused her until the doorbell rang again.

Sitting up in bed revived less pain in her neck than she feared. She dashed across the landing to grab her father's robe and spy out of his window. A man and a woman, neither of them many years older than herself, were standing on the gravel. Their uniforms were as dark as their jagged dwarfish shadows. Both were police.

She tied the cord of the robe around her waist as she padded fast downstairs. As she edged the front door open she was unnerved to realise she hadn't chained it last night. "Miss Logan?" the policewoman said.

Her sharp eyes and thin prim lips seemed designed to contradict the snubness of her nose. Daniella heard her own voice grow as stiff as the rest of her did. "What is it?"

"Miss Daniella Logan?"

"That's all of me. What—"

"May we have a word with you?"

"Go ahead. I mean, sorry," Daniella said, opening the door wide. "What do you want?"

The policewoman's eyes were saying she'd already answered that. There appeared to be more chance of a response from her colleague, who had freckles and unconquerably curly red hair and a not entirely humourless gaze, while his holding his lips straight only emphasised the broadness of his snout. Before he could speak, Daniella's confusion made itself heard. "How did you know I was here?"

"We called the number we had for you in York," the policewoman said.

"Why?"

"May we talk inside?"

"Wherever. Come in. Come in here," Daniella said, retreating to the front lounge as the policeman shut the door. She hurried to perch on the edge of the couch and waited for her visitors to sit opposite. The policeman broke the silence. "Can you tell us why you're here, Miss Logan?"

"Why shouldn't I be? It's my house."

"We understood you were a student."

"It can still be my house, can't it? My dad left it to me."

"You were here last night," the policeman said, raising a flat hand.

"Can't you tell? What's happened now? There's been too much, my dad getting killed for a start."

The police didn't quite glance at each other, but the man let his colleague respond. "Were you anywhere near his grave last night?"

"Why shouldn't I have been? He was my dad."

"A child said she was attacked with a knife in the graveyard by someone who was disturbing the grave."

"You've seen what you're saying was a child."

"It was an anonymous call."

"And that's enough?"

The policewoman only sharpened her gaze while her partner said "Enough for what, Miss Logan?"

"Enough for you to come after me because you think it was me with the knife."

"Was it?"

"I didn't attack anyone. They were going to attack me. They were getting in my way, I mean, they were trying to stop me getting away, so I defended myself."

"With a knife."

"I don't carry one around with me if that's what you're thinking. I carry an attack alarm."

"But you had a knife last night."

"That's because I found it. There were three girls, I don't know if she told you that, and I wouldn't call them children, less than I was at their age, believe me. They wanted to take the knife off me, and that's how one of them got scratched, just scratched. I bet she didn't bother going to hospital."

"You say you found the knife," the policewoman said.

"I found it where it was hidden. I'd figured out it had to be there. You know what I saw the night of my dad's funeral."

The policeman brought the pause to an end. "And now you're saying . . ."

"The men I saw weren't stealing from his grave, they were putting something in."

"A knife. Why do you think somebody would do that?"

"Not just any knife. I can show you."

Her visitors stood up as she did. "Where is it?" the policewoman said.

"Like I say, I don't carry it around. It's in my room."

The policewoman preceded her out of the room and paced her on the stairs while the policeman stayed close behind. Daniella didn't care how nearly arrested they were causing her to feel. They couldn't make much of her encounter at the graveyard, not when the girl who had tried to get her into trouble didn't want to be identified. All that mattered was her having something to show at last. She strode into her room and waited for her audience to catch

up before she walked to the bed, doing her best not to
appear too theatrical, and pointed in the direction of the
weapon. Then her finger curled towards her palm as if her
nerves were dragging it. Lying on the carpet was an ordinary carving-knife.

"No, that's not it," she said, shaking her head so hard
that pain blazed through her neck into her skull. "Wait,"
she protested as the police advanced, flanking the bed.
"Someone's taken the one I found and put this there. Did
you see anyone near the house? Wait. Don't touch."

This was addressed not to the policeman, though he
was reaching for her with a slowness that might have been
intended to be reassuring or even unobtrusive, but to his
colleague, who was stooping to the knife. She was stretching out a hand. "Don't touch it," Daniella heard herself cry,
"fingerprints," and seized the surgical collar to catch hold
of the knife.

The policewoman might have meant to capture her
wrist or the handle. Her grab missed both as Daniella
snatched the knife. She felt the edge of the blade slash the
young woman's palm and saw crimson drops appear on the
bed, but her mind seemed to have retreated from all this,
to have found somewhere it hadn't happened yet and
couldn't happen. "Sorry," she nevertheless said, "only you
mustn't touch it, or—My neck. Mind my neck."

She was speaking to the policeman now, whose hands
had closed like manacles around her wrists. She let the
knife fall on the increasingly reddened sheet to demonstrate
she wanted to cooperate. She did her best to make it clear
she was sharing the pain that was wetting the policewoman's eyes. The policeman yanked Daniella's wrists behind her and squashed them together with one hand, but

this wasn't America or a film in which English police behaved as they did over there: he wasn't going to handcuff
her wrists in the small of her back or wrench her neck in
the process. But he did.

TWENTY-ONE

H i. I'm still here. I haven't gone anywhere. I haven't hurt myself. One of you did that. I'm not going to do anything. I'm not even going to shout or bang on the door, because someone has to come and tell me what's happening soon. I'm just going to sit here so you can see what a good girl I am. I didn't do anything very bad, and it wasn't all my fault either."

By now whoever had looked through the spyhole had gone, and Daniella was alone with the cell—with the pale green walls and the door quite as blank except for its lidded hole that let her be seen and not see, and the window too small to be worth looking through even if it had been low enough, and the bench that was also a bed with a single sheet and a pillow not much less flat than a board, and the seatless metal toilet with a roll of harsh paper standing guard beside it. She wasn't going to let any of this affect her. She knew she didn't deserve to be locked up.

The police had been doing their job, she told herself. The policeman hadn't hurt her as badly as she'd injured his partner, whose white handkerchief had been red by the time they reached the police station. Daniella only wished they had allowed her to get changed instead of just putting on shoes. Even the cord of her father's bathrobe had been taken from her before she was led to the cell. She wished

she hadn't used her one phone call to try and contact her
mother, whose taped voice sibilant with static had made her
feel more alone. She'd asked the police to get in touch with
Chrysteen's father—surely they would. She would have lain
down to wait for him, she felt so tired and helpless and
devoid of any thoughts she cared to have, except that she'd
found that lying down put her in mind of how someone
must have crept into her room, so stealthily that she hadn't
even dreamed of a presence. Perhaps they had stood watching her while their eyes adjusted to the dimness, and if
she'd jerked awake, what face would she have seen peering
at her? What expression would it have worn? When she
heard the lid of the spyhole move, a sound not unlike the
shifting of a hidden knife, and the lens grew a glazed observant eye, it wasn't only the pain in her neck that made
her reluctant to turn her head. She would have had time
to take more breaths than she managed before Chrysteen's
father admitted himself to the cell.

He shut the door and leaned against it. Beneath the
crewcut his face looked less concerned than determined,
and squarer for it. "Well, Daniella," he said.

"How is she?"

"I take it you're asking after my young officer."

Daniella wondered if she'd forfeited his concern by injuring someone else about whom he felt paternal. "Yes, how
is she now?"

"She needed stitches. She'll be off work for several days
even though she didn't want to be. She's an asset to the
force."

"I didn't mean to hurt her."

He raised his head, tugging the jowls straight. "Perhaps
you can tell me what you did mean."

"I was trying to see she didn't get prints on the knife."

"And that was a reason to send her to hospital."

"We both tried to get hold of it. I could have been cut too."

"The difference being that she's a police officer."

"You'd rather it had been me that was hurt, you mean."

"I said nothing of the kind."

His gaze rested heavily on her until she had to speak. "What's happened to the knife?"

"It's evidence."

"Somcone will see if there are prints on it, then."

"What kind of evidence do you think I had in mind? I'm talking about the injury to my officer."

Daniella would have clutched at her head if her neck hadn't been aching so much. "Why won't anyone ever believe me?"

"As a matter of fact the knife was checked for prints."

"And?"

"Apart from my officer's, the only prints on it were yours."

"They couldn't be. I never touched it."

"Daniella, I'm going to have to suggest—"

"No, listen. Obviously I touched it, but I got hold of it with something. You ask her, no, you can't, she isn't here. Ask him."

"What would be the point? Your prints are there."

"Okay." For a moment her failure to find an explanation seemed capable of pushing her mind apart into the darkest recesses of her skull, and then she regained her hold. "I know what it was. I thought I recognised it. It's from the kitchen at the house. That's why it's got my prints."

"If you had it by you for fear someone would break in, you wouldn't be the only girl who did."

"I never expected anyone to break in. Didn't you hear how shocked I was when I found what they'd done?"

He drew a long slow breath that resounded in the cell, then he approached her as though his gaze was weighing him down. Folding the pillow in half, he rested his shoulders against it as he sat on the far end of the bunk from her. "Tell me what you say happened," he said.

"Where am I supposed to start?"

"With why you came back to Oxford."

"Nobody was going to believe me unless I had something to show them."

"Such as what?"

"What I found in my dad's grave."

Chrysteen's father turned his head as though he meant to shake it while keeping his gaze on her, but held it still. "You dug up his grave?"

"Only this much," Daniella said, pinching a few inches of air between one thumb and forefinger. "Maybe not even that. Just enough to find what they hid after he was buried. The girls who hang round there at night saw me find it, the real knife. You've got to believe they exist, they rang up about me. Can't you try and find them?"

"How do you suggest we go about that?"

"I can tell you what they look like."

"No, tell me what finding them would change."

"They saw the knife, so they can say it's not the one that was at my house."

"I've read the record of the complaint. The girl said nothing about seeing the weapon dug up."

"She mightn't have though, might she?"

"I should have thought she would have found it significant enough to mention, yes."

"She was just trying to get me into trouble."

"You seem able to do that all by yourself."

Her shoulders writhed but failed to dislodge her tension. "No, somebody's trying to make it for me."

"Who is?"

"Whoever got into my house."

"Then answer me one question." As he sat towards her, the unfolding pillow nodded over his shoulder before slithering down the wall. "Why would anyone switch knives?"

"So I couldn't show people what I found. So nobody would believe me, and it looks as if that worked."

He reached behind him for the pillow and held it between his hands. It took him some seconds to begin to say "I want to do the best I can for you as Chrysteen's friend."

"Thanks."

"You'll accept that."

However he meant the question, not that it sounded like one, she said "Sure."

"Then I'll do it provided you promise to agree to whatever I can arrange for you."

"Like what, do you think?" When he only gazed at her, sadness growing more apparent in his eyes, she gave in to saying "All right, I promise."

He dropped the pillow on the bunk and stood up at once to rap on the door. A middle-aged constable opened it and twitched his bristling black moustache at Daniella. Soon the door scraped its eye wide to peer at her, and it did so again, having transformed its pupil from brown to

blue, before Simon Hastings returned. He left the door ajar
as though to give her a glimpse of freedom but blocked the
gap. "I've told them you promised," he said.

"Who?"

"My young lady officer for one. I've explained the situation and she concedes her injury may have been acciden-
tal. If you do as I told her you would I believe we won't
need to take that any further."

"What did you tell her?"

"That you'd go in for counselling."

"Okay, I'll see who I can find."

"I've done that for you. I heard Eamonn Reith offer it
to you at Teddy's funeral. He's an old friend, and I've just
spoken to him."

"Oh," Daniella said, and meant it somewhat more than
"Right."

"He'll contact you in York tomorrow." Simon Hastings
watched her stand up, but remained in her way as he added
"That's a condition of letting you go."

"I know that."

He swung the door open slowly enough to be har-
bouring some doubt. He waited while she collected her
handbag and the cord that allowed her at last to stop holding the robe shut. He drove her back to the house and
lingered at the gate until she unlocked the front door, and
left her with a long unblinking look as his car inched out
of sight beyond the hedge. She thought the look was intended to remind her of her promise, and she could only
think that was why, although she was miles from the police
cell and stepping into her father's house, she didn't feel even
slightly released.

TWENTY-TWO

W hen Daniella realised she was trying to decide if her clothes would impress Eamonn Reith with her normality she almost lost her temper. If her baggy shorts and the T-shirt that barely tucked into them were good enough for her, they should be for him. In the park beyond her window two young mothers were agreeing vehemently and competing to produce the largest gestures with their silver-nailed hands while two toddlers dressed like miniature sumo wrestlers staggered about the sunlit grass. The spectacle seemed to be out of her mind's reach. She was too busy feeling that Eamonn Reith's visit was yet another reason for her to be furious.

She mustn't just sit and grow angrier. Her neck was growing so tense she wished she hadn't left the collar at her father's house, even if it had made her feel like a dog let temporarily off the leash. She still had to bring her essay on belief to a conclusion, but the prospect felt like rough lumps in her skull. Instead she opened her old school book that was lying on a corner of the desk.

Her mouth tried on a variety of smiles—wry at the sight of handwriting that appeared to be struggling to resemble hers, then nostalgic followed by wistful—as she read. *What I Did In The Holidays* had been to go to Jersey, which she'd noted solemnly was in the Channel Islands for the benefit of her English teacher, though she'd failed to mention it had been the farthest she had ever gone abroad. The aspect of *A Day In The Life Of A Star* she'd found most significant had been that Nana Babouris had someone else put on her makeup. She remembered watching Nana on the set—remembered not only her own awe at the glamour of a ballroom scene but a glimpse of her father blinking his eyes dry as she'd caught him watching her. That wasn't the only time she'd had such an impression of him: there had been her first formal dinner—a Care For Children bene-fit—and other occasions when she'd worn an evening dress, not to overlook several school prizegivings, at the last of which he'd dabbed at his eyes with his sleeve while her mother had turned a fond look from Daniella to him. He must have kept feeling he was losing Daniella as she grew up, but she found herself imagining that he'd foreseen the way she'd lost him. She turned the pages and came to the last few sheets, which were blank. Except that one wasn't— the last page. It had been written on by her father.

SMITHS, he'd written at the top with a red ballpoint that had dug into the paper. Below the word was a list that seemed to make at least as little sense.

Goldsmith
Talksmith February 14 1992
Healsmith
Jokesmith April 30 1969
Courtsmith December 19 1961
Lawsmith
Talesmith May 1 1956
Newssmith
Caresmith 20 December 1990

Stocksmith June 12 1955
Playsmith October 30 1994
Meatsmith
Flysmith March 4 1991
Booksmith August 28 1981
Banksmith November 1 1958

There was at least as much more, but her gaze had snagged on the last words, which were "Filmsmith" twice, neither dated. She knew at once who they were: Alan Stanley and her father. She was about to see who else she could identify when she was distracted by the dragging of the gate, and Eamonn Reith came striding up the path.

He was a small neat man, unobtrusively dressed except for a diamond tiepin as bright as his eyes. His face looked compact and assured beneath carefully brushed short but thick black hair, more of which framed his pale pink lips and covered the front of his round chin. He didn't glance up before ringing the doorbell. She shut the exercise book in a drawer of her desk and was making by no means hastily to answer the bell when Chrysteen let him in.

Daniella hadn't finished taking her time when she heard his carefully modulated tones, which sounded as though he was preparing his professional manner. She hurried downstairs, sandals clacking angrily. He was seated at the kitchen table and facing the hall. A few purple veins in his aquiline nose went some way towards spoiling the neatness of his face. When he stood up to reach across the table for her hands, his proved to be firm and cool as meat not long released from a freezer. "Would you rather not talk in front of your friend?" he said.

"Why should I?"

"Why should you . . ."

"Mind, obviously, not talk."

"Would you prefer to adjourn to somewhere more comfortable?"

"We're comfortable in here, aren't we, Chrys?"

"We must be when we're always in it."

"Then it's ideal." The psychoanalyst let go of Daniella's hands but left his gaze on her while she sat opposite him, and then he fed himself a precise sip from a glass of water. "Shall we begin?" he said.

"I thought we had."

"Very good. Is there anything either of you would like me to know at the outset?"

"Danny's been hurt."

"Indeed she has. I don't know if she's let you see how deeply."

"I meant her neck."

"I'm sure that's part of the problem. She's lucky to have someone so attentive as a friend. What effect do you think her injuries may have had?"

"Shouldn't you ask me that?" Daniella objected.

"I was going to, of course. I thought you might welcome your friend's views. By all means have the floor."

"Right now they're making my head ache, you know I mean the injuries, but maybe it's not only them."

"Any other symptoms? Dizziness?"

"Not now."

"And how has Daniella's behaviour lately struck you?"

"I've already told her I wish she'd give it up."

"I'm interested in your choice of words. Give what up exactly?"

"All the stuff about her father," Chrysteen said, and

turned to Daniella. "Whatever it is I don't see what good finding out can do."

"Maybe you would if it was your father."

"Do you think that sounds as if you're trying to displace her observation onto her?" the psychoanalyst intervened.

"No I don't, and do you wonder if I am, and anyway so what?"

"Just suppose for a moment you didn't see what you thought you saw at your father's grave."

"When?"

"Start with the first time."

"I didn't. I thought I saw men holding lights up, but they were really knives."

"Men holding up symbols that now you say were knives." He nodded as though she had agreed with him. "You're reading psychology, Chrysteen. You'll know your Freud."

"Well, I don't," Daniella said, further enraged by Chrysteen's understanding look, "so maybe you can let me in on the secret."

"I'll ask you to consider something purely as a hypothesis, not even a possibility if you'd rather it wasn't. Just suppose for the purpose of argument that the men you saw were, let's call them mythical. What do you think you might be saying then?"

"I'd be saying it was crap, because it isn't true."

"Remember I'm only asking you to imagine."

"I can imagine crap all by myself if I want to without you helping," Daniella said, and had to laugh at how that could be taken, though the laugh sounded more like a gasp at the ache that was claiming most of her head, thoughts included. "Fine, right, tell me what I'm supposed to say."

"It really ought to come from you, otherwise it loses some of its point." Nevertheless he extended one empty hand to her and the other to Chrysteen as if to demonstrate no trickery was involved. "If you leave out the men," he said, "wouldn't it seem you were talking about an urge to dig up your father, though of course you'd know you couldn't? Except what you really wanted was to have everything back the way it had been, and you knew that was a wish nobody could grant."

"You mean everything's been about wanting my dad back."

"If that's what you feel."

Nearly all she was feeling was a shoulder-length headache, but she said "You bet I want him back, only I know he won't come, and you're leaving one thing out."

"Remind us."

"I really found a knife."

"Did you?"

"I thought you were supposed to be counselling me. This doesn't feel like counselling."

"I'm afraid it may not until you open yourself up to it."

"What, what stuff have I got to open up to now?"

"There's no doubt there was a knife or that you dug up the grave—"

"I'm glad to know they're real at least."

"Or that you injured two people, but that's something Teddy Logan's daughter would never normally do."

"I didn't mean to harm anyone. They were accidents, both of them."

"What does psychology say about accidents, Chrysteen?" When Chrysteen only looked unhappy Eamonn

Reith answered his own question. "That there aren't any. There are just actions we perform to distract ourselves from truths we'd rather not admit."

"What are you trying to say I won't admit now?" Daniella said in a voice squeezed high and tight by the ache in her skull.

"It might have to do with the knife, do you think? The one Chrysteen's father tells me was an ordinary kitchen knife from your house."

"It wasn't and I'm sick of saying it wasn't. I hope that's enough counselling for one day, because it's going to have to be. My head hurts and I want to lie down," she said, and stood rapidly up.

It was dark up there—so dark that she could locate her head only by the pain. Her body was stumbling about somewhere in the distance without any help from her, and not doing very well. She heard Chrysteen cry out, but she seemed to be left alone in the dark for some time before hands grasped her arms. Even Eamonn Reith's voice was welcome when it said "We've got you. Let's have you sitting down."

After some awkwardness a kitchen chair met her body, which might have been quicker to seat itself if those holding onto it hadn't differed over how it should. Once they let go she was able to concentrate on the firmness of the chair. She heard Eamonn Reith mutter "Worse than I expected" and Chrysteen utter a sound sadder than words. Daniella closed her eyes and watched the darkness start to fade, and opened them to see two bedside faces. "I'll be okay," she said, gripping the edge of the table to lever herself to her feet. She had raised herself only a couple of inches when her arms shook and she sank hastily onto the chair.

"You aren't okay," Chrysteen said more forcefully than Daniella had ever heard her speak.

"I'm afraid your friend is right."

"What are you going to say is the matter with me now?"

Reith looked only slightly pained by her response. "How long would you say your neck was trapped?"

"Too long."

"You haven't any idea—"

"I don't know." The threat of darkness felt too reminiscent of the safe—it even tasted metallic. "It seemed like minutes," she said.

"It may have been close to that, judging by your state just now. You were taken to a hospital, surely. Did they do any tests for oxygen starvation?"

"I don't think so. They kept me in overnight and saw how I was in the morning."

"And then sent you packing without even a neck brace so someone else could have the bed."

"I had a collar but I got sick of it. Maybe someone else needed the bed more than I did."

"Not if you were in as bad a way as I believe you are. I hope at least you won't have to be convinced of that."

She no longer had the energy to continue to be hostile. "What are you saying is wrong with me?"

"The oxygen to your brain would have been cut off, and now you're suffering the effects."

"Chrys, could you drive me to the university clinic?"

"Is it open this afternoon? I'd better check."

Daniella closed her eyes so as not to feel bound to interpret Eamonn Reith's frown. She heard Chrysteen pick up the receiver and dial, and nothing else apart from the psychoanalyst's almost inaudible breaths until her friend hurried back. "Danny, there's only a message. There's nobody there till tomorrow."

"Then could you take me to the hospital?"

"I wonder if it would be any better than the one that left you like this," Eamonn Reith said. "Would you feel happier with one I recommend?"

"I should think."

That was Chrysteen, but Daniella couldn't find much disagreement in herself. She opened her eyes to see Eamonn Reith slipping out his wallet. "I have their card here," he said. "They're an easy drive south."

Her headache blackened with the effort of focusing on the card. THE COPPICE HOSPITAL AT HARESBOROUGH, it said in discreetly embossed silver letters, together with a postcode she didn't recognise and a lengthy phone number. "Shall I call them?" Eamonn Reith suggested. "I really wouldn't feel I'd done my job if I didn't try to get you the optimum treatment."

Daniella attempted to relax in case that helped her think, but her throbbing skull felt clenched on her mind, and she wasn't due for another brace of aspirins for hours. "Call them if you want," she mumbled, closing her eyes against the sunlight that had begun to feel sharp as a knife.

Chrysteen set about massaging her shoulders as the friends often did to each other. Just now it didn't help, perhaps because it reminded Daniella of Mark's hands on her. Even reaching to take a gentle hold of Chysteen's aggravated the ache that felt capable of engulfing all her sense of herself. "Is Julian available?" she heard Eamonn Reith murmur, and almost immediately "I've diagnosed a problem with a young lady I'm helping. Daniella Logan."

She would have liked to hear everything, but Chrysteen
was breathing words of comfort in her ear. She heard the
psychoanalyst say only "That's most kind." He trotted into
the kitchen, beaming like an uncle who had brought a present. "Good news," he declared. "They've a bed for you and
they'd like you to go to them at once."

TWENTY-THREE

Daniella was less than halfway upstairs when it became apparent that each step she climbed was jerking her towards more pain. She clung to the banister while she retreated to the hall, along which she fumbled almost blindly to the kitchen and lowered herself onto the chair she'd recently vacated. "Chrys," she said without being able to judge how small her voice was, "would you mind packing for me?"

"Of course I don't. You stay with Dr Reith and I'll be down before you know it."

"Just throw my night stuff into my old case and a few things to wear."

"How long do you think she'll be there, Dr Reith?"

"I should make provision for a few days to be safe."

"Nothing special," Daniella called after her friend as if that might help her regain some control, and closed her eyes until Chrysteen brought the small suitcase to exhibit the contents. "I don't expect I'll need all that, but lots of thanks," she said as Chrysteen zipped the case up.

Eamonn Reith took charge of it while Chrysteen helped Daniella stand up and held her arm all the way to his car. It was a Bentley almost the same grey as his suit and double parked, trapping Daniella's Ford. Though the bodywork gleamed with newness, the interior smelled old as well as leathery—perhaps it was the dryness of the air. She sank onto the front passenger seat, keeping her head upright like a vessel capable of spilling black pain, and lowered the window to talk to Chrysteen while Eamonn Reith shut the case in the boot. "Will you tell the university why I won't be there?"

"I'll call them in a moment and the Trencher as well."

"Oh, Chrys, I hope I won't lose my job."

Eamonn Reith sat briskly beside her, tugging his seat-belt half out of its niche to indicate she should don hers. "Try and leave your worries behind," he said. "They won't improve your state."

"I'll ring and find out how you are," Chrysteen said, patting the hospital card in her pocket, "if you don't ring us."

The Bentley crept forward and emerged with scarcely a whisper into the traffic. The road and the houses slid backwards, but the sun ahead couldn't be bothered to move, while the sky carried on being nothing except blue. Houses crouched to expose more of it before fields pulled it down to the horizon. Daniella had been concentrating on feeling no worse, but her condition seemed to have stabilised because of the smoothness of the ride. "Thanks for looking after me," she said.

"The least I could do. It's on my way home anyway, and I'm glad to be of some use at last."

She closed her eyes as the Bentley turned south, away from the road that had led to the wreck of her father's car. For a while she was lulled by the subdued monotonous chord of the engine and the wheels. She must have dozed, because the next time she looked, an upright page of giant childish print made her aware that she was no longer in

the county south of Yorkshire but well into the one below
that. "I thought you said it wasn't far," she protested as her
headache raised itself.

"I rather think I said it was an easy drive. I've been
doing my best to ensure it was that. In any case, here we
are."

They didn't appear to be. They were no longer on the
motorway, and the sign she'd glimpsed turned its back on
her as he swung the car onto a narrow unsignposted road
that wound between thick spiky hedges too tall for her to
be able to see beyond the curves. After at least a mile the
Bentley crossed a deserted unmarked junction, allowing her
a glimpse of a line of poplars ahead, after which the route
treated her to a succession of bends that challenged her to
keep her head steady on her neck. "Sorry," Eamonn Reith
said at more than one, and "Not much further" as the first
of the poplars reared above the next bend. They stepped
out from behind one another, their dark green plumes waving so stealthily she couldn't be sure she was seeing the
movement, especially since not a leaf seemed to stir in the
hedges. Also revealed was the long high white stone wall
above which they towered, and a gateway with a pair of
gates held open, their elaborate iron scrollwork painted silver. "I'm sorry it took us so long," Eamonn Reith said.

A small gold plaque on the left-hand gatepost identified
the Coppice Hospital. Otherwise she might have taken the
broad white symmetrical two-storey building for a country
house. On either side of the generous front door the windows were high and wide and elegant; one of them was
sending forth a stream of trills on a piano. Above the steep
red roof two slim chimney stacks described a gesture on
the sky. A gravel drive on which two cars could pass abreast

snaked between gradually sloping lawns where a few
shrubs squatted on their own shade and nurses in white
uniforms sat with patients in day clothes on benches scattered about the grass. The drive led around the house to a
parking area by no means crowded with half a dozen cars
and a brace of minibuses bearing the hospital's name. Daniella heard a clatter of utensils and smelled boiled vegetables
in the midst of the scent of mown grass as she straightened
up slowly while Eamonn Reith retrieved her suitcase from
the boot. "Let me see you safely in," he said.

The stout front door was hooked back to show a vestibule smaller than the building warranted. Several exits led
from the anonymous space: doors in both the walls that
were also occupied by couches, presumably for visitors, and
an enclosed staircase beside the window of an office that
must have a door elsewhere. A brawny young woman with
a smile that would have survived any number of close-ups
slid the window open with a clink like a meeting of wine-
glasses. "You're Daniella," she said firmly enough to be informing her of the fact, and immediately glanced past her
as the left door opened with a faint squeak of its elbow.
"Phyllis, this is our new friend Daniella. Are you free to
show her up?"

"I'm here for her. I saw her coming," said the nurse,
another sturdy short-haired blonde, whose face—large
mouth ready with a smile, broad nose, blue eyes set wide
apart—reminded Daniella how big her mother's face had
looked to her as a child. "Will you follow me, Daniella?
Let me have your case."

"Is Julian here?" Eamonn Reith was asking the receptionist.

"He's away on outreach this afternoon."

"Of course, he did say. Would you like me to take care of the essentials?"

Phyllis, whose name was stitched in silver letters on the left breast of her crisp white uniform, picked up the suitcase and let go of the handle with all except one finger as though to demonstrate how little it weighed. "Shall we?" she said.

The interior of Daniella's skull felt as if it had yet to leave the moving vehicle. She supported herself with one hand on the wall, which was unnecessarily warm, as she followed the nurse up the stairs. A mirror above the bend in them showed her a foreshortened version of herself, a diminutive figure whose face was blank with introspection beneath a swollen cranium. At the top the nurse turned right along a broad bright corridor, at both ends of which the windows of fire exits gave views of fields. She led Daniella past a bedroom that exhibited a town on the horizon, presumably Haresborough, before ushering her into a room at the front of the hospital.

It was decorated in a floral pattern of pastel pinks and greens that was elaborated by heavy curtains ungathered by cords and by a bedspread that hung down to the poplar-coloured carpet. Phyllis swung one large-fingered hand to indicate the furniture—a wardrobe squaring the corner farthest from the door, a dressing-table full of drawers and with a mirror bolted to the wall above it, an item that seemed uncertain what its place was in the room and whether it was a straight chair or an armchair—as she twirled Daniella's case one-fingered onto the bed and backed around her to the door. "Enjoy your time with us," she said.

"I'll try," said Daniella, and started by lying down next to her case on the bedspread and closing her eyes. The

inside of her cranium had begun to catch up with her still-
ness when she heard footsteps climb the stairs and approach
her room. "Daniella?" Eamonn Reith murmured. "Are you
asleep?"

"Resting."

"Here's something to help. Can you sit up for a moment?"

She opened one eye and saw him holding out a capsule
and a miniature plastic cup. "What is it?" she wanted to
know.

"A relaxant they've sent up with me. It should ease your
neck."

She took her time over raising herself towards the pain
that was hovering in wait. She swallowed the capsule and
drained the cup of water, and was fumbling to deposit it
on the bedside table while she returned her head very gradually to the pillow when Eamonn Reith said "Before you
get too comfortable, can we just take care of the formalities?"

She watched him take a form out of his jacket. "Do I
have to fill all that in now?" she pleaded.

"It's your medical history, any allergies, next of kin, that
sort of thing, and of course these days a waiver," he said,
leafing through the form to show her. "I really oughtn't to
have given you that medication till it's completed."

"Can you write it for me so I can just sign?"

"Certainly, if you'll tell me what to write."

Long before the questions came to an end her eyelids
were drooping and the rest of her was well on its way.
When he handed her the form to endorse, the pages seemed
to glare a threat of even more pain than was already hatch-
ing in her skull. She flicked quickly to the last page and

scribbled her name, and sank towards the pillow as she let the form flutter to the bedspread. "Well done," Eamonn Reith said. She only heard him leave the room, and his last words were so quiet she wasn't sure whether she was meant to catch them. "I know Teddy would be glad you're in our hands."

TWENTY-FOUR

W hile Daniella failed to sleep, she did grow more tranquil
as the ache lost its hold on her shoulders and neck
before dwindling within her head. She heard Eamonn
Reith's goodbyes downstairs, followed by the slam of the
car door and the receding purr of the engine. Like these,
the sounds of the hospital seemed comforting in some way
she was content to leave undefined: laughter from a television and a more haphazard version from people watching
it, kitchen clatters, the hollow irregular brittle ticks of table
tennis and then the claps of bats slapping a table, the soft
snug thuds of the doors off the vestibule, releasing footsteps
that never had anything to do with her. Once the pain
shrank to a point between her eyebrows and vanished, its
absence felt like an insubstantial soothing medium in which
she need only lie. It had occurred to her several times that
she ought to unpack before she pushed herself upright with
a sigh and, having sat against the headboard for a minute
or a number of them to confirm that her headache was
buried too deep to be easily revived, wandered over to the
window.

The sky had lowered a grey shutter like a vow of rain.
Cars on the road along the horizon jabbed ineffectually at
it with flashes of sunlight from their roofs, while the fields
grew luminous to compensate. The poplars were absently

fingering the sky, though she couldn't hear so much as a whisper from them. She hauled the window open as far as it would go—the breadth of her hand at the top of the frame—and watched a car reappear at several bends: a toy car, then a model, then one no larger than a pendant. When the swaying of a poplar wiped it out she turned to unpacking, which didn't take long even at her new untroubled pace. She unfolded her nightdress on the bedspread and observed its resemblance to a flattened limbless doll with a pale green tousled pillow for a head. It was time to see more of the hospital, she thought. Having finished a survey of the room from the corridor, she closed the door and made her way downstairs.

The receptionist was slipping bills on headed notepaper into envelopes. The spectacle halted Daniella until a question whose belatedness struck her as vaguely amusing suggested itself. "Am I going to have to pay?"

The woman glanced up long enough to flash an undirected smile. "I believe Mr Logan's estate is taking care of that."

"It could be a while before it's sorted out."

"So we've been told."

Presumably Eamonn Reith had spoken to Daniella's mother. Daniella searched within herself for resentment but couldn't locate much. "Don't let it bother you. You aren't here to be bothered," the receptionist advised, letting her gaze lift her face. "Why don't you go and meet the others? They're a good crowd, most of them."

The door at which she nodded gave onto a long corridor containing three doors. The jolly television was beyond the first on the left, through which she found a lounge at least as broad as a third of the hospital. It and its fur-

niture were the colours that the view beyond the floor-
length windows would have been except for the greyness
of the sky: blue walls, upright soft-backed chairs and sofas
striped grass-green and darker. Only a few of the couple of
dozen seats were occupied, mostly those facing a large shallow television squatting on a ledge across the corner farthest
from the door. Three shaggy puppets were making rudi-
mentary gestures on the screen. She was trying not too hard
to identify the children's programme when a male nurse
standing near the windows announced "Everybody, this is
Daniella."

Those who weren't intent on the television were already
looking up—a woman Daniella would have thought too
young to be knitting or so grey-haired, a rather more than
middle-aged one with eyes that stayed narrowed by wrin-
kles as she covered her bony knees by inverting the gold-
covered novel—*Foiled*, a Midas book—in whose margins
she had been minutely writing. "Here she is," cried the
smallest of the women in front of the television, and shuffled along a sofa, her short thick bare legs swinging. "Come
and join the girls. I'm Hilary."

"Hilary the Hilarious," amplified her companion, a
woman with fat drooping from her pallid arms and legs,
a larger portion imperfectly concealed by her big top of a
white dress, and took a laborious breath to name herself.
"Alison."

"Hilarious Hilary," the last of the trio declared with
enough force to be correcting the previous speaker, and half
raised herself on one lanky dark-haired arm to hitch her
body round inside her long loose swarthy dress. "And me,
I'm Cynth, you know. Sit with us, do."

"Here's a spot for you," Hilary declared, patting the

cushion beside her before jabbing a stubby finger at the television. "Come and watch this. Looks as if someone's hand is where it shouldn't be."

Alison sat forward so vigorously her whole body wobbled. "Like some doctors do to people," she said with a fierceness that trailed off into a wheeze.

"Not ours," Cynth assured Daniella. "They aren't that sort."

Daniella found herself observing with detached amusement not only the women but also her own ability to fit in with them. "I should hope not," she felt she ought to respond as she took her place on the sofa.

Hilary unleashed a protracted chuckle of agreement, which at some point shifted to addressing the television. Her companions seemed equally entertained by the way the legless cloth-faced figures jerked about as though struggling to uproot themselves. Daniella supposed it would be polite to emit the occasional laugh, but hadn't seen a reason to produce any when Hilary gurgled "Watch out, here comes grief."

She might have been referring only to the first of the patients who were straggling in through the windows, a tall woman in an opaque black dress that hid all of her except her head and feet and large raw hands. Under hair that resembled a dusty reddish mop her oversized piebald face was slack with preoccupation, and she seemed to have to remember how to use her limbs. She stared at Daniella while the room filled up, and Daniella couldn't help hoping that everyone was coming in because of the threat of a storm, not to scrutinise her. It became apparent that neither was the reason when Hilary let herself down onto the floor and stumped rapidly towards the exit. "You stay with us, Daniella. You can be at our table."

The dining-room was across the corridor. There was space in it for more tables than the seven round ones it contained, most of them attended by four chairs. Hilary and her party hurried to a table by the window, beyond which the parking area gave way to a lawn that stretched to a wall and a taller thorny hedge obscuring any view of distant Haresborough. Once all the patients were seated, which took some time as the oldest hobbled or limped doggedly to their places or in two instances were wheeled to them, a pair of young women uniformed in green even paler than the walls began serving dinner: bowls of soup, salad as a centrepiece for each table. "That's it, give her plenty," Hilary exhorted as Daniella was brought soup.

"That'll warm you up," Alison assured her.

"It'll fix your cockles for you," Cynth said.

It was chunky vegetable soup with just enough pepper not to draw attention to itself. Daniella supposed she was hungry, since she was the first at the table to finish. She was only opening her mouth to demur when Cynth and then Alison poured into her bowl the remains of their soup, which she couldn't very well not sip. Hilary ensured she had the largest portion of the salad. Daniella's companions were exerting themselves to make her feel accepted, but she could have done without the behaviour of the woman in the long black dress, who was facing her at the next table— indeed, had argued her way around from the seat with its back to Daniella. She was apparently so concerned with how Daniella was eating that she kept forgetting to lift her fork past her chin.

The main course was slices of chicken in a creamy sauce that added very little flavour but lent the vegetables the look of pudding and cloaked their tastes. As the green-uniformed women cleared the tables Hilary kicked her legs up and lolled back on the chair, drumming her palms on her stomach. "What shall we do now? Are you a cardy girl?"

"Bridge, she means," said Alison.

"No I don't. You're the bridgy one. She always tries to make us play because she likes all that talking in code," Hilary told Daniella. "Just makes us sound like spies, and then she sulks if I laugh. Whist's our game."

"I can play Solo."

"That's not right," Cynth objected. "You don't want to be by yourself."

"Solo whist, she's saying, aren't you, Daniella? We've played that. We'll make you wish you had a partner," Hilary declared and flapped a hand to urge her towards the lounge before stumping in her wake.

The women seated themselves near an unobtrusively blue phone that had an alcove opposite the windows to itself. Cynth extended a lanky arm to snag a pack of cards from the highest of a set of wall shelves scattered with paperbacks, many of them Midas paperbacks like blocks of gold or silver. Victor Shakespeare would be pleased and, Daniella thought with muffled rage, Mark too. That almost obscured a thought she'd just had. "I ought to let my mother know where I am."

"Ah," the women chorused.

She was taken aback by having forgotten to call until now, but the emotion felt observed more than experienced. She took hold of the receiver only to find the dial was blank. "What do I need to do?" She felt distantly childish for having to ask.

Hilary appeared to be expanding with hilarity. "Try picking it up."

At first lifting the receiver brought merely a guffaw from Hilary and giggles from her companions, and then the receptionist said in Daniella's ear "Hello? Who's on?"

"It's Daniella Logan."

"Yes, Daniella. What can I get for you?"

"I need to call my mother."

"Nothing simpler. Tell me the number and I'll put you in touch."

"Isn't there a pay phone?"

"The charge will go on your bill. Don't worry, we don't mark it up much."

Daniella assumed all that meant no. She told the receptionist the number and in a few moments heard a trilling interrupted by her mother's stale taped voice. She told the machine where she was and conveyed to it the phone number she obtained from a nurse who was sitting by the windows, and could think of nothing more to say. She was taking the fourth seat at the table, where a sprawl of cards hid its faces while it awaited her, when Hilary protested "That wasn't much of a chat to have with your own mother."

"She wasn't there."

Cynth looked ready to argue until Alison wheezed "Daniella means she was a robot like the one in the office."

As Daniella reached for her cards the phone emitted a solitary pair of notes. "There's the robot now," Hilary cried, spluttering with so much mirth she had to wipe her chin.

Daniella smiled politely and began to sort her hand as

the nurse answered the phone. "Daniella?" he said.

She had barely greeted the receiver when the receptionist said "Just hang up when you've finished. I'm off for the night now."

There was indeed darkness beyond the windows and their welcome mats of illuminated turf. Daniella heard a click and said "Hello?"

"Daniella Logan?"

It was a man's somewhat Californian voice, which she felt she should recognise. "That's me," she admitted.

"You called my machine."

She had to disentangle this from Hilary's suggestion. She leaned one hand against the wall, to find it disconcertingly not much less warm than flesh. "Did I? When?"

"It can't have been two days ago."

Realising who he was felt like nearly waking up. "You're—"

"Timothy Turner. I called the number you left and your friend, is it Chrysteen, she told me you'd had an accident that put you in the hospital."

"I'm just here for observation."

"So long as you'll be doing some as well."

She glanced at the women, who were watching her over their fans of cards. "How do you mean?"

"Don't take a scrap of notice. Too curious for my own good, that's Professor Turner. I'm sure hospitals in my old country still lead the world."

"You're English, then."

"As Cambridge could make me. Read theology and taught it for a while and then came to Hollywood after they wanted my advice on a project that never got made. So I stayed here to teach."

"If you'd been here you could have advised my dad. He made *The Flood* and *David and Goliath*."

"You still have a few guys who know what it takes to make it in the world." So wryly it was clear he wasn't claiming to be one of them, he said "Where did you find my book that nearly had me thrown off the faculty?"

"*The Bible Decoded*, you mean."

"It's the only one I've written, and I ended up wishing I hadn't."

"How come?"

"Too contentious for some of the worthies of Orange County. I wasn't too unhappy when it disappeared. You have to keep quiet sometimes if you want to get ahead. I guess it doesn't matter if a copy surfaced where you are. Too far away for my paymasters to notice."

"It was one of Victor Shakespeare's copies."

"Whose?"

"The man who runs Midas Books. He bought all of your books he could."

"Got you, and then he didn't publish it. He isn't giving them away now, is he?"

"All I know is he gave my dad one."

"Because of the kind of film he was making, you mean."

"That's what I thought."

"So tell me what you made of my little volume."

"I didn't make anything."

"Well, I can't say that isn't honest." The author seemed uncertain how amused to sound, and put up his accent like a shield. "Kind of a weird thing to ask me to call you to hear, though."

"I didn't mean it like that. I haven't read your book."

"Then I'm bewildered. Why the message?"

"Because I saw your book at my dad's house but now I can't find it, and maybe you heard he's dead."

"It was all over Hollywood. Let me tender my sympathies." He gave her a silence to go with them before saying "You'll pardon me, but I'm still not clear on why you called."

"To ask about your book."

An electric crackling beside her terminated in a loud report. "We're starting without you," Hilary warned her, brandishing the cards through which she'd dragged an impatient finger.

"I'll join you soon," Daniella said, having covered the mouthpiece, as Timothy Turner prompted "Any question in particular?"

Daniella watched Hilary collect all the cards and deal three hands, leaving one card face down in the middle of the table. The only question she could find among her indolent thoughts was "Is there anything in your book about smiths?"

"Myths, did you say?"

"Smiths. People being smiths."

"Why do you ask that?"

"Because some people may have got the idea for a secret society out of the Bible or maybe even—how old is your book?"

"Just an infant. Less than four years."

She remembered some of the dates her father had written against the list of mysterious names. "Then it couldn't have been you that gave them the idea."

"I should very much hope not."

Hilary hooted with laughter, apparently at having lost a queen. "Why not?" Daniella said.

"Because the only smith in my book is the first one. Cain."

"I thought he was—" Daniella searched her memory for bits of the Bible from school. "Wasn't he supposed to be a farmer? Didn't he sacrifice some of his animals and God didn't think much of it?"

"Offered portions of the firstborn of his flock, that's the text. There's no doubt he was a farmer, but we have to assume that isn't all the people the Bible was originally written for would take from it. The name Cain means a smith, a worker in metal."

"A forger of metal," Daniella thought aloud.

"That would be another word for it."

"So you think if people started calling themselves smiths because of him their brothers had better watch out," she said, remembering her father had been an only child.

"No, I wouldn't think that."

"Why not?"

"What kind of a society did you say you were talking about?"

She didn't want to risk scaring him off. "Maybe just one in a film my dad was planning to make."

"It doesn't sound the kind of movie he was known for."

"Maybe he could see how things were going."

"Reverting to savagery, you mean."

"I don't know. Do I?"

"I'm sorry, I forgot you hadn't read my book. The point is it can be argued Cain didn't kill his brother."

"How?"

"One clue is the brother's name. Abel means meaning-less. It means that in Ecclesiastes too. That's one reason you can wonder if Cain ever had a brother."

"If he didn't, what was supposed to have happened?"

"My question exactly, and I think the answer is in what you said before."

"What I . . ." She glimpsed Alison quivering as if with panic, but she'd only shrugged off the loss of a trick. "What did I say?" Daniella had to ask.

"The reference to sacrificing the firstborn. That was the first thing Cain did that God objected to, if you remember. I conclude the Cain and Abel story is a disguised account of an early human sacrifice, redesigned by the writer so as to put his audience off the practice. Just as history is re-written by the victors, you know, religions are rewritten by the priests. Maybe the writer recognised how primal the urge to sacrifice is and so he didn't want to risk having it appeal to the reader, which is why he makes it into a mur-der story instead. But it's like any murder story, there are clues in it if you look hard enough."

"Don't you think you may have been looking too hard? It seems a whole lot to squeeze out of just a few words."

"That's how some writers try to write, you know, and I don't think any scholars would deny that about the writ-ing in the Bible. Besides, Cain and Abel's not the only pas-sage with that ritual hidden in it. Some passages hardly conceal it."

"Like which?"

"Most of the major figures in Genesis are second chil-dren, and nobody seems to ask what might have happened to the firstborn, but you'll certainly remember the story of Abraham and Isaac."

"Isaac being saved from getting sacrificed, you mean."

"Was he?"

"Saved? Of course he was," she said, though arguing had started to feel like the threat of an elongated headache. "I can't remember what it says God said exactly, but he told Abraham not to touch Isaac."

"It was actually an angel, not God, but he's reported to have said that, I grant you. Only the Bible also has him saying Abraham and his descendants will succeed because he didn't withhold his firstborn, and I have to point out that it says Abraham returned from the sacrifice but nothing about Isaac. In the Midrash, which is the nearest thing to a source for the Bible, Abraham either spills his blood or kills him, in which case Isaac returns from the dead."

Daniella felt as if a story she hadn't known she valued was being stolen from her. "So?" she said as Cynth clawed at the table to gather up a trick.

"So I deduce that Moses, if we accept he was the author of Genesis, that he couldn't alter the story too much because it was too well known, but he went as far as he could towards pretending the sacrifice didn't take place."

"Doesn't the Bible ever mean what it says according to you?"

"Well, you might wonder what to make of all the first-born of Egypt having to die when it was God who made the Pharaoh ignore Moses telling him it was going to happen. Some readers could figure it was okay to kill someone else's firstborn to get what you want, do you suppose? I don't know what message they would bring away from the New Testament, Herod killing nearly all the children and then God sacrificing the one Herod missed, God's own son."

"What are you saying anyone could make of that?"

"It's the ultimate sacrifice of the firstborn, isn't it? Do you think that's what your father had in mind?"

"I can't tell, can I?" she said tightly and high. "He didn't leave any notes."

Of course he had, and her mind was trying to grasp what they implied when Timothy Turner said "For the film he was planning, you mean."

"That's what we've been talking about, isn't it?"

"Do you mind if I ask why it has such importance for you if it won't be made?"

Hilary shrieked with laughter as Daniella heard herself say "I want to hang onto everything I can about him."

"Excuse me. I understand." After a pause apparently meant to demonstrate he did he added "Was that all you need from me?"

"Where's all this stuff in your book? Which bit is it in?"

"The middle chapters. The rest of the book—"

She didn't hear what he went on to say, her hand with the receiver having sunk away from her face. She was remembering the copy on her father's shelf, the copy that someone had nearly killed her to prevent her or anybody else from reading—remembering how the Midas Books compliments slip had marked a place in the middle of the book. As she became aware that several of the patients in the lounge were watching a television show about a morgue, the offscreen laughter that identified it as a comedy seemed to lurch at her. When Timothy Turner's voice stopped and recommenced she found the energy to hoist the receiver. "Hello? Have you gone?" he was saying.

"Where?" Daniella hardly knew she said.

"I have to be off now to enlighten my students. I hope I've done the same for you."

Light seemed to have very little to do with the ideas he'd planted in her flimsy skull, especially when he said "Is it dark there yet?"

She might have imagined he was wishing this on her. By the time she understood that he meant it was morning in California he'd finished telling her "I won't say good-night in case. Just goodbye."

"Goodbye," Daniella mumbled. She felt as though the handset had gained a weight that dragged her grasp to the hook. She dropped the receiver on it and gazed at her blurred shadow pinned in the alcove by the lights. As a confused mass of thoughts began to bear upon her neck, Hilary tugged at her wrist. "Come and tell us all about it," she cried.

TWENTY-FIVE

D aniella turned to see the women scrutinising her with an eagerness that seemed to wrench at her thoughts. She had no idea what response might have escaped her if Alison hadn't wheezed "You didn't say your father was famous."

"Sit down and tell us what he was like," urged Cynth.

"I don't know any more."

Perhaps Hilary didn't mean to dig a finger into her wrist, but it felt like a sly schoolyard pinch. "How can't you know about your own dad?" she demanded, adding a laugh that contained less mirth than usual.

"I don't want to talk about him just now," Daniella came close to pleading.

Cynth scratched her scalp and then her forehead. "Hasn't he been gone long?"

"That's right," gasped Alison, and took a breath. "When was he on the news?"

"He died a couple of weeks ago," Daniella said, one of the few facts she was sure of.

Hilary's eyes filled to their brims as she produced an incomplete smile. "Don't say any more if it hurts," she advised, still not releasing Daniella from her clammy grasp. "Just sit quiet if you like. It'll be your turn soon."

"Turn for what?" Daniella blurted.

"To play, of course. You haven't forgotten you're playing."

Daniella restrained herself from jerking her wrist free, but she had to be alone to think. "I wouldn't mind going to bed," she tried saying.

Hilary's grasp tightened as her face searched for an expression, and then she gaped, tilting her face and her gaze up while keeping her chin level. "You should have said if you're tired out," she protested, letting go of Daniella. "You get those eyes shut and don't you open them till morning."

"We'll tell you how the game worked out," Alison promised.

"It won't be how you think," Cynth told Daniella or her fellow players, not without ominousness.

It struck Daniella that far too little was. She was heading for the corridor when a stocky crop-haired blonde whose breast pocket named her Doreen glanced up from a game of draughts with the oldest of the few men in the room. "Leaving us?" she said.

"She's off to the land of Nod," Hilary called.

"Ah," said voices all over the room, and the draughts opponent raised his eyes to Daniella, followed more effortfully by the rest of his blotchy bald head. "You get your sleep while you can," he advised her.

"He means while you're young enough to sleep through the night," a woman knitting with blunt needles said, and began to unpick her shapeless work as if talking had made her go wrong.

"Just wait there for me," the stocky nurse told Daniella, and hurried out of the room.

Daniella found there was nowhere she wanted to look,

especially when she would have had to manufacture an expression if she met anyone's gaze. She was aware of being watched by the tall woman almost entirely concealed within a black dress. The click of jerky needles was plucking at Daniella's nerves when Doreen reappeared, bearing a capsule and a gulp of water in a plastic cup. "Just take these for me before you leave us," she said.

The capsule was a duplicate of the one that had helped Daniella relax. Anything that would relieve the ache her thoughts were threatening to become was welcome. Beyond that she couldn't think for the moment, and she barely hesitated before swallowing the capsule. "Thanks," she hoped she was justified in saying as she pursued her thoughts out of the room.

She was on the stairs when it occurred to her that the land of Nod was Biblical, a parched place where Cain was supposed to have roamed after killing his brother. In the mirror at the bend she saw her head swell as if its load of half-formed thoughts was close to exploding. She hustled herself to her room to grab her toiletry bag and dodged into the bathroom diagonally opposite.

It smelled of invisible flowers and was white as marble except for a green carpet that reminded her of turf. In a large wall mirror opposite the pale trough of a bath she saw herself not knowing what to think or almost what to do. She finished as fast as she could, not least because there was no lock or bolt to keep anyone out, and retreated to her room, where she seized the chair and stood it against the door. A thought had grown clear as a light that was finding others in her skull. She'd identified one of the dates her father had written in the back of her schoolbook. Cer-

tainly the year, and on reflection the month, listed next to
Caresmith were those during which Norman Wells' child
had been murdered.

She remembered that December—she could feel its
chill. She remembered her mother telling her father how
dreadful it was about the little Wells girl, as though the
Wellses hadn't suffered enough with the collapse of Norman Wells' catering firm that had provided all the fare on
several Oxford films. At the time Daniella had thought her
father had changed the subject swiftly in order to protect
her ten-year-old self, but now she seemed to remember his
glance at her—a glance so uneasy she'd assumed her imagination had exaggerated it. Why had his last words been
that it was her day? What might he have planned to confide
to her that he'd needed to drink up so much courage? More
of what Timothy Turner had implied without knowing, she
thought—more and worse.

She had to be grateful for the medication that was in-
sulating her from most of her distress, or was it also preventing her from grasping all she should? Why had
Norman Wells killed Alan Stanley's child? Could it have
been meant as some proof of loyalty after he'd been caught
talking to Daniella? Might he have been tortured to death
because he hadn't proved enough? She wondered if she had
yet to understand the worst, and a surge of muffled panic
sent her to the window as if it might offer some comfort.

Beyond the lawn the poplars were enacting a stealthy
dance, executing movements that grew more secretive the
further they were from the lights trained on the gates. Miles
away a road was stringing a very few headlights. She felt
trapped by all the darkness, and had to tell herself she had
no reason to believe she was in danger: nobody could think

she was one since she'd been robbed of both the book and
the knife. Perhaps the shock and dismay she ought to be
experiencing would assail her once she'd slept, but then she
ought to be able to think what to do. She changed into her
nightdress and slipped between the unexpectedly chill
sheets under the bedspread.

While she felt relaxed to the point of stupor—indeed,
was unable not to—that stopped short of slumber, and
switching off the light didn't help. All the thoughts her
conversation with the writer had provoked began to scram-
ble over one another, and it became clear that until they'd
finished reiterating their antics she wouldn't be able to
think past them. They were nowhere near an end when
the hospital set about demonstrating how many toilets it
had to flush and how often, including several encores after
she'd been treated to as many performances as there had
been diners. When at last there was silence she found it
had quieted her thoughts, and before long she was unaware
of the silence.

A memory jarred her awake. Further down her schoolbook page than she'd had time to read before Mark had
interrupted her, hadn't she glimpsed "Mindsmith" and a
date? She'd been distracted by Eamonn Reith's arrival, and
while it would be paranoid to the point of insanity to think
that had been his intention, the secret name might very well
be his. She didn't want to consider the implications until
she moved the chair; she ought to have jammed it under
the doorknob rather than just pushing it against the door.
She set about raising her burdensome eyelids as she estab-
lished that to switch on the light she needed a hand to
emerge from under the bedclothes, where both hands had
retreated while she was asleep. Then her eyes sprang open

so wide that they stung. The chair was no longer against the door. Whoever was sitting in it had moved it to the foot of the bed.

Daniella's mouth gaped to release a cry that she barely managed to choke back. She clamped her lips between her teeth and almost succeeded in making no sound, but a snort of panic stung her nostrils. She tried to hold herself so motionless it set her trembling until she saw the intruder hadn't moved, or at any rate was no more agitated than the room itself, which was restless with faint shadows that the poplars must be casting. The seated figure was a woman— the tall woman who'd watched Daniella at dinner and in the lounge from the concealment of her long black dress. Her face looked slacker than ever, so loose that her dim jowls appeared to have merged with the front of her ankle-length white nightdress, where her chin was propped. Daniella flattened her hands on the mattress to inch herself up the bed. Neither of her arms was free when the mattress gave a creak that the bedclothes failed to muffle, and the woman's head reared up.

She might have been asleep, or almost. Her eyes blinked themselves wide as though she had to regain her sense of where she was. As they squinted at Daniella they seemed close to resenting her presence, and certainly to be finding recognition difficult. Daniella dragged an arm from beneath the sheet so awkwardly it revived the pain in her neck, and groped about the floor for the handbag that contained her attack alarm. Here was the bag, but it was the back of her hand that encountered it and knocked it out of reach—no, only nearly. She clutched at it and heaved it onto her chest and fumbled in it for the alarm. "What do you want?" she said, letting go of the bag with her other hand to find the light-switch.

"Daniella."

It might have been an answer or a rebuke to her for having switched the light on, although the woman seemed determined not to blink, unless she was unconscious of the need. Daniella had to narrow her own eyes at the light as she said "Right, that's me. You're in my room."

"I know."

The woman sounded proud of it and resentful of the suggestion that she mightn't be aware. "So what do you think you're doing?" Daniella enquired, closing a hand around the alarm.

"I wanted to talk to you," the woman said, and as if this completed her explanation "I'm Winnie."

"Why couldn't you before?"

"You were with them. This is just for us."

"If you need to tell me something," Daniella made herself say, "go ahead."

Winnie crouched forward, erecting her spread fingers on her knees, then seemed to have left her thoughts behind. She rocked back as if to retrieve them, and forward again, and said with some triumph "Dr Eamonn brought you."

Daniella withdrew her hand from the bag for fear her tension would set off the alarm. "You've got something to tell me about him?"

"I should think you'd know."

"Maybe I do, but say it anyway."

"You know how good he is."

"Suppose I do."

This was intended to persuade Winnie to complete her

observations about him, and it took quite a pause to demonstrate she already had. By then she had nodded vigorously several times, her cheeks growing pouchy and then
thinning at the end of each nod. All this allowed a question
to occur to Daniella, however little she wanted to ask it.
"Does he work here?"

"Of course he does. Not all the time," Winnie said,
impatient with the interruption to her thoughts. "Did he
say about me and knives?"

Daniella had to prise her lips open with her tongue.
"What about them?"

"I haven't got to hide it, he says," Winnie said, raising
her arms in a prophetic gesture that let her sleeves sag to
her knobbly wrinkled elbows. "I'm not bothered who
knows as long as you do."

Daniella swallowed hard, not only at the sight of the
thin arms, each crisscrossed with a dozen or more pinkish
scars left by cuts. "Why as long as I do?"

"Because you've got a thing about knives as well."

Daniella's words felt like sand in her mouth. "Who told
you that?"

Winnie only looked conspiratorial, and Daniella was
dismayed not to need to hear the answer. A desperate hope
to be proved at least partly wrong made her almost plead
"What kind of a hospital is this?"

"You've never forgotten that, have you? You must be
worse than me. The kind they put people like us." Winnie
tried on her conspiratorial grin again, but her mouth was
impatient to talk. "Shall I show you where some knives
are?"

Daniella had to know how immediate the danger was.
"Where?"

"Don't make any noise. Come on with me."

As Winnie lurched to her feet Daniella shoved a hand into her bag. "Tell me where."

"It needs us both."

"What does?"

Winnie looked bewildered, then laughed or at any rate let fly a sound she might have uttered in her sleep. "You can't get any by yourself," she said smugly. "I've got to be there to lift you up."

"Then there's no reason not to tell me, right?"

Winnie leaned forward and peered at her, apparently to be certain Daniella wasn't playing a trick. "I bet you've guessed where," she said at last. "They lock the kitchen when there isn't any staff, but I saw out of my window there's a window we can use."

"Right."

"Come on then. You oughtn't to have kept me talking all this time. It'll be light soon and then we'll be too late."

"Not now. I'm too tired now, I'd only make a noise. Wait till tomorrow."

"You can be careful and then you won't make any." Winnie frowned and produced a series of pouts that twisted her lips. "I'm only doing this for you, you know," she said with something rather fiercer than reproach, "because you keep looking for a knife."

"Thanks," Daniella made herself say so as to add "But not now, thanks."

"You're going to stay there and sleep, are you?"

"I'm going to try."

Winnie pouted harder. "Don't bother saying I was here or anything I said. I'm meant to be nearly cured but you've only just come, so they'll believe me, not you. They'll think it's you being mad."

Having delivered herself of all this, slowly and with increasing triumph, Winnie folded her bare scarred arms. Some time passed before she finished watching Daniella, who was beginning to grip the alarm when Winnie shuffled backwards to the door, her bare feet slithering over the carpet. As the door closed on the sight of her face, still watching Daniella as though it had forgotten how to stop, she unleashed a parting whisper. "It was for me really. You've had your turn. I cut people too."

TWENTY-SIX

D aniella didn't move until she heard a door shut along the corridor, and then she kicked the bedclothes off. A spasm of her entire body left her seated shaking on the edge of the bed. So Mindsmith hadn't tricked her into committing herself to the hospital merely in order to discredit her or keep her out of the way, but then what had been his plan? She was struggling to feel as much in danger as she knew she was, an inability that frightened her less than it should. Even grasping how the medication was affecting her failed to bring her feelings closer. If it prevented her from being overwhelmed by panic, surely she ought to welcome the effect. She pushed herself to her feet and did her best to make no sound as she tiptoed to the door.

She inched it open and made herself lean into the corridor, which was deserted. Winnie hadn't pretended to return to her room so as to catch her in the act of sneaking downstairs. Daniella switched off her light and crept the door shut, though the knob was almost too slippery to hold, and took her time about setting each foot down on the lukewarm prickly carpet as she headed for the stairs.

She couldn't simply flee the hospital. Even if she managed to open the front door and the gates without alerting anyone, she would never reach the town or the distant road before dawn. Whichever direction she took she might well encounter someone from the hospital on their way to work, and how determined would they be to return her to the Coppice? What might Eamonn Reith have told the staff about her? It wouldn't be long before some of them were about. She stole downstairs as swiftly as she could. Her face bobbed up towards her in the mirror that magnified her nervousness, and then she was past the bend and listening for sounds from below. There was none. She succeeded in taking a couple of breaths as she reached the foot of the stairs and ventured to the receptionist's window.

The office was unlit, but the light from the lobby showed her the desk with the switchboard on it. It looked unreal as a set with actors waiting offstage. She mustn't let herself think anything around her wasn't real—wasn't capable of betraying her. She used both hands to edge the door to the corridor out of its frame and sidled around it, hanging onto it as it subsided into place, urged by its metal elbow. She released it when she thought it had stopped moving. It still had an inch to travel. It halted with an exhalation and a soft thud.

She clenched her fists and stood where she was, legs pressed together so that they wouldn't shake, until she was convinced that none of the doors along the corridor was about to spring open—that the noise she'd made hadn't alerted anyone else in the hospital. The medication was deserting her just when she might have been gladdest of it, and every one of her paces towards the office door seemed excessively loud. Two of them were underlined by creaking floorboards. As she closed her clammy hands around the doorknob she willed the door not to prove to be locked. It swung open with a squeak no louder than her shivery breaths. She dodged around it and inched it shut to keep her noises in the office before she tiptoed to sit at the desk.

The light through the receptionist's window illuminated the switchboard, but it also made her feel on show. Anyone entering the lobby would see her at once. All she needed was an outside line and then she could dial for help. The board bristled with switches, the first of which was marked EXT for external. She grabbed the headset and draped the earphones over her ears and depressed the switch. The headset didn't respond, but a phone began to ring somewhere in the hospital.

She fumbled the switch off before the second pair of rings was finished. She snatched the headset free of her ears and sat with her eyes squeezed shut like a child who thought that would hide her, listening for any sign that the phone had wakened someone. It took her far longer than she would have liked before she was able to conclude it had not. She lowered the earphones into place as she opened her eyes to see that most of the extensions were EXT with numbers underneath. Only the last one was unmarked. Something like a prayer made the inside of her head ache as much as her neck while she poised a finger on the switch and flicked it down. In a moment she was listening to the most welcome sound she'd ever heard: the dialling tone.

She might have phoned her mother, but only the answering machine would be awake. Her finger trembled as she dialled the house in York. As the phone set about ringing, a sound that seemed too distant even though it was on both sides of her head, she crouched low as if that could render her invisible from the lobby window. Six rings, a dozen, eighteen . . . Of course nobody at the house would be up yet, but surely one of her friends had heard the phone by now and was trudging sleepily, not to mention resentfully, downstairs. Six more rings and they still weren't there, and she felt as if her medication had cut her off from the world. Then she heard a silence that suggested she had been cut off. She was about to force herself to speak when a voice blurred by sleepiness complained "Who is it?"

"Is that Chrys?"

"Just about. Danny? What's wrong with your watch if you've got one? It isn't even six o'clock."

"I know. I'm sorry, but—do you think I should be in a mental hospital?"

"If you're going to start phoning people at this time of night or day or whatever it is, maybe. Can you speak up a bit? I can hardly hear you."

"I'm trying not— Is this better?"

"Not much."

"You heard what I asked you, anyway, and I'm really serious. Do you think I should?"

"Be in a mental hospital? I shouldn't think so."

"Well, I am."

"You mean that's what the, what is it, the Coppice Hospital is?"

"Right, where Dr Reith brought me."

"I thought he was taking you to just a hospital."

"So did I. That's what he made us think because he knew I wouldn't have come if I'd known and maybe you and the others wouldn't have wanted me to."

"I don't like it that he tricked you. That wasn't fair. Danny? Are you still there?"

"Yes." It was mostly a hiss of a whisper, because footsteps were tramping overhead. They sounded well on the way to the office when she heard a door shut upstairs, bringing them to an end. "I can't talk much more," she

said, struggling not to let Chrysteen hear her panic. "I want
to come back home. I'm not committed or anything, but
you know I haven't got my car and there's nobody who can
drive me. Will you fetch?"

"When are you asking me to?"

"As soon as you possibly can."

"Today, you mean? There's things I'm supposed to be
doing, like finishing an essay for a start."

"Please, Chrys." Upstairs a toilet flushed, and the footsteps retraced their route. They were all Daniella could hear
except for herself saying "I'm scared."

"Oh, Danny, what of?"

"The people here. There's one I really don't like who's
after me."

"That sounds awful. It is." A pause let Daniella appreciate the awfulness before Chrysteen said "All right, I'll get
dressed and come and find you."

"Oh, thanks," Daniella said, surely not too loud.

"I'll be off in just a few minutes, so don't fret. Where
are you, in your room?"

"I'm going back there now," Daniella said, aware that
the question showed how little sense Chrysteen had of the
situation. "See you in a couple of hours," she said, and made
herself cut Chrysteen off.

She was taking far too much time over trying to leave
the headset exactly as she'd found it when she managed to
grasp that the receptionist wouldn't notice. She replaced it
more or less where it had been and hurried to the door.
The hinges kept their squeak to themselves, but the lobby
door was less discreet; it rubbed its snugness against the
frame while it opened and while it shut. She dashed on
tiptoe up the stairs and into her room, where she wedged

the chair under the doorknob. There was no point in trying to persuade herself that made her safe, however. All too soon she was going to have to pretend she wasn't waiting to escape.

TWENTY-SEVEN

D aniella was staring through the reinforced glass of her window in the hope that one of the cars on the distant road might already be Chrysteen's when a set of footsteps failed to pass her room. Knuckles tapped discreetly or stealthily on the door, then rapped more firmly before determining to knock. By this time the knob was being twisted, and once the perpetrator decided this was insufficiently effective it was rattled so that the door shook.

The kitchen must be open by now. Perhaps Winnie had managed to steal a knife and brought it to show her. Daniella was retreating from the window and about to lean her weight on the chair under the doorknob when she heard her name. There it was again, in the identical petulant almost accusing tone. "Are you there? Are you awake?" Hilary also said.

"Yes."

"Is that you in there, Daniella? Did you speak?"

"I said yes."

"That is you, isn't it? I can barely hear you. Are you coming for it, then?"

"What?" Daniella demanded—she was shocked by how loud.

"Breakfast," Hilary said in two halves rendered jagged

by laughter. "What else are you expecting this early in the day?"

The answer was Chrysteen, but that was only hope. Daniella grabbed her handbag and jerked the chair from under the doorknob. The door lurched towards her at the end of a muscular arm and showed her Hilary's untypically disapproving face. "We aren't supposed to do that," Hilary said, nodding hard at the chair.

"Why not?"

"We might be ill in the night and they wouldn't be able to get to us. Were you afraid of something?"

Daniella tried not to answer but heard herself say "All sorts of stuff."

"That's why you're here though, isn't it? I know they'll see to you and you won't be afraid any more."

Daniella had to restrain herself from jamming the chair under the knob again. As she followed Hilary along the corridor she murmured "I wish." An aroma of scrambled eggs rose upstairs to accompany the mechanical progress of doll-sized Daniella and her toy handbag in the mirror. It smelled like childhood—like lying ill in bed, surrounded by cloying warmth, and being brought soft food. It didn't help that Hilary said "You just keep wishing and it'll come true."

As Daniella stepped into the lobby the receptionist glanced across the switchboard—glanced, then gazed hard at her through the inner window. She felt her face stiffen, and was struggling to relax her mouth so that it would be able to deny whatever it would have to when the receptionist said "How was your first night with us, Daniella?"

She had only been taking time to remember the new patient's name. "I slept," Daniella admitted, however little benefit she was experiencing. At least the receptionist's answering smile proved she wasn't too observant, and Daniella tried to find some encouragement in that as the lobby door shut behind her with a sound rather too reminiscent of the thud of metal on her neck.

The women seated by the window greeted her arrival across the dining-room. "We didn't know if we should wake you if you were having such a good sleep," Cynth told her, and Alison called "Trust Hil not to let you miss anything you've paid for." Presumably that meant breakfast, served by the girls in green, one of whom was intervening in an argument at the table nearest the kitchen. As Daniella sat with her back to the window she saw Winnie being ousted by the woman who did little except knit. "That's yours," the knitter said for all to hear, and pointed straight at Daniella.

She was indicating the seat behind Hilary, Daniella told herself. Very little reassurance was to be gained from that as Winnie stared at her while tramping across the room. She folded her long body onto the chair and picked up her utensils only to let the fork drop and raise the blunt knife between her fingers, clenched together prayerfully in front of her empty plate. "Her and her old knives," Cynth scoffed.

"Looks like one herself," Alison wheezed, and expressed mirth by quivering.

Hilary sat up so as to present Winnie with more of her back. "She's just trying to make you like her."

Daniella didn't know which way to take that, nor which would be more dismaying. Her view was obscured by one of the kitchen staff, who moved away to reveal Winnie lifting a yellow chunk of egg on the flat of her knife into her loosely gleeful mouth. Daniella looked away so as not to be sick, but couldn't prevent Hilary from ladling a generous portion of glistening egg onto her plate. As soon as Daniella managed to swallow rather less than a forkful, Hilary cried "Eat up or you'll never be healthy."

"We wouldn't want that," Alison said, thrusting the toast rack at Daniella.

"Nobody would," said Cynth, snatching two slices out of the rack to plant them with belated delicacy on Daniella's plate.

Not eating might betray her uneasiness. She succeeded in dealing with the rest of her toast and enough of her egg to be able to say that she'd finished—she even produced a smile as she fended off another helping. "Now what shall we do?" Hilary said.

"I think," Daniella said as though it was only one possibility, "I'd like to go for a walk."

"She's just like us, isn't she? We always go for a morning plod when the weather lets us."

"We don't like it when it doesn't," Cynth said as if to the culprit.

"There were twenty-nine days last year when it didn't let us," said Alison, "and thirty-three the one before, I remember that because it's how many years they let Jesus live, and the one before that, what was it . . ."

Hilary laughed hard with impatience. "We'd have gone before breakfast but we were waiting for you, Daniella."

Daniella had hurried ahead of the women as far as the vestibule when the receptionist clattered her fingernails against the window. "Hold on, please."

Daniella told herself she wouldn't care if anyone was on the phone for her so long as it wasn't Chrysteen calling to say she couldn't pick her up, but she was hoping to be contradicted as she asked "Do you want me?"

"Don't go anywhere just yet."

The three women had moved in their various ways between Daniella and the front door. "Why not?" she said less evenly than she liked.

"Take this first."

A nurse had appeared beside the receptionist and was holding out a tray that bore another of the capsules along with a gulp-sized plastic tumbler of water. "I will," Daniella blurted almost before she thought to add "When my breakfast's gone down."

"No," the nurse said, "we need you to take it now."

Daniella picked up the capsule and placed it in her mouth. How many films had she seen in which someone only pretended to swallow a pill? The staff were watching her closely enough to suggest they'd seen some too. If she turned away she would be confronted by Hilary's insistence on the rules. She couldn't manoeuvre the capsule under her tongue unobserved, and she could think of no other ruse. If it helped her keep her fears to herself while she awaited Chrysteen, mightn't it even be desirable? She used the water to send it down and returned the tumbler to the tray. "That should keep you happy till you see Dr Julian," the receptionist said. "You haven't forgotten your appointment, have you?"

"I don't forget anything," Daniella said and immediately, with a sensation that felt like stepping into quicksand, was sure she had. "When is it? Not now."

"Not right away. Ten o'clock. You see, you can forget things."

Daniella was struggling to recall what she had as she

trailed Alison out of the hospital. The effort made her skull feel as hot as the sunlit grounds, though much darker. Surely Chrysteen would arrive before the doctor came looking for Daniella, even if no car was to be seen on the road outside the gates. Those were open, and she was trying not to head for them too fast when Hilary stumped in front of her and grinned at her neck. "Where do you think you're trotting off?"

Daniella's hand strayed towards her bag and the alarm. "Where should I?"

"Not out. We aren't allowed out unless they say we can have a pass."

Daniella told herself that wasn't going to include her, but perhaps she ought not to risk making for the road until she saw Chrysteen's car, particularly since a nurse had sat down with a patient on the bench closest to the gates. "Where, then?"

"Round and round the hospital," Alison said, wheezing at the prospect.

"Like a teddy bear," said Cynth, jerking her chin up as though to invite tickling.

Daniella remembered that game from her childhood— remembered her father intoning "Round and round the garden" while his fingers traced her palm before scuttling up her arm to play with her throat. Just now she hoped walking would help her forget it. Cynth overtook everyone else in a flurry of gravel before they reached a corner of the hospital, and forged ahead in an awkward extravagant loose-limbed jog, her long cream silk dress flapping, while Hilary plodded red-faced after her and Alison wheezed behind Daniella. A cloying smell of petrol from the parking area mixed with a taste of eggs in the air. Winnie was still

seated in the dining-room, her head rotating like a doll's so
that her fixed eyes could keep Daniella in sight. The pale
bulk of the hospital engulfed Winnie none too soon, but
also blocked Daniella's view of the road. She caught up with
Cynth as they rounded the third side of the building. There
was no sign of Chrysteen's amber Accord through the poplars. "Eh," Alison wheezed in protest, "you don't need to
race."

Hilary was next to speak. "There's one."

She was addressing Daniella, who thought for a panicky moment she had somehow betrayed she was waiting
for a car. Apparently Hilary was counting their rounds of
the hospital, since they had just passed the front door. Daniella didn't know if the day was growing hotter, but she
was, if not from the pace of the walk then from straining
to recall what the receptionist had made her aware of forgetting. The back of the hospital cut off the sight of the
road, and she was almost abreast of the dining-room window when she heard a car prowl up the drive.

Would it stop in front of the hospital, or might Chrysteen realise parking was at the back? Daniella slowed so
abruptly that Alison bumped into her, quivering. "I said
don't race," Alison protested, "not stop." In a moment the
car appeared around the corner of the hospital—a blue
Volvo driven by a man. Chrysteen was on her way, she
must be—except that instantly Daniella knew what she'd
been struggling to recall.

It was another name on her father's secret list. It could
mean a lawyer or a judge. But it had been Chrysteen's
father who had insisted Daniella came to the hospital, and
if he was Lawsmith— Had Chrysteen's voice on the phone
sounded unusually distant? Weren't phones supposed to

sound like that if they were tapped? Daniella was striving
to visualise whether Lawsmith had been followed by a date
as the man climbed out of the Volvo. "Good morning, Dr
Julian," the women said one after the other.

"It is." He pushed his oval golden spectacles higher on
his well-fed pinkish face to examine Daniella. "Is this my
new patient?"

"She's looking forward to her date with you," Hilary
took it upon herself to say, and the other women murmured
eagerly on Daniella's behalf.

"Ten minutes, then."

"I'll remember," Daniella told him, and urged herself
around the hospital. The stretch of road beyond the gates
was deserted, as were the scraps of it between the poplars.
"Are we sitting down soon?" Alison complained with a
wheeze after every word.

One bench facing the gates, though not the nearest to
them, was unoccupied. "Now, if you like," Daniella blurted.

"Don't let us down when you're the youngest," Hilary
said with several laughs. "Got to sweat out our brekky or
the things they put in it will make us worse."

Daniella wasn't sure if the food producers or the hospital were being accused of this. She would have headed
for the bench if she hadn't feared that Hilary would make
a fuss when Daniella was still hoping to have reason to be
unobtrusive. Alison panted after Cynth towards the side of
the hospital, and Daniella tried to appear to be glancing at
them once she passed them, not at the road. The thickened
smell of petrol caught at her throat and parched her mouth
as she hurried along the rear of the building. Winnie wasn't
in the dining-room.

That wasn't why Daniella stumbled. The door was

open on the corridor, and so was its twin, through which she could see fragments of road beyond the open windows of the lounge. Past a poplar, and then another, she glimpsed an amber car.

It flashed like a traffic light—like the colour of being unsure whether to go or stop. A third poplar extinguished the gleam so as to reveal it again, and Daniella realised the car was nearly at the gates. She didn't quite run, but walked to the corner of the hospital as fast as she could. Chrysteen was braking at the gates and about to drive between them.

Daniella nearly waved. Instead she thrust out her left hand at chest height and wagged it vigorously while she jabbed the other leftward to tell Chrysteen to wait for her outside the wall. Had Chrysteen understood? Apparently not, because the car cruised onto the gravel between the gates. Daniella was about to break into a sprint, a panicky attempt to outrun anyone who intervened, when the Accord continued its turn and passed out of sight behind the right-hand wall as though it had merely been using the gateway to reverse its direction. Just because Chrysteen had parked, that didn't have to mean she would stay outside the gates. Daniella had started for them, surely not so fast as to draw attention to herself, when Cynth said almost in her ear but loud enough to be heard by everyone in the grounds "Where are you off now?"

"Time out on the bench," Daniella said not much more quietly and kept moving, not looking back.

"Give Ali a hand over to it, then," Hilary said, no longer jovial, "since she can't take your pace."

She could have been addressing Cynth, Daniella told herself. She felt mean but too vulnerable to slow down. She was beyond the side of the hospital now and striding across the grass. There was no route to the gates that didn't lead her past a bench with a nurse on, but surely she appeared to be heading for the empty bench. She was within a few yards of the back view of a broad-shouldered thick-armed female nurse with a cap of glistening hair like brown moss growing black when the women, even wheezy Alison, shouted "Daniella."

It felt as though they'd seized her by her aching neck. The nurse rose into a crouch. "Hello there," she said, shoving her large face forward, stretching her lips wide in an expression that hadn't time to be a smile.

"Hello," Daniella responded, not slowing, telling herself she mustn't slow.

"Hello there," the nurse said more firmly, proving to be taller than Daniella as she took a step towards her. "Where do you want to go?"

"I told them," Daniella said in a wild attempt to distract attention from herself, and swung round to point at the women. They hadn't been trying to delay her by shouting, they had wanted to warn her. Winnie had emerged from the lounge and was stalking jerkily across the lawn, a carving knife upraised in her clasped hands and flashing a message with every step.

Daniella backed towards the gates. "She's got a knife," she cried.

"I see her." For a moment the nurse seemed prepared to leave it at that. "Just stay there," she told Daniella, and advanced on Winnie, arms stretched wide. "Drop it, Winnie," she said like an aunt to a young child. "You know you're not allowed anything sharp."

Her weighty glance had made sure Daniella knew she was also told to stay, but Daniella was racing for the gates.

"Look," Winnie wailed, a child robbed of a treat.

"Don't run off, Daniella," Hilary called. "She's being stopped."

Daniella could only pray that even if the nurse realised she was fleeing, she would be too occupied with Winnie to give chase—that all the nurses would. She heard her name called in a voice she didn't recognise as she dashed through the gates. Chrysteen's car was a hundred yards away, and she was climbing out of it. "Don't get out. I'm coming," Daniella said, doing her utmost to sound only breathless. "You can start the car. Here I am."

Chrysteen remained neither quite in nor out of the car. "What's wrong? What's the rush?"

"There's a woman with a knife."

Chrysteen gazed at her as Daniella reached the car. She looked anxious for her, but that wasn't the same as convinced. Daniella clutched at the handle of the passenger door and was wondering desperately what else to say that wouldn't make her sound more deranged when she heard a man shouting beyond the wall "Watch out for the knife."

Chrysteen heard it too, and her face grew dismayed, perhaps at having doubted. She took her seat as Daniella did, and yanked her belt across herself while starting the car so hastily it almost stalled. In a second they were speeding away, and in not many more the poplars in the driving mirror were the only signs of the hospital, though not before Daniella glimpsed someone at an upper window, too briefly to identify the watcher. "All right, Danny," Chrysteen said, and squeezed her hand. "You're safe."

TWENTY-EIGHT

Daniella was watching the poplars dwindle in the mirror when they halted, because the car had. She felt as if the fingers they resembled had seized the vehicle and her. "What are you doing?" she gasped.

"We've forgotten something."

"What have we? What now?"

"Didn't you bring a case?"

"It's my old one. I can live without it. Go on, Chrys, drive."

"But you had some clothes in it. You won't want to leave them."

Daniella slid her window down. The road was as hushed as the poplars, which could mean they were concealing the sound of pursuit setting out from the hospital. "They weren't much. They weren't my best or anything," she said fast. "All I know is I'm not going back there. You heard some of why. If you don't want to drive me, let me out and I'll walk."

"Of course I'm not letting you out." Chrysteen released the handbrake, and the Accord started to coast, too slowly for Daniella's nerves. "They'll have to send your clothes or bring them, won't they?" Chrysteen said.

The car picked up speed at the next bend. The spiky hedges in the mirror dragged the poplars down, leaving themselves only a blue sky to scratch. Out of their reach a sun that seemed harsher than a floodlight paced the car. The brow of every stretch of road revealed by a bend gleamed like a knife. Traffic flashed ahead, travelling south towards London or north towards York. "Which way am I supposed to go?" Chrysteen said.

"Back to the house."

"Ours in York? Aren't you worried he'll realise you'll go there?"

"Who?"

"Dr Reith, of course."

It wasn't of course or by any means only, Daniella thought, but said "I won't be worried if you and everyone are there."

"He'll have to admit what he did, you mean."

At first Daniella couldn't answer for knowing how little her friend thought that involved. Chrysteen was waiting for an answer, and Daniella managed to mutter "Some."

Chrysteen braked hard at the junction. The traffic opened a gap she didn't use, and Daniella was biting the inside of her lip so as not to urge haste when Chrysteen rushed the car through a larger gap, across the centre of the main road and into the northward lane. "Sorry," she said.

Daniella waited until the car matched the pace of the traffic. "So you believe me now."

"I mostly did."

"But now you know I was telling more of the truth than you thought. You can see I'm not mad."

"I never thought you were. None of us did."

"You thought I was ill and that was messing with my head, though, didn't you?"

"We may have."

"So long as you don't any more. I'm not saying I wasn't ill. Only do you think Dr Reith tried to upset me so I'd look as if I needed to go to hospital?"

"I'm not sure."

Perhaps Chrysteen was loath to say no, but Daniella couldn't insist on knowing—she was too conscious of how much worse she had in store for her friend. Eventually she made herself say "Chrys?"

"Anything."

"Has your dad got another name?"

Chrysteen made a surprised noise that seemed unsure whether it was a laugh. "What would he want another name for?"

"A middle name."

"My mother said once his middle name was methodical. Another time it was regimentation. He just likes to know where everything is and not have anybody touch his private stuff."

"What stuff?"

"Files he brings home from work. Sometimes he gets ideas about cases at night, so he likes to read over them in his room. He's ended up catching a few people that way, him and his staff."

"So hasn't he got a real middle name?"

"Why are you keeping on about that?"

"Because I only realised at my dad's funeral he had a name he never told me."

Chrysteen was silent while she overtook a yellow piece of farm machinery holding up teeth stained with earth, and then she said "No reason why he should, was there?"

"You think it's okay to keep secrets from your family."

"I wouldn't call that much of a secret. Anyway, didn't your mother know?"

"I suppose, but you're saying you don't know if your dad has one."

"Of course I do. I saw it when he had to fill in all the forms for my grant he's too rich for me to get and so he has to pay it all like your dad. It's Christopher."

Daniella saw the huge soiled teeth recede only very slowly in the mirror, and felt as if they or worse might be poised to descend on the car. "So that's where your name comes from."

"That's what he told me. Shows I'm a bit of him, he said."

"And you are of your mother."

"Funny, that's exactly how she told him off."

When Daniella spoke again it sounded like a plea. "Chrys?"

"I'm sorry," Chrysteen said and stroked her arm. "Am I reminding you of when you had both your parents?"

"Did yours ever have anyone before you?"

"I'm all they had and all they've got. Are you thinking it'd be easier for you if you had a sister or a brother? Remember you've always got me."

Not for much longer, Daniella thought sadly. She was going to lose her best friend. No, not her friend, just her friendship—she wouldn't expect to keep that once she told Chrysteen the worst. She could imagine not wanting to have any further contact with such a messenger. She mustn't let herself care about that, only about ensuring Chrysteen was safe, she thought as her friend said "Don't if you'd rather not, but do you feel like telling me what happened?"

"Somebody wanted me out of the way. Somebody wanted me dead."

"Daniella."

There was no mistaking her distress, but was it with believing Daniella or the reverse? "It's true," Daniella insisted. "It isn't just me who could tell you it is."

"All right if you say so, but it's behind you now, isn't it? I already said you're safe."

Their exchange had caused her to stray a little too close to the vehicle in front before regaining her distance. Daniella saw herself making her friend crash by trying to warn her. She couldn't quite keep silent, however. "I'm trying to believe you, Chrys," she said.

That seemed to leave them nothing to say to each other. When at last the car turned along the road into York she was no closer to knowing how to warn her friend. "Nearly home," Chrysteen said, which left Daniella's spirits where they were.

The fields began to edge themselves with houses and then covered themselves with streets. As familiar places streamed past the car she found herself missing them as if she had already gone to ground. When the car veered into her street she glanced nervously about, but none of the parked cars was expensive enough to be ominous. Two young mothers smoking in the park had it and their frenzied children to themselves. The Accord nosed into a space behind her car, and she was hurrying to the gates when she saw the path had been cleared. "Duncan did that for you to come home to," Chrysteen said.

Daniella felt as if she was being treated like a convalescent, and found she'd quite liked the unselfconscious sprawl of colours on the path. She couldn't help treading

gingerly on the raw pale patches of old concrete like a child
at a stepping game. She unlocked the front door, which at
least nobody had repainted, and had to dab away a tear at
the sight of the hall. Duncan's bicycle had gone, presumably
to his room, and the party hat had been replaced by a plain
yellow Chinese paper globe. Brighter than its dusty pre-
decessor though this was, it had nothing in the way of
memories to offer. When she called "Who's here?" her voice
let her down by wavering.

"We are," Maeve said, stepping out of the kitchen to
frown at Daniella.

Duncan sidled past Maeve and threw her a sharp
glance. "What did someone try to do to you?" he asked
Daniella, losing force after the first word.

"Chrys can tell you. She was there."

"The doctor wanted us to think it was just an ordinary
hospital," Chrysteen said, "and then someone went after
Danny with a knife."

"Why?" Duncan demanded.

"Because they were mad."

"You're saying your dad's friend took you to a mental
hospital and didn't tell anyone," Maeve said slowly enough
to be encouraging Daniella to correct her at any point, "and
they let one of the other, one of the patients tried to what?"

"I'm saying it. I was there," Chrysteen intervened. "I
expect they went for Daniella because she was new."

"Something like that," Daniella found she said.

"So I rescued her and I'm glad I did. You wouldn't like
to think she was somewhere they didn't keep dangerous
people away from her, would you, Maeve?"

"Nobody would want that," Maeve said with some
pique.

"Then we'll need to agree what we're going to do when they come looking for her."

Maeve frowned at Daniella. "Did they find out what was wrong with you while you were there?"

"Lay off her a bit," Duncan objected. "Chrys just told you—"

"Don't you want to know if Daniella's well?"

"It's okay, Duncan, I can look after myself." Daniella knew she was hearing the continuation of an argument that had started while she was away. "Whatever it was, I'm over it now. Just tension, and no wonder, right? I'd have driven back and not bothered Chrys if I'd had my car."

She sensed that Maeve was holding disagreement in, and perhaps not only Maeve. "I don't mind that you called," Chrysteen said. "I'm glad you did."

"So am I," Daniella said, and the phone rang at her back.

She felt as though the sound was drilling through her neck. Nobody moved or spoke until the phone had shrilled twice, and then Duncan strode to it with some defiance— of whom, Daniella wasn't sure. "What shall I say?" he said, closing his hand over the receiver.

"You could say you haven't heard from me. That isn't really lying."

"I don't mind lying if it helps you."

Maeve expelled a long loud discontented breath. "I hope you never lie to me."

"I hope I never have to," he said, and lifted the receiver. As he listened his face grew blank. "Who's asking?"

He was gazing at Daniella as if practicing not to see her. After a pause during which his lips crept open he said "She isn't here."

Maeve stalked into the kitchen, only to emerge in time to hear him say "We don't know where Daniella is, do we?"

Chrysteen shook her head. Maeve kept hers still and stared at him, which might have made him a little too swift in answering the caller. "She didn't go in her car, did she? So maybe she's walking. You'd be best looking for her round by where you are if you ask me. Do us a favour and let us know when you find her," he said, and shouted the end of a goodbye as the receiver found the hook.

Maeve folded her arms, levelling her breasts at him. "I'd like to know why you're so pleased with yourself."

"He's given me a bit of time. Thanks, Duncan," Daniella said, partly to control her voice. "Who was it?"

"He didn't say, just he was calling for the hospital. Maybe you ought to have listened in. He sounded a wee bit familiar."

"That's how you were with him," Maeve said, "and I don't know how you think it'll help."

"Never mind," Daniella said. "You'll have been telling him the truth. Just a few minutes and I won't be here."

"Where will you be?"

"You'll excuse me if I don't say, Maeve. I don't want people arguing about whether they should tell anyone."

"I expect we'll argue about something else," Duncan said.

"So long as you don't about me."

Maeve refrained from speaking, but not for long. "We already have."

"Try not to, okay? I'd hate to think I was responsible for any of my friends splitting up. If anything made me ill again that would, even thinking it could happen."

She felt as if the undertaking she sought to extract was

the preamble to a last farewell. "It won't, will it?" Maeve said.

"It hasn't yet," Duncan said, and took her hand.

Daniella was conscious that there was no hand for her to take. She hurried upstairs to retrieve her old exercise book and stuff it into her handbag. She stood on tiptoe to drag down from the top of the wardrobe another of the suitcases that had travelled full of clothes to York, and was throwing in a hasty selection when Chrysteen put her head around the door. "You can come in," Daniella murmured.

Chrysteen shut the door and gazed at the suitcase. "You can ask," Daniella said.

"Do you know where you're going?"

"Oxford."

"Will you be all right to drive?"

"I'll have to be, won't I?"

"Would you like me to drive you in case you aren't? I've been meaning to go home for a weekend."

"I'll need my own transport, Chrys. I may not be staying there long."

"Then shall I ride with you? I can always get the train back here."

Daniella had a fleeting impression that life had begun to organise itself in her favour. "I'd like you with me," she said, and zipped the case shut. "Chrys is coming with me," she called on her way downstairs, and saw relief on the faces that came to the front door to watch her departure. She only wished, having slung her case into the boot and locked herself and Chrysteen in the car, that she could share the relief. It wasn't just that her sense of being prey roused itself before she had even started the car. It was the knowledge that she had scarcely begun to tell her friend the truth.

TWENTY-NINE

Once the motorway swung westward from the road that veered east to the Haresborough junction Daniella told herself she could forget the hospital. It was at least half an hour's drive further south, by which point the routes would have splayed apart like a wishbone twenty miles wide, about to snap with a wish. If that took away one threat, her present situation was another. When the mirror showed her a police car hurtling in pursuit along the third lane of the motorway, all its lights throbbing like a migraine set off by its siren, she had to restrain herself from crouching low over the wheel. She couldn't hide her registration number, though she kept wishing she could even after the police car winked out over the brow of the motorway. As soon as a procession of lorries let her glimpse a sign for a service area she sought refuge in the inner lane, between a pair of trucks almost huge enough to mask the car. "Are you all right?" Chrysteen said as it followed the first truck onto the slip road.

"I will be," Daniella said, only to feel she might have been too eager. The truck swerved into the parking area reserved for giants, and the gasp of its brakes seemed to greet the sight it had exposed: the police car in front of the clump of fast-food restaurants that surrounded all the telephones. She had to believe the police hadn't yet been told to watch out nationwide for her, otherwise she would find herself fleeing without a plan or a destination. The first parking space she was able to locate was no more than half a dozen heavy-booted strides from the police car. She had to reassure herself that was empty of police as she maintained control of the wheel and the pedals and her body and her mind. "I'll come too," Chrysteen said as the handbrake rasped.

She must think they had stopped for the Women that would have been called the Ladies when they were as young as the child at a table by the window of a Burger King, his chin and throat red with a trickle of ketchup until his mother wiped it off. As Daniella straightened up from the car, two policemen emerged from the lobby between the restaurants. Her face had just risen into view when the right-hand policeman waved to someone behind her. She twisted round to see another police car gathering speed along the exit road—she turned back in time to watch the vehicle outside the restaurants race after it, lights flashing. "I wonder who's unlucky," Chrysteen said.

"Not me," Daniella murmured, and tried to believe it. She let Chrysteen precede her into the tiled lobby that was jangling with fruit machines and exploding with video games, all of which rendered the piped music more than usually irrelevant. "Don't wait for me," she said, halting by the phones.

"Who are you calling?"

"Tell you later."

Chrysteen lingered over disappearing into the toilets. She was only on her way when Daniella snatched the address book out of her bag. The card Nana Babouris had given her at the funeral was in the book under B. She had to slide her credit card twice along the slot before the phone would acknowledge it. She dialled and heard an introverted whisper of static that put her in mind of all the sea between her and Greece. The ketchup-lipped child she had seen at the window ran into the lobby, chased by a girl with an even redder mouth and a mother bent on erasing the traces with a paper napkin. As the chase spilled into the car park the waves of static sank, beaching Nana's voice. It sounded much as it did on the screen, except that it was speaking Greek until it came intimately close. "Hello?"

Daniella turned to the wall and the instruction plaque, the plastic covering of which reduced her image to a vague pale mask, before she risked identifying herself. "Hi. It's Daniella Logan."

"Daniella!" There was enough joy in that for the climax of any one of several of her films. "How are you?" Nana cried.

"I'm—" Sensing too much unseen activity at her back, Daniella turned to survey the passing faces, none of them familiar, none of them to be trusted on that account. "I'm a lot of different things right now," she said, cupping her hands around the mouthpiece.

"Better than being just one, would you say, or not?"

"I don't know," Daniella said, and protested "I haven't got long."

"A little longer, I certainly hope. Why am I hearing from you?"

Daniella did her best to trap more of her voice in the receiver. "You know what you said at my dad's funeral."

"That I owed my career to him? That's as true as ever."

"No, if I needed to get away . . ."

"You could be sure of a Greek welcome? Nothing truer in the world."

"Would it be okay if that was soon?"

"The sooner the more perfect. Fly over now if you need to, like the angel you are," Nana said, and aimed some Greek at whoever was with her.

All at once Daniella felt spied upon and hardly able to speak for it. "Nana?"

"Child."

"Do you always answer the phone in English?"

"To stay international, do you mean? I'm not all European yet or American either. My roots are here. There's quite a lot of old Greek in me still."

"So how did you know to say hello to me?"

"Because the display showed it was a call from England. You're at a public phone, aren't you?"

"You mean," Daniella had to say, "it shows that too?"

"I expect I may have one soon that does, but I was saying what I could hear. Isn't there some kind of game going on around you?"

"Pinballs and video games."

"Are you in a pub? Cheers if you are, or shall I say to absent friends? I'm taking it you won't be there much longer."

"Why do you say that?" Daniella asked, nervous again.

"I thought you'd be on your way here. When will that be?"

"As soon as I can get a ticket, if that's all right."

"Far better than. You'll be flying into Athens. I'll make sure you're met if you let me know when."

"I will. Thanks, Nana. Really, thanks," Daniella said,

and had to make herself let go of the lifeline the phone and its cord seemed to have become. The uproar of the lobby flooded back into her consciousness, and she felt as if it was helping the medication slow her down as she hurried in search of Chrysteen.

Beyond the door sporting a red silhouette with a round blank head and a triangle above its parted legs was a long room no less whitely tiled than the lobby. Four of the eight cubicles displayed Engaged signs like miniature down-turned crimson mouths. Chrysteen was shoving at a metal nozzle above a sink to persuade it to exude a handful of snotty soap. Seized by a need that felt like panic, Daniella dodged into the nearest empty cubicle. Eventually her stream dwindled to a desert trickle, and she dabbed at her-self and zipped up her jeans. "Did you speak to whoever you wanted?" Chrysteen said over the lungless exhalation of a hand dryer.

"Yes," Daniella said and hurried to the car.

She locked the doors as soon as she and Chrysteen were inside. The face that reared up at her back as she pinned herself down with her safety belt was a child's, not on the back seat but at the rear window of the car behind hers. The Ford put on speed as it reached the motorway, then almost froze like a rabbit snared by headlamps when a vast oncoming truck flashed its headlamps at her to accelerate. Driving was enough of a strain on her nerves without the task of robbing Chrysteen of her innocence, but she had at least to prepare the way. "Chrys, can you reach my bag?" she said.

Chrysteen craned around and fished it off the back seat. "What do you need?"

"There's something in it I want you to see. My old school exercise book."

Chrysteen gave a small laugh of surprise and, Daniella was dismayed to hear, relief. "What am I looking for?"

"You'll know it when you see it," Daniella said, by no means certain that was true or even if she hoped it was.

The rustling of pages put her in mind of a mouse in a nest of paper—a pet that must think it was safe. "What we did on our holidays," Chrysteen mused aloud, "how many years did we have to write about that? The last time I made it up. Said I'd been to America. Got all the details out of some of your dad's films."

"Why did you want to do that?"

"Because old Miss Packet And A Half said I'd made up a story when I hadn't. She didn't even apologise when my dad told her I hadn't. Don't you remember?"

Daniella remembered Miss Paget's lined unenthusiastic face, the lay teacher's grey hair and greyer cardigan that always smelled of thirty cigarettes a day. "I don't believe I do," she said.

"I never thought she cared what really happened, to me or any of us. Half the time I don't think she even listened once she'd asked a question. Too busy waiting for the next smoke."

"What would you have wanted her to know?"

"Nothing bad. There never was anything bad."

"What did she say you'd made up, I mean?"

"The time we were riding in the back when my dad chased that man. She said he wouldn't have put us in danger, and she wouldn't accept we hadn't been in any because he'd been taught how to drive that fast. And she didn't want to hear the man was a child molester who'd escaped from court. You tried to say but she told you to sit down."

"Shows people ought to listen to me."

"I have, Danny. I have more than anyone. Really I was angry with her for making me feel I hadn't been safe. Do you know what she made me dream? That he wanted to kill me so it would look like an accident. I never forgave her for that."

Daniella's response got no farther than pressing against the backs of her eyes and the inside of her mouth while her friend leafed through the book. As a truck with a bright red cab and a steep-roofed bungalow on its back grew in the mirror, Chrysteen came to the list of secret names and peered at them. "Is this your dad? It looks like all the cheques he sent you."

Daniella returned the car to the least fraught lane and made her cramped fingers relax. "It was him."

"What's it all meant to be?"

"What does it look like to you?"

Chrysteen took a breath that emerged as a sigh before she admitted "A lodge."

"Masons don't use names like that."

"Something like a lodge, anyway," Chrysteen said with even more reluctance. "Some kind of society where only the members know who's in it."

"Unless you can work out who they are."

Chrysteen ducked her head towards the page as if seized by a realisation. "Do you suppose he wrote Film-smith twice because that was him?"

"Him and his partner. They're two I'm sure of."

"Jokesmith might be Larry Larabee, and Newssmith could be Bill Trask. Mindsmith, is that Eamonn Reith, do you . . ." She was silent for some moments, and when her voice revived it was lower. "Who do you think Lawsmith is?" she said.

Daniella had already glimpsed the absence of a date beside the name. She saw the cab of the truck fill her mirror with crimson. "What's your guess?" she countered, and felt she was the worst coward she knew.

"You're going to say it's my dad."

"It might be."

Chrysteen sat up straighter as if to brace herself for the next answer. "Do you think he's got one of those knives?"

The truck swerved into the middle lane and roared alongside. The front door of the bungalow twitched between blank windows as if it was about to fly open and launch an occupant of the house at the car. The truck thundered onward, trailing its oily exhaust, and Daniella pretended it had been the reason why she had delayed answering. "Are you saying you believe in them now?"

"I never really didn't, not completely, not when it was you saying it. So that's why Dr Reith tried to make me doubt you." Perhaps it was unwillingness to consider the implications that made her say with some haste "They'll be like aprons, won't they?"

Daniella saw herself surrounded by men wearing butchers' aprons stained with blood wiped off their knives. "What do you mean?"

"Masons wear aprons, don't they, when they do their stuff. This lot must have knives instead to show they're; it looks as if they call themselves smiths. They'll hold them up like you saw them doing. Can you imagine my dad and yours carrying on like that? What a sight." She was close to laughter, however uneasy or defensive it might have proved to be, but it subsided as she blinked at Daniella. "I expect we'd have liked to see it, though," she said.

She must think Daniella was subdued because she'd been reminded of having lost her father. Daniella could only follow the truck, which vanished over the crest of the motorway before Chrysteen said "What do you think these dates are?"

"That's what I have to be certain of, Chrys."

Chrysteen turned the page and held the schoolbook closer to her face. "What's he written here?"

Daniella had been sure the reverse of the page was blank. When she glanced at the book she saw Chrysteen peering at the back cover. "I can only just read it," Chrysteen complained. "It's red like what it's written on."

"Can you read it to me?"

"I'll try." Chrysteen was silent for so long that Daniella was beginning to fear the words were indecipherable when her friend said "It must be about how he got involved."

"Go on then," Daniella said urgently.

"It starts 'A. introduced. Said since was enjoying benefits should commit too.' Could A. be Alan Stanley, do you think?"

"That—" Daniella couldn't find a word sufficiently harsh to convey her dislike. "Yes," she said.

"There's more about him. 'A. suspected uncle had secret. Never talked about how prospered in Depression. A. kept investigating till found evidence. Nothing escapes A.' Is that true?"

"Yes." Daniella practically spat the word.

Chrysteen blinked at Daniella's vehemence before she continued reading. "I don't know if that's the end of him. Next it says 'Wasn't married then.' Why should that matter?"

Daniella knew her father had meant himself, and she had to struggle through an inflamed tangle of emotions to say "Is that all?"

"Not yet," Chrysteen said, slanting the book towards the sun to catch glints on the ink. " 'Some have more to ease pact. Should have,' and there's a question mark."

He'd been wondering if siblings might have made up for Daniella. " 'Victorians revived,' " Chrysteen read. "Victorians are underlined. 'Some never called on to keep pact.' What's wrong?"

What was nearly unbearable was Daniella's sense that her father had tried to justify his promise in every way he could, presumably even to believing its Victorianism rendered it somehow more acceptable. As she clenched her fists on the wheel to keep it steady she couldn't tell how much of her was aching; she only knew the medication had begun to ebb, leaving her mind raw. "I don't want to say," she blurted, "not till I can prove it to you."

Chrysteen closed the book and let her be silent even when they left the motorway and swung southwest towards Oxford. Half an hour's worth of fields and villages, some with new streets crystallising irregularly around them, brought her to Chiltern Road. A silver hearse followed by two limousines twice its length was entering the churchyard. Even if the girls who had seen her find the knife hung around the churchyard in the daytime, no doubt the funeral would have driven them away. In any case she had enough to do before anyone tracked her down.

The thought made her accelerate, only to have to brake at every bend. As the house poked its chimneys above the hedges she told herself she would be there no longer than it took to fetch her passport. She was almost at the gates when she trod on the brake so hard it jerked her neck. She heard the wheels release a screech too reminiscent of a cry of panic as Chrysteen said quite unnecessarily "Someone's at your house."

THIRTY

For a moment Daniella thought the police had raced her to the house. The two cars parked outside were white enough for theirs—white as a pair of teeth just cleaned in technicolour. They bore no insignia, however, and their roofs were bare of lights. She was hesitating over which pedal to tread on when the front door opened, revealing three people. The foremost, a youngish man with a round face several shades of pink and a bush of red hair an inch wider than his head, shaded his eyes as a preamble to waving to her. She had never seen him before, and his calling "Miss Logan?" with some unsureness didn't help. Nevertheless she seemed to have no option but to steer into the drive.

He left the front door open and stayed by it as she and Chrysteen unbent from the car. "Key?" he said.

As she grasped that was an offer she realised who he was. "I've got mine," she told him.

"Capital," he said with more enthusiasm than she thought the information warranted, then flattened his hand above his eyes again to scrutinise her. "I ought to be asking how you are."

"Better than last time you saw me."

"I should very much hope so. I was just telling Mr and

Mrs Purslow about how I found you after the, the incident with the safe. Manners," he said.

By the time she understood the rebuke had been aimed at himself he was introducing the couple, a determinedly bald middle-aged man who squared his shoulders as he delivered a handshake, and his child bride or at least a woman devoted to looking like one with pigtails and a short thin dress on her short thin self. "Mr and Mrs Purslow, Miss Logan," the estate agent said, "and you are..."

"She's my friend," Daniella intervened, perhaps more hastily than made sense.

"Mr and Mrs Purslow are planning on a family."

"What did you think of my house?" she had to ask them.

"A bit cold," Mrs Purslow said with a reminiscent shiver.

"Needs kids in it," her husband seemed to be agreeing.

Daniella might have pointed out it had once had her, but the words died in her dry mouth. She had found no substitute for them when Mrs Purslow said "We'll have a conference and let you know. You'll be here, will you?"

"I'm going in right now."

"Is your friend staying with you?"

"We'll be together if it's anything to do with me," Daniella said, and even more awkwardly "Why?"

"Just in case you need someone."

"All of us do," Mr Purslow said, caressing his wife's bare neck.

The estate agent lingered by his car until the Purslows departed with a sporty spurt of gravel. As he drove away he made a circle of one finger and thumb and curved three fingers over them, a sign that reminded her too much of the shape an adult might have used to cast the silhouette of a rabbit to amuse a child. Once she'd heard his car brushed away by a wind in the hedges she said "Wait outside if you like. I'll only be a minute."

"Aren't we staying here, then?" Chrysteen said.

"Not after I told them we were."

"They're just people, Danny. You can't suspect everyone."

"I can't risk staying anywhere someone knows I am." When Chrysteen opened her mouth Daniella interrupted "Except for you. We mustn't waste time arguing, okay?"

"Up to you. Is there something you don't want me to know either?"

"No, Chrys. There can't be."

"Then I'll come in with you," Chrysteen said with some bravado.

Though the front door had been left open the house persisted in smelling deserted, smells of dust lying low in the carpets, of furniture where only sunlight had sat for weeks. Perhaps there were spiders in the darkest corners, weaving their traps for blood. Daniella hurried into the study, to the safe. She had to keep trying to swallow as she typed the digits of the birthday she had no idea how she would celebrate. They released the lock, and she was starting to haul the door open when Chrysteen came to help. The door swung wide. The safe was empty of anything but darkness, a darkness that wouldn't have been misplaced in a grave. Then Chrysteen and her shadow stepped back, and Daniella saw the passport lying face down at the back of the safe.

She opened the passport at the photograph of herself, which was less than a year younger but which looked to her now as innocent as Chrysteen, for reassurance that it was hers. She shouldered the metal door closed, not caring if her neck ached, and slid the passport as deep in her bag as it would hide. "Are you thinking of using that soon?" Chrysteen said.

"I may have to. Where's yours?"

"Still at my house. You're thinking I shouldn't have given in to my dad."

"Something like that."

"We couldn't have afforded to go abroad last summer, though, could we? He was right about that. I know our parents spent more on that party for us than they'd have needed to give us for the holiday, but it was their money, after all."

At the time Daniella had thought the party at her father's house had been intended as a consolation, but now it struck her as a way of ensuring she and Chrysteen stayed at home. Too many of the guests had been men listed in her schoolbook. "Never mind," Chrysteen said, "we'll go away somewhere soon, won't we?"

"I hope so, Chrys. I really hope we will."

"Let's promise, shall we?"

"Let's," Daniella said and took her hand, only to find she didn't want to let go. For as long as she held it she was close to being able to believe that could be a substitute for saving her friend with the truth. She made herself relinquish it and hurried from the room, mumbling "I've got to pack."

Her battered old suitcase patched with names of English holiday resorts was nesting on top of her wardrobe. As she pulled it down it bestowed a sprinkling of dust on her. She threw in clothes, by no means enough to fill it—

T-shirts printed with outmoded legends, skirts uncertain if their length was presently acceptable, a couple of sweaters sufficiently thick for the dying of the year, some faded underwear—while Chrysteen watched. Daniella snapped the pockmarked locks, having tugged the rusty key out of its socket, and was hefting the case, which felt hollow as a promise, when Chrysteen said "Are you going away now?"

"I have to make some phone calls first, but I don't want to do it from here."

"Phone from my house."

"Won't anyone be there?"

"My mother doesn't get home from the bank usually till at least six, and my dad hardly ever comes home during the day."

"Could you make sure?"

"I suppose I better had," Chrysteen said almost more agreeably than Daniella could bear.

In the study Chrysteen listened for significantly fewer seconds than Daniella would have before hanging up. "Told you, nobody."

"Do you think you might be able to find out where your dad is going to be?"

"Danny, come on. He isn't hiding somewhere waiting to jump out at us." When Daniella let a plea surface in her eyes Chrysteen sighed and dialled another number. "It's Chrysteen Hastings," she said as though apologising for it. "Is my dad there?"

Daniella was instantly afraid that he might be—that Chrysteen would fail to manufacture a convincing reason for the call. Even when Chrysteen said only "Thanks" that wasn't reassuring until she put the phone down. "He's gone to London," she said. "May not even be back tonight."

"Okay," Daniella said, though it felt more like a prayer.

Half a mile into Oxford the hedges alongside the lane fell away, and she saw the skyline of the city bristling with spires yellow as a desert and shaped like tapering saw-toothed blades. She wasn't sorry when that image was blotted out by the roofs of a suburb. "You can park in the drive," Chrysteen said.

She seemed less than happy when Daniella left the car several buildings distant and walked back. The suburb was offering up noises to the sun: the ruminations of lawnmowers, the shouts and shrieks of a school at play. Nobody appeared to be watching as Chrysteen unlocked the house, one of a white pair as broad as a small church, and switched off the alarm by typing a six-digit formula that reminded Daniella of the dates in her exercise book. The capacious hall smelled not unlike a bathroom, and boasted a wide staircase leading up to a window veiled with white lace and framed by wallpaper that barely admitted to a pattern. Chrysteen hurried past a wooden stand in which two petrified snakes of sticks balanced on their tails above a quartet of walking boots, and slapped the kitchen door with both hands to open it. "Ow," she said. "Here's our phone."

Daniella followed her into the long bright metallic spotless room—followed a step and faltered. The phone had a cord and was mounted on the wall in full view of the curtainless window, beyond which, over a low fence, a furry-backed man in shorts was trotting after a mower with its snout buried in unkempt grass. He would turn and see her in no more than a few seconds. "Isn't there another one?" she wished.

"Only in my dad's room."

"Can I use that if it's more out of sight?"

Chrysteen looked close to refusing until she saw Daniella take cover in the hall. "You won't touch anything else, will you?" she said.

"What else do you think there'd be I'd want to touch?"

She retreated in the hope that would bring her friend out of the kitchen, which it eventually did. Chrysteen reached for the nearest doorknob not much less timidly than a child venturing to handle a forbidden object, and let go of it as soon as the door began to swing inwards. Daniella pushed it wide. The room was smaller and barer than she was expecting. The walls were even more secretively patterned than the hall, and there was nothing on them that could hide a safe, unless it was behind the shelves laden with law books, fat leathery volumes whose spines were identical except for numbers. They massed opposite a heavy squat oak desk attended by a leather armchair reminiscent of a gentlemen's club. The desk bore a telephone in the form of a white slab, an address book brandishing the alphabet on yellow plastic tabs, a computer slumbering in the light from a window that displayed the side of the next house. Daniella sat in the chair, which drew attention to her with a protracted creak, and removed her schoolbook from the bag she had dropped like a challenge on the desk. She was turning to her father's list when Chrysteen, who had ventured only just into the room, murmured "Danny?"

Daniella used a fingernail to prise the receiver out of the slab. "Chrys."

"I don't understand something. If they're like masons, why didn't they help your dad when he was in trouble?"

"We're going to find out. They're the calls I have to make."

"I thought you needed to get away. What are you planning to do when you've found out?"

"Shall we decide that together?" Daniella suggested, feeling far too deceitful. "There's one way I can save some time. Let's see if any of these are in your dad's address book."

Chrysteen lurched towards the desk and raised her hands as though to grab the book or plead for it or fend it off. "Like who?"

"Who do you think Talksmith has to be?"

"It could be what's his name who does the evening show on Metropolitan," Chrysteen said reluctantly, "who is he, I hardly ever watch it, Reginald Gray."

"Here he is. There's even his direct line. Chrys, you aren't going to like what I do, but don't stop me till you've heard what happens, okay?"

"Happens to who?"

"Happens on the phone," Daniella said. She laid the receiver, which put her in mind of a flattened white slug, on its back and poked the squares cut out of its underside. When the number she'd summoned began to ring she lifted the receiver and motioned Chrysteen closer. Her friend had leaned across the desk when a light young male voice announced "Reginald Gray's office."

"I'm calling on behalf of Care For Children," Daniella said, and saw Chrysteen's eyes and mouth start to open wide. She put her free hand over Chrysteen's lips and felt them shift against her palm. "He's supported our work in the past," she said.

"I believe so, but he isn't here just now. I'm his assistant."

"That's all right," Daniella said, thinking it was at least

that welcome. "Have you been at Metropolitan long?"

"Seven years, but not all with Reg."

"I expect you'll be able to give me what I need," Daniella said, and turned the receiver to be certain Chrysteen heard him. "I'm just updating our database."

"I'll help if I can."

"I know you'll find this question less upsetting than he would. He and his wife lost their first child, didn't they?" she said, and felt Chrysteen's mouth work like her own unease made flesh.

"Their only child."

"Only, right, that's what I meant. You wouldn't remember when they did, would you?"

"I shouldn't think anybody who was here then would forget. It was Valentine's Day."

"And just a few years back."

"Nineteen ninety-two. I know that because it was the year nobody sent me a card."

"I'm sorry," Daniella had to say as Chrysteen straightened up, freeing her mouth. She looked about to speak, but instead twisted the schoolbook around so as to glare at the list. Planting her hands on the desk, she jerked her head close to the phone as Daniella said "Can you remind me how they lost, I don't seem to have the name . . ."

"Felice."

"That's unusual. I wonder where they got it from."

"From Reg. He never uses his middle name, but it's Felix."

"I thought it might be," Daniella said, feeling not at all triumphant, wondering how much longer Chrysteen would be able to contain herself. "So you were saying Felice was . . ."

"The Grays were on holiday in Africa and one day while his wife was sick in bed Reg drove too close to the border with Felice. Ran into a terrorist ambush. They slashed the little girl to death. Afterwards the troops shot a whole village full of them, though I don't know if it was ever proved they were the ones. Reg still blames himself, of course, and his wife did and left him. In a way the worst part was his career was failing just then, but after the tragedy so many people knew about him and wanted to see him survive it, not only people here but the public, that he landed the job he's got now."

Daniella didn't know whether her gaze was trapped by Chrysteen's or the reverse—knew only that neither of them could look away, even when Chrysteen stepped back from the desk. "Am I telling you too much?" Reginald Gray's assistant said. "I'm not quite sure what you're after."

"We were wondering if he'd want to talk about his experience at one of our functions."

Chrysteen mimed shock and disbelief so violently that Daniella heard her friend's lips snap shut as the assistant said "I'm afraid I can't speak for him on that. He'll be here in a couple of hours."

"I won't be," Daniella only mouthed, and said "We'll track him down later, then. No need to trouble him about any of this till we contact him."

"I understand," the assistant surprised her by saying. She snapped the receiver into its slab and raised her eyes to Chrysteen, who was waiting to demand "What are you supposed to be doing?"

"What do you think, Chrys?"

"I'm asking you to tell me."

"Listen to another call with me first. Maybe then it'll be easier."

"Easier."

"For you," Daniella said, realising at once that she was talking about herself. "For you to believe," she tried saying as she observed that the next name followed by a date was Jokesmith. In the address book Larry Larabee's name was followed by two numbers, one of which she recognised as belonging to a mobile phone. She preferred not to speak to him—to any of the men behind the names. She dug out the phone and typed the other number. It had shrilled thrice when the comedian cried "Hello there" and giggled in her ear.

"Say who you are and what you want and when you did," he exhorted, by which time she'd grasped that he was on tape, "and while you're at it, why don't you leave me a laugh? Go on, give me a bit of a chuckle. Tell me something I'll want to share with the world. There can never be enough fun about."

His monologue was succeeded by a beep that almost provoked her into uttering the response that had swelled within her like a breath held too long. Instead she squashed the cut-off button with a fingertip, wishing she were doing so to part of him. The next identity she felt certain of was Booksmith's. She was even less anxious to speak to Mark's father than to the rest of them, but she was scanning so many esses in the address book they seemed to hiss in her brain when Chrysteen said "What are you trying to prove?"

"One won't be enough, will it, Chrys? One could be a coincidence. Just hear one more, and then . . ." She caught herself preferring not to think past that as she keyed the publisher's number and gazed at the computer screen, whose blankness was so monolithic it might have been exhibiting or prefiguring her non-existence. "Victor Shakespeare's phone," a woman's sharp brisk voice said.

"Is he there?"

"He is not. He's at lunch."

"That's fine," Daniella said rather too enthusiastically. "Are you his secretary?"

"I'm his assistant," the woman said, sharper than ever.

"That's what I meant, sorry. I expect you know he's helped us in the past."

"Helped whom?"

Chrysteen's stare weighed on Daniella, requiring of her an effort to lie that stiffened her neck. "Care For Children," she said.

"I think he may have mentioned it."

"Now that Norman Wells is gone we're checking whose support we still have."

"I imagine that may depend on the kind of support you're looking for."

"Maybe he could give a speech at one of our dinners soon," Daniella said and braced herself for more of Chrysteen's disapproval. "Or maybe not so soon, because doesn't he have a sad anniversary coming up? I shouldn't think he'll want to talk about that."

"What makes you say so?"

"Doesn't it upset him to remember?"

"Of course it must."

"Then I expect he'd want to keep it to himself."

"Surely it's a question of what you would be asking him to say."

"I don't know. I wouldn't be responsible for that." Daniella was aware of appearing more knowledgeable than was any use, and retreated so hastily towards ignorance it felt like panic. "I'm just looking, I'm looking at—we don't seem to have his child's name."

"It's Mark."

"The child they," Daniella said, and had to soften her voice, "lost."

"Philippa."

"That's from Victor's middle name, is it?"

"Philip, you mean."

"Right." She gazed a plea at Chrysteen, who looked unprepared to stay quiet for much longer, and said "It's the twenty-eighth, isn't it, the anniversary of her death? She'd have been twelve."

"I thought you said you had no details."

"It was just her name we didn't have for some reason. Well, no, actually I don't think we know how she died."

"Why would you need that?"

"Because . . ." Daniella saw the challenge reiterated in Chrysteen's eyes, and had never seen them so unfriendly. "In case it would be too painful," she said, "for him to go through, that is. Wasn't it quite a violent death?"

"Quite." A silence left the word suspended, and Daniella was struggling to think of a way to proceed that wouldn't be too obviously inquisitive when Victor Shakespeare's assistant made the reason for her pause clear. "Ah, I thought so. He's back. Victor?"

Her voice moved away as her hand closed over the mouthpiece. Daniella heard voices bumbling like two flies trapped in the hand. She had distinguished no words when the discussion ended and the assistant told her "I'm transferring you, Ms—"

Daniella felt as though Mark's father was about to seize her by the neck. She jabbed the cut-off button so hard she almost cracked her fingernail. Chrysteen took her time about only staring at her. "What a performance," she eventually said. "You could be an actress all right."

"There wasn't any other way to do it." Daniella made to press the receiver into its hollow, then felt as though it had turned lethal in her hand. "Oh, Chrys, what have I done?"

"You tell me."

"I forgot to dial the numbers to stop anyone calling us back."

"You won't need to worry about that."

"Why not?" When her friend seemed to have given up speaking Daniella insisted "Why not, Chrys?"

"Because my dad fixed the phone so nobody we call can get our number. Are you going to make something out of that as well?"

"As well as . . ."

"As the rest of the stuff you've been trying to get at without coming out and saying it. Only I noticed the woman you were talking to didn't say as much as I expect you want me to think she did."

Daniella found she was still clutching the receiver, and rammed its face into the slab. "Chrys, all I want—"

"She never said there was anything wrong about the way the girl died, did she? She didn't even really say she got her name from her dad's."

"I think she did, Chrys."

"Like you were asking me if I did," Chrysteen said angrily.

"Like me."

"So, like you. So what? What's meant to be so bad if that's what they did?"

"That isn't all. You know that by now."

"No I don't. Gob it out if you've got anything to tell me. What else are you saying your father did?"

"He didn't. That's the point. He didn't do what he was supposed to."

"Then you can't know what it was."

"I can. I do. I wish I didn't."

"Go on then," Chrysteen said, and immediately raised her hands towards her ears. "No, I don't want—"

"Either they wouldn't help him fix things because he wouldn't make the sacrifice they have to make or that was why his money went wrong, because he didn't."

Chrysteen looked determined not to speak, then grimaced furiously. "Which sacrifice?"

"You know which. You heard."

"No I don't, and you can't even say it. You can't really think it's true, or if you do I'm sorry but you have to be, to be ill after all."

"You don't believe that. I know you. I can tell."

"Then maybe you don't know me as well as you'd like to think. You're certainly making it clear you don't know my dad."

"Chrys, I know how you're feeling," Daniella pleaded and reached across the desk for her friend's hand, only for Chrysteen to flinch back as though from a threat of infection. "How do you think I felt when I had to realise about mine?"

"I couldn't say. I'm not sure I know you any more."

"Yes you do. I'm still the friend I've always been. I'm just trying to look out for you like we do for each other."

Chrysteen knuckled the outer corners of her eyes before glaring at her. "Go on then, show me some evidence my dad's involved in any of the stuff you're so anxious to get me believing. And don't say my name, because that doesn't prove a thing."

"Chrys?"

Chrysteen's eyes grew fiercer, perhaps to keep themselves dry. "What?"

"Do you know where your passport is?"

"I told you before I do."

"How about fetching it and we'll go away somewhere for a while like we promised each other we would? It won't cost much once we're there."

"You really have to be ill to say that now."

"Okay, if I am then I need someone to come with me to make sure I'm all right, and there's only you."

"You know I can't, so maybe you shouldn't go either."

She ought to have asked Chrysteen to accompany her hours ago, Daniella thought too late. Could she have persuaded her to leave the country without her knowing why or even their ultimate destination? It might have been easier than the task that faced her now. A surge of frustration, mostly with herself, sent her hands off the desk to grab the handles of the top drawers. "What do you think you're doing?" Chrysteen demanded.

"You said show you some evidence."

"Don't," Chrysteen cried, but Daniella had already pulled the drawers out. The left-hand drawer was almost full of items: a stapler and a box of refills, a packet of paper handkerchiefs, a tin of paperclips, a message pad displaying a crude doodle of a swordsman, his blade poking up from a fist like a knuckleduster. The other drawer contained only a collection of Father's Day cards nesting inside one another as though to form a book. "Those are all the cards I sent him since I was little," Chrysteen said with savage protectiveness. "Just you be careful unless you want him knowing I was in here, and leave—"

She gasped with rage. Daniella had slid the top drawers shut only to pull out those beneath them. On the left were dozens of transparent boxes of computer disks, but the right-hand drawer claimed all her attention. Lying there with its cover upturned, exhibiting an image that was both a knife and a cross, was *The Bible Decoded*. "That's the book that was taken from my house," Daniella said.

"Don't you dare start accusing my dad of that."

"I'm not saying it's the copy, but it's the book."

"So why shouldn't they read the same book?"

"Why this one? Is it the kind your dad normally reads?"

Chrysteen pressed her lips together until they grew pale, then parted them too late to forbid Daniella to lift out the book. It fell open on the desk at a page where a sentence had been underlined. "Whosoever slayeth Cain, vengeance shall be taken on him sevenfold." Timothy Turner interpreted this to mean the performer of the sacrifice was regarded as sacred, but she hadn't time to point that out to Chrysteen. Her lifting the book had revealed a rectangular mahogany box about eighteen inches long. "Chrys," she said gently, "what do you think that is?"

"I've no idea, but don't you touch it. You've touched enough."

"Then you open it. You have to see."

"I certainly do not, and you don't either."

"Chrys, we don't have time," Daniella protested, reach-

ing for the box. Chrysteen knocked her hand aside and
snatched the box out of the drawer. She looked ready to
hug it to prevent Daniella from seeing inside it—ready to
find it and herself a hiding-place—but perhaps she was
unable to escape her friend's dismay. She set the box on the
desk, only to make such a performance of being unable to
open it that Daniella had to clench her fists to prevent herself from intervening. She was nearly convinced that it was
protected by a secret catch when Chrysteen abandoned trying to lift any lid and attempted to slide it off. The lid
yielded so readily that it clattered on the desk.

Daniella saw Chrysteen stiffen so as not to draw back
from the sound, or the gleam of reflected sunlight that
sprang from the box to illuminate her instantly blank face,
or the source of the gleam. Lying on a puffy strip of dark
red velvet at the bottom of the box was a knife with a
smooth black handle as thick as a small child's wrist, with
a polished silvery blade at least a foot long. "So?" Chrysteen
demanded.

"You tell me, Chrys."

"So it's their symbol. I never said he wasn't one of
them."

"It's more than—"

"No, Daniella, it isn't. You've got no proof it is because
there isn't any. You just can't let go of thinking it's more,
but you have to. You saw them waving their knives about
because that's all they do with them. It's mad to believe
anything else. I'm not saying you're mad, but that is,"
Chrysteen said and stepped back with a small tight cry that
might have been of fear or rage or both.

The phone had begun jangling as if to warn her and
Daniella they'd been found. She stared not much less than

tearfully at it, then accusingly at Daniella, before running out of the room. Daniella thought she was fleeing the call until she heard Chrysteen grab the phone in the kitchen. "Hello?"

She sounded as though she hoped not to be noticed. From the hall Daniella saw her friend's face waver, then try to borrow some steadiness from her voice. "Hello, dad."

Daniella faltered for only a moment. She ventured as far as the end of the hall, just out of sight of the man whose mower was snarling at the grass, while Chrysteen said "How did you know I was here?"

Though microscopic, her father's response was clear. "Would you rather I didn't?"

"Of course not. I said I'd be coming to see you and mum soon, and here I am."

She had turned away from Daniella, perhaps to avoid being shown how convincing she sounded. "Is your friend there?" her father said.

"Which one? I've lots."

The tiny voice grew sharp as a knife-point. "Daniella Logan."

Tension extended its grasp from Daniella's neck to her spine and her arms, although Chrysteen barely paused before saying "No."

"But you know where she is."

"I think . . ." Chrysteen turned her head towards her friend and gazed into her eyes as if uncertain what they hid. "I saw her at her house," she said.

"Which house?"

"Her dad's. The one here."

"I'll want to talk to you further. You'll be there when I come home?"

It was scarcely a question. "I expect," Chrysteen said.

"I'd like to be sure of it," the minute voice said, and was gone.

Was that an order in the form of a wish or an indication that he was on his way to make sure? Daniella couldn't tell if Chrysteen was preparing herself for that as she hung up—as she said "That's all I can do. Go away now. Go wherever you're going and don't tell me where it is."

"Chrys, won't you—"

"What I'll do if you don't go now, I'll call him back and tell him you're here."

Her voice and her eyes were calm as stone. Daniella knew her too well to imagine that persuasion had a chance. "Be careful, Chrys," she said helplessly, "don't..." Unable to finish, she retreated along the hall to stuff her schoolbook into her bag. It wasn't sunlight that almost blinded her as she let herself out of the house. She dabbed her eyes with the back of her hand so that she was able to see as she glanced at the house from the gate.

She was hoping to see that Chrysteen had relented and was waiting for an excuse to follow her. Chrysteen was indeed watching from the front door that Daniella had left open, but waved her violently away with one hand while she mimed using a phone with the other. Her face was stiff and blank as a mask, and Daniella couldn't bear to look. She had only started towards the car when she heard the house shut like a trap.

THIRTY-ONE

As soon as Daniella was locked in the hot parched cage of her car she wanted to go back for her friend. She had to remind herself that while she knew she was in danger, she had no reason to believe Chrysteen immediately was— Chrysteen or any of the children of the men whose names on the secret list weren't trailed by dates. Of course the children signified only by dates weren't in danger either— had ceased to be. The thought seemed to focus on the suburb an illumination brighter and harsher than the sunshine, but she couldn't tell if it suggested how much the houses and their occupants would never admit or how much one might conceal. She twisted the ignition key and trod on the pedals as though to crush something underfoot. The car had surged forward no more than the width of a spotless white house and its partner when she tramped on the brake, jarring her neck.

Which way did she mean to go? She still had to book a flight to Greece. If she drove into town she might encounter Chrysteen's father coming home. If she returned to the motorway she would have to pass her own house, where she'd told the estate agent she would be. Rage at her indecision and her plight sent her towards the motorway by another suburban route, only for the maze of smug fat houses dazzling as laundered sheets to bring her to Chiltern

Road. She took it, too desperate to be other than defiant, past her house with not a car outside, past the churchyard where a funeral was sprouting bouquets. She was in sight of the motorway, and exposed by the sky the fields had spread around her, when she had to pull onto the rutted verge that other vehicles had rendered patchy as an adolescent boy's chin. Which direction on the motorway could she risk?

She dragged her driver's atlas out of the glove compartment and peered at a flayed Britain, blue veins of motorways, red arteries of major roads. The nearest airport was Heathrow, but wouldn't that be her obvious point of departure? If she turned north she would come to an airport in Birmingham and eventually another in Manchester, but wouldn't that course be predictable too? She had no idea which airline Flysmith might work for, if indeed he didn't own one. She had to force her mind to hold onto the knowledge that the longer she delayed the sooner someone would discover that she wasn't at her house. She sped to the motorway and drove north. As soon as she saw the first town—Banbury—she turned along that road.

She remembered an old children's rhyme about riding a cock horse, although the cross to which it had been ridden had been demolished by the Puritans and rebuilt later. Much of the market town had been renovated, a mass of new buildings that failed to conceal glimpses of houses black and white as her father's early films. She was still on the outskirts when she reached a block of shops, the first of which strewed the pavement with flowers and vegetables as if the ancient landscape was reclaiming ground. Next came open-air racks of clothes in which actors on location might have costumed themselves, and then a travel agency. She backed the car fast into a gap outside and dodged into the shop.

A bell sprang its tongue above the door, and both people seated behind the squat counter looked up. The middle-aged woman with a black parting in her blonde hair and PARADISE TRAVELS printed on her tight white T-shirt only blinked at Daniella, but the young man similarly if more loosely dressed raised his large face, which was tanned enough for the tropical poster above him, and offered her a dimpled smile as a prelude to asking "Where do you want to escape to?"

It took her only long enough to swallow hard before she was convinced he knew nothing about her. "Do I look as if I do?" she wished she hadn't said.

"Most customers do when another year gets to them. That's why we're here."

"Well, I just need to be in Athens."

"Greece."

"It has to be Athens."

"No, I mean not Athens, Georgia."

"No."

"Or Athens, New York."

"Not that either."

"Or Ohio."

"Terry," the woman said, screwing up the side of her face nearer to him. "Don't tease."

"Those Greeks get everywhere," he remarked, presumably not about her, since he added "History's scattered all over the place."

He'd been flirting with her, Daniella realised, and she

had been close to enjoying an encounter with someone she
had no reason to fear or fear for. "I should be in Athens as
soon as I can," she said.

"We'll see you are." He performed a brief virtuoso im-
provisation on his computer keyboard and glanced at her
as though to declare himself unworthy of applause. "Can I
take your name?"

She didn't need to use her credit card when she had so
much cash left in her bag. "Eve," she said. "Eve Cain."

"Can't get much more historical than that," Terry's colleague commented.

He was tapping the information as he said "And your
address?"

"Before we go through all that, do we know if you can
get me to Athens today?"

"If we can't nobody can," he vowed, his fingers hovering eagerly over the keys. "Where are you looking to fly
from?"

"Wherever I can drive to in time."

"Let's try Heathrow." He was already typing, and his
face grew so preoccupied she couldn't judge what success
he was having until he very eventually admitted "There
doesn't seem to be much."

"How much?"

"Not at all much. Actually, not a seat. Pity they don't
have standing room." He was typing again, but delayed
letting her into the secret of why. "Is Birmingham too far?"

"I told you, I don't mind how far I drive so long as it'll
take me."

"Then we'll have a scan of Birmingham and Manchester."

Doing so consumed several minutes, by the end of

which the clack of plastic keys felt like dice being shaken inside her skull. "Do you think," he said at last, "you could be at Birmingham International in, this isn't looking too advisable, less than an hour and a half?"

"I'm not sure."

"I wouldn't be. It was only a possible, anyway. Wait now, here's a likely. This might be more your style. Can you get yourself to Ringway, that's not Ringworm, that's Manchester, in three?"

"That's in, not for," his colleague either said or asked.

"I'll have to," Daniella said. "What are you calling likely?"

"There are a couple of standbys. Shall I ring Delphic Airlines in case they'll hold one for you?"

"That'd be—" It would be impossible, she saw barely in time, since the name she'd given him wasn't on her passport. "It'd hold me up. I'm best just going," she said.

"Don't forget us whenever you need a break."

"I'll remember."

She flashed a smile at him as she opened the door, and his colleague gave them both a mother's knowing look. The bell went off like a cartoon bubble's exclamation above Daniella's head as she retreated onto the pavement. A policeman was reading the number of her car.

Her feet set off to walk her past him and keep on walking, but where could she go without the car? She sucked in a breath that smelled of hot traffic before she paced over to him. "I haven't done anything wrong, have I?" she said.

He didn't turn to her until his irrelevantly sky-blue eyes had scrutinised the tax disc inside her windscreen. He had a broader nose than his thin mottled face warranted, and prominent teeth almost too large for the mouth his reddish moustache and baby-hedgehog beard seemed to be holding small. "I'm afraid you have," he said.

"Who says?"

His inspection fixed itself more firmly on her. "Are you local?"

"Not quite. Oxford," she said and almost amended it to "York."

"That's hardly an excuse."

"I wasn't trying to make one. You haven't told me yet what I'm supposed to have done."

"If you can drive you must be able to read."

"They're two of the things I get up to, sure enough."

"Couldn't you be bothered to read the notice, or did you think it meant everyone but you?"

His eyes gave no hint of where it might be. She had to turn her back on him so as to locate the sign further along the block. Gossiping shoppers watched her have to trudge to scan it—no weekday parking between nine and six on the yellow line she saw crushed beneath her nearside wheels and those of half a dozen other cars—and return to him. "I didn't see it," she said. "I didn't get that far."

"It's your responsibility to check whether there are any restrictions. You must have seen the line."

"I didn't, honestly. I just saw a space and all these cars. It looked as if it was okay to park."

"Just because other people break the law—"

"I know. No excuse. Sorry. Do I have to pay a fine? Tell me how much and I will."

He took almost as long to begin to answer as she'd taken to say all that. "Is there some hurry?"

"I need to catch a plane. I've only just got time."

He glanced at the travel agent's, no doubt wondering why she hadn't booked a flight in Oxford. His lips shifted in their nest of hair before he showed his teeth again. "I'm afraid I'll have to see your licence and insurance."

"Here they are," she said, but they weren't, not until she'd rummaged in her bag so urgently that her schoolbook flapped the upturned edges of its pages, revealing the dates her father had listed. "Here," she repeated as she handed the documents to the policeman, but seemed only to succeed in rendering him more deliberate. He'd slipped the papers out of their transparent plastic envelope and was unfolding her insurance certificate when the Paradise Travels bell announced Terry's intervention. "Shall I make that call for you?" he said.

She had no answer she could risk, but the policeman raised his head though not his gaze from the certificate. "Can you confirm this young lady has a plane to catch?"

"She has, and pretty soon too."

Some seconds passed before the policeman refolded the certificate and slipped it together with her licence into the envelope, which he proffered to her. "I'm letting you go this time, Miss Logan, but in future please keep an eye on the signs. Drive carefully. We don't want you putting yourself at risk."

She didn't look at Terry while she thanked the policeman and shoved the documents into her bag and took refuge in her car. She was signalling to pull out when she saw him hold the door open for the policeman to precede him into the shop. She wrenched at the steering wheel to swerve back towards the motorway as soon as the traffic would allow her. Headlamps flared like flashbulbs, and as the car screeched in a tight trapped arc she thought she saw the

Paradise Travels door spring open. Perhaps only the slant of the sunlight had made the glass rectangle glare at her. She could see nobody racing in pursuit, on foot or in a vehicle, as the road shrank away from her in the mirror. Nevertheless Terry might have heard that she'd lied about her name.

THIRTY-TWO

She had been driving for not much less than an hour when planes started to appear. They rose from the murky horizon over Birmingham, tiny bright knives that seemed hardly to move and yet left white scars on the blue sky. There were shapes of planes on the motorway signs, silhouettes so basic they might have been drawn by a child. If she was too late for the flight from Birmingham, or if the seat Terry had found for her proved to have been sold, surely she would still have time to drive to Manchester. Beyond the signpost for the airport turnoff the traffic had slowed to a crawl and was breaking out in hazard lights, and she sped onto the slip road as fast as her sudden escort of several large cars not much swifter than a funeral would allow.

A dual carriageway led half a mile to a knot of concrete roads. She sped over the knot and down to a car park beside which a train snaked, an airliner swooping hawk-like above the last carriages on its way to land. She found a parking space between two vans that did their best to hide her car, only a few hundred yards from the airport terminal. She was retrieving her suitcase from the boot and preparing to sprint to the terminal when someone ran up on tiptoe behind her and seized her arm.

No, not on tiptoe, she saw as she twisted around. She'd

been clutched by a small sandalled girl wearing a swimsuit
and a T-shirt over it as though she had just left a beach.
Her parents, fat and pink in luxuriantly floral shirt and
shorts and a dress large even for them, added to her urging.
"Leg it, love," the father shouted at Daniella, "while you've
got the chance."

"He's waiting for you," cried his wife.

They were making sure she saw the dumpy bus that
was holding its doors open behind them. She ran after the
holiday girl and slung her case into a recess in front of the
seat she sprawled on, but the vehicle didn't move. "Which
terminal?" the driver wanted her to tell him.

"Whichever's for Athens."

"You'll be for the big one," he said and shut the doors,
which gave a sigh that sounded replete. "What's your
flight?"

"Any that'll have me."

"You haven't got a ticket."

"Not yet," Daniella said in an attempt to ward off the
ominousness in his voice. Having to hear the little girl whisper "Hasn't she got a ticket?" and see the parents shake
their heads as though the situation was too dismaying for
words didn't help. The bus followed a series of roads that
struck Daniella as wilfully indirect—surely no faster a route
to the terminals than she could have run. Here, having
withheld itself as long as it was able, was the Eurohub
Terminal, and she was about to protest that the bus hadn't
stopped and lurch at the doors when she saw the vehicle
was bound for a terminal large enough to have given birth
to the other. The bus halted outside with a gasp at her haste.
By the time it had finished folding its doors open she was

clattering down the metal step. "Good luck," the driver called after her.

The automatic doors only just slid out of her way as she dashed into the elongated hall full of queues at check-in desks. Monitor screens displayed announcements no more detailed than could fit on a single line. Flight AE 21 was bound for Athens in less than half an hour. As she read that, it was erased by the information that the flight was being boarded and the gate number. She stared desperately about and saw Aegean Airlines beyond two queues that began as one—not unlike, she couldn't help thinking irrelevantly, the tongue of a snake. Neither of them led to the Aegean Airlines desk, to which she ran, struggling past an argumentative family's entourage of luggage. Behind the desk was a young woman with a long face framed by blonde hair that aided her white blouse in emphasising her spectacular tan. She appeared to be exhibiting her long-lashed sea-green eyes more than seeing Daniella with them as she said "Not checked in yet?"

"No ticket. Any left?"

"For Athens?"

"Right."

The airline clerk began to type on her computer with a slowness that might have been intended to rebuke Daniella's brevity. She hadn't finished typing when she asked "Have you a passport?"

"Course," Daniella said, snatching it out of her handbag and slapping it on the counter.

The clerk reached for it without looking at her, then glanced past her. "Is it just you that's travelling?"

Daniella turned before she could be arrested from be-

hind, and felt as if she'd been twisted around by a grip on
her neck. At her back was only an out-of-breath pensioner
who'd crossed her hands to drag ticket and passport out of
her grey suit. "Just me," Daniella assured the clerk.

"Lucky you," the clerk said, then seemed to think better
of it. "You understand it's only one way. No return."

"That's for me."

"How will you be paying?"

"Cash," Daniella said, and spread her wad of notes on
the counter.

The clerk must have been pacing herself, because now
her fingers put on speed for the last lap. A few breaths'
worth of plastic chattering produced a ticket and a boarding
card. "Go straight through security," the clerk said as Daniella's case blundered away along a conveyor belt, "and then
race for the gate."

Whenever she'd raced at school Daniella had come close
to winning, but that meant there was someone in pursuit.
She remembered her parents cheering her on—remembered her father cupping his hands to shout something she
had either forgotten or never heard, another of his secrets.
Now she felt as if a band of men he'd led was gaining
silently but inexorably on her, her father having fallen out
of the race. She sprinted for the security check she seemed
to have been told she could ignore, only for a guard to
display one large thick palm until she sent her handbag
along a belt under a mass of trailing thongs and paced
through an arch that withheld its alarm as she held her
breath. After barely glancing at her passport, an extravagantly moustached civil servant waved her to start the last
lap of hundreds of yards to the departure gate.

The gate was deserted, attended by dozens of empty seats, or rather it retained just one young woman dressed like the check-in clerk and not much less tanned. She examined Daniella's boarding card and passport with a wordless interrogative murmur at each before directing her along a boxy tunnel that might have led to an arena but proved to be stuck to the doorway of a plane. A stewardess took a few steps towards escorting Daniella to her seat, and several passengers greeted her appearance with a faint ironic cheer. Presumably they were suggesting she had delayed the take-off, which she thought was unfair: once she was seated and belted she noticed an empty seat diagonally opposite her. It didn't take her long to panic over who might occupy it, and the small lemon-scented towel a stewardess passed her with tongs failed to cool her clammy hands.

She'd been seated for at least fifteen minutes, and was realising her suitcase might be to blame for the further delay, when the airliner beyond the token window on the far side of the extensive flowered mounds—breasts almost half as big as the stomach below them—of her snoozing neighbour began to crawl forward, so tentatively that Daniella had to keep reconvincing herself that in fact her plane had gone into reverse. At last it stopped, and paused until she was certain the pilot had been advised not to take off, either so that she could be removed from the plane or for whoever was due in the empty seat to catch up with her. Then the plane stirred and inched forward and even gathered some speed. She gripped the arm-rests so hard to urge it onward that she wakened her seat-mate. "First time, sweetheart? Nothing to fret about," the woman assured her, and immediately settled deeper into sleep as beyond her the

world dropped silently away, shrank as if squeezed by the
cramped window—as if, the camera having swooped sky-
ward, it was the final image of a film.

Daniella was in flight, and the seat across from her was
empty. Chrysteen could have sat in it—would have been
safe. Daniella reached for the phone embedded in the seat
in front of her, though she was saving only herself. She
activated it with her credit card and told Nana she was
bound for Athens. "Look for a man with your name," Nana
said, and was gone before Daniella could ask her to explain.

Four hours later, after wakening dry-mouthed over the
Adriatic from a dream of being met at the airport by her
father with a bright razor-sharp knife in his hand, she saw
the swarthy shirt-sleeved man holding to his hirsute chest
with his equally hirsute arms a placard bearing all of her
name except for one "l." She might have laughed at her
doubts or at feeling far enough from home for safety, except
that she feared he would think she was laughing at him.
She couldn't explain, since he spoke no English. Before long
she didn't miss that. She was too busy trying to ignore the
fumes of the hot dusty car as it bore her through streets
above which she kept glimpsing ancient pillars that gleamed
like teeth. Then came the harbour, and the incessantly
lurching sea, and the boat that would pitch for over an hour
towards Nektarikos.

THIRTY-THREE

The morning after Daniella had been unable to buy water by the harbour she awoke feeling eager and had to remind herself why. Not because Nana's friend was returning to the mainland—Daniella didn't care whether she went or stayed, despite what Daphne had asked her at dinner. As the setting sun had left the sky raw, Daphne had grown drunker, smoking before every course and regularly forgetting not to offer Daniella a cigarette. She spoke Greek to Nana before translating each comment, perhaps as yet another reason to touch Daniella's hand or stroke her arm. Her translations had concerned the wine, the food, the company, the wine, her childhood friendship with Nana, her work as a research chemist in the laboratory of Nana's Glamour Range ... Daniella had taken her to be praising in Greek the Metaxa that came with coffee as dark as the sky had grown when Daphne planted an unexpectedly cold hand on her arm. "What was he really like?"

"Who?"

Daphne had frowned before forgiving Daniella for needing to ask. "We were saying without him, who knows what path Nana might have followed in life. Who else but your father."

"Right."

She had been hoping the woman would be drunk

enough to drift onto another subject, but Daphne had taken a firmer grip on her arm. "So tell us about the man. Tell us things only his daughter knows."

Daniella's lips had stiffened as if clamped shut from within. Until that moment she hadn't known how hard it might be to tell a stranger that her entire relationship with her father had been a pretence, a trick with her as the victim. Her lips had begun to tremble with tension or grief before Nana had said "Forget it, Daniella. We understand. It's too soon."

Though Daphne's apologies had been so effusive she'd left some of them in Greek, Daniella had retreated to her bedroom as early as seemed polite. As she'd lain at the edge of waves of sleep that kept withdrawing from her, leaving her stranded on the bed, she'd heard the women chattering and laughing like schoolgirls, first outside her window and then in Nana's room, where their sounds had grown more intimate. She couldn't avoid being reminded by their friendship of how she had failed to rescue Chrysteen, but now that it was morning she had a chance to reassure herself. She could phone her friend without the risk of encountering Chrysteen's father, since Chrysteen would be back at York.

As soon as she was dressed she made for the terrace. Nana was reading a computer printout at the skeletally elegant table, which was bare except for a bowl of dusky grapes and the cordless receiver not unlike a bone club. She greeted Daniella with a smile as white as the single fleecy cloud that was being drawn down the blue sky towards the knife-edge of the sea. "Did we disturb you last night?" she said.

"How would you have done that?"

"We were having such a time we didn't realise it was so near your bed at first, and then we took it to my room."

"I must have been asleep," Daniella said before they could find themselves embarrassed.

"You look better for it. Ready to be fed? I'll call Theo and you can tell her what you want, or rather I'll tell her for you."

"Could I possibly phone someone first? I really ought to pay you. It's England again."

"You pay me just by being here. Shall I leave you alone?"

"No, don't. I don't want to keep anything from you any more."

"Then I'll have to be the same," said Nana, handing her the receiver and turning to the horizon, where the sheepish cloud appeared to have been chopped in half lengthwise. As Daniella dialled York, Nana's cook tramped floppy-sandalled onto the terrace and gestured so fiercely to indicate how thin she thought the guest was that Daniella felt bound to mime breakfasting. The old woman hobbled into the villa as the distant phone began to shrill in imitation of the cicadas, whose chorus sounded capable of engulfing the pulse of the bell. When the ringing ceased there was such a silence in the phone that Daniella was afraid she'd been cut off. Then Maeve said none too welcomingly "Hello?"

"Guess who this is."

"Daniella." Her tone hadn't changed, and only sharpened as she said "Where are you?"

"I'd still rather not say, Maeve. You can't wonder if you ought to tell what you don't know. I'm trying not to make any trouble I don't have to for my friends."

"It's a few days too late for you to start."

"Oh, Maeve, I thought you and Duncan promised not to fall out over me."

"We didn't know then what you'd done, and anyway I wasn't talking about me and Duncan."

"So you haven't . . . you're still . . ."

"Seems like we're stuck with each other."

"I'm glad. Can I speak to Chrys now? I don't expect she'll mind if you need to wake her up."

"No."

"Sorry, no what?"

"No, you can't speak to her."

"Why not?" Daniella heard her own voice growing childishly plaintive, but hadn't time to care. "What's wrong, Maeve?"

"She isn't here, and I'm sorry, Daniella, but it's your fault she's not."

Daniella dug her fingertips into the metal lattice of the tabletop, and Nana covered her hand with hers. "How?" Daniella pleaded.

"They got her registration number when she was fetching you from the hospital, and the police found out it was hers, so now her father's keeping her at home."

The rasping of insects seemed to drill deep into Daniella's ears and meet in a black space inside her skull. "Keeping her for what?" she a hardly knew she said.

"For helping you when she knew he wouldn't want her to, I should think."

"He can't lock her up for that, for Christ's sake. She's nearly as old as me."

"Maybe he thinks like your father did, that you're not an adult till you're twenty-one. I don't suppose he has to

lock her up to keep her there. She's never been as much of
a rebel as you."

Daniella thought she herself had been far too little of
one for altogether too long. "Have you spoken to her?" she
said as calmly as she could.

"Once."

"When?"

"Last night."

"And?"

"We didn't talk long. What do you want me to say?"

"How she is. Can't you tell me how she is?"

"She seemed all right. More embarrassed than anything,
but she tried to joke about it till her father came along."

"Why"—Daniella swallowed hard—"what did he do?"

"Told her to keep it short like fathers do when we're
on the phone, I should think. Don't try and make it sound
as if he's hidden her away somewhere so nobody will know
what happened to her. She called us."

"How long is he supposed to be keeping her there?"

"Till he thinks she's been punished enough, I expect.
She'll have to come back soon, she's left work here she has
to finish. Unless he fetches it for her, I suppose."

Nana's cool hand withdrew across the table as though
the actress had flinched from the inadvertent implications
of Maeve's words as Daniella had inwardly. Nana was making way for the trayful of breakfast Theo had borne out of
the villa: orange juice, Sticky Rotters in an individual
packet, blank dominoes of feta cheese, hard-boiled eggs in
swarthy shells, foiled ingots of butter, hot bread . . . Daniella
pressed the receiver against her cheek with both hands.
"Will you keep in touch with her?"

"Don't you think it might be better to leave her alone for a while?"

"I don't at all. I think she needs to know her friends care about her, so I hope you'll call her whenever you can to let her know."

"I suppose there can't be much harm in that."

Theo stood back from the table, folding her arms. Daniella grabbed the glass of juice and tipped it into her dry mouth while the phone let the cicadas have the stage. "Thanks," she told Maeve, "don't worry about me," and put the sea between them. As the cicadas turned up their volume she asked Nana "Could I make one more call?"

"So long as you don't disappoint us."

"Disappoint how?"

"How else but not feeding yourself?"

"I will."

Whatever translation Nana gave Theo was insufficient to move her. The old woman refolded her arms more firmly over her black-dressed breasts and frowned at Daniella for continuing to hold the receiver. Daniella thumbed the digits before nervousness could drive them or her resolution out of her head. She heard a bell pretending that Chrysteen was within her reach, that it was ringing only in the kitchen rather than hiding like so much else in Chrysteen's father's study, while the pulse in Daniella's ears scurried to keep pace with the sound. A pair of shrill notes, another pair that felt but could hardly be shriller, a single ring or almost the whole of one—"Hello?"

It was Chrysteen's father. Perhaps he was merely impatient, but Daniella couldn't help feeling pounced upon by his quick sharp voice or, worse still, that she had interrupted him in the midst of some activity he would rather nobody saw or heard. "Yes?" he said, more brusquely still. "Hello?"

She took another mouthful of juice. It knocked on her teeth with its ice cubes and found nerves in her jaw with its chill and went down harsh. She planted the glass on the tray so as not to crack it in her fist, and was parting her lips to speak before he could cut her off when she heard Chrysteen. "Who is it, dad?"

She was calling across a room too big to be his study—the kitchen. She sounded unconcerned, so careless that Daniella had a sense she was feigning it. Or did she only hope that Chrysteen wasn't as unafraid, as trusting, as she seemed? Daniella was resisting a useless temptation to shout a warning to her when Chrysteen's mother said "Can't you tell who it is?"

Chrysteen wasn't alone with him. That had to be enough for now. Daniella broke the connection, and the cicadas fell silent too. She passed Nana the receiver and, in the silence the sea was too placid to trouble, set about buttering half a loaf as warm as a hand, shelling an egg, transferring crumbly lumps of feta to her plate. When she began to eat Theo clapped her hands and stumped into the house. The egg and the bread tasted as if they had only just been created, and Daniella would have liked to have time to savour them. Instead she informed Nana "You won't believe what I'm going to tell you."

"You might be surprised what I've come to believe in my life."

"I don't mean that kind of believing. I know I've hardly got here, but I'm going to have to head back."

"Now that I don't believe. Is there anything we could have done to make your time more pleasant?"

"I don't see how there could be, Nana. It isn't that. It's nothing to do with you or here."

"Forgive me if I wasn't intended to, but I couldn't help overhearing what you said to your friend. I gained the impression you didn't want people to know where you are."

"I still don't."

"Then excuse me once again, but won't they know if you go back?"

"There's something more important than whether they do."

"If you'll allow me to ask, is there trouble at home?"

This struck Daniella as so inadequate that she almost burst out with the truth. "Kind of," she confined herself to admitting.

"You seemed to be concerned about someone close to you."

"I am."

"There isn't any way you could have someone intervene on your behalf."

"I don't see how. I really need to be with her myself."

It wasn't only Chrysteen she had to keep safe—there were all the others to persuade they were in danger. If she convinced just one, then she would have help. Surely someone had to believe her—someone she could trust more than Mark. She could do without Nana's doubtful look, though her hostess said "Then I mustn't seem anxious to keep you."

Daniella thought it polite to deal with another mouthful of breakfast before asking "How did Daphne get here?"

"By boat. Her own."

"Do you think she'd mind taking me over with her?"

"You might," Nana said with not much of a laugh. "Her boat is smaller than the one that brought you."

"The sea's a lot smoother."

"Sadly you won't have the chance to make the comparison."

"I don't get it."

"Precisely," said Nana, raising the left side of her mouth to acknowledge that was all the joke was worth. "You won't be sailing away with my friend. She left with the dawn."

That sounded to Daniella like a line from a film, and not a good film either. "So can I get a ride on your boat? I'll pay whatever you ask."

"I ask nothing. That isn't how I operate. You're a guest in my house." Only when she'd finished saying that, and slowly too, did Nana add "It may be too late."

"What?" Daniella demanded, and had to restrain herself from repeating it at once.

"Not all the work was acceptable. I have to send my boat back to the mainland. It may already have gone."

"Can you find out?"

"I'm about to, of course."

Nana gave her a look not far short of reproachful that lasted perhaps a second—long enough for Daniella to begrudge the time it wasted. She saw her hostess pick up the receiver, and found she was too nervous to wait and watch. She pushed back her chair with a screech of metal on marble and hurried through the villa to run along the path, from which shiny flies flew up at her approach. She could see the white boat dwarfing the vessels strung like a half-drowned necklace across the middle distance of the sea. It appeared to be retreating from her, but then the perspective was changing as she ran. She had dashed to the end of the marble path and skidded to a halt on the dusty patch of ground, her hand recoiling from the heat of the bonnet of the solitary white car, before she was sure that she was watching the wake of the boat, the ripples sweeping it relentlessly out to sea.

She was stretching out her hands as if they might be capable of retrieving the boat they encompassed when she heard Nana's voice grow hollow as it approached through the villa. Daniella stared across the trees, praying to whatever power the ancient landscape harboured that she would see the boat start to turn. When the ripples multiplied like fish-bones on either side of its inexorably straight wake, she swung round to meet Nana. "It's coming back, isn't it?" she pleaded.

"It doesn't look like it," Nana said, abandoning Greek.

"I know it doesn't, but is it? What does he say?"

"Who?"

"Whatever you call him, what he does. The boatman. The captain."

"I'm not speaking to him. Give me a moment."

She lifted the receiver and went back to haranguing it in Greek. The boat was receding with such minuteness that surely it could be stopped. It needn't be as close to the line of fishing vessels as it looked, Daniella thought until there was no doubt that it had passed beyond them. "I'm afraid it's gone," Nana said, and cut the phone off.

"But why couldn't you—" Daniella was beginning to sound helplessly childish to herself. "Who were you talking to?" she said not much less than accusingly.

"The boy who takes care of the store. I think you met him. You'd have found him slower than you seem to like. By the time I managed to persuade him to leave the store my man was too far away to notice him, as I expect you saw."

The boy could have been any of several figures down by the harbour, too distant for Daniella to identify which of them was or had been trying to beckon the vessel back. Why couldn't he or someone else have used a boat to chase it? There seemed to be no point in asking Nana, but rather "Why couldn't you speak to the captain?"

"Because the communications on my boat aren't working. That's what has to be seen to. I must say I wouldn't have been happy for you to be on it while it was incommunicado."

Daniella saw the latest ripple in the wake gleam like a knife, and turned her back on it. "Can you do me one last favour instead?"

"I hope it's not the last. I wouldn't like to think we've come to an end."

"Okay, maybe not the last, maybe just on this visit if you'll let me come again, but could you change some of my English money for me?"

"Into . . . ?"

"Greek, obviously." In case there was some way in which it was less than obvious Daniella repeated "Greek."

"You know you've no need of that here."

"I have now."

"May I know why?"

"I'll have to get one of the fishermen to take me to the mainland."

"It saddens me to tell you that you'd be wasting your time."

Daniella felt as if the dusty heat had closed around her skull and filled her mouth. "How do you know?"

"Because, why, because not so very long ago, in fact the last time I had guests, someone needed to leave while my boat was picking up another couple and nobody down there would take my guest."

"They would if I paid them enough, wouldn't they?"

For the first time that Daniella had seen it outside a film, Nana looked offended. "If they wouldn't do it for me they aren't going to do it for money."

"Couldn't you get them to do it for you if it's really important?"

"Some things are more than favours, and you can't just ask them. None of those boats would be safe to go that far." She gazed past Daniella, then focused on her. "Try and find a reason to be calm," she said. "Is there anything you can achieve by phone?"

"I don't know what. I don't think so. I'd have to think."

"Take time and do that while I make some calls and then tell me if you see your way."

Daniella trudged into the villa and sat on the edge of the bed. Her thoughts seemed inhibited by the aching of her breasts as she supported her head, hands on cheeks, in an attempt to relieve the tension of her neck while she stared at the marble floor, a slab without a message. It occurred to her that the younger the children, the more open they might be to believing they were in danger, but she didn't know if she could cope with the distress she would be bound to cause them. Ought she to call some of the men on the list and confront them with their secret? It struck her as only too likely that they would have planned a response to any threat of exposure—Norman Wells' fate suggested how ruthless they would be—but suddenly she knew who would be unprepared, who would have to keep the children safe if they had the slightest doubt that Daniella wasn't lying or insane: the mothers. This wasn't why her head rose, however. Beyond the vestibule Nana's voice, shrunken to a murmur by the distance but just clear enough to be understood, had mentioned Oxford Films.

"Any change at Oxford Films?" That, as she pushed herself quickly but quietly to her feet, was what she grasped Nana had said. She slipped her feet out of her sandals and padded well-nigh soundlessly into the corridor in time to hear Nana say "When, then? How soon can we expect some?"

Daniella halted just inside the corridor. Beneath her feet the marble couldn't decide whether to be warm or chill. "That's far too long," Nana said. "How much does that mean I'll have to sell?"

The kitchen emitted a clatter of pans that might have been an inarticulate expression of anger, enough to make Daniella retreat a pace. Her foot unstuck itself from the marble with a noise like an amplified smacking of lips, and she froze, flattening one clammy hand against the wall. Now her heartbeat was the only sound until Nana said "Never. I won't lose control. I'll instruct you when I've taken steps."

All at once Daniella was tired of hiding, not least because it seemed utterly irrational. She donned her sandals and marched out to the accompaniment of their applause as Nana said "You'll hear from me in a few days, maybe less."

She was watching her boat glint like a knife the horizon had raised before letting it drop. She turned, hooking the receiver onto the belt of her ankle-length white dress, as her guest descended the steps. "Yes, Daniella," she said.

"Like you couldn't help before, I couldn't help hearing. Do you mind if I ask what you were saying about the studio?"

"Nothing I'd expect you not to know."

"Can you tell me anyway?"

"I'm sure they must already have. You'll know what's come of how your father and his partner structured their distribution deals and subsidiaries."

"Not when you put it that way I don't. What are you saying?"

"Simply that until they've finished investigating Teddy's affairs all the income from Oxford Films and anything to do with them is locked up."

"Nobody told me."

"Maybe they thought you were upset enough, or maybe . . ."

"Say it. Say everything."

"When I was your age there were things some people wouldn't bother telling a young woman."

"There still are. Nana, don't think I'm being rude after you've been so kind to me, but what does it have to do with you?"

"You're my concern while you're here."

"No, I mean how does Oxford Films being in trouble affect you?"

"Weren't you aware I get a percentage every time any of my films are shown?"

"I wasn't. Lucky you."

"Not so lucky any more unless I turn out to be. If my percentages aren't released very soon I'll have to sell shares in Nana's Glamour and then I won't have control."

"Can't you borrow till things are sorted out?"

Daniella blurted that because she felt unfairly accused, but it brought her an ostentatiously patient look from Nana. "Forget I said it," Daniella told her. "I don't know much about how business works. I wasn't allowed to know."

"Teddy must have wanted you innocent," Nana said and gazed at her as if she thought Daniella was. Or perhaps her steady patient gaze meant she had more to say to the phone and nothing else for Daniella, who retreated, feeling embarrassed and confused and out of place, only to be met by Theo in the doorway of the villa. The old woman frowned a fierce question at her. "Sorry, but I think I'm finished," Daniella said.

Nana hadn't completed the translation when the old woman threw up her hands as though she'd been jabbed in the back with a knife and stumped to fetch the tray while Daniella sought refuge in her room. Her thoughts were trapped beneath everything she'd just learned about Oxford Films, weighed down by the very irrelevance of it. She sat on the bed and attempted to squeeze some ideas out of her head with her hands, she lay back in case inspiration was to be met down there, she shoved herself into a sitting position when she found only a quicksand of drowsiness, she stood up once her neck began to ache from propping her unhelpful head against the wall. She paced around the room and then to the window. Beyond the beach at the far side of the island from the harbour, a largish motorboat was rocking gently at the edge of the waves.

It was the boat that toured the islands. She counted at least a dozen people on the beach or in the sea. She must have been unable to hear its arrival because of the cicadas, but couldn't help feeling as if the island had done its best to keep her unaware. She grabbed her handbag and a light

jacket, which she tugged through the handles of the bag.
There had to be room on the boat for her. She didn't mind
how cramped or choppy or otherwise unpleasant the voyage
might be so long as it took her to the mainland.

She couldn't see or hear Nana from the vestibule. She
thought of calling out, but suppose that only attracted
Theo? Daniella hadn't time to waste in struggling to explain—no time to waste at all. She dodged onto the terrace
and shuffled softly to the corner furthest from the kitchen,
and stepped off it onto baked earth.

For hundreds of yards down the gradual slope the trees
were surrounded by nets that she told herself only looked
like an elaborate trap. If they sounded electrified, she was
hearing the beetles concealed in the trees. Between the nets
was a labyrinth of paths—either that or no paths at all. She
followed one that appeared to promise to screen her from
the villa, to relieve her of the threat of having to explain.

The trees were farther apart than they'd seemed from
above. Whenever she glanced back she was still in sight
from the building, while the slope kept cutting off her view
of the beach. Below the lowest nets the slope grew treach-
erous with rubble, and she couldn't find anything like a
continuous path. She had to search for routes that didn't
lead to rock too sheer for her to climb down in sandals.
Every time she was forced to detour, the cicadas rasped in
what sounded like mirth.

There were fewer trees now. Even more sunlight was
riding her scalp, coating her back, glaring from the pale
earth and paler rock to parch her eyes. She'd left the sunglasses in her room. She felt as though the dusty heat was
escorting her, silencing the cicadas as it paced her, and she

yearned for a drink. She must be halfway to the boat, she told herself.

From a miniature plateau flat and rectangular enough to have been a natural altar she saw the boat nodding in its sleep while most of the passengers appeared only as heads chopped off by the sea. The path she was following led to the beach, but tortuously, between walls of rock that prevented her from keeping an eye on the boat. She hurried down, slithering on rock that was too smooth, climbing and sometimes clambering over falls of rubble, the straps of her sandals skinning the arches of her feet and the backs of her ankles. Her neck ached from raising her head whenever a shape loomed above her, clinging to the rock as it shrilled in triumph—yet another tree that was vocal with insects. The wall dipped low enough to let her see that some of the passengers had boarded and were lying on their backs on the deck. That surely couldn't mean they were about to leave, but it sent her running down the path, which doubled back on itself several times without allowing her another glimpse of the boat. Rubble played at tripping her or piled itself up in her way, sprouting weeds not much less pale than dust and with thorns that caught at her jacket, scratched her arms and legs. The narrowing passage protruded sharp bits of itself she had to duck beneath or contort her body around. She was having to sidle, her bag held at arm's length, by the time the passage reluctantly widened and came to an end. A salty breeze ruffled her hair and stung her eyes as she dashed out of a cleft in the horseshoe of rock that enclosed the pebbly beach. She was several hundred yards from the edge of the whispering sea, and alone on the stark pebbles. All the day-trippers had re-

turned to the boat, which was chugging away from the
beach.

It was already further from the land than she was from
the sea, but she could move faster. "Wait," she called at the
top of her voice, and sprinted across the beach. She had
run no more than a few yards when she lost her footing
on a mass of slippery shifting pebbles and sprawled on her
knees. Pebbles took turns to bruise them as she grabbed the
schoolbook that had flown out of her bag. "Wait," she was
able to shout no louder as she dashed limping down the
beach. "Ask him to wait for me."

The passengers had seen her. Those who were sunning
themselves on the deck raised their heads while those at
the rail waved to her. They were waving goodbye, but as
she stumbled at a run across the unstable pebbles, the
watchers started to bat the air with the backs of their hands
as though they were fending off insects. They were trying
to wave her away. "I need to leave," she cried, exerting all
the energy she could spare to prevent herself from sounding
hysterical. "I'll pay, tell him."

Two men at the rail above the bubbling wake and grey
fumes turned to each other, and she saw them shrug. They
cupped their hands about their mouths to answer her, and
several of their fellow passengers added to the clamour. She
wouldn't have understood even if just one had addressed
her, any more than they had understood her cries, because
they were haranguing her in Greek.

They had to be advising her that it wasn't a ferry, that
it didn't pick up extra passengers, even though she could
see there was room. "Wait," she cried, pretending not to
grasp their meaning. "I'll come." She skidded down the
sloping beach, almost kicking off her sandals when they did

PACT of the FATHERS

their best to trip her up, except that injuring her bare feet on the pebbles would only slow her further. The passengers had hushed and were contenting themselves with the spectacle of her when she heard a sharp harsh clatter of rock at her back. Someone was climbing swiftly down the slope beside the path she'd used. It was Stavros, Nana's man.

His eyes were wrapped around with sunglasses, which blazed like molten metal as they caught the light, then blackened as he set foot on the beach. He strode at Daniella, pebbles clacking dice-like beneath his heavy boots. She jabbed a finger at herself and at the boat, she pointed at her mouth that was miming words in no language and swung the finger towards him, then to the boat again. His broad square thick-lipped face stayed impassive as a chunk of rock. She hadn't finished gesturing when she decided not to care what he did so long as he didn't hinder her. She had stepped into the unexpectedly icy water, which fell not far short of cramping her legs, when he started shouting in Greek.

He was addressing the captain, a rotund swarthy fellow with a massive head and a bare chest almost as thoroughly bearded as his prominent chin. He hurried to the stern to answer Stavros as Daniella slithered over the submerged pebbles, only to discover that the sea floor dipped steeply no more than a few yards from the water's edge. She would be out of her depth before she was halfway to the boat, and how could she protect the list in her schoolbook from the sea? But the captain had done talking to Stavros and was returning to the wheel. As she floundered as far as was safe, the boat emitted a choked throaty roar and a prolonged gob of smoke. Through the fumes dissipating in the still air she saw the boat was moving—was turning so gradually that she had to convince herself it was swinging towards her. She wasn't even seeing that, she was merely trying to believe she was. She wavered at the top of the drowned slope while the boat sailed with a mocking slowness further and further out of her reach.

An undertow caught at her ankles as she sloshed around to confront Stavros. He stood at the edge of the beach, arms folded, face expressionless as the visor of his glasses. She was doing her infuriated utmost not to seem even the least unsteady as she marched out of the waves when he unhooked a flask from the belt of his slacks and extended it to her. She was tempted to knock it out of his hand, except that it was full of water. Despite the taste, she emptied it down her throat before gasping a reluctant thanks that made him show his teeth.

THIRTY-FOUR

By the time Daniella came within shouting distance of the villa she wanted only to complain about Stavros. It didn't matter that he'd helped her up a brief steep incline to a path easier than the one she'd descended, nor that he kept offering his arm whenever they came to an even moderately difficult stretch. She clambered between the highest trees, where a few black olives glistened like eyes in the nets. Before she could call out to her hostess Nana said "I'll see you then" and laid the receiver flat on the table. "Daniella," she cried, jumping to her feet with a silky rustle of her long dress, and helped her onto the terrace. "We were worried about you."

"Why?"

"Why," Nana said, frowning gently at Daniella's abruptness, "because Theo thought she saw you fall on the rock down there."

"Well, you can see I'm all right."

"I sent Stavros to make sure you were."

"That's not all he did."

Nana's frown deepened as she turned it on him while he leapt deftly as a goat onto the terrace. "No? What else?"

"Maybe I should have told you what I was doing, but I couldn't find you and there wasn't time. I wanted to catch the boat that comes to the beach. He told the boatman not to take me, I know he did."

"We'll soon discover." Nana aimed a stream of jagged words at him and received as many back. "I thought so," she said as he stalked into the villa.

Daniella dumped her bag on the table and lifted a chair so that no screech scraped her nerves. "What?" she demanded, seating herself opposite Nana.

"Why do you think he should want to hinder you?"

"I don't know," Daniella said, struggling not to feel she'd reverted to being simply paranoid, since that had never been her state. "It just looked as if he was."

"As a matter of fact he was trying to help."

"Then why did the boat leave me?"

"In a word? Insurance. More comes down to that than you might think. The boat is only insured to carry passengers who have a round trip ticket. It's not allowed to collect anyone along the route."

Daniella let her hands slump palms upward on the table. Exhaustion must be overtaking her: she felt lightheaded. Her gaze sank from Nana's watchful face to the printout her hostess had been reading earlier. "What's that?" she thought she might as well ask.

"Something I was going to discuss with you." Nana fingered the pages as if she meant to slide them across to Daniella, but instead aligned their edges with her nails. "What would you think of me for a mother?" she said.

"I've got one."

Nana laughed at her or at herself. "I was wondering if I'm too old."

"You don't seem it to me."

"I've made a living out of seeming, and perhaps I'm at the age to stop."

"Is there someone?"

"Only Daphne." Before Daniella could decide whether that meant yes, Nana said "It can be managed if you're prepared to pay."

"For a donor."

"And a good deal of care."

"Would you have a baby here?" Daniella said, and interrupted any answer, having realised what the pages signified. "Are those off the Internet?"

"Everything's there if you know where to look."

"Nearly everything." It had to be how she could share the secrets of her father's list with the world. "Could I go on it for a while?" she blurted.

"I'll have to know what you want to see."

"Nothing bad. I mean, nothing that's illegal to look at."

"I'm not making myself clear. I'm saying I need the details."

"I want to send a message."

"I'd have to know what, Daniella."

"Why, because people would see it was coming from here? Isn't there a way of hiding that? There has to be."

"No."

This sounded final as a parent's answer to a child, one Daniella felt unreasonably like until Nana said "That is, your message wouldn't be coming from here."

"Why not?"

"Because I'm not on the Internet. Daphne printed this out for me to see." Nana turned the pages face down and said "There shouldn't be too much of a delay. I'll phone your message through to her."

"I'd have to write it out."

"Do by all means."

That Nana would have to read the information seemed altogether more daunting than typing it onto a screen. "I want to cool off first," Daniella said.

"There's my pool."

Daniella was out of it again before long. Whenever she moved the water seemed reluctant to stop glittering like knives. If she floated she felt as though she was laid out on a soft almost insubstantial altar beneath the immense ancient gaze of the sky. The beetles gave her the impression that she was surrounded by a loud but invisible audience. Soon those notions sent her to wrap herself in a towel and trudge into the villa.

She had showered and was donning some more of the few clothes she'd brought when Nana tapped on the door of her room. "How long do you think you may be writing your message?"

Daniella tugged her shorts up and her T-shirt down before opening the door. "I haven't started yet."

"Daphne will be leaving her office for the day in half an hour or so."

"I won't be finished by then."

"Tomorrow?"

"I suppose."

"Would you like to watch a film before dinner?"

Daniella found she lacked the energy to refuse. "Which was the one I saw when I was little where you rescue the girl who's been sent down the mine?"

"*Sunshine for Susan?* That was my first big success. Come, it'll make us both feel younger."

The viewing room was opposite Nana's bedroom. She

used a remote control that lay on the projection console to summon concealed lighting as she closed the door. Two rows of six seats deep as armchairs faced a screen about twelve feet wide and framed by velvet curtains. Daniella took a seat in the middle of the back row while Nana inserted a disc into the player. As the Oxford Films symbol, a golden-armoured knight brandishing a sword that blazed like a flame, appeared on the screen she sat next to Daniella and extinguished the lights.

In not many minutes Daniella wished she hadn't asked for the film, and not only because it reminded her how easily deluded she must have been as a child. The Victorian mine was an art director's dream—she didn't need to be told the dripping black tunnels were under a studio roof—and how, if the supposedly eight-year-old girl picturesquely smeared with sweat and grime was meant to be so ailing in the scenes where she tended a tiny garden behind the family hovel, was she able to haul a wagon piled with coal? Daniella had forgotten that it was the girl's father who'd sacrificed her to the mine for the sake of the impoverished family—who justified his actions to the unlikely village schoolmistress Nana played. When Nana heaved a sigh at the scene that made it even less bearable, and Daniella's neck ached with her forcing herself to watch. The school-mistress marched down the crooked cobbled street of ramshackle cottages streamered with black smoke, on her way to teach children too ill to work in the mine, and Nana expelled another long sigh. It struck Daniella as grotesquely self-indulgent, and she turned to peer at the actress. Nana wasn't sighing, she was breathing loudly in her sleep.

She could hardly expect her guest to sit the film out if she was incapable of watching it herself. Daniella eased her-

self off the seat, holding on to hush it as it tilted up. As
she inched the door shut she saw Nana raising her head
with a look of secret purpose, but only on the screen, in
front of which she might have been modelling a statue,
robed forearms propped on either side of her in the posture
of a queen or a priestess. Then the door shut up a triumphant surge of music and Daniella wandered out of the
villa.

For a vague but significant length of time the dullness
that had settled on her mind seemed determined to prevent
her from grasping what she saw. Beyond the skein of fishing boats a vessel of about their size was heading either for
the horizon or towards Nektarikos.

The slow unfolding of the ocean drifted into her mind,
so that she had to recollect what she was supposed to be
observing before she was able to perceive that the boat was
coming in. If it had made the trip from the mainland, surely
it could take her back. She had to reach Chrysteen. Nobody
would dare to harm her friend then. She removed her sandals and left them by the steps as she padded quickly into
the villa.

She was halfway across the vestibule when she heard
Stavros and Theo laughing in the kitchen. They were still
finding reasons for mirth when Daniella crept out of her
room, having washed out her flask and refilled it from the
jug of water by the bed and collected her handbag. She
hung the flask around her neck and carried her sandals to
the end of the marble path, where she slipped them on to
hurry downhill.

As she reached the trees the cicadas fell silent around
her. She held her dry breath until she was out of sight of
the windows of the villa. The ocean kept reappearing as

she tramped around the bends of the dusty road. Before she was halfway to the church the incoming boat had threaded its pale wake between two fishing vessels, which lifted their heads to acknowledge it and then went back to sleep. She needed the view to remind her why she was hurrying. Each time it vanished her awareness shrank, confining itself to the flat repetitive impacts of her footsteps, the aching of her soles, the chafing of sandal straps on her raw skin. She would have fed herself a drink more often if each sip hadn't tempted her to halt—even drinking on the move slowed her down, so that she had to make more of an effort each time to regain her painful speed. At least the monotony of her trek appeared to be dulling her aches; she couldn't think what else might be.

Over the highest of the haphazard unrelated roofs she saw that the boatman and his passenger were almost at the jetty. She did her best to sprint around the last bend and down the parched harsh road. As the harbour sank behind the houses she heard the slam of a car door. It was up by the villa. The car gave a roar that struck her, surely inaccurately, as the kind of sound an animal might utter on sighting its prey, and started downhill.

As she dashed past the cottages old women raised their tortoise faces to peer black-eyed at her. Two naked female toddlers ran out of a doorway ragged with vines and danced around her until she managed to stumble out of their way. A threadbare kitten almost as pink as it was black darted with a yowl across her path. A wizened oldster with a rusty metal stepladder slung wide over his shoulder trudged to meet her and took a generous amount of time to stumble aside. When at last she limped onto the stretch of pebbles along the harbour, the boat had its stern to her and was chugging out of her depth. That wasn't why she staggered to a halt without shouting to the boatman, nor did she because Nana's car had sped down behind her. Standing on the jetty, one hand resting indolently on the handle of a small wheeled suitcase, was Mark.

THIRTY-FIVE

M ark didn't move until she stalked towards him, and then he raised his free hand. It might have been a greeting or an attempt to quieten her or even some more secret sign. His face was as earnestly concerned as she remembered, but that no longer meant anything to her. Before she could exact an explanation, Stavros drove past her with a spurt of pebbles and stopped the car in front of Mark. "Shakespeare?" he said.

"That's me," Mark agreed with a nod. "What do I call you?"

Stavros appeared to have understood only the nod. "He's Stavros," Daniella said. "What do you think you're doing here, Mark?"

"I told Ms Babouris I wanted to talk to her about your father."

"So why didn't I know you were coming?"

"I asked her not to tell you. I thought you mightn't want me to come."

"You were right about that at least. And she said she wouldn't, did she?"

He only glanced at Stavros, who had stepped out of the car to plant Mark's case on the front passenger seat. "How far to where we're going?" Mark asked him.

The shrug and upturned hands this prompted appeared

to satisfy Mark, apparently because it showed that the driver
didn't understand English. Stavros held the rear door open
and Mark motioned her to climb in. The gesture looked
like an unvoiced apology, which only angered her. She
hadn't decided between not offering him another word and
treating him to a selection from the clamour in her head
as Stavros shut him in beside her. The driver had presented
his disinterested back to them when Mark murmured "I'm
sorry."

"Well, that fixes everything." Being provoked to respond enraged her. "What are you feeling sorry for?"

"Not telling you my whole name the first time we met.
I didn't after that because I thought it would make you
suspicious."

"Why would you think anything like that?" Her sar-
casm fell short of satisfying her, and she demanded without
wanting to hear "Why am I supposed to believe you didn't
tell me in the first place?"

"Truthfully? I don't think of myself as a Shakespeare.
I tried to get rid of all that when I started writing."

The car swerved away from the harbour so fast she
would have been flung against him if she hadn't grabbed
the top of the hot door. "All what?"

"All the stuff I found out and you have."

The church sank beyond him as she studied his face.
Even his earnestness looked apologetic now, which confused
her. "You have to tell me what you mean," she said.

He pointed a finger at Stavros out of reach of the
driver's mirror. "Maybe it should wait till we're alone," he
suggested, almost managing to sound casual.

That his wariness exceeded hers was disconcerting, not to mention his inability to fake his tone as much as she'd assumed he could. "You saw he doesn't understand," she said, and with an urgency that felt like praying for an ally "Tell me."

"What your father and mine were part of."

"How do you know about that?"

"Really I've known ever since my sister died."

"When?"

"Coming up to nineteen years ago. She was seven and I was six."

"I'm sorry." Daniella wasn't only that, since she was recalling the date her father had written next to Booksmith. "What happened to her?" she said.

"My father nearly went bankrupt when he left the publishers he worked for and started Midas Books. The day he launched Midas a lot of the people who were at your father's funeral came back to our house afterwards."

"Did my father?"

"I'm afraid so. That was the night my sister was supposed to have walked out of the house in her sleep and a train killed her on the crossing down the road where there weren't any gates."

"And you don't think she did? Wasn't anyone suspicious?"

"Not when she was supposed to have started sleepwalking that year."

"You keep saying supposed. Didn't your parents take her to a doctor?"

"My father did that all right. He took her to Eamonn Reith."

Daniella's mouth was growing dryer, perhaps from dust stirred up by the car. "I wouldn't trust him, but I don't see how he could make her walk in her sleep."

"I don't think she ever did. She kept waking all over the house and not knowing how she'd got there. Except one night when I wasn't quite asleep I thought I heard someone go in her room and carry her downstairs, and that's where she woke up."

Daniella drank from her flask and offered it to him, and made herself say "What was her name?"

"Philippa."

"And your father's middle name is . . ."

"You know."

"Did you try and tell anyone?"

"Who was going to believe me? I tried all right, and the family hardly spoke to me for weeks. I gave up trying a long time ago, but I kept on keeping watch. I know that isn't much. I only came to see you for the magazine at first, and then you told me what you saw after the funeral and I was sure we could find out more."

"How, by not telling me anything?"

"I was trying to work up to it. I didn't think you'd believe it all at once."

"It wasn't all you were trying to work up to, was it, Mark?"

She was glad his face pinkened a little as he said "So long as you believe me now."

"I'm still not sure what we're believing." When he blinked at her she muttered "Why are you saying they do what they do?"

"Sometimes I think it's just a way of making sure they all have to keep one another's secrets, or maybe it's how they show they're totally committed to doing whatever the others ask them to do. Only it looks as if they have to make, you know, a sacrifice when they're in bad trouble before the others will help them out, or sometimes just when they want to be helped to succeed."

"It has to be more than that. It can't be that pathetic. I think it started before the Bible, when they used to make sacrifices to all sorts of things."

"Always virgins, weren't they, sacrifices? They'd be to the desert back then, to ask it to feed the people and give them water."

"There's something in the Bible about anyone who harmed Cain dying seven times. I think that's what they tried to do to Norman Wells for talking to me."

Mark glanced uphill. "We're almost there. Have you still got a list of them all?"

"And the dates any of them did what they did."

"What were you planning to do with it?" he said with some urgency, then peered at her. "Are you feeling all right?"

She saw Nana on the steps of the villa, crouching forward, hands on knees. Presumably she was watching the car, but looked as though she was preparing for a marathon. "As much as I'd expect to," Daniella said. "Why?"

"You seem slower than you were."

It occurred to her that the car did too, no doubt because Nana had rebuked Stavros for his driving. "Too much walking and not enough sleep," she said. "I wanted to put the list on the Internet, only Nana doesn't have access."

At that moment Nana reached the car, having strode to it so fast her scent preceded those of the flowers beside the path. "What are you saying about me?" she said.

This was apparently a greeting, because Daniella hadn't answered when Nana turned to Mark. "So you're Victor Shakespeare's boy."

"Can't say I'm not."

"I shouldn't think you'd want to, would you? It's a reason to be proud, and I'm sure he must be proud of you." Nana rested her gaze on him while she said "Do you mind explaining one thing?"

"It's good to meet you. Thanks for letting me come," Mark said, shaking her hand without stepping out of the car. "What's the thing?"

"You didn't want me to tell my other young friend you were going to stay with us, but I see you're together."

Daniella had managed to anticipate this, and said "He wanted to surprise me" almost swiftly enough to prevent Mark from declaring "We'd had a disagreement but now we've made up."

"I'd say you still have your disagreements." Nana gave each of them a faint lingering smile and said "Will you be sharing a room?"

"I shouldn't think so." Mark began and ended that with a laugh, and with even more of one Daniella said "No."

"Forgive any embarrassment. I had to ask so I could choose Mark a room." Nana reclaimed his hand as she opened the door on that side of the car, and held onto him as she addressed Stavros in Greek. Perhaps she was telling the driver to lift Mark's case out of the car, since he did, but they had more to say to each other—enough that Mark snatched the chance to whisper "Daniella."

"What?"

"She—"

Nana pushed the front passenger seat forward and

helped him out of the car. "Let me show you where I'm putting you so you can get ready for dinner."

As she led him by the hand into the villa he shot Daniella a frustrated glance, and she could only follow. Stavros was directed to wheel Mark's case into the room across the corridor from hers and Nana's. As Daniella made to pursue Mark into the room Nana put a cool hand on her arm.

"Are you planning to change for dinner, Mark?"

"I didn't realise it was going to be formal."

"It won't be. Whatever makes us comfortable, isn't that so, Daniella? I just thought you might like to feel fresher, Mark."

"I'll have a shower and then I will."

"We ladies will respect your modesty," Nana said, closing the door behind him. "We'll start with cocktails on the terrace," she called through it. "What will you have?"

"Any chance of a lager?"

"Of course, a lager," she said as though that was only to be expected of a man. "And you, Daniella?"

"I don't feel like drinking much."

"You won't let me drink alone or you'll have me thinking I'm a desperate woman. Take some water with it and all will be as it should."

"Just a glass of white, then."

"White for a lady." She steered Daniella by an elbow into the kitchen, where she poured a large olive-eyed gin and it for herself while Theo mumbled over mouthfuls of the casserole she was stirring. Nana handed Daniella the gin and a substantial glass of wine, and followed her onto the terrace with a jug of water and an empty glass. "You need ice in your water," she said and swept back into the villa to emerge with the glass jingling like Christmas.

The nets around the topmost trees glistened red as if they had caught more than olives. The shrunken sun extended a crimson trail from the horizon to the deserted beach. Nana leaned back on her skeletal chair and closed her eyes, suggesting that she was enjoying a peace the cicadas weren't about to allow. Her face looked monumental in its calm. If Daniella could have been sure she was dozing she might have stolen away for a word with Mark, except that she felt too comfortably inert to move, no less so for taking a drink of iced water instead of wine. In any case, here came Mark in a shirt and slacks, even if she couldn't ask him what he had fallen short of saying in the car. "Here's the gentleman," Nana announced, opening her eyes as soon as he stepped out of the villa, and clapped her hands.

Prawns that Daniella found herself comparing to fat copyright signs or symbols for cold water or Roman numerals, and starting to count how many centuries they would represent, made up much of the steaming casserole Theo ladled onto plates. "Saginaki," she said of it and stumped into the villa.

The sauce was spicy enough for Daniella to have recourse to both water and wine. Having watched to see all went down well, Nana continued to watch Mark. "Why haven't I seen you before?" she said.

"Where would you have seen me?"

"At Teddy's funeral, I should have thought."

"I didn't know Danny then."

"And her father?"

"I'd met him just a couple of times."

"So you want to know whether I've any revelations about him."

Daniella had been watching Nana's eyes appear to swell red with the sunset. A surge of fury and distress made her blurt "Have you?"

"I've a few things I'd be happy to tell the world. Are we doing the interview now?"

Mark opened his mouth but glanced at Daniella. "That's up to you," he told her.

"Then I'd rather you didn't just yet."

"Poor girl. Still grieving," Nana said. "Has my island brought you no peace?"

"Some."

"I'll be happy if you end up feeling no pain." Nana closed her eyes, momentarily extinguishing their glow, then blinked at both her guests. "So what's your story?"

"Story," Daniella said in case it made time for a thought to form, and Mark said "About what?"

"What brought the two of you together?"

"Same reason I'm here. I wanted to talk to Danny about her father."

"You couldn't have."

"Why not?" Daniella and Mark demanded in chorus.

Daniella manufactured a laugh—Mark's sounded more genuine, and Daniella wondered if that was why Nana addressed her response to him. "You just saw how she feels. She isn't ready yet."

Daniella fed herself more seafood and more water while she thought up a contribution to the dialogue. "We found we had other things in common."

"Would it be indelicate of me to enquire further?"

"We both know what we want," Mark said, "and we're going to get it together."

Daniella supposed she ought to admire his conversational skill but thought it was a little too glib. Teeth gleamed in Nana's smiling silhouette with the last of the afterglow. "That's information, isn't it?" she said.

"Absolutely," Mark said. "About your films."

"We were losing ourselves in one today, weren't we, Daniella? I was, anyway. What would you like to hear about them, Mark?"

"Give me some background. Tell me what went into making them."

"That would involve Teddy again."

"It's all right," Daniella managed to say, and "I don't want to stop people talking about him."

"I'll tell you about my best years," the actress said.

Daniella finished her seafood and a couple of glasses of water while she listened. Not only the films but also Nana's idyllic account of how they had been made struck her as a myth that concealed a much grimmer reality, and once she'd swallowed her portion of the fibrous honeyed dessert Theo served she felt she'd had more than enough sweetness. "Do you mind if I go to bed? I'm dead tired," she interrupted, not at all far from the truth—close enough that she barely remembered to signal to Mark with a lift of her head as she passed behind their hostess.

His expression didn't alter. She had wandered less than steadily into the villa when she heard him say "Just let me go to the loo and then I'd like to ask you some questions." She loitered outside his room, and as soon as he left the vestibule she murmured "What were you going to tell me in the car?"

"Shall we talk about it in your room?" he said, even lower.

"Wherever, so long as you tell me."

"Fine, so let's . . ."

His ushering gesture annoyed her, not least by implying a need for stealth. She stalked into her room and switched on the light and sent herself to draw the curtains. Theo was muttering at Nana, who flashed a smile at Daniella as the curtains hid her classical profile, luminous against the night. Mark had stayed just inside the room, and beckoned Daniella over. "So say," she hissed.

"You said you thought of putting your list on the Internet."

"So?"

"Why didn't you?"

"I told you. Nana isn't on it."

"Who says she isn't?"

"She does."

"That's what I thought. She mustn't have wanted you to go on it, because she wasn't telling the truth."

"Who says she isn't?" Daniella whispered fiercely, feeling childish for repeating a question of his.

"Danny, she has a site on the web. I hit it before I came here."

"That doesn't mean she writes her page herself. It'll be one of her fans that does."

"It isn't. When I visited her page she'd just written about how all her royalties are frozen."

"Okay then, she must have meant she doesn't have access from here. She must write it when she goes over to the mainland."

"Has she been over since you got here?"

"No. So?"

"How long is that?"

"Three days. So?"

"The news about her royalties was only posted yesterday. I know because it was the second time I visited her site."

Daniella glared at him, not knowing whether she felt more betrayed by Nana or by him, nor what to do in either case. He was acting equally loath to make a move when the phone rang on the terrace. She heard Nana say "Babouris" and Theo's footsteps tramp into the house, and then Nana's voice again, not as loud as her greeting. "She is," she said.

She could be talking about Theo, Daniella told herself as she heard a chair being pushed back with a faint screech. "I've told nobody except you and whoever you'll have told," Nana murmured. "He couldn't bear not to tell someone, but it's been my secret since."

When she spoke again her voice was more distant. "Exactly what I said I would, to show you I can. And if I need to I will again once I have one of my own."

She was barely audible. Mark moved to the window and gazed at Daniella, who lurched after him in a fury at the assumptions she refused to make. "Don't think I won't because I'm a woman," Nana said among the trees. "We Greeks remember longer. Women were there at the start, and it's time you realised. It's time we reclaimed some of that power."

Daniella leaned one reluctant ear close to the window, and froze. Her shoulder had brushed a curtain, which stirred as though impatient to reveal a last act. She found she couldn't breathe until Nana's voice returned unaffected. "Just wait till I send you a tape. It won't be much of a film, but I promise you'll see it's real. It's coming very soon, my new image."

Daniella was clenching her fists and straining to hear more when she was rewarded by the sound of Nana's footsteps on the terrace. "I'll have to go," Mark muttered, "or she'll wonder where I am."

"Now you've got me on edge and confused you're off."

"I'll settle this Internet business as soon as I can at least, and then—"

"How do you think you're going to do that?"

"Wait till everyone's asleep, everyone except you if you want to come, and find the terminal."

"I doubt it. If it's anywhere it's in her room, because I've seen everywhere else."

"Can you get her talking now so I can look?"

"You just said she's expecting you." For a moment the dullness that was continuing to gather in Daniella's skull made that seem to be all the answer she needed to give him. "You keep her talking," she said, "and I'll look."

"Are you sure?"

"I want to be."

His uncertain smile at that only underlined the concern in his eyes as he hurried to his room. The toilet was still flushing as he crossed the vestibule. As the downpour faded Nana said "There you are. I was starting to think I'd lost my charm."

"I heard you were on the phone. I thought it might be private."

"You're very thoughtful. It was a business call."

"Important?"

"Life and death."

Daniella was becoming angrier by the moment with the mistrust he'd sown in her and left to grow. It didn't help that she felt she ought to recall something he'd recently or

perhaps not so recently said. She stole into the corridor at
least partly to escape his voice and Nana's. There was silence within the villa. She took hold of the knob and edged
Nana's door open, and saw Nana at once.

She had her back to the uncurtained window. Mark
saw Daniella, however, and fixed such a determined gaze
on their hostess that Daniella was sure Nana would guess
something was wrong. "Tell me about her father now she's
gone," he said.

"He helped me become myself," Nana began, and Daniella made herself tiptoe into the room, to be out again
before she heard too much that she might be unable to bear.
The room was illuminated only by the light in the corridor
and a faint indirect glow from the terrace. It contained a
bed big enough for at least two people, an enormous fitted
wardrobe, a dressing-table glittering with jewels. In the corner farthest from the window and the door, and out of sight
from both, a computer terminal stood on a desk.

Nana hadn't meant to hide it, she told herself; it had
been placed there simply to keep the screen free of direct
sunlight. She crossed the room swiftly and stealthily as
Mark held his gaze immobile so as not to own up to seeing
her. She glimpsed posters on the walls, magnified versions
of Nana's face surrounded by words the dimness rendered
vague. "He taught me what I had to do to succeed," Nana
said as Daniella reached the desk. Two leads were sprouting
from the computer. One carried power to it, but the other—
she saw and continued seeing as she leaned closer in the
hope she was mistaken—belonged to an Internet modem.

As she sank to her knees to trace the lead, trying to
believe it might be awaiting connection, she understood that
she felt very much as Chrysteen must have while denying

there was any reason to suspect her father. The lead ended at a junction box for the phone line. It was indisputably connected to the Internet, but that wasn't why her head jerked up. She'd grasped at last what she had failed to comprehend. It felt as though the ache she'd jarred into her neck had set her skull ablaze. To know about the list in her schoolbook, Mark must have spoken to Chrysteen— must have convinced her of at least some of the truth.

Daniella sprang to her feet, or tried to. She wobbled between standing and kneeling, and almost made a panicky grab at the wheeled office chair in front of the desk. Instead she splayed a hand on the closer of the pair of pillows on the bed. It steadied her, but not before it slithered inches across the silk sheet on the mattress. She stooped to ease it back into place so that Nana wouldn't suspect any intrusion. She hadn't touched it when she stiffened, hands outstretched in a vain attempt to fend off what she was seeing, head bent as though it was being dragged down by her throbbing neck.

She crouched like that for seconds, but glaring so fiercely her eyes burned couldn't alter the sight. She had to fling the pillow back to reveal the rest of the item she'd exposed. It gleamed only dimly, much like her sluggish thoughts. Nevertheless there was no mistaking that it was a knife far too much like the one she had found in her father's grave.

THIRTY-SIX

Daniella had been lying awake for hours imagining someone had crept into the room, and she thought at first she was dreaming when someone did. Or was the faint soft regular sound only that of the sea, carried across the island by a stray wind? No, the sound was approaching—the hushed soft shuffle of bare feet—and so was Nana's discreet yet insidious perfume. Daniella's breath caught in her nostrils as the perfume slunk closer and she sensed a presence looming over the bed.

She didn't know whether her eyes were burning to squeeze themselves tight shut or spring open. The hardest task was keeping them and the rest of herself absolutely still except for the breaths she was struggling to control, to make them regular but not so loud it would be apparent she was conscious, to overcome their shakiness that would reveal she was aware of the intruder. Each of them drew in a trace of Nana's perfume—any more, and she was sure it would lodge in her throat and set her coughing. An ache gripped her neck and shoulders, and she felt the bed pressing against the side of her face through the mattress and the pillow. A hint of a hot dry breath found her upturned cheek. The heat of Nana's body hovered above her as though the sultriness of the night was concentrated there, and she knew the actress was naked. She heard herself swallow the taste of perfume, and didn't know if her throat was visible—if its movement was. She felt the actress stoop to her, she felt her own body straining not to shrink away from Nana's touch or to betray that it was nerving itself. Then, releasing a sigh so muted it might almost have been a scented breeze that had drifted into the room, Nana prowled away from the bed.

Daniella seemed to have to focus her entire consciousness in her ears to listen for the closing of the door. She was by no means sure she'd heard it when she was able to distinguish only silence around the bed. Had Nana lingered to watch? Certainly her perfume was loitering at the bedside. Daniella let her eyes open a slit and did her best to make out more than dimness. "Has she gone?" she whispered, barely hearing herself.

A lump of the dimness rose in front of her face, and she widened her eyes. As it returned to its half of the mattress she saw beyond it the scrawny luminous outline of the closed door. Mark turned on his back, taking care not to touch her. "Yes," he less than hissed.

She didn't quite believe it until she heard the door of the next room shut surreptitiously, and then she swallowed hard. "I wish I had some water."

"You don't want to risk it, do you?"

"I don't and nor do you."

"It could just be in the ice."

"Whatever she's been giving me so it won't hurt when it happens, you mean."

"Or it's been slowing you down and making it hard for you to think."

She felt as though it still was. "I need to leave," she whispered harshly, "and now she's awake and she'll hear me."

"You don't have to go till nearer dawn. There won't be anyone about till then."

"It's easy for you to say wait," she muttered, though he hadn't. "It isn't your friend who's in danger."

"If she is," he said, and added hastily when Daniella tilted her furious face to him "I only mean if she's in any more because I went to see her."

"I wish you hadn't. I don't understand why you did."

"I tried calling your house again in case you'd talk to me."

"About the fathers."

"Mostly about them. I got your friend Maeve and she told me how Eamonn Reith pretended he was taking you to an ordinary hospital and then someone nearly got you with a knife."

"Because he put me in her mind."

"I knew it had to be something like that. You think they'd have made it look as if she escaped and blamed her for whatever happened to you."

"And maybe me for bringing a knife. You know, they didn't even check in my bag. It was all to shut me up or give themselves more power."

"I believe. So I managed to get Maeve to tell me you'd gone to Oxford with Chrysteen and when I couldn't find you at your house there I went to see her."

"And she told you I was here?"

"She'd guessed because she'd heard Nana Babouris inviting you at the funeral."

"All right, you needed to find that out, but why did

you have to tell her about her father? You must have for her to let you know about the list."

"Because she asked. Not about her father, about the whole thing when she realised whose mine was."

"Asked what?"

"She wanted to know if I thought you were imagining stuff because you were still upset over losing your father."

"Did she say what stuff?"

"Yes, so I had to tell her it was all true."

Though Daniella saw he had, everything he told her made her want to dash to the harbour. "How did she take it?" she whispered.

"I thought not too badly."

"What's that supposed to mean?"

"She thanked me for making her see there was nothing wrong with your head, and then she told me you were most likely here and she wanted me to leave her alone to think."

"But how did she *seem*?"

"Pretty calm, considering."

"Was she really or didn't she want you seeing how she felt?"

"I can't be sure. I don't know her that well."

Daniella was reduced to wishing Chrysteen hadn't trusted him or that she herself hadn't stopped. At least she did now, sufficiently to have allowed her to take refuge in his room after she had found the knife. He'd appeared both surprised and pleased to find her seated on his bed, and had shown nothing but concern as she'd informed him of her discovery. It had only been to help herself feel in control of the situation that she'd insisted they retreat to her room once they were certain Nana was in hers, and then she'd trusted him to lie beside her. "Is she asleep yet, do you think?" she murmured urgently.

"Chrysteen?"

"Her." Not far short of choking on Nana's name, she jerked her thumb at the wall between their rooms. "How can she mean to . . ." she muttered, and was unable to say the rest of that either. "How can anyone?"

"Mothers did sacrifice their daughters to oracles in ancient Greece, you know."

"You're a historian as well now, are you?"

"I just read it somewhere."

"I'm sorry, I don't mean to be a bitch." She squeezed his hand and with the same movement pushed herself up the bed. "It's got to be near enough to dawn now. It's time to go down."

"I'm ready if you are."

"That'll have to be ready enough," she decided, but a question occurred to her. "Can you speak Greek?"

"Not a word."

"You're no more use than I am then, are you?" she said as lightly as possible under her breath, easing herself out from beneath the sheet. "No more talking till we're on the road."

She was in her underwear. She groped shorts and a T-shirt out of a drawer. She donned a light jacket as well and picked up her sandals and handbag. By that time Mark had regained the clothes he'd worn before stripping to his boxer shorts and was standing with his sandals in his hand. She touched his shoulder and put a finger to her lips, then tiptoed to the door.

The marble corridor was deserted and unexpectedly

cold. The villa and the island seemed transfixed by the spectacle of her sneaking out of the room. She had taken three
hesitant paces that chilled her bare feet, and was halfway
to Nana's door, when she heard a muffled exhalation and
glimpsed movement in the vestibule ahead.

Her pulse had begun to fill her ears and set her body
throbbing before she located the movement and the sound—
the trembling of a vine-leaf in a breeze that had crept
into the villa. Mark had just finished closing her door. She
held up one thumb and turned it around and joined its
forefinger to it, and felt as if she was trying to discover a
secret sign. She headed for the vestibule as fast as stealth
would allow, suddenly afraid that the chill underfoot might
cramp her muscles and render her unable to suppress a cry,
to do anything other than hop in agony until Nana came
to see what the trouble was. She had to walk the last few
steps on her heels while her feet considered curling up. She
steadied herself against the wall beside a vase brimming
with vines, and saw that the double doors of the villa were
shut for the night.

Surely they weren't locked. Who on the island would
dare trespass in the villa? She pressed her hand against the
clammy marble or her clammy hand against the marble and
leaned back to see why Mark hadn't caught her up. He'd
halted outside Nana's door, his head cocked towards it, his
sidelong gaze fixed on it. Daniella unstuck her hand from
the wall. She was about to gesture to him in case he could
quieten her nerves with some mute hint of the problem
when the door opened and Nana stepped into the corridor.

Daniella covered her mouth to trap a gasp and snatched
herself out of sight. She was sure her movements had been

impossible to miss. "Have we fallen out of favour?" the actress said.

Mark was silent for a couple of thumps of Daniella's pulse. "Have what, sorry?"

"Have we, have you been cast out into the wilderness?"

"Not that bad. Just my room."

"That's where you're bound."

"Going back there, right."

"Good night then. Do sleep well for the rest of it."

"Good night." There was a pause for a solo for Daniella's heartbeat, and then he said "You were in her room before, weren't you?"

Daniella let go of her mouth and almost of the gasp she had been suppressing. What was the question supposed to achieve? The actress responded before Daniella grasped that he meant to give her time to creep out of the villa. "I was," Nana said.

He couldn't know the doors were shut, any more than Daniella knew how much noise they would make. Only the possibility that the voices in the corridor might waken Theo or Stavros sent her stumping on her muted heels across the vestibule. "What did you want?" Mark said.

"Why, to see my guest had everything she could desire."

A spasm of disgust at the pretence nearly overbalanced Daniella, and her toes flinched from the threat of touching marble. "I'd say she had," said Mark.

Daniella tottered on her bare heels as she planted her sandals on top of her bag in front of the left-hand door, a smooth pale massive hunk of pine, and closed both hands around the right-hand knob above the lock. "Then why are we here?" Nana said.

"What are you saying? I don't . . ."

"Why are you with me and not with your, I'm taking it I should still call her a friend?"

The indentations of the chilly knob felt capable of snaring Daniella's fingertips. As she twisted it an inch it gave a squeak not as loud as her heartbeat seemed—she had no idea how audible that meant it was. "She wants to rest now," Mark said. "She was asleep."

"You mean I disturbed her."

"Let's say we both did. Now she doesn't want anyone to wake her. She doesn't want anyone going in her room. She'll see us when she comes out, she says."

He was making too much of it, Daniella thought, close to panic. Nana would guess why he was insisting—perhaps she already had. Daniella bent her fingernails against the doorknob until it refused to turn further. It didn't squeak again, and the hinges were as discreet while she inched the door towards her. She lifted the bag and her precarious sandals on top of it and transferred her burden to the top step. She was sidling out of the villa when Nana said "Then we'd better put an end to this."

"To what?"

"To talking out here if it's keeping her awake."

Daniella closed the door faster than she had opened it. The hinges made no sound that she could hear. Any answer Mark gave Nana was shut in too. Daniella turned just in time to see her sandals toppling off the bag. As she saved them from falling their soles met with surely only a faint clack. She gripped them in her left hand and hefted her bag with her right, and padded rapidly down the steps, which were colder than the floor of the villa. So was the marble path, and as she set foot on it a bush in front of her blazed up like a flame.

Her approach had triggered a concealed light beside the path. Every few paces, as she clenched her toes against the growing threat of cramp, another mass of leaves and vegetation sprang unnaturally bright to signal to the villa. Whenever she looked back the doors were still closed, the curtains gave no sign of having stirred, but suppose Theo or Stavros had seen the glow? She hadn't left the lights behind when the imminence of cramp became unbearable. She thrust her feet into her sandals and stooped awkwardly to buckle them, then kicked away a dead cicada no heavier than a leaf before shuffling to the end of the path with as little noise as the sandals allowed.

She was tramping past the parked car when the light nearest the villa went out. By the time she reached the road, darkness had reclaimed half the path. Though it was covering her tracks, the night seemed also to be pretending she had never come to the villa, so that she felt less safe than she would have hoped as she saw the last light die. The sky appeared close to beginning to glimmer, and more than one window was lit near the harbour to lure her down the road.

The trees looming over her were voiceless now. The beetles weren't biding their time before raising the alarm. The dim road lifted its dimmer banks to cut off her view of the harbour and of the villa white as a temple or a tomb. For minutes at a time she saw only the road sloping to yet another bend. Her flight was starting to seem unreal, a dream of trudging once more down the island, as if she might be compelled to repeat that until she died. She kept encountering patches of heat in the dark, and when the nocturnal chill returned she had an impression that the desert dryness was pacing her. Unseen dust parched her mouth, but there was no use wishing she had the flask she'd made sure to leave in her room. At least she was halfway down the island, and couldn't see any boats leaving the harbour. The thought of being left behind sent her stumbling faster along the road. She was close enough to the harbour to distinguish the jagged mass of roofs against an obscure shifting of waves when she heard a sound up by the villa.

At first it was the merest whisper, impossible to identify. She had grasped that it was coming after her before she knew what it might be. As she strained her stinging eyes she glimpsed movement through the trees, and then the same movement reversed on the next stretch of road. Nana's car was coasting swiftly downhill, its engine silenced, its lights off.

She dashed towards the harbour, her sandals scraping her feet raw. The road turned back on itself and turned back on itself as the blind but purposeful car halved the distance behind her. Now she was directly above the highest roofs, and nearly slithered down the rocky slope beside the road, but it was too steep to risk. She sprinted limping past the church and the dark huddle of the houses, past small lit windows intent on keeping to themselves all the light they could, and skidded onto the pebbles beyond the street. Five men were at the jetty, untying or loading their boats, except for a man talking to a woman, presumably his wife, with her back to Daniella. Daniella raced across the beach, her sandals catching pebbles to bruise her feet, and heard the car halt behind her with a triumphant rasp of its handbrake. As the fishermen turned to stare at her she groped in her handbag. "Athens," she called, waving Greek notes and fifty, sixty, a hundred pounds in the air.

The fishermen stared and shrugged virtually in unison. The woman swung around, her outline fluttering with the restlessness of the sea, and planted her hands on the parts of her shapeless black dress that must conceal her hips. Her long face resembled old cracked inflexible leather buttoned with eyes black as basalt. It didn't alter as Daniella added a hundred pounds to her offer and thrust the money at whoever was prepared to earn it. "Athens," she pleaded.

The woman jabbed a stubby forefinger into the wad of cash. As she separated each pair of notes, Daniella heard footsteps clattering across the beach. The woman closed her fingers and thumb on the notes and addressed some swift words harsh with consonants to her husband. Daniella kept hold of the wad and twisted her upper body to see who was running towards her. It was Mark.

The woman tugged at her wrist and asked an urgent question that Daniella comprehended once she saw that the questioner was nodding hard at Mark. "Both of us," she said, grabbing Mark's hand to ensure she was understood. It was hot and dusty and eager to be held, and she didn't relinquish it until the fisherman and his wife had finished chattering and shrugging, at which point the man helped Mark hand Daniella into the small boat.

The vessel lurched as she sat in the prow. It wallowed as Mark took his place beside her. The sea spat at them as the boatman yanked the cord of the motor in the stern. The boat surged forward, slicing the dark skin of the water to reveal the soft pale flesh of the sea, and the island shrank, displaying the white bulk that squatted on top of it. Long after the villa lowered itself over the horizon she sensed its existence as if threads of an invisible web had attached themselves to her and would cling to her wherever she journeyed in the world.

THIRTY-SEVEN

C hrys, I'm sorry."

"For what?"

"For not making you believe me."

"You nearly did."

"I should have stayed till you had to. I should have been there when you did."

"You couldn't have. You mightn't have been safe."

"Neither were you, Chrys."

"I know that now. Mark made me see."

"And then he went off and left you too."

"So we can blame him if we need to blame someone, but we don't."

"Don't you hate me, then?"

"Danny, how could I do that when you were only trying to protect me? It isn't you I hate, just the truth, and there's no point in hating that."

"Still friends?"

"Best. What do you think?"

"So long as we look after each other and make certain we're safe."

"And all the others. We have to warn them too. It has to be easier now both of us know, and Mark."

Daniella hoped that was the situation, but she was getting ahead of herself. As she swung the car she'd hired at

Heathrow off the motorway onto the Oxford road, all that
mattered to her was Chrysteen's safety. Nobody would dare
to harm her friend now that Daniella was back to expose
them if they tried—even if they didn't try, once she figured
out how she could. Mark would be with her soon—would
have been now if the first flight out of Athens hadn't offered just one standby seat. Perhaps it was best that she
would be meeting Chrysteen alone; at least some of the
conversation she'd imagined might ensue. She'd tried to call
her twice from Heathrow, but each time the line had been
engaged. She managed to derive a little reassurance from
knowing it could hardly have been Nana on the phone,
since Mark had cut the cable before riding down the island
in the car.

The horizon brandished spires at her as she drove into
Chrysteen's suburb. Though she had slept throughout the
flight, the lack of sleep preceding it was eager to be recognised, so that she kept feeling she was dreaming or about
to dream. That was why the spires put her in mind of the
tips of stone crowns worn by enormous unseen heads. She
was glad when the spectacle was screened by pairs of houses
white as blocks of salt. Here was Chrysteen's house with a
car in the drive, not her father's car or any Daniella knew.
She parked outside and slammed the door and strode up
the drive to lean on the doorbell.

She let go once its tune from *William Tell* reminded
her of the child who had trusted his father not to injure
him. In the silence she heard sounds from a tennis court
somewhere close, the taut slap of a racket followed several
breathless seconds later by the opponent's sloppy pat and a
cry of triumph. She thought she heard footsteps approach-

ing the door, but the noise was only the bouncing of the tennis ball. She was about to thumb the marble bellpush into its gilded surround when a woman she had never seen before peered at her through the front window. For a moment she thought she'd mistaken the house. She might almost have wondered if she had never left Nektarikos, the woman was so blackly and severely dressed and coiffured, all expression drawn out of the long bony face by the tight hair. Her thin whitish lips parted only to press themselves straight as she turned abruptly and made for the hall. When the door swung open Daniella said at once "Is Chrys here?"

The woman's gaze moved from Daniella's sandals to her face via her shorts and T-shirt with no gain in cordiality. "May I ask who you are?" she eventually said.

"Her friend."

"Will I have heard of you?"

"Who from?"

"From whom."

It was the automaticity of the response that made Daniella demand "Are you a teacher?"

"I was a lecturer. Do I take it you're a student?"

"Just like Chrys."

The woman fingered her forehead as though to count the lines appearing there. "Have you known her long?"

"Since we were . . ."

Daniella's voice trailed off, not simply because a girl of about eight had wandered out of the kitchen with a sketchpad in her hand, not even because she resembled Chrysteen at that age, especially her bright quick friendly eyes. "Nana," the little girl had said.

"Not just now, Dawn," the woman told her, and gave Daniella a look that was almost confiding. "My other granddaughter."

The little girl had called her by a pet name for a grandmother, Daniella realised as Dawn said "But I've finished, look."

"Very nice," her grandmother said with barely a glance, so that Daniella felt bound to appraise the crayon drawing of a rickety red house with a smiling face at every window. The faces were so round and similar they put her in mind of badges or masks, but she found enough enthusiasm in the midst of her increasing nervousness to say "It's good."

"Of course it is. Go and draw something else now, Dawn, and then I'll come and see. We shouldn't be more than a few minutes."

Daniella took that as an admonition, and was struggling to understand its brusqueness as Dawn asked "What shall I draw?"

"Something pleasant. Something pretty," her grandmother said, which struck Daniella as so inadequate that she told Dawn "You."

"I'll try," the little girl said and made for the kitchen, using a crayon to push her lips into a thoughtful grimace.

"Close the door, please." When Dawn had, her grandmother glanced along the street at a man who had just wheeled a barrow full of tools into his front garden. "You'd better come in for a moment, Miss..." she said, wagging her fingertips at Daniella.

"Can't you just tell me where Chrys is?"

"Please."

Her voice was gentler, which only made Daniella more nervous. When Chrysteen's grandmother turned she had to follow. The bathroom scent of the house caught in her throat like the threat of some reaction. A pair of walking-sticks rattled in their stand as she hurried into the front room, where she was gestured to sit in a wing chair. Its pale leather cushions were floppy as soft toys, but she perched on the edge in too much sunlight while her reluctant hostess sat up straight against the light. After some preparation, not least of the blankness of her face, all the woman said was "Will you have anything to drink?"

"I'm driving."

Chrysteen's grandmother nodded in approval, then kept her head bowed. "Tea or coffee? A glass of water?"

"Nothing, thanks. I just want—"

"Pardon my interrupting, but when did you last see my granddaughter?"

"Just a few days back," Daniella said, though it felt distant enough to have been a previous life.

"And you said you'd been friends for how long?"

"Since we were younger than Dawn. We still are, friends, I mean."

The woman sat forward and folded her hands in her black lap before lowering her voice. "Can you prepare yourself for some very sad news?"

"I don't know if I can or not. Just tell me."

"My granddaughter, your friend Chrysteen, has passed away."

At moments like this, Daniella knew, people in films yelled "Noooo." Sometimes they threw their heads back as they did so or clutched their skulls with their fists or both. She felt like doing some or all of this, except that as well as being wholly inadequate it would reinforce her impression that the situation was no more real than a film, than

392   Ramsey Campbell

a dream her mind had been aching to have, which had
turned into a nightmare. "When?" she pleaded.

"Yesterday."

It must have been while she was trying to leave Nektarikos to rejoin Chrysteen, Daniella thought, which made
it even harder to bear. "How?"

"My son-in-law was driving her back to the house she
shared with friends in York."

Daniella saw that Chrysteen's grandmother kept having
to pause to hide her grief—her own was close to robbing
her of speech. "And?" she succeeded in saying.

"It isn't clear what happened yet."

"What is?"

"It may never be. The police are still questioning witnesses."

Daniella found she had room for fury in the midst of
her grief. "To what? Did they see Chrys..."

"Both."

"Both..."

"Chrysteen and her father."

"You're saying they're both..."

"Passed on."

Though Daniella saw that the phrase was meant to be
comforting, she found it intolerably vague. "But what did
anyone see?"

"My son-in-law was supposed to have been trained as
a police driver." Chrysteen's grandmother blinked at the
closed door to the hall. "They're only meant to drive so fast
to prevent a crime or catch a criminal, aren't they?" she
said.

"How fast?"

"Over a hundred miles an hour, people have been saying. This was on the motorway, you understand. He did
like to drive fast according to my daughter." She gazed at
nothing or a memory and then squeezed her eyes shut in
order to dry them. "I still don't understand why he couldn't
brake in time. The traffic was halted in all three lanes and
witnesses say he didn't brake until he was no more than
the width of this house away. They went into a skid and
under one of those huge lorries we see too many of these
days. The whole top of the car—You'll excuse me if I don't
go on." She dabbed hard at her eyes. "Something must have
distracted him," she said.

It was fierce enough to be an accusation, one that Daniella levelled at herself. Nothing could have distracted him
so badly except being confronted by Chrysteen with some
or all of what she'd learned about him. Daniella had intended the knowledge to protect her, but it had killed her
instead. She thought she was going to own up to her guilt
until she heard herself ask "How's Chrys' mother?"

"She needed treatment, as you can imagine. At least
she's in the best hands."

"Whose?"

"You may have heard of him. He has the highest reputation. Dr Eamonn Reith."

Daniella could think of no response there would be any
point in uttering. "He's been the soul of kindness," Chrysteen's grandmother said. "He's with her at this moment,
helping make the funeral arrangements."

"Are they coming back here?"

"Quite soon, I should think. Would you mind terribly
not waiting?"

"No."

"Only I can see you're liable to be upset, and I'd rather not be, not while Dawn's here."

"Fine."

"She wouldn't be except for her parents being on a business trip. She hardly knew her cousin."

"She never will," Daniella said, standing up before she grew unable to see for tears. She was in the hall and turning hastily towards the front door when Dawn ran out of the kitchen. "See what I've made now," the little girl invited.

Daniella glanced back to see her exhibiting the next page of the pad. Though or possibly because the self-portrait was primitive, with squiggles of blue crayon bearing little similarity to Dawn's long black curly hair, it looked painfully like Chrysteen—like, Daniella thought with sudden awful clarity, a sketch of a victim produced for the police by a child. "Maybe you'll grow up to be an artist," she managed to comment as she grabbed the latch.

She was fumbling not too blindly with the gate when Chrysteen's grandmother stepped onto the path. "Will you be all right to drive?" she called just loud enough for Daniella to hear.

"I'll have to be," Daniella told her, and took refuge in the car from the worst of the irrelevant sunlight that was rendering the houses bright as Greece. "I'll be all right for whatever I need to be," she vowed as Chrysteen's grandmother returned to the house. She couldn't give in to her grief yet, not until she was far away from anywhere Eamonn Reith might appear. She swung the car out from the kerb and saw Chrysteen's house dwindle in the mirror to be erased by the whiteness of its neighbours. All that was constant in the strip of glass was her own stunned sleepless dry-eyed face. When it opened its mouth she felt as though she was watching a widescreen film of herself. "I'm sorry, Chrys," she murmured, or it did.

THIRTY-EIGHT

H ealsmith."
  "I beg your pardon?"
"Healsmith."
"Who am I speaking to, please?"
"The only woman it could be."
"I need your name."
"I don't have one like yours yet. You know that's what I want to earn. I favour Glamoursmith. What do you think?"
"Can I call you back in let's say an hour?"
"Why would you have to do that?"
"This is hardly the best time. I'm at a funeral."
"It sounds to me as if you've stepped out of the church by now."
"The service is starting in a few minutes."
"That's long enough. I'm only sorry I can't be with you. I expect I could have made this call to half the people there. That's one of the times you meet, isn't it, when any of you dies."
"What of it?"
"I was just remembering that was the last time I met you all. Of course Caresmith's family had to do without any of you at the funeral because he'd given you away."
"May I ask if that's what you're planning?"

"Why should I want anything except what we all want?"

"Which you're suggesting is?"

"To succeed."

"That sounds commendable enough."

"I'll tell you something that will sound much better. I have what you've been searching for."

"Perhaps you ought to tell me what you think that is."

"Both her and what has to be used."

"Have you plans for them?"

"One that I needn't explain to any of you, and I want you all to see it carried out, otherwise there'll be no point, of course."

"Are you asking to be told where?"

"I believe I've thought of the perfect place."

"I take it you're in no danger of being overheard."

"Nobody except you and the others would understand if they heard. It's where the Filmsmiths made me what I became."

"That place is tied up in litigation, as you know."

"There's nobody in it at night, is there?"

"I understand only a man on the gate."

"And the Filmsmith who's left can send him away, can't he?"

"I suppose that may be possible."

"See that he does. Waiting makes me nervous. I want this done tonight before anything can go wrong."

"You'll forgive my saying this, but you're talking as if you're in one of your films."

"You have my word tonight's show will be real."

"I don't know how many people would be able to be there."

"All of the smiths who are where you are, I hope. It isn't far to go, and I can't speak for what might happen otherwise."

"That sounds like a threat."

"Blame my nervousness. This is newer to me than it is to you, remember. Shall we agree a time?"

"When have you in mind?"

"The earliest tomorrow gets. There won't be anybody passing then to spy on us. You'll understand if I stay hidden till then. You won't be able to contact me, so I trust you to gather the brethren tonight."

"I hope I can."

"A man of your stature? I know you can. Go to your funeral now and don't let anything put you off mourning. At least he didn't leave a child to find what you'll hide in his grave."

The first of the cars almost as dark as the night had reached the open gates of Oxford Films when the phone rang in the unlit gatehouse. The car halted in the gateway, staining the vehicle behind it crimson with its lights. The driver hurried around it to snatch the gatehouse door open and seize the receiver. "Which of you is it?" the phone said.

"We spoke earlier."

"Healsmith."

"You'll be Glamoursmith."

"That's agreed, is it? I couldn't be happier. Are you all here to celebrate?"

"Every one."

"I should feel honoured, but you're early, aren't you? It's still the same day."

"Only just. Now may I ask—"

"True enough, it's about to be the future. Don't worry, I'm at least as eager as you are."

"Then may we know where to find you?"

"Drive straight ahead till you see the light."

"I'm looking, but I can't see any."

"We're at the end of the road. We're waiting for you. This is exciting, isn't it? It's like another film."

"Rather more serious, surely."

"What's more serious than succeeding? The lights are on and I'm ready for the action. Come and be the audience. Come and participate."

Daniella lay on her back on a waist-high altar. It was rough as sandstone and of that colour, but felt like the plastic of which it was composed. It was longer and wider than a grave. Above it half a dozen lights shone brighter than the Greek sun. At her feet was Nana's knife.

For the moment nobody was to be seen, and not much else either. The altar was left over from an early scene in *The Flood*, where some primitive people dressed in ragged skins had made a sacrifice to a god that sounded like a grunt and got themselves washed away for it. Items in the gloom beyond the lights had been used in the film too: olive trees withered by the intervening months, man-high dunes that could be moved about to simulate a different landscape. She could distinguish little of this if she raised her head, but she glimpsed the eager gleam of the knife. Her head was sinking back onto the hollow pretence of a slab when she heard vehicles creeping to a halt outside the open door of the sound stage.

She drew a shaky breath that tasted of hot dust. As she stiffened, arms outstretched by her sides, plastic squeaked beneath her nails. A car door closed stealthily, then another and another—so many echoes she might have thought the sounds were retreating down an excavation. She heard men murmuring like visitors to a church, and then there was silence except for soft footsteps crowding towards the doorway. Her skin prickled as though specks of heat were falling from the lamps. She couldn't move—she could scarcely keep up her short dry breaths—as the first of the players stepped onto the set.

It was Anthony St George, the surgeon who had failed to save her father. His bald head gleamed beneath the lamps like a huge pinkish jewel wrapped in a wad of silver hair. He blinked rapidly about, his small mouth drawn inward through the shadow of his beaky nose, his long oval face glistening a little. He saw the knife at Daniella's feet, though he hadn't seemed to bother seeing her. He strode forward, reaching inside the jacket of his elegant black suit, and the others followed him: Bill Trask of the *Beacon*, Reginald Gray from Metropolitan Television, Alan Stanley with a curt appraising glance at her, a dozen more men preceding Eamonn Reith . . . Only he had the grace to look even faintly embarrassed as they brought out their knives and raised them high to acknowledge the blade on the altar.

Daniella clenched her fists at the explosion of flashes of metal, so bright and sharp she imagined she could feel them on her skin. The men's uniform lack of expression made it clear that they'd chosen not to be aware of her as a person. She was nothing but the offering they needed. She didn't know how long they stood like that—long enough for her chest to start aching with her struggle to breathe—before some of the knives began to waver and some of the faces turned not quite so inexpressive. At that moment Nana's muffled voice said "I'll be there directly. Look after her till I come."

The knives sank in response or at least in a lessening of tension, but the men had lost the option of ignoring Daniella. Anthony St George met her eyes with a look that declared he had every right to do so. "You poor child, have you been kept waiting long?"

Her stiff lips pinched themselves together, and Eamonn Reith peered at her face. "I believe she's been given something to help," he murmured.

She was gazing dully into his eyes, in which concern or a pretence of it was visible, when Alan Stanley emitted a shrill cough. "Hold on a second. What did she say?"

"Nothing," Reith assured him. "Shall we let her stay quiet? It'll be easier for all concerned. She may not even know what's going on or where she is."

"Not her. I'm not talking about her," Alan Stanley said, and stalked past the altar. "Where's Miss Babouris supposed to be? If I'm not mistaken—"

He gasped in fury or triumph and slapped the top of the altar as he crouched. Daniella strained her eyes to their corners and saw his hand poised on the plastic like a spider lacking several legs. On the back of the hand were scratches that made her nails tingle. He straightened up, brandishing the tape recorder he'd found in a recess beneath the altar. "What's this?" he cried in Daniella's face.

She let her fist unclench, exposing the remote control, and sat up to swing her legs off the altar. She managed to grin while she said "It's what you thought. It's Nana in *Say Yes to Tomorrow* and a line from *Sunshine for Susan*."

Anthony St George appeared to want to point his blade at her for emphasis, but perhaps it was too sacred. "And who was on the phone?"

"That was me. I can sound like her if I have to," Daniella said, and did.

"She spoke to me from her island. I wouldn't have been fooled," Alan Stanley said in a rage that seemed to be directed solely at Daniella, and shook the tape recorder until its pair of cassettes chattered in their housings. "What was this meant to achieve?"

Daniella splayed her fingers against plastic on either side of her and tried to relax so that her arms wouldn't tremble as the men surrounded the altar. "What do you think?"

"You surely couldn't have imagined we'd be stupid enough to let you tape us."

"I don't know why not when you're so stupid you believe killing your children brings you luck."

"It's not just luck," Larry Larabee protested. "A damn sight more than luck put me where I am."

All of Daniella was threatening to tremble, and she fought to hold herself still. "You must be joking, Jokesmith."

His face darkened despite the lamps. "You'll find out there's some things I never joke about. Stands to reason the oldest beliefs are the real ones, love. They never went away if you know where to look."

"It wouldn't hurt you to show a bit of respect," Bill Trask told her. "Respect for tradition for a kick off. I don't suppose you read the Bible. Lot would have given the Sodomites his virgin daughters to save the angels. Don't try and tell us that was about nothing but luck."

"That's how you sell people what you do, is it, News-smith? Or maybe sell it to yourself. Only you haven't had to kill your own child yet, have you? I wonder how you'll feel when you do."

She had to force the words up from the depths of her-self. An uncontrollable shiver passed through her, and she restrained her clammy hands from sliding away from her along the edge of the altar as several of the men advanced on her. The flashes of their knives stabbed at her eyes. Then Larabee uttered a snort that sounded squeezed dry of mirth. "Wait," he said. "Where's she getting our names from?"

She saw blades rise as though to probe the answer out of her. As she told herself the men would have to do worse than wave their knives about to make her flinch, Reginald Gray darted forward and snatched up the remote control she'd dropped on the altar. "That's not important now," he gabbled. "Where was the recorder?"

"There," Alan Stanley said, using it to indicate.

"Keep quiet then. Everybody keep quiet."

"What's the hush for, Talksmith?" Larabee enquired as if he saw a chance for a joke.

"Someone else is here. She couldn't have controlled the tape from where she was with this. It wouldn't have worked."

Alan Stanley slammed the tape recorder down on the altar with a splintering of plastic. He was glaring at Dan-iella while his companions stared about at the gloom beyond the lights or made to search it when two dunes beyond the head of the altar were trundled apart, revealing Mark. He shied the control of the tape recorder onto the altar before anyone did more than snarl, and then a stout man with a face not unlike a swollen version of Mark's, its cheeks two veinous bruises, peered through almost invisibly thin gold spectacles at him in disbelief. "What the devil are you doing here, Mark?"

"Making sure nobody else ends up like Philippa."

"Never mind trying to show off. You may impress your friend, but we've seen it all before. Some of us have known you since you were born." Every vein in Victor Shakespeare's face was etched purple under the spotlights. "What did you imagine you were going to achieve? Do you want to throw away your life?"

"Are you going to kill us both now? Try making that look like an accident now you've got nobody in the police."

His father glared at Daniella as though to hold her responsible. "You haven't let your friend think you've no reason to be grateful, Mark."

"For what?" Mark demanded more harshly than she found reassuring.

"You may have taken a dislike to my name, but you didn't mind the kind of life you could afford to live with us, if you remember."

Mark's shoulders moved uncomfortably or with rage. "I remember everything there is to remember about Philippa, and you didn't let that be much."

"You remember fighting half the time and screaming at each other and breaking each other's toys? Do you remember how often you said you wished we could send her back where she came from?"

"If you're trying to make me feel guilty for what you did," Mark said through barely parted teeth, "don't bother."

"Maybe he hopes you'll see how much of your life you owe to the sacrifice your sister made," Eamonn Reith said with a gentleness that left Daniella unable to swallow.

"What are you saying she did?" Mark little more than whispered. "She never had a choice."

"You can't know till you've seen it," Bill Trask told him.

"Do you think I could live with everything she brought us if I didn't know she was happy?" Mark's father said. "She's somewhere we can't imagine. You have to believe that, whatever you think of me, and maybe you can accept I knew that was where she had to be going."

"Anyone who's sacrificed with love goes straight to paradise," Larabee said, using a knuckle to dab at his eyes.

"We know all that," Alan Stanley said, and used his knife to indicate Daniella and Mark. "How much more time are we going to waste?"

Anthony St George coughed like a butler in a film. "This isn't right," he said.

His discomfort communicated itself to at least some of his associates. Apparently that made them determined to overcome it, since they moved to trap Mark as well as Daniella. The surgeon took a step that brought him back into the circle, though protesting "It shouldn't be like this."

"Tell us the alternative," Alan Stanley said.

"There has to be one," Victor Shakespeare wished aloud. "Doesn't there, Mark?"

"To what?"

His father seemed about to step forward and clutch him by the shoulders, but stayed in place, his hands and the knife retreating behind his back. "Forget everyone else," he said. "Just think of you and me. Imagine how you'd feel if you destroyed me and my life, and remember it's your mother's too."

"What are you asking me to do instead?"

"You're only at the start of your career. Everyone here

is impressed with your work. In a few years you could be one of the leaders in your field."

Daniella saw several heads nod a tentative agreement. It seemed to her that the air beneath the spotlights had grown as thirsty as her mouth—she might even have thought the studio dunes had grown more real and more concealing. "If I do what?" Mark said.

"Make a promise you may not even have to keep."

His father glanced at the faces behind Mark. He parted his lips and held Mark with a solemn gaze before intoning "We pledge our firstborn in token of our brotherhood. Let their sacrifice confirm their sacred innocence and our faith."

An indeterminate number of voices murmured some of this in chorus with him. As Daniella swallowed the nausea that had risen into her parched mouth, Mark said "Do you say it again when you murder them?"

"Enough," Alan Stanley said not far from triumphantly. "You've had your chance."

He might have meant either of them, but it was Victor Shakespeare who demanded "What are you—"

"I'll take him. No offence, Booksmith, but just in case you aren't up to it when it comes to the task. Who's with me? Talksmith, Healsmith, you can handle him. We'll decide where and what as we go, and Mindsmith can take her back to his hospital."

"Unless our young pair both had an accident," Larry Larabee suggested.

For a moment Daniella thought indecision might distract their captors. Perhaps the possibility occurred to them too; Eamonn Reith and the comedian each stepped towards her as if she had become a magnet for their knives. She could only cleave to her belief that she and Mark had done all they were capable of. The television personality and the surgeon converged on Mark as Victor Shakespeare brought his hands out from behind his back. "Maybe that's the only answer," he said, "but I'm sorry, Filmsmith, you're not taking him."

Alan Stanley raised an eyebrow at the others. "Looks as if I was right to want to."

"No, because I think you'd enjoy it too much. That's never been what we're about. Some of us thought you got a taste for it after your sacrifice. You seemed a bit too ready to take your time with Caresmith."

Daniella swallowed hard so as to be able to speak. "You mean he killed Norman Wells."

"Eventually."

Alan Stanley's face darkened with rage, then appeared to brighten with the gleam of the knife he raised. "All right, we won't go anywhere," he said. "Let's do what has to be done. You two hold the boy."

Reginald Gray and Anthony St George each seized Mark by an arm. The spotlights seemed to blaze into Daniella's skull, and her mouth grew almost too parched for words. She was about to blurt the only thing that could save Mark—if it could, if the men believed her in time—when Victor Shakespeare lurched between his son and Alan Stanley. He threw out a hand to oppose the knife. "Wait, you can't—"

Alan Stanley's grim blank-eyed smile told him he was wrong. When Victor Shakespeare didn't step aside, Stanley jabbed the knife at the outstretched hand. Rather than flinch—more as though, Daniella thought, he meant to prove himself to his son—Shakespeare lunged for Stanley's wrist. Stanley wrenched it free, dragging the blade through his opponent's grasp. In case that failed to make his point he sawed it back and forth. Perhaps pain or his emotions left Shakespeare nothing except instinct. Just the first drop of blood had swelled out of his fist when he jerked up his own knife and slashed Alan Stanley's throat.

A slick red bib appeared beneath Stanley's chin, and a vein began to spurt under his right ear. He spent only a moment in gazing at the other man as though refusing to believe the situation. With a lopsided grimace that announced he could give as good as he'd received—that put Daniella in mind of an overgrown schoolboy confronting a schoolmate—he cut Victor Shakespeare's throat from one ear to the other.

Shakespeare clutched at it with a hand that was already streaming crimson. The knife slithered out of his grasp, and the blade snapped in two as it struck the floor. The impact released the other men from their apparent momentary paralysis. Reginald Gray disarmed Alan Stanley, who was stumbling on the spot, while Anthony St George took Victor Shakespeare by the elbows to support him. "Mind out of the way," the surgeon snarled at Mark and Daniella as if they'd provoked the violence. "Give them room."

Mark looked stunned and ready to accept the guilt. When Daniella gripped his arm to ease him towards the door, he resisted. He watched in something like dismay while the surgeon led his father to the plastic altar and helped him sit on the edge. Reginald Gray ushered Alan Stanley to the far end and sat him as far as possible from Shakespeare, though the injured men seemed wholly unaware of anything except themselves. Anthony St George tramped from one to the other, tugging gently at their hands for a view of the gaping throats. "Should we get them to a hospital?" Bill Trask urged.

"Too late for either." The surgeon's tone remained accusing. "We need to think what happened here," he said, turning to stare at Daniella and Mark. "Something that will explain how these two died as well."

Daniella held onto Mark's arm, although there was no longer any point in trying surreptitiously to retreat towards the door; several of the men were blocking that route. She felt the spectacle on the altar had immobilised her and Mark—the sight of his father and her father's partner trying to hold in their blood while they sagged into an identical crouch as if the crimson fistfuls they were losing had robbed them of any other posture. If they would just do something that would draw the attention of their cronies—or was it time for her to risk speaking up? The appearance of so much blood and the imminence of death—anyone's death—had begun to make her feel sick, and she was afraid of growing faint. The threat of this parted her lips, but she was interrupted before she had a chance to speak.

Neither of the men slumping lower on the altar raised his head, but all the others did like hounds. As the chorus of sirens on the main road grew louder, Anthony St George declared "They won't be coming here." It seemed he was right, because a drop in the pitch of the leading siren betrayed that it had bypassed the studio gates. She had let go of Mark's arm and was about to dash for the exit from the sound stage when the sirens crowded through the gates.

It was Mark who sprinted to the exit, having dodged the men and a slash from one knife. He flung the door open and ran only just onto the road through the studios, waving his arms as headlights found him. "Here," he shouted.

Eamonn Reith was the only father to make a purposeful move. He lurched to head Daniella off as three police cars and two vans screeched to a disarrayed halt outside the sound stage. First to emerge from the foremost car was a tall hulk of at least an inspector, who held up his splayed fingers to direct Mark into the building. The youthfulness of his face was contradicted not so much by a receding hairline as by his look of resignation to whatever might confront him. Mark rejoined Daniella as the policeman was followed by more officers than she could count. "Will you please put your weapons on the floor and step away," the policeman said.

Reith took it upon himself to speak for all. "Chief Inspector, is it? I don't know how this must look . . ."

The policeman was frowning at the men slumped on the altar. Their chins rested on their raw throats, and they'd slumped helplessly against each other as though exemplifying fellowship to the last. "Can you call an ambulance?" Mark pleaded.

"There's one on the way," the policeman said, and turned his frown on the fathers while motioning his men to stay back. "Please drop your weapons now."

"Stand back, everyone," Eamonn Reith urged as if he couldn't quite believe the policeman had ignored him. "Let these officers see to the victims if there's anything to be done."

"For the last time, drop your weapons or we'll be forced to disarm you."

He was being too cautious, Daniella thought in dismay;

perhaps he was secretly overawed. When he gestured his men to move in, they stopped short of the fathers, waiting for them to comply. "To the grave," someone whispered— Anthony St George must have, since he glanced around him for support. Everyone else was silent except for Bill Trask, who jabbed his upturned empty hand at the leader of the police. "Do you know who we are?"

"Film stars," remarked the policeman nearest him.

Trask grew unsure what expression or even what colour to assume. "What kind of nonsense is that?"

It was Mark who couldn't resist answering. "You've all been on the Internet ever since you came in here."

They almost hadn't been, Daniella thought as she saw their faces grow enraged or expressionless. Maeve and Duncan had needed more time than they'd anticipated to find a vantage point from which the camera would broadcast everything, and then they'd had to hook it up. Until this moment she'd been afraid Maeve might have had second thoughts, even if Mark had seemed to help persuade her, but wherever she and Duncan were now, she must have alerted the police and the media. The policeman in charge was watching for reactions to Mark's words. Abruptly Reginald Gray paced towards him, holding out his knife with his finger and thumb on the blade. "You'll have seen I didn't harm anyone," he said.

Bill Trask released a mirthless laugh followed by a mutter. "Not here, that is."

Eamonn Reith was next to offer the policeman his knife. "The girl's my patient," he confided. "You know you can't rely on anything you see on the web. She's the one who attacked our friends, and that's what you should be dealing with, isn't it? You'll have it in your records that she injured more than one person with a knife."

"That's right," his fellow fathers said, and "She did" and "It was her."

The policeman waited until all the knives had been collected and contained in plastic bags. "Why would you want us to think that?" he then mused aloud.

"Because some of them killed their children and the rest promised to," Daniella said, "and they wanted to kill me tonight."

The policeman only glanced at her before facing Reith. Her head had begun to throb with the breath she was holding when he said "I have to warn you gentlemen that anything you say—"

The fathers reached almost in unison for their concealed weapons—their mobile phones. "Please hand those to my officers," the policeman said. "You'll be able to make one call each from the station, but I have to advise you that I am arresting you on suspicion—"

Daniella didn't know if he'd forgotten this was being broadcast or was ensuring it was. He completed the ritual as the phones were confiscated, not without some argument, and an ambulance drew up outside the sound stage. "Can I ride with him?" Mark asked the attendants who hurried in with the first stretcher. "He's still my father."

Neither paramedic looked at him until they'd finished checking pulses. "I'm sorry, son, they're both gone," the older and wearier attendant said.

The police were escorting out the last of the fathers, all of whom seemed to have aged decades, as if their power had suddenly deserted them. Daniella was certain it hadn't entirely, however. "Can you come with us instead?" the leader of the police asked Mark.

"We'll stop them," Daniella murmured as she followed a policeman to her car behind the sound stage. The spotlights died all at once as though the desert had at last revealed its falseness, and the door slammed on the dark. Undoubtedly the fathers would use all their contacts to blur the truth, but it was out there now, and people had to see it. It was time for the mothers to be heard, and herself too, and Mark. She gave him a quick encouraging smile in the mirror, and he did his best to respond as she joined the parade of lights. She'd seen today how the fathers feared the truth, and surely they were right to be afraid. That was her belief.